# Where Did All That Love Come From?

## The Love in That Man

By Joe Green

First Edition

PAGE PUBLISHING, INC.
New York, NY

First originally published by Page Publishing 2014

ISBN 978-1-62838-353-9 (pbk)
ISBN 978-1-62838-354-6 (digital)

Printed in the United States of America

# Preface

Something continued to gnaw at me to write a novel. I kept putting it off. The persistence remained. I finally asked myself: "What am I to write about, and do I have the discipline in me to write a novel?" There was this recurring dream, so I was determined to make the attempt.

This has been written for those who enjoy a love story. I hope you will enjoy reading this novel as I, surprisingly, enjoyed writing it.

To Joyce
Too Long Apart. It's been Love seeing you after so Long. Love to you & the boys.
Hope you enjoy the read!
Joe Green

# The Power of Love

When I look at what is happening in the world and around us, when I listen to the news, and read and hear how men, women, and children are destroying others and themselves, I ask myself, "Why?" My answer is, "lack of Love!" Lack of love causes us to destroy. Love causes us to build (takes after our creative Father!)

This novel is about a young man and his love for a girl, a horse, the people close to him and for those with whom he comes in contact. The love in him affects almost everyone he meets. It drives him to fight to live, build, share and draw people as well as animals to him. This is what love will do—it builds, it does not destroy!

The girl has that same love in her. At times it is misdirected, but not misused. There is a reason for her misdirected love, but her love is there. As always, if love remains it will win out in the end. Go with them on their journey of love. Love is not always that warm fuzzy feeling. Love can hurt and sometimes seem cruel, but if you remain true to it, it will remain true to you.

How does love affect you? Look deep within yourself, and ask yourself these questions: "Am I a builder or a destroyer, and can I love my fellow person?" If the answers are, "Builder, and yes, I can," then you will know that where all that love comes from is from God. Because God is Love!

Dedicated to my sons, granddaughters, and family with all the love that is in me!

# Jay's Soul Mate

Exiting the classroom, I noticed some friends gathered near the water fountain. As I approached, my heart began to skip, for there, in the midst of the group, was the most gorgeous young lady. She was understandably the center of attention. She stood in the middle of four guys and a girl—Mike, Tommy, Ben, Roy and Jamie.

As I entered the group, Jamie said, "Hi Jay," as she gave me a big hug and a kiss on the cheek. Then she turned to the new girl. "Ronnie, this is the friend I mentioned." and then turned back to me. "Jay, this is Ronnie she has just moved here from California."

"Hello Ronnie, welcome," I said, extending my hand. "I hope you will be happy here. If I can be of any help, feel free to call on me." I couldn't help but notice that her stare and handshake was very cool if not cold. Then with a laugh I said, "But you seem to be well cared for in this hothouse of male egos." As I exited the group, I didn't know it but I had just met my soul mate!

* * * *

When the group broke for the next class, Jamie asked Ronnie, "What did you think of Jay?"

"I didn't particularly like him," responded Ronnie.

"Oh, I was hoping the two of you might hit it off!" said Jamie.

"He has a beautiful smile, but he's not very good looking. He's what I would expect to find on a blind date," Ronnie answered.

"Oh Ronnie, you're looking for pretty but you're going to learn that beauty is on the inside and that it is what's inside the wrapping that counts! I don't know of any one else that doesn't like Jay."

"Yes I noticed you like him a lot. I saw it in your eyes, and the way you looked at him." Ronnie answered,

Jamie replied, "I'll tell you about it sometime. Anyway I think Jay is quite handsome."

* * * *

After school we all met at Roscoe's as usual. Jamie had not yet arrived, but I saw Ronnie with four other girls and approached them. The four girls all said, "Hi Jay, would you join us? Jamie is going to be a little late, so we have an empty seat here." I sat down and asked if I might order a round of sodas.

Immediately Ronnie said, "I won't have anything."

The other girls accepted, with a "thanks Jay." Conversing with the other girls went great, but I could feel Ronnie's uneasiness with me being there. So I excused myself saying I forgot I had something else to do.

"But you haven't finished your soda!" they said.

I replied, "I don't have time," and left.

I heard the girls say, "That's unlike Jay."

Outside, I saw Jamie crossing the street. She waved and hurried across to greet me with her usual loving hug and a kiss on the cheek. She asked why I was leaving so early.

"I'll tell you about it sometime," I said,

Knowing me as well as she did, she asked if I had seen Ronnie. I replied that she was inside.

"You really like her don't you?" Jamie said,

I replied. "What in the world makes you think that?"

"Because of your reaction the first time you met her, and your leaving so early now. That's not like you Jay. Tell me the truth," she said,

Well I guess I can't lie to you even if I wanted to. Yes, she does stick in my craw.

"I was afraid of that, said Jamie. She told me she didn't like you. So Jay why don't you just forget her?"

"I wish I could. There is something about her that has just crawled inside of me!" I said.

Jamie responded. "Oh God, Jay I can't bear to see you hurt!" I smiled, and touched her cheek gently and said, "Don't worry. See you later."

Every time I saw Ronnie after that, I greeted her with a warm smile and a "Hello love." I wrapped myself into baseball to take my mind off Ronnie. I didn't know why she did not like me but I accepted the fact that she didn't and just lost myself in playing baseball. Then I saw Ronnie at one of the baseball games. To my surprise, she was going with the second baseman. It made me sad, but it caused me to concentrate more on baseball and enhanced my already wonderful season. I was the leading hitter and all glove, all-star third baseman.

Soon the semester was over and school was out for the summer. Summers were spent at the stables with my horse, or roller-skating, swimming, bowling, and going to the Teen Dance Club. It was a long summer and I had put Ronnie behind me, or so I thought. I spent the summer with Jamie and her boyfriend Mike, my best friend. I could tell that she was happy that I had forgotten about Ronnie.

Finally, summer vacation was over and football practice had started. The first day back in school brought back the memories of Ronnie. Ronnie had gone back to California for the summer. That is why I never ran into her. Surprisingly, it did not bother me much at all. I guess I had accepted that she had a boyfriend and wanted no part of me. Then one day I was coming down from the third floor and she was coming up. I just smiled and nodded and she nodded as we passed on the steps. I thought to myself I got a nod where I expected a snub. Hum—. After that whenever we met, I would just smile and nod. Sometimes she would nod and other times not.

Three games into the football season I had scored five touchdowns on the ground and caught a pass for another. I had forgotten about girls and threw myself into football and schoolwork. I only stopped by Roscoe's occasionally. One day I stopped by Roscoe's and the jukebox was playing a favorite song of Jamie's. As I walked into Roscoe's a big roar went up "Jay"! At that moment, two of the girls sitting in the booth with Ronnie jumped up and ran towards me, one was Jamie. The other girl, Marge got to me first and asked me to dance.

I apologized to Marge and said, "You know this is Jamie's favorite song, but if you like I will play it over so we can dance." Marge smiled, nodded her head, gave me a hug and went back to the booth. Jamie and I danced and everyone seemed to have their eyes on us. You would have thought that we were lovers the way we danced and looked at each other, but we were not.

* * * *

Ronnie muttered to Marge "Why did you accept him shoving you off like that? And look! There must be something between those two the way they dance together."

Marge just smiled and said, "One day you'll understand." Ronnie said, "Gosh is he a smooth dancer!"

Again Marge smiled and said, "You're beginning to get it. He's not only a smooth dancer he is such a gentleman."

When the dance was over, Jay played the song over again and danced with Marge. And at the end, Marge kissed him long and hard in the middle of the floor. When she sat down, Ronnie commented,

"You kissed him like that in front of everyone?"

Marge said, "Yep every chance I get."

Ronnie asked, "Are you two—?"

Marge said, "Nope. I just love that beautiful smile! It makes my heart flutter."

Jay danced with some of the other girls, socialized with the fellows for a while, and then went over and kissed Jamie and Marge on the cheek. He would have had to reach across Ronnie to kiss Mary, so he just winked and blew her a kiss and she blew one back and he left.

Ronnie asked. "What does everyone see in him?"

Jamie seemed rather irritated, and responded, "You don't like him for your reasons, but let me tell you he is the nicest, kindest, and most loving person you could ever hope to meet."

Marge added, "Yeah, and the best friend anyone could ever have. Plus he is the most humble person I've ever met. Whatever he does he seems to do it better than anyone else. Yet he never brags or ever tries to impress anyone. If you ever mention anything he's done, he just says, 'It's Gods gift,' and he'll try to change the subject."

* * * *

The Canteen dances were going on but during football season I didn't go to them—early to bed, you know. I hadn't run into Ronnie for a long time. Although I had put her on the back burner, I had not gotten her out of my system. I had a great season in football, second season in a row. My last game was the highlight of the season, with 214 yards and 3 touchdowns. I thought

I'd go home and rest, but Mike called and said he and Jamie wanted me to go roller-skating with them.

I hadn't seen much of Jamie during football season although Mike and I played football and baseball together, so I said, "Why not?"

He asked me to call Jamie and tell her that we would pick her up.

Jamie congratulated me on the game. She said that Ronnie went to all the football and baseball games with her. She mentioned that Ronnie loved football and baseball. Then she told me that Ronnie had said that I was the most beautiful running back she had ever seen, but that she'd never seen anyone so brutal.

"She also thought that you were the most graceful third baseman she has ever seen, but you even play baseball too hard."

Roller-skating was fun. It was dancing on skates. Mike, Jamie and I always had a ball skating.

"Now that football is over, will you guys be coming to the Canteen dances? "Jamie asked.

We said, "Of course!"

So Friday evening, we all went to the dance at the Canteen. When we walked in, everyone rushed Mike and me to congratulate us on the game and winning the season. Mike had caught two touchdown passes. Marge immediately grabbed me for a dance. When the dance was over, I was near Ronnie so I asked her to dance, but she refused. In fact, I asked her to dance four different times and she refused each time. I danced with a number of the girls during the evening and hardly had to ask any one of them.

During the evening, I noticed a girl sitting with another group of girls and I had only seen her dance once. She was a bit homely, but not an ugly girl; in fact, she was pretty. It was the way she dressed, the way she wore her hair and the eyeglasses she wore. I wondered why she was not being asked to dance. The next dance, as I made my way towards her, Mary asked me to dance.

I said, "Mary, Can I beg off this dance and we catch the next dance? I have something to do. She said, "Yes." So I kissed her forehead and continued toward the girl sitting alone.

All her friends had been asked to dance. I approached her and asked her to dance.

She said, "I don't dance well and I always step on my partner's feet. I'm a bit clumsy."

I said, "So am I. But maybe we can make it through the dance without stepping on each other's feet."

She responded, "Oh no, I have been watching you dance! You are not clumsy! I could never dance with you!"

I said, "Please, give me a chance. Maybe we will do all right together." Reluctantly, she agreed.

As we began to dance, I whispered, "Just relax and let your body follow mine." We flowed around the floor without mishap. When the dance was over, she was elated. She could hardly wait to get back to her girlfriends. I told her we would dance some more and kissed her on the forehead.

"Thank you so much," she said and gave me a big hug.

The next song I danced with Mary and she said, "That was sweet of you to dance with Alice. Most of the guys won't dance with her because they say she is so clumsy. We have tried to work with her but haven't had much luck."

Alice and I danced three more times before the night was over. She was quite confident by the end of the evening.

I didn't know that Alice knew Ronnie.

When Ronnie said to Alice, "I thought that you couldn't dance well." Alice replied that she had nothing to do with it.

"It was Jay. He told me to relax and let my body follow him. So I did. Gosh! Is he nice! I've never met any one like him, so patient; he persisted even when I refused to dance with him. He just insisted and I am glad he did. He said that I just lacked confidence. He is not like the regular run-of-the mill-guys. It's not like he wants something from you. It's more like he wants to give you something. I don't know—he's just different. We danced four times. He would just come over and ask me and each time when we finished, he would bring me back and kiss me on the forehead."

The next day Jamie called and said, "I heard how you handled Alice Hutchins. That was sweet and so typical of you. I guess that's why I will always love you."

I said, "Hey, don't talk like that Mike might get the wrong idea."

She laughed and said, "Mike knows how I feel about you." Besides if it wasn't for you, Mike and I might never have gotten together."

I said, "Yeah, my loss."

She laughed and said, "Liar! By the way, Alice told Ronnie how you helped her. I just found out that she and Ronnie are cousins."

I said, "I just tried to give her a little confidence that's all. She's really a pretty girl. The way she wears her hair, the clothes and those eyeglasses, is all that's wrong. If she would pick some more feminine eyeglasses to set off those beautiful eyes, change her hairstyle, and choose some pastel colors that would bring out her beautiful complexion, you'd have to beat the guys away with a stick! You girls could help her with that."

Jamie said, "Maybe I'll tell her that. Would you be one of those guys?"

"I like her without her being made over. Remember, anyway, I'm spoken for you know!"

Jamie laughed.

I asked Jamie, "How is Ronnie?"

Jamie said, "She's OK Jay. I just wish that you could put her behind you. She is not worthy of you. I don't know why I like her so much! I heard that she refused to dance with you a number of times. Why do you bother?"

"Don't worry Love," I said. "I'm the only one in the group she doesn't like. Personality conflict I guess. You like her for the same reason I like her. She's nice."

Jamie said, "Jay, you're impossible."

I made many attempts to talk to Ronnie. Most of the time she acted like I had the plague. However, I continued to speak and on one occasion, I happened on her at her locker. I approached her and asked if I could talk to her for a moment. She said nothing so I began to talk for about a minute and a half. She just stood there looking straight ahead at her locker. I was saying all kinds of nice things to her. Then I asked why she did not like me.

She said, "I've got to go," and walked off.

From then on, I just smiled or waved, but never tried to talk to her any more.

She and Jamie grew closer and closer together. But she could never understand Jamie's attraction to me. I suppose she thought if Jamie lost her attraction to me, I would never come around her at all.

One day, I overheard Ronnie asking Jamie with a scowl, "What in the world do you ever see in him?"

Jamie answered very angrily, "You can hate him all you want, but If you want to remain my friend, don't ever speak negatively about him in my presence again, and to think that I wanted you two to hit it off. He really likes you and I wish he didn't. You don't know how lucky you are. He could have just about any of the girls in school and here he is mooning over you."

Ronnie began to cry because she saw how she had hurt her best friend.

Jamie apologized for her anger and said, "You'll never understand how much I love him."

Ronnie asked, "Are you in love with him?"

Jamie said, "No, I'm in love with Mike, but I love Jay! Maybe one day I'll explain it to you." They hugged each other.

I enjoyed myself for the rest of the year at the stables, or dancing, swimming, roller-skating, and bowling, and ice-skating during the winter. Sundays were always spent in church before going to the stables. During the winter I saw more of Ronnie, because we spent more time at the canteen dances. It did not help the ache I had in me for her. I began to ask her to dance again. I thought she might have had a change of heart. I was wrong, but I continued to ask her. Her cousin Alice had become quite a dancer by now. Jamie and Ronnie had a talk with Alice, and what a looker she is now! Like I said, the guys were around her like flies. She and I danced a lot together.

One time while we were dancing, she whispered, "Thanks!"

I asked, "For what?"

She said, "Never mind," and kissed me softly on the cheek and whispered, "Now I know why everyone loves you so much!"

In all that time we had never mentioned Ronnie. Alice was from another school that is why we had never met before. She usually hung out with the girls from her school. Occasionally she would sit with Ronnie, Jamie and the girls, as on this occasion. I approached and asked Ronnie to dance and as usual she refused. So I asked Alice and she gladly accepted.

While dancing, Alice asked, "Why does Ronnie always refuse to dance with you?"

I responded, "I have no idea. Obviously she doesn't like me for some reason. I wish I knew her reason. Maybe I could fix the problem."

Alice said, "You really like her don't you? Maybe I can help."

I said, "Yes I do, but don't tell her that."

Alice said, "I think she knows it."

"Well I appreciate your offer to help, but I'd rather leave it as it is," I responded. The next dance I saw that Ronnie was sitting alone. All the other girls were dancing. As I walked towards her, she started to get up and walk away but she sat back down.

"I know that you are fed up with me constantly asking you to dance," I said.

She gave me a look that said, "Then why do you persist?"

I said, "Would you like to get rid of me permanently?"

"I would enjoy it if you stopped annoying me." She replied.

"I'll make a bargain with you," I said. "Dance with me once and I will never bother you again." She said nothing.

I said, "Wouldn't one dance be worth it, never to be bothered again? Surely you could suffer through one dance."

She asked, "How do I know you will keep the bargain?"

I said, "Because I'm a man of my word."

She said, "Let's dance."

I said, "No, no I get to pick the dance."

She said, "If that's the way you want it—as long as it's only one dance."

So I walked away as the song was ending. But not before I had heard Jamie ask Ronnie with a pleased smile, "Did I see you and Jay conversing?"

Ronnie said, "He promised if I would dance once with him he would never bother me again. So I agreed. Will he keep his word?"

Jamie said, "Oh Ronnie you didn't! Yes he will keep his word. He will not bother you anymore. You may be sorry you made that bargain."

Ronnie said, "Good. I doubt if I will ever be sorry about that!"

I drifted around the Canteen dancing with different girls. Jamie's song came up so I made my way over to her and as we danced she said,

"So Ronnie has agreed to dance with you?"

I said, "Yes, for a price."

Jamie said, "Oh Jay she doesn't really know you. Don't hold her to that."

I said, "I have come to realize that she really doesn't like me and I want to honor her feelings. Besides, wasn't it you who said, 'Get her out of your system'? Well I am doing just that!"

Jamie said, "Jay I know you better than that. You will still pine after her."

I said, "I have to do what I have to do."

I had asked Tim the DJ to play a specific record for me and to give me the nod when he was going to play it.

He said, "Jay it's been a long time since I've played that one. I'll have to find it." I told him when that song was about to end to put on a second song and start it towards the middle as if the first song didn't end and to start a third song close to the beginning the same way so that all three would seem like one continuous song.

He said, "I got you! This must be something special."

I said, "Yeah, you're right."

When Tim nodded I made my way towards Ronnie. It seems as if he must have watched me because just as I asked her to dance and she stood up, the record started to play. There seemed to be a hush over the whole place and Jamie looked at me with her mouth open. I took Ronnie in my arms and started to slide very smoothly around the floor. All eyes were on us. I don't know if it was because of the way we were dancing, or that I was dancing to that song. You see I hadn't danced to that song for a long time.

Ronnie fit in my arms like a well-tailored sleeve. She must have felt the magic of our dance because her soft hand went from my shoulder to the nape of my neck. I handled her as though she would break. My every touch was as light as a feather as I guided her through this move and that move. She followed me as though she was part of me. I would move her out and bring her in without our bodies ever touching. We glided over the floor as though we were on ice-skates.

I whispered in her ear, "You fit in my arms as though you were made only for them." I told her how gorgeous and soft she was, and how beautiful her eyes were like pools of deep cool water, in which a guy would gladly drown. I mentioned that her fragrance was like the summer breeze blowing the mixed scents of evening flowers—jasmine, roses and honeysuckle—into the nostrils of a man, and making him as intoxicated as would warm wine of evening and that her nose was like a sculptured masterpiece.

"The sculptor could make it over ten thousand times and not match it," I whispered. "Your lips are like the reddest rose that slowly opens its sleepy petals to the kiss of the morning sun."

Although she seemed to enjoy the dance, her attitude was as cold as the North Pole. The second song began just like I told the DJ. We continued to dance. Ronnie said, "You asked for one dance!" I responded, "Right, the music hasn't ended." I could tell that she was enjoying the dance as I moved her in out and around sometimes briefly pausing. I continued to speak softly and sweetly to her but I could not break that iceberg attitude.

Suddenly, the last song, "Spanish Harlem", began to play. Shortly after, when we began to dance to the rhythm of the song, I could feel a change in her throughout her body. I said nothing to her during the entire song. I began to combine a couple of different dances. I carefully guided her and she followed me completely. She moved with my lightest touch. I combined cha cha, mambo, and tango all in one song. The floor emptied and all were watching.

As I guided her through certain moves, there would be a roar from the crowd as we moved side by side. I made a couple of Paso Doble moves with her like a torero, or matador would do with a bull, as she spun by, which drew great applause from the gang. I had Ronnie do a spinning turn like a top and all the girls gasped as did Ronnie as she came out of it, I pulled her close, and paused, our bodies now touching, at which Ronnie threw her head back and her arm left my shoulder and flew out, and we went into a tango move that brought the roof down. I knew then, she was truly enjoying the dance.

The song was coming to a close, so I maneuvered her back toward her friends. Nearing them I apologized for anything that I had done to create the animosity she felt towards me. As the song ended, I spun her around and brought her close and into a dip. Her face was close to mine and our lips were almost touching. I looked into her beautiful eyes for a moment as I held her. I brought her up and thanked her for the dance and walked away. I thought I could feel her staring after me but I never looked back.

Closing time was approaching and I was being swamped with girls trying to get a dance with me. That is not unusual but tonight they wanted to know about me dancing with Ronnie to that first and last song. I danced until closing, but I didn't once look at Ronnie. And I kept my word. I never bothered her again.

* * * *

The girls all gathered around Ronnie and questioned her. She was bewildered by all the questions. They asked Ronnie if she and Jay were a couple.

"Just because I danced with him?" She asked.

"No," they said. "Because he danced with you to that song." At that moment Jamie walked up and squashed the conversation. Ronnie wanted to know want the song had to do with anything. Jamie just put her off.

Jamie said, "The two of you really looked marvelous out there. Jay really pulled out all the stops for you. No one has ever seen him dance like that before, except with one person. He showed you how much he loved you with his dancing. He opened his heart to you out there for all to see. That's why all the girls were asking. First of all he hadn't danced to the first song in a long time. I'll tell you about that some time and they have only seen him dance with one other person to that last song. I'll tell you about her too, sometime. Did you enjoy the dance?"

Ronnie said, "It was all right I suppose—nothing so special. Maybe he will leave me alone now."

Jamie reminded her, "Oh he will! He will never go back on his word as you will find out!" She added, "Ronnie, if you can sit there and say that the dance with Jay was just all right, I suppose you are either the biggest liar in the world, or you are as dead as that chair you're sitting on, or you really hate him. If you hate him that much, I'm glad he's through with you. Now tell the truth!"

All the girls began to say, "Yeah Ronnie tell the truth."

"Well I guess I have to be what you said I am Jamie. I still say the dance was all right," said Ronnie.

One day after school, Ronnie asked Jamie these questions: "What is it about Jay that makes him so special to you? What is this hold he seems to have over everyone? Why were you so set on him and me getting together?" Then she said, "Frankly I don't see any thing so special about him. You said you would explain and tell me about him sometime."

Jamie asked, "Do you honestly mean that you have not noticed a difference between Jay and most of the other guys?"

Ronnie replied, "Well I have noticed some things about him."

Jamie asked, "For instance?"

Ronnie said thoughtfully, "He's polite, has a nice demeanor, kind, and respectful."

Jamie said, "I can mention a number of other qualities: like a positive attitude, loving, sweet spirited, helpful, a friend, dependable, and sensitive to others. For example, I am sure Alice must have told you how he treated her. I suppose you are used to finding all these qualities in the guys you hang around, right?"

Ronnie shrugged her shoulders and said, "Well, no."

Jamie said, "To answer your questions; I wanted the two of you to get together because I see a lot of the same qualities in both of you. You only act like a "B" when it comes to him. Because he is not the pretty boy like that second baseman you were going with. You don't like Jay. And where is he now, your second baseman? As far as Jay and I are concerned, for some reason, I always had strong feelings for him ever since I met him, even when he was going with a girl name Denise. We have always been close just as we are now. After Denise, I think he seemed to sense my true feelings and I had a feeling things were beginning to move forward. When we danced he held me very differently. Although neither of us said anything, there was a sense of loving tenderness. I think the silence was due to the breakup of him and Denise. It was too soon. In the meantime, Mike, a childhood friend of Jay's transferred to our school. One day Mike asked Jay if we were a couple. Jay told him no, so he asked Jay to introduce him. So Jay introduced me to Mike and Jay stepped out of the picture. I was hurt because I loved Jay so much, yet there was a magnetic attraction to Mike. In time, I fell madly in love with Mike."`

"Did you ever find out if Jay loved you or not," asked Ronnie?

"Yes," replied Jamie. "One day Jay told me he stepped aside because he felt Mike and I were meant for each other." He said, 'I will always love you, but it will be a different kind of love from now on.' I didn't understand what he meant about feeling Mike and I were meant for each other until now. You see, that's the same feeling I have about you and Jay!"

Ronnie asked, "How come you and Jay didn't hit it off before him and Denise?" "When I first met Jay, I was going with someone else. I introduced him to Denise," said Jamie.

* * * *

The spring semester was approaching and baseball season would soon be at hand. I thought that I wouldn't enjoy the Canteen dances after my dance with Ronnie. For a long time, no girl except Jamie seemed to fit in my arms but that passed. I think it was the sixth Canteen dance after my dance with Ronnie; I was sitting out a dance when suddenly, "These Arms of Mine" the first song to which I had danced with Ronnie started playing. As before, the whole place became hushed. I looked toward the DJ, and there she was, walking towards me, my old girlfriend, the beautiful Miss Denise Winters. I quickly looked towards Jamie and shook my head no, because Jamie was about to cut her off.

At one time, she had been Jamie's best friend. Now Jamie couldn't stand her. Denise walked right up to me and stepped into my arms and we began to swirl around the floor. She was a great dancer and she knew it. I knew only one better. I absolutely loved to dance with her. There was no match for us in the Canteen except when I danced with Ronnie. We looked like one person on the floor. I had spent a lot of time teaching Denise to dance. Most of the other girls didn't like her because she would have monopolized all my dances, if I'd let her.

* * * *

Ronnie asked Jamie, "Who is that dancing with Jay? Gosh! Is she beautiful? They're dancing to that same song. Wow! Are they gorgeous together?"

Jamie said, "Not as gorgeous as you and Jay were."

"I could never dance that like that," said Ronnie.

"She only looks that good because of Jay," said Jamie. "One day you will meet someone who will make her good looks and dancing look fourth-rate."

Ronnie asked, "Who?"

"You'll see," replied Jamie.

"Gosh, look how she's lying against him," said Ronnie. "Is that his girlfriend?"

"Do I detect a bit of jealousy?" asked Jamie.

"Heavens, no! Just curious," said Ronnie.

"She used to be," said Jamie. "But he won't have her anymore."

"Why?" asked Ronnie.

"It's a long story," said Jamie. "I'll tell it to you some time when it's important enough to you.

"It's important right now," said Ronnie. Look how she's swooning against him. She'll win him back. No way will he be able to resist her advances."

"You wanna bet?" said Jamie.

"Who is she anyway? And why hasn't she been around?" asked Ronnie.

Jamie responded, "That, my dear girl, is the cheating Miss Denise Winters. She used to be my best friend. She's been in New York for over a year. I heard she was coming back."

"What happened?" asked Ronnie. "Like I said, when it's important enough to you," said Jamie.

"I told you it's important enough now," replied Ronnie.

"No it's not," answered Jamie.

"Well cheater or not, I am willing to bet that he won't be able to resist for long," Ronnie retorted. "See how she snuggles up to him! His knees are probably knocking right now."

Jamie responded, "I'll take that bet. Like I said, you don't know Jay. And I bet you're a bit more interested than you're making out. Are you sure there isn't a bit of jealousy showing up?" asked Jamie.

"Huh, are you kidding? I want no part of him," replied Ronnie.

* * * *

One Friday we decided to go to the roller rink. I didn't know Jamie had talked Ronnie into coming with us. Jamie wanted Ronnie and me to sit together in the car. I insisted that it would be better if Mike and I and she and Ronnie sat together. I did not know that Ronnie could not skate. She had heard how much fun we had and thought that she'd like to try it. I had no idea that Jamie and Mike were planning to have me teach her. Their plan was for me to teach Ronnie with the hope of getting us together, and her being dependent on me.

Jamie suggested to Ronnie that I teach her. "Jay is an excellent skater and a wonderfully patient teacher," She said. However, Ronnie was not having any of that. She decided that she would rather wait in the lounge until we finished. But Jamie and Mike put her skates on and began to teach her. They were both great skaters. They got Ronnie to the point where she could skate along the railing.

I had put my skates on and was skating with a couple of girls. We were dancing and having a great time. As we passed by, Jamie pointed to us and said to Ronnie,

"See those girls Jay is skating with? They were beginners like you last year. Jay taught them in a short time. Look at them now! Why won't you let him teach you?"

"I just don't want him to," Ronnie replied. "Isn't there anything he can't do?"

Mike answered, "Not much."

Ronnie asked, "Doesn't that bother you?"

Mike answered, "Heck No! You see Jay is Jay and Mike is Mike! Jay taught me that. Besides, he is the best friend a guy, or girl for that matter, can have. You'll find that out one day."

Ronnie was practicing along the railing so I told Mike and Jamie that I would keep an eye on her while they enjoyed themselves for a time. So I stayed near a post out of sight and kept watch on Ronnie. She seemed to be getting the hang of it and would get a bit away from the railing occasionally. I was kind of proud of her determination.

It was one of those times that she was away from the railing that Wild Willie came ducking in and out skating backwards and heading right towards Ronnie. I put on a burst of speed and arrived just as Willie crashed into Ronnie sending her toward the railing. I lunged forward to prevent her from going over the railing. The collision with her sent me face first into the railing but threw Ronnie away from the railing. Ronnie hit the floor and I was holding on to the railing trying to keep from going over. I felt losing consciousness and myself slipping. I thought I was going over, when I felt a hand grab me and pull me back. It was Mike. I remember putting my hand up to my face because of the pain. Ronnie was still on the floor. I was dazed, but I felt myself reach over to help her up, but she slapped my hand away. I partially lost my balance and braced myself using Ronnie's shoulder. She flung my hand off her shoulder and yelled, "You clumsy ox!" My arm felt wet.

Mike said to me, "You're bleeding badly let me get you to the locker room."

I must have passed out because the next thing I remember was Mike saying, "We need to stop this bleeding!" I was bleeding from my nose and a large gash just under my eyebrow.

Someone reported that as they helped Ronnie off the floor she screamed, "I'm bleeding somewhere!" there was blood all over her shoulder, arm and hand that I had reached for.

"That's Jay's blood," they told her. "See that trail of blood leading to the locker room!"

"That's what he gets for knocking me down! I think he ran into me intentionally." Ronnie said.

They said Jamie was furious. Shortly after that, the medics arrived, stopped the bleeding and took me to the hospital.

Someone told me later that Jamie was so angry with Ronnie that she called her a little "B." She told Ronnie that the only reason she and Mike left her skating along the railing was because of me.

"Jay told us to go and enjoy ourselves for a while and he would watch out for you. All the while we were gone he was standing behind that post keeping an eye on you. When he saw what was about to happen, he skated as fast as he could and threw his body between you and that railing. Yes, you are right; he is brutal. Brutal enough to almost give his life to save someone whom he felt hated him."

Mike told her that I had risked my life to protect her from going over the railing—the other side of which was a deep stairwell to the emergency exit. He told her that after Wild Willie had knocked her toward the railing and I had thrown my body between her and the railing to protect her, I would have gone over the railing myself if he had not grabbed hold of me. They told me that Mike had grabbed Ronnie and pulled her over to the railing and showed her where she would have fallen if she had gone over. He told her that she could have been seriously injured or even killed. Apparently he called her an ungrateful "B" and said that I could possibly lose an eye. They said Ronnie cried like a baby.

She said, "Oh Mike, Jamie, I'm so sorry, I thought he had knocked me down! I thought he just had a nosebleed! I didn't realize how serious it was until the ambulance arrived. I pray that he doesn't lose his eye! When they carried Jay out I was so afraid of what may have happened to him! Please forgive me!"

I was in the hospital for eight days. The gash required stitches. I was going in and out of consciousness with a concussion and they had to wait to be sure there was no damage to my eye. The loss of vision was temporary. After being released from the hospital I had to recover from the swelling around the eye and nose area of my face. I didn't look so good. When my outpatient visits were over and the stitches were removed, I had a scar over my right eye and a damaged nerve that caused my right eyelid to be slightly closed. Jamie said it made me look sexy. The doctor said that the nerve would probably heal itself in time.

I spent my time preparing for the coming baseball season. I chose not to go back to the Canteen or Roller rink. I started playing golf and spent more time at the stables to take up any time I had on my hands. I really liked golf and became rather good at it. Mike and Jamie continued to pressure me return to the canteen and rink, but I refused. They said how the gang missed me and were hoping that I would return soon. They did not mention Ronnie and neither did I. The truth of the matter was that I wanted no part of Ronnie. Word was going around as to how much I had changed. They said I was not the old Jay. I suppose they were right. Except for Mike and Jamie, I didn't socialize at all.

When the baseball season was over, I spent the summer vacation in Virginia with an old friend. We played a lot of golf together. He was a scratch golfer and taught me quite a lot. He also helped me to find my old self. We use to walk and talk for hours just traipsing through the woods.

By the time summer vacation was over, I had not only found myself, but had gotten myself in great shape for football. But I still did not socialize very much. I kept my concentration on the season's games ahead, the stables, playing golf and going to church. I did socialize with my friends in the halls, but I would not go anywhere near Ronnie. If we passed in the halls, I would not look in her direction. She would seem to pause as if to speak, but I would keep moving. After school I either went to practice, or to the stables, or the golf course, or bowling, or home. I didn't even mingle very long after games.

One day Mike came by the house.

"Jay," he said. "I know that things have hurt you, but it is time for you to get past that and get on with your life. I've never known you to lie down on anything. You have the strongest constitution of any one I have ever met. I've never seen you let anything beat you. The Canteen is as lifeless as a morgue and the roller-rink is almost without laughter. Jamie and I are bombarded with questions about you. They miss your spirit Jay. Perk up buddy, I expect to see you at the dance in a couple of days." He hugged me and left.

I was pondering what Mike had said, when Lori came into the room.

She said, "I thought I heard Mike's voice."

"You did," I responded.

"He didn't sound like himself," said Lori. "Is something wrong between you two?"

I said, "No, nothing's wrong. He's just disappointed in me."

She said, "Oh!"

I said, "In a few words he made me realize that I have been acting like a kid. He said he wanted to see me at the dance Friday."

Lori said, "Hooray for Mike! Now I don't have to get at you. I know that I've been away on business for a while and don't know much about your accident, but after watching you for the past few days I was on my way in to find out what was wrong with you. You've been almost lifeless. Not your vibrant self."

I said, "I know, but Mike has just snapped me out of that."

Lori said, "So what are you going to do."

I said, "Go to the dance like Mike said."

Lori said, "Good. I'll go with you, if you don't mind. I need some time for myself and it's a long time since I've been to the canteen, and it's been a long time since we've danced together."

Jamie and Ronnie had long since made up. Jamie really loved Ronnie but it disturbed her that Ronnie did not like me. When everyone began to turn away from Ronnie because of what happened to me, Jamie came to her defense big time. When Denise attacked Ronnie, cursing her and saying how insensitive she had been to my injury, Ronnie broke down in tears. Jamie slapped Denise and warned her to stay away from Ronnie. That brought the whole group to Ronnie's defense and pulled her back into the group.

* * * *

During the dance Friday night, Ronnie began to confide in Jamie. She told Jamie that she had not told her the truth the night that she first danced with Jay.

"When Jay put his arms around me, I tried to remain as cold as I could knowing that I had been dying to dance with him ever since the first time I saw him dance with you. When he had them play that song "These Arms of mine" and took me in his arms, it was wonderful. His touch was so light. It was like I was dancing by myself." I remember thinking, 'How can anyone I thought was so rough have such a feathery touch?' He held me, but it was as though he wasn't holding me. I could feel every move he wanted me to make, even though his touch was as light as a feather. His voice was so soft. His words were so tender. He said so many sweet things to me. I wanted to just melt in his arms. Every fiber in my body tingled, but my pride wouldn't let me say anything. I acted like a bump on a log."

"So the seeds of love did take root!" said Jamie.

"Huh?" asked Ronnie.

"The seeds Jay planted when he danced with you." answered Jamie.

Ronnie continued, "I know he was holding me, but it was like I was dancing around by myself. He moved me around so smoothly it was like we were on a cloud just floating along. It was as if I knew every move he would make by heart. I wanted to dance with him forever. Then another song, "Adorable" began and I tried to act like he had gone back on his word, but I was happy when he said that the music had never stopped. He continued to say so many sweet things to me. I felt myself weakening. I knew I couldn't continue to resist him.

When that song "Spanish Harlem" began to play, he didn't say a word; he just danced the way he danced. He touched my very soul and every fiber of my body was on fire. I had never danced or felt anything like that in my life. I was breathless. It was like I was some famous Spanish dancer. His touch was so light yet I knew where and how he wanted me to move. I don't know how I was doing what I was doing. All I know is that I didn't want it to end.

Just before the last song ended, he even apologized for anything he had done to create the animosity that I felt towards him. I felt so bad! I wanted to just turn my head and kiss him! You know how I said I didn't like him? Yet, here he was apologizing. I wanted to tell him to just hold me and never let me go. I wanted to continue dancing with him. I didn't want to let him go.

When the song ended, and he was holding me in that dip, our lips were so close and he was staring into my eyes. I thought he was going to kiss me. If he had I would have surrendered all. I wanted him to kiss me but he just smiled that beautiful boyish smile of his and walked away. I could not take my eyes off him. He never looked back. My heart was aching so, because I realized at that moment that he would keep his word.

Oh! How I have hoped that he would once again ask me to dance. When I saw him coming towards us, I kept hoping that he would ask me to dance, but he always asked someone else. He wouldn't even look at me. When our eyes did meet, he would just smile that beautiful smile and turn away. I keep remembering when you told me that, 'he will keep his word and you will be sorry.' I have cried a lot of tears since then. Now that song just haunts me day and night. It's as though I can hear him pleading to let him hold me. But now, he doesn't want to. What hurts most is that I don't think I have ever smiled at him.

When you asked me to go skating and wanted him to teach me, I really wanted him to. I was really being a little "B" like you said. I thought he would come over when I was practicing along the railing. I so wished he would and now look what a mess I have made. When I see him in the school halls, I want to say something to him but he won't stop or even look at me. My heart feels as though it will crumble into a thousand pieces. He said that he would never bother me again. He really meant it! He won't even look at me! Oh! Jamie, what have I done?"

"Maybe nothing that you can't fix, but you have to do it. I told you he would keep his word. You see, he meant it," said Jamie.

Ronnie said, "Jamie, I don't think I could ever face him now."

"Well, he left the ball in your court. It's totally up to you now. If you want him you've got to tell him because no one else can."

"I've messed up so badly that I'm sure he will go right into the arms of Denise if and when he comes back," Ronnie replied,

Jamie responded, "I told you that will never happen."

Ronnie started to ask Jamie something when a couple of guys asked them to dance. Ronnie started to refuse, but since Jamie was going to dance she accepted.

When the dance was over, Ronnie asked Jamie, "Will you tell me now what happened between Jay and Denise? Why do you say he will never go back to her?" Jamie looked at Ronnie and said, "You really do care now don't you?"

Ronnie said, "Oh yes Jamie, if you only knew how much! I remember asking you what everyone saw in Jay. Now I know. I'd be satisfied just to see him, even if he never wants me."

Jamie said, "I think that I can tell you what happened now."

"Jay was madly in love with Denise. You should have seen the two of them dance together then. What a beautiful sight. Remember I told you how beautiful the two of you looked dancing together? Well it was because he loved you. The two of them did not compare to you and him dancing together that night. I told you everyone was in awe watching you two dancing. I have only seen him dance to "Spanish Harlem" with one other person. Believe me his dance with you was something special. To continue with Denise: One day, Jay stopped by a mutual friend's house, no names of course. Jay later said that he noticed that our friend seemed uncomfortable, but he didn't pay much attention to it. Jay was about to leave when he heard Denise's voice laughing as she exited a bedroom. Right behind her was another friend. When they saw Jay, they were shocked. Jay just looked at the two of them, then turned and walked out. She has been begging for forgiveness ever since. Jay says he has forgiven her, but she could never mean anything to him again. Believe me, she won't. Now you know."

Suddenly tears began to stream from Ronnie's eyes. "I know now that he will never have anything to do with me either. But I would be satisfied just to see him like he used to be. No one seems to be happy anymore. This place used to be overflowing with laughter. You guys were right when you said I would learn one day. I'd be satisfied just to see him even if it meant his being with Denise."

Jamie hugged her and said, "You've finally made it! Don't worry she won't get him!"

Suddenly, a great roar went up, and everyone began to chant Jay, Jay, Jay, and Jay! Ronnie's heart suddenly leaped in her throat and fell back. As she looked towards the entrance, there stood Jay and one of the most gorgeous young ladies she had ever seen. She was not only beautiful, she was very elegant. Everyone rushed and gathered around Jay and his young lady. Tears began to slip into Ronnie eyes. She knew she had no chance against this gorgeous young lady. As she looked around, she realized that she had been left by herself. Even Jamie had deserted her. She had never felt so alone.

Finally, Jay gestured to the DJ to begin playing and suddenly it was the Canteen of old. Every one was joyously dancing. Jay was still standing with his new girlfriend and surprisingly to Ronnie, the girl and Jamie were hugging and laughing. Ronnie thought, "She's probably an old girlfriend?" When the record stopped, Jamie left Jay and the young lady and walked back towards Ronnie. As the next record began to play, Jay took his partner in his arms and they began to swirl around the floor like nothing you've ever seen before. What grace and beauty they exhibited. Everyone seemed to move off the floor. Watching the two of them dance was a delightful treat.

Ronnie said to Jamie, "I thought Denise could dance but that girl is the most beautiful I've ever seen on a dance floor. She and Jay look as though they have been dancing together forever! She makes Denise look like an old witch. Look at the way she moves. See how graceful she is! I can see why he wouldn't want Denise. No wonder Jay loves her."

Jamie said. "Yeah he sure does! Remember I told you that you would meet someone that would make Denise look fourth-rate!"

With Jamie's words, Ronnie's heart almost dropped completely out of her chest. Her chance with Jay was certainly gone. With tears in her eyes she wanted to run out and cry, but she felt everyone would know why she was leaving. Ronnie pulled herself together and commented to Jamie that Denise looked jealous.

Jamie said, "Yep, she sure does."

* * * *

# Ronnie

The next record that played was one of Jamie's favorites, "I've Been Loving You Too Long to Stop Now", her other being, "Kiss and Say Goodbye". She loved to dance with Jay when either of those songs played. True to who he was, Jay excused himself from his date and started towards Jamie. As Jamie started to meet him, Denise made a beeline for Jay. I thought that Jay would let Denise have her way, but I was wrong. He politely excused himself and continued to meet Jamie. Boy! The way Jamie and he danced together you would think that they were in love. Now I understood what these songs were saying for Jamie. When the dance was over, Jay escorted Jamie back to her seat. I suddenly realized how much of a gentleman he was. A lot of the fellows did not escort you all the way back to where they had picked you up, but he always would. She sat right next to me. He bent and kissed her forehead as usual. He did not look at me. My heart was about to jump out of my chest it was pounding so. This was the first time I had been near him since that night at the roller-rink. I saw the scar over his right eye and realized how close it was to his eye and how it had left his right eyelid slightly closed. Realizing that he could have lost his eye, I was nearly to tears, and moved by compassion, I reached up and gently touched the scar and the side of his face as he was kissing Jamie. He paused briefly, looked into my eyes and walked away. I could not hold back the tears as I watched him walk away. He walked over to Denise and began to dance with her. I realized at that moment, that he had probably promised her the next dance.

After his dance with Denise, Jay walked over to the DJ and whispered something. He then walked toward the young lady who had been swamped by the other guys. About that time, the song "Spanish Harlem" began to play. I turned and looked at Jamie.

Jamie said, "Remember I told you that I had only seen him dance to that song with but one other person? Well that's her! That song is very special to the two of them and Tim won't play it for anyone but Jay. That's why everyone was so shocked when he played it and danced with you. They all knew you were special when that happened. If you want to know how you looked out on the floor, you will see when you see her dance. You just didn't have all the flare that she has, but otherwise, that's how you looked out there! He will also do dances with her that he did not do with you."

When they took to the floor every one left the floor. What transpired on that dance floor during that song would be ingrained in my mind forever! They were like one person out there. I could not take my eyes off her. She moved with the grace of an antelope. Every move was perfectly executed. Jay looked as though he was a matador fighting a bull, as she would pass gracefully by him. What beauty, grace and love of dance they exhibited. The whole canteen was electrified. In that one number they executed different dances: Cha-Cha, Tango, Mambo, and others. Jamie had to tell me the different dances as they were performing them. I had never seen anything so beautiful. When the dance ended there was a roar that could be heard in the next county.

I told Jamie as tears streamed down my face, "She is a lucky girl and, as hard as it is, I'm glad Jay has someone like her. Gosh! She is so beautiful!"

Jamie said, "Yes and she loves Jay very much!" Jamie did not look at me when she said that.

I continued to hope against hope that he would come back by me but he did not. Each time I saw him dance with the girl he had brought with him, my heart sank. How could I match her?

I told Jamie, "Each time I see him dance with her I die a little. I know that I have lost any chance I ever had."

Jamie said, "I told you the ball was in your court."

I said, "How can I compete against her?"

Jamie said, "Yeah, I guess you're right."

There was something about the way Jamie said this that spurred something in me. I walked up to the DJ and asked him to play "These Arms of Mine." I asked him to wait until I was over by Jay before starting the song.

He smiled and said, "Got yah."

Jay was standing with the young lady and some other friends. Once I reached Jay, the record started to play. I was afraid of two things: That the young lady would be offended, but most of all that Jay would refuse. I excused myself to the girl with him and asked Jay if he would dance with me. To my surprise, the young lady, who was even prettier up close, just smiled and nodded yes, and Jay, who was always a gentleman, did not refuse. I noticed the surprised look on his face when the song began and I was standing there. He'd had his back to me. I supposed he had expected Denise.

He took me in his arms and we began to dance. He stared straight ahead. He did not look at me at all. I began to talk to him. I talked to him through the whole song. I told him what a "B" I had been. I told him that the last time we had danced together, I had heard and remembered every word he said. I told him how I had wanted to just melt in his arms but I had let pride stand in the way.

I said, "This song is saying everything that is in my heart."

When the song ended, he maneuvered me back to where Jamie and I were sitting. He turned and walked away and I called, "Ja—ay!" Tears were streaming down my face like a water faucet turned on. Suddenly the song started to play again. As he turned around, I ran and jumped and threw my arms around his neck. At first he didn't respond but I wouldn't let go. I was crying profusely. Slowly his arms slid around me tightly, but ever so gently. After he lowered my feet to the ground, he raised my chin with his fingers.

As he looked at my tear-soaked face and water-filled eyes he said softly, as he dried my eyes with his handkerchief, "These eyes are too beautiful to have tears!" Then, holding my face in his hands, for the first time, he began to kiss me. He lightly kissed my forehead, then he softly touched his lips to my right eye, then lovingly kissed my left eye, then he so softly kissed my nose, then he gently touched his lips to the right side of my mouth, then feather-like kissed the left side of my mouth, then very softly he kissed just above my upper lip, then warmly kissed under my lower lip, I was trembling so, and my heart was pounding in my ears so loud that when his soft lips fell upon my mouth like a butterfly landing on a rose petal, I went completely limp. Everyone was watching and let out a tremendous roar of approval. They said that I fainted. I only know that I have never known such ecstasy. My heart was still pounding like a jackhammer. I opened my eyes and looked up to the most beautiful, loving smile.

I had totally forgotten about the beautiful girl that Jay was with. I could not believe that he had kissed me. Who was she? Where was she? Then I saw her. She was talking to Denise. Denise did not look at all happy. Then she came towards Jay and me and said,

"Hi, I'm Lori. So you are little Miss Heartthrob! I can see why Jay is so taken with you. You are absolutely lovely!" Then she put her arm around me and said, "You be good to my little brother. I don't like it when he is not happy. I love him very much." I could not believe my ears. I looked at Jamie and she just nodded and smiled. His sister! I could have screamed for joy! Wow! Did Jamie and I have to talk! Gosh! Lori was so cool!

Then I noticed that Jay had walked over to Denise. She was crying. He took his handkerchief and dried her eyes. I am not sure what I was feeling. I wasn't angry, jealous, or hurting, but yet I was not pleased. Wow! What a way to feel. I continued to watch them. Then as he took her in his arms and began to dance, I felt so strange.

At that moment Lori, who had been watching me, said in a whisper, "Never worry about Jay," and she smiled.

Suddenly, all my apprehension disappeared. I continued to watch them and she had her head laid on his chest as she usually did when they danced. When the music ended, he continued to talk to her for a while, kissed her forehead and came straight to me. He lifted me up, let me back down and kissed me ever so soft and sweetly.

Then he whispered in my ear, "Never worry about Denise or anyone else."

My heart was about to burst open. How could I have ever not loved him? I don't believe my feet touched the floor for the rest of the evening!

When the dance was over, Lori asked Jamie and Mike to take her home. Then she came over to Jay and me.

She put her arms around me and said, "Goodnight little sister" and kissed me on the cheek. Then she hugged Jay; you could see the love she had for him, and she said,

"I'm so happy for you. She's a doll."

As she walked away, I thought, "How lucky I am that she is his sister." Then my eyes turned to Jay and I thought, "What a guy, how lucky can a girl get?" So I reached up and kissed him. When he took me home, I think I just floated into my house.

The next morning I could not wait to call Jamie. We were both so excited; I think it was two minutes before we realized that one of us had to stop talking.

Jamie said, "Wait, wait, wait, wait! I think I had better let you talk first."

I said, "Jamie, you were so right all along. How could I have been so stupid? My heart is still pounding in my chest. Jay is such a wonderful person. I never thought any man could be so loving and tender. Now I know why everyone loves him."

Jamie responded, "For a while I was beginning to think there was something wrong with you."

"Yeah, I guess I was acting like a 'B,'" I answered.

Jamie said, "I worried about you when Jay went over to Denise after Lori told her off. I noticed how you were watching. What did Lori say to you?"

Oh Jamie she is so cool! She just whispered, 'Never worry about Jay.' Speaking of Lori, I was shocked to find out that she was Jay's sister."

"Well," said Jamie. "She is not really his sister. She is his cousin. Lori and Jay's mothers were sisters. Both Lori and Jay are the only children. Jay's dad was a war hero killed in the Korean War. When his mother died, Lori's mother adopted Jay so Lori finally had the little brother she wanted. They both love him something awful as you could see."

"Gosh!" I said. "I've wondered. Where did all that love come from?"

Jamie said, "I understand he is a lot like his father, and his mother was even more loving than Lori's mom Loren."

I asked, "Do you know Lori's mother? I bet she's beautiful."

Jamie responded, "Yes and yes."

Then I asked, "Did you know Jay's mother?"

Jamie said, "No, but I've seen her pictures and she was absolutely gorgeous and Jay looks like his father. He has his mother's eyes and mouth."

I smiled and said, "Maybe that's why his lips are so soft." Then I asked, "Why hasn't Lori been coming to the dances?"

Jamie replied, "Lori is a professional dance instructor and she travels, teaching around the world."

My jaw dropped. "Gosh! No wonder she's such a great dancer! Does she skate also?"

"Yes," said Jamie. "She was Jay's teacher in both. She said he is the best student she's ever had and not because he is her cousin. She wanted him to turn professional. Jay said no. She said Jay has the lightest, yet firmest touch of anyone she has ever taught or danced with. She said that is not teachable, it's a gift."

"Wow! I am so glad I met her!" I said.

Jamie said, "When they first came to the dance last night, she asked me if you were there. When I told her you were the one standing alone over there. She asked if you were as pretty as you looked. I told her yes, you were. She's home because when she heard that Jay was in the hospital, she immediately canceled all her appointments and flew home. I dare say that she was quite upset because he was hurt. If you think I love him, it is doesn't compare to her love for him. She and her mother absolutely adore Jay!"

"Does she know that I was the cause?" I asked.

Jamie said, "No! Jay just said it was an accident. He said he was trying to prevent a girl from going over the railing and hit his face against the railing. Which is exactly what happened. So you see you were really not the cause. Everyone was more upset by your attitude. Lori really likes you. You can tell she does not like Denise. I am so happy for you and Jay. I knew the two of you would make a great couple."

I said, "Thank you for sticking with me. You are a good friend and I will always love you."

Jamie said, "You have a better friend in Jay. You take good care of him. You will never have anyone who will love you more or be a better friend."

With tears in my eyes, I thanked Jamie and said, "I know now!"

# Ronnie Meets Rance

The next four years were the happiest in my life. Jay and I were together constantly. He had so many ways of showing his love, and they were mostly little things. Things you would not expect from a man. He would just look at the clouds and talk softly to me about them. One day while looking at the clouds, he was holding me, I had my back to him, and he began to talk to the clouds. He asked them where they were going. He acted as if they were answering him. As he talked to them, he described how they looked and I could see what he saw. I had never seen clouds in that way before. Some of them looked like people. He finished by saying, "Have a safe trip".

Then he turned me to him and said as he lifted me, "You are my little cloud. You are so light and soft and sweet." Then he lowered me and kissed me with such tenderness that I thought my heart would burst.

Jay loves horses, but I am deathly afraid of them. The one place I did not want to go with him was to the stables. He knew my fear of horses so he never asked me to go with him, but he would always ask if I would mind if he went. He went to the stables often and I couldn't bear to be away from him. One Sunday, after church, I asked him to take me with him. He asked if I was sure. I was afraid, but I wanted to share everything about him; I even wore his school sweater.

I was surprised when we arrived at the stables. They were nothing like I had imagined. It was a beautiful place. With white fences all around, the stables were red with white shutters, and there was a beautiful white house with red shutters. The owner, Mr. Ross, was sitting on the porch. He welcomed Jay and me.

Jay introduced me and he smiled and said, "I've heard a lot about you." He turned to Jay and said, "She's more beautiful than you said!"

I couldn't help but blush. I kept hearing a horse whinny.

Mr. Ross said, "I think that horse knows you are coming when you are miles away. He's been acting up for the last fifteen minutes." He looked at me and said, "I have never in my life seen any thing like him and Rance!" He looked at Jay and said laughing, "Well you'd better get back there before Rance tears the stable apart."

Jay led me to a place that was like a grandstand where people can watch what is going on in the arena.

He kissed me and said, "Now don't be afraid. You are totally out of harm's way here." He left me there and went to the stables. Then I saw Jay leading this magnificent, beautiful black horse into the arena. At first glance I was afraid because I thought the horse was trying to bite Jay. Later Jay told me that he was only kissing him, to show his affection.

The two of them continued to show their affection for each other for a while. Then Jay waved his hand and I never saw anything like what I witnessed for the next few minutes. I was in awe of the speed, power, and grace demonstrated by that animal. He acted as though he had never been out before. During the whole scene Jay was standing in the middle of the arena. Jay told me later that it was called a corral.

Finally, he ran full speed at Jay and my heart almost jumped in my mouth, but Jay just raised his hand like a traffic cop and the horse slid to a stop right at Jay.

At that moment, Mr. Ross asked, "Have you ever seen the like?"

I had been so intent on watching that horse and Jay that I hadn't noticed Mr. Ross come out onto the grandstand.

He said, "They are like two kids." Then Jay and Rance began to play tag. Each in turn began to chase the other. Again Mr. Ross said, "Have you ever seen anything like that? Jay has a gift I have never seen in all my years around horses."

I said, "He's like that with people too." Mr. Ross looked at me and smiled. We continued to watch Jay and Rance play until they tired. Then they began to share their affection for each other again. I felt jealous. I wanted to be a part of that.

When I told Mr. Ross that I was afraid of horses, he said, "Here's your opportunity to get over it, with Jay and Rance."

I asked how Jay happened to have Rance. And Mr. Ross told me a fascinating story. He told me that Jim, Jay's father, had been a great horseman. Lorna, his mother, had also loved and been good with horses, but Jay had something beyond what they had. He said that Jay's father first brought him to the stable when he was eight years old. Jay was very excited when he first saw the horses. His father took Jay in with the horses right off and Jay showed no fear of them. He took to petting them right off.

He said, "I had a mare that was the meanest horse I have ever seen. She wouldn't let anyone come near her. Even Jay's father couldn't handle her. Jim went to put his horse up and left Jay sitting on the grandstand steps. One of the hands put that mare in the corral. When I looked out to check on Jay, I saw Jay at the corral fence and started to yell for him to get away. To my startled senses, I saw that he was petting the mare. Her ears were not laid back and she was enjoying his petting. Jay was running up and down the fence and she chased along with him. I called the stables and asked Jim to take a look but not to get upset. He looked out of the stables, then walked to the fence and just watched the two of them. Later when we questioned Jay, he said he had wanted to pet her, so he went to the fence and called her and she came. Afterward every time Jay came here she would come right to him.

A few years later, we got Rance. That was not his name at that time. He was a young stallion and meaner than that mare. We had made plans to sell him. He had hurt one of the hands. It wasn't bad but he was a risk to keep around. One day Jay and his dad came out. Rance had just chased one of the hands out of the corral. Jay and his dad stood at the fence just looking at the horse. Finally Jay called to him. He hesitated and Jay continued to call him. Finally he came over to the fence and Jay began to pet him, and later his father was able to pet him. Jay walked along the fence and the horse followed him. His dad tried it but the horse did not follow him. We knew then that it was Jay. I told them that I had the horse marked for sale. Jay begged for me not to sell him. I told him that I had to sell him. He hugged his dad around his waist, but didn't say anything. His dad put his hand under Jay's chin, raised his head and just looked into his eyes. Then he held Jay to him and asked me what I would take for the horse. Jay named him Rance."

When Jay came and told me he was going to take Rance in and clean him up, I asked if I could go with him. Jay looked shocked and asked if I was sure, I responded, without a doubt, and he said to come on down. When I went down into the corral, fear began to build in me. Rance seemed huge up close and much more powerful. There was no rope or halter on him. Jay sensed my fear and so did Rance because he snorted and sort of backed up.

Jay said, "Rance, this is my friend." He put his arms around me and kissed me; then he told Rance, "Bow to the lady," and made a bowing gesture. Rance followed suit and did the same with his head. My fear seemed to slowly leave me.

Jay said, "Say hello to the lady, Rance." Rance nodded his head as if to say OK, walked up to me and lowered his head. Jay lifted my hand and placed it on Rance's forehead and I began to stroke his forehead. Rance seemed so pleased, almost as if he was happy for Jay. From that moment on I had no fear of him.

I helped Jay clean Rance up. I loved brushing him. His coat was so smooth, soft and shiny. Jay cleaned his hooves and put him in his box stall. Then he told me to fill a can with oats and give them to Rance. Wow! Did Rance really go for that! Jay was so proud of me. He said that one day he hoped that I would want to learn to ride. I told him I would. We shared everything else. Why not riding horses? I knew from that moment on I wanted to see as much of Rance as I could. How could I have lost my horrible fear of horses in that little time? Now, I needed to learn to ride.

We walked around for a while and I stopped Jay at the big vacant field next to the Rosses home.

"I looked at Jay and said, "What a beautiful place to build a home."

He just looked at me and kissed me and said, "Yeah!"

As I snuggled up to Jay on our drive home, I realized that I had just seen another side of this remarkable person. Where did all that love come from? Jay and Rance. Gosh! How I loved them both. I cry sometimes when I think of what I almost lost. I reached up and kissed his cheek. He glanced at me and smiled that beautiful smile. I continued to snuggle close to him.

When we arrived at my home, Jay walked me to the door. He held my face in his gentle hands and kissed me so softly and then held me closely. I could feel his love just pouring into me and I knew that he was saying, "Thanks for overcoming your fear and accepting this part of my life." Although he had never said it, I knew he wanted so much for me to be part of his life with Rance.

Those four years were glorious: watching Jay and Mike play sports, and us dancing, roller-skating, bowling, and totally overcoming my fear of horses; learning to ride, learning to fish and the excitement of catching my first fish, even if it was—as Jay teased—a minnow; strolling through the park, spending time with Mike and Jamie, the occasional night dinner-dance cruises, and ice-skating.

Two of those four years we were in college and yet our lives did not change that much. Since we lived close to it, the four of us decided to stay home and go to the State University. We were so close we did not want to be separated from each other. We were all happy we had made that choice. Although we chose different career fields, we sometimes had classes together and we studied together.

It seemed so strange, because we would be in the same room together sometimes for what seemed like hours and no one spoke a word. We were all serious about our studies. Finally someone would say, "Let's take a break." Then we would laugh and enjoy each other. Usually it would be Jay who would say, "OK guys! Time to get back to the books." Someone would say, "Yes master." And we would all laugh.

One day while walking hand-in-hand with Jay around the campus, I saw Jamie and Mike necking. I thought to myself how much they loved each other. Then I looked at Jay and thought how much I loved him and how lucky I was to have him. I thought, "I will make him happy for the rest of my life." Jay and I talked about getting married after we finished college. Jay had received a large sum of money from his parents' death, so we would have a nest egg to get us started. Wow! Was that a shock when he told me about the nest egg! He said no one knew about it outside of his family. I thought to myself, "That much money and still be so humble. He is remarkable." He said that he would not touch it until we were married. When I think about how remarkable he is, I think about the time I wanted Jay to make love to me.

He said, "Not until we are married. I will not degrade you. If you feel you must, feel free to walk away from me. Just tell me that's what you need. I will not hold it against you. Don't do it behind my back. I suppose that was Denise's problem."

When he finished, I cried tears I didn't know I had in me; mainly because I realized how much he loved and respected me, partly because I felt I had embarrassed him, and partly because I was embarrassed.

Being the remarkable person he is, he gently pulled me to him and spoke softly in my ear saying, "My love, do you think I don't have the same feelings that you have? I constantly have to fight them off. Because I love you so much I want our consummation to be in ecstasy." Then he kissed me in that way that caused my legs to turn to jelly and my senses to leave me.

# Then Came War

In our third year of college, something seemed to come over me. I kept feeling that I would lose Jay. I knew it was silly because we were happier then ever. Jay had taught me to ride on one of the other horses at the stable using a saddle. I even learned to love, trust and get Rance from his box stall and he had learned to love and trust me. This made Jay extremely happy because now I shared every part of his life. He taught me to call Rance and stand as he raced full speed toward me and then raise my hand like a traffic cop and stand still while Rance slid to a stop right in front of me. Rance would then lower his head and sort of nuzzle me with his nose. Jay said this was his way of showing his affection.

It took me a while to get the nerve to stand there, but Jay's love and patience paid off. Now I would go into the corral alone and call Rance to me. He is such a loving animal. I sometimes thought how much he and Jay were alike personality-wise. In spite of this, that feeling of losing Jay would creep over me every so often. I kept telling myself that it was just because I was so happy and that deep inside of me I felt I didn't deserve Jay because of the way I had treated him in the beginning.

Then one day, my fears became a reality. On the news was the escalation of war in Vietnam. Our men were being drafted and some were enlisting. Jay and Mike decided to enlist. They both wanted to go into the service and decided if they enlisted they could stay together. In spite of the pleas and tears of Jamie and me, their minds were made up. We even enlisted the support of

Lori and Loren, Lori's mother. I thought their tears would make a difference, but the guys said that it was every man's duty to defend our country.

After their enlistment, we spent all of our time together. We included Jamie and Mike and Lori and Loren. Jay wanted all of us to be together as much as possible before they had to report.

One day Loren went to Washington. When she came back, she called all of us together. She had gone to see a friend of hers who happened to be a General. She got his assurance that Jay and Mike would be kept together while in the service. She did not trust the regular service people to keep their word. That made all of us so happy. We all hugged and thanked Loren.

Loren said, "Thank Lori it was her idea." So we did.

"Why don't you guys get married before you have to leave?" Lori asked Jay. Jamie and I thought that was a wonderful idea and so did Loren. Jay did not agree. Mike and Jamie did and got married. I pleaded with Jay, but he said we would make our plans for when he returned. I told Jay about the feeling that I had been having about losing him, but he said he would return, just to love and trust him. So we spent the next few days planning our life for when he returned.

The night before they had to leave I could not sleep. The next day at the train station, Jamie and I could not hold back the tears. I thought between us we would float the train station away.

Jay said, "I want the two of you to finish college." He turned to Lori and Loren and said; "Take care of her and Jamie for us until we return." They promised that they would. When it was time for them to leave, he turned to me and held me close.

I thought, "What will I do without his love? How can I exist without him?"

Then he said, "I told you before, these eyes are too beautiful for tears!" Then he softly kissed my forehead, then kissed my tearful right eye, then my tearful left eye, then softly kissed the tip of my nose, then gently touched his lips to the right corner of my mouth, then the left corner of my mouth, then feather light he touched his lips to the top of my upper lip, then under my lower lip, then holding me gently but firmly, he let his lips settle so softly on my lips, that there was a pounding of my heart, a rush to my head and blissfully, my senses drifted away from me.

When I regained my senses Lori and Loren were holding me and Jay had gone. Jamie was standing by the tracks looking longingly after the train. I could not believe that they had gone. Loren asked if I was all right. I nodded my head, yes.

She said, "I have never seen such a loving kiss as that. Now I know the love that my son feels for you."

I realized two things at that moment. I realized why Lori calls Jay her brother and that Loren had never seen Jay kiss me before. Loren put her arms around me and held me like a mother.

She said, "We will bear this pain together;" I looked and saw the tears in her and Lori's eyes. They would also miss Jay. The four of us comforted each other as we drove home from the train station

We spent the next two months trying to fill the void left by Jay and Mike. I had been so concerned with my own feelings that I had not realized how much Jay was a part of Loren and Lori's life. Lori canceled all appointments for two months so that she could be with Loren. On occasion I would see Loren crying, though she would never do so in front of Jamie and me. I knew then that I would have to be strong around them from now on.

Finally, Loren told Lori that it was time for her to get back to work. She told Lori that she was all right now and that getting back to work would get her mind off Jay. Before Lori went back to work, she said one day, that she wanted to talk to Jamie and me. She told us that Jay had asked her to assist us in any way she could. Lori said that she had a lot of connections and that she could help us when we finished college.

She asked what area of music I wanted to venture into. I told her I wanted to study voice and look towards theater and acting. She said I was easy and then asked Jamie what she wanted. Jamie, who was a wonderful artist and painter, also loved real estate. Lori said she could be of help to both of us. Boy, that really made us smile! We hugged Lori and thanked her.

She said, "What could I do? Jay's wish is my command."

I missed Jay so much it was like half of me was missing! I wanted so to be close to him. My thoughts turned to Rance. He was so much a part of Jay that I felt being close to him would be the nearest thing to being with Jay. I visited Rance as often as I could.

I remember the first time I went to see him. It caused me to realize that a horse had the same type of feelings that we have. When he saw me, he ran and jumped the same way he did the first time I went with Jay and saw him. He was happy to see me, but after he greeted me he ran to the fence and looked. He came back nudged me and then ran back to the fence and looked. Then

I began to understand. He was asking me, where was Jay? At that moment I remembered what Jay had told me, "If you pay attention you can read the actions of an animal."

So I began to rub his fore head and say softly that Jay had told him he would be gone for a while but he would be back. I almost believed that I could see a tear in his eye. It made tears come to my eyes as I told Rance, "I miss him too!" He put his head over my shoulder and stood there. I continued to stroke his neck. It was as if we were consoling each other. It was at that time that I knew that I had been totally accepted by Rance. He showed his acceptance each time I went to see him but he always looked to see if Jay was with me.

Three months passed. Then one day my phone rang. I answered and Loren said she needed to see me as soon as possible and hung up. Frightened I made haste to Loren's. As I was parking I noticed Jamie arriving. My mind began to race and I tried to fight off thoughts. I waited for Jamie and we both wondered what could be so urgent. We rang the doorbell and Loren let us in and invited us into the sitting room.

She said, "Now both of you, sit down."

All kinds of wild thoughts were running through our heads and our hearts were pounding. Just as we sat down, Jay and Mike entered the room. We both screamed. I don't remember leaving the chair. I just remember my arms around Jay's neck and him holding and kissing me, the same with Jamie and Mike. Loren just stood there smiling.

Jay held me for what seem like an eternity. After asking me how I had been, He drew me back close to him and asked softly, "How's Rance?"

I said, "Missing you! Let's go see him!" Jay held me at arm's length and looked at me, puzzled.

I said, "Yes! I love him too. He has been my consolation since you have been gone."

Jay laughed and picked me up and spun me around like a top. He lowered me and kissed me ever so gently and said, "I love you more than life itself! Lets go see Rance!"

When we arrived, Mr. Ross was standing on the porch. He was smiling and hurried to the gate to meet Jay and me as we got out of the car.

He hugged Jay and said, "I had a feeling you were coming. Rance is going crazy back there."

Mr. Ross had let Rance out so we hurried to the corral. Rance was looking over the fence and saw Jay. He seemed absolutely hysterical. Just like the first time I saw him, he ran and jumped and kicked his hind legs all the time whinnying. Finally, he stopped and came to Jay. It seemed he could not stop nuzzling Jay. Then he laid his head over Jay's shoulder just as he had done to me. Jay stroked his neck and said, "Yeah, I've missed you too." After a while, Rance walked over to me and began to nuzzle me.

Jay said with a smile, "Ah ha! I see you two have become good friends." You don't know how happy that made me to hear Jay say that. I looked to the porch and saw Mr. Ross give me the OK sign. I remembered what he had said to me when I told him about my fear of horses. After a few minutes with me, Rance went back to Jay and did something that I had never seen before; Jay was standing with his back to the fence. Rance walked up to Jay lowered his front legs as if he was kneeling down and invited Jay to get on his back. Jay climbed on and Rance took him for a ride around the corral. That was the first time I had ever seen Jay ride Rance. They had always enjoyed playing, but there he was atop Rance— no saddle and no bridle—Jay had never put a bridle or saddle on Rance. He just sat there with his hand on his thighs even when Rance went into a canter. They really seemed to be enjoying each other. It was unbelievable to see the love between the two of them, but it was easy for me to understand.

Finally Rance came to a stop by me. Jay slid off and said to me, "Up you go!" I held back, but Jay said, "It will be all right." I had never ridden without a saddle but I had learned to trust Jay and my fear subsided although it did not leave me. Jay boosted me atop Rance, gathered a handful of his mane for me to hold onto and told me to relax.

"He will be very gentle with you, OK?" He said.

I said, "OK!"

Jay turned to Rance and said, "OK Rance." Rance started to walk away.

I felt terrified but that suddenly left me. Rance walked so easily. It was as if he knew I was frightened. He also seemed to know when I felt totally comfortable because he suddenly broke into a slow canter. There I was atop this powerful mass of horseflesh, no saddle, no bridle and just a handful of mane, and feeling totally secure. As I approached Jay, I saw that beautiful smile of his. I wanted to hop off of Rance into his arms but I was enjoying this immensely. It was unbelievable that I could be doing what I was doing. Not me, who had such a dreadful fear of horses. It was as if I was going to wake up any minute and find out I was dreaming. I could have continued on forever. I guess Rance knew that too because just like he began everything else he came to a stop right by Jay.

Smiling from ear to ear, I slid off into Jay's arms, and hugged and kissed him as though it was for the last time.

He said, “Whoa, I‘m not the one who gave you that wonderful ride!” So I immediately went to Rance and hugged him and told him thanks. It seemed I couldn’t stop hugging him. I felt so wonderful inside. I wondered if this is what Jay felt and why he loved to spend so much time with Rance—Wow! Then it was time for us to go. Now we both hated to leave Rance. I told Jay that I would like for us to spend every day of his leave with Rance.

He just smiled and said, “Thanks so would I.” It made me so happy to please Jay. I loved him so much. I cry every time I think of what I would have missed if I had lost him. We brushed Rance down, cleaned his hooves, gave him some oats and left. Jay turned around and stood looking back toward the stables.

I asked, “What’s the matter?

He said, “In a few days, I won’t see him for some time.” I thought I detected a tear in Jay’s eye. My heart almost stopped. I had never seen that sadness in him. I just held him.

As we promised, we spent every day with Rance. What a wonderful time that was! It was almost as though Rance was a person. In fact, that horse had more personality than most people! Then came that dreaded time when we had to leave. We stayed with Rance as long as we possibly could. Jay had to leave the following day and we wanted to spend some time with Loren and Lori.

That evening was the most wonderful.

Lori said, “Now I have a little sister.” She took Jay aside and told him that he should have married me before he had to leave. Later that evening she told me that Jay just said, “I will not marry her and leave her. When I marry her I don’t intend ever to leave her.” He asked Lori and Loren to take care of me while he was gone.

The next day was the saddest of my life. Jay and Mike left Loren, Lori, Jamie and me in floods of tears. I had never seen Lori or Loren cry like that before. All we could do was console one another.

Letters began to come and I would read and reread them. I treasured each and every word. His letters were so gentle and sweet just like him. I told him how Rance looked for him each time I went out to see him. I told him how Jamie and I really supported each other. She was really shocked to see how close Rance and I were.

She said, “And you were the one who said no one would ever get you close to a horse, and Rance, of all horses. Now, look at you!”

I told him how close Loren, Lori and I had become. That made him so happy. Each day I waited for the mailman. I could not wait to get my letter. Receiving a letter and sometimes two, made two months go by fast.

Then suddenly, there was no letter. I thought that something probably had happened to the mail and that the following day I would get two letters. Not so, nor did any come the day after that, or the next. I was frantic. I went to see Loren and asked if she had received any mail. She had not. We were really worried so Loren called her friend in Washington. He said he would get back to her. The news came that Jay and Mike's company had suddenly been shipped overseas. Jamie and I cried for days.

Three weeks passed and still no word. One day my phone rang. It was Jamie, and she was very excited.

"I got a letter from Mike," she said. "He says, 'We were in our barrack writing letters, when Jay was told to go to the C.O.'s office. He was gone about 40 minutes. When he came back, he tossed me a set of corporal stripes. Jay had a set of sergeant stripes. He said we had both been promoted. Because of the need, the lieutenant had recommended the two of us. Something must be in the wind because the lieutenant just called Jay into his office. I am writing this as fast as I can just in case. We haven't been allowed to mail letters until now. We have been writing them in secret, but I will be able to mail this one. We have a feeling that something is going to happen because of the promotions. So I am glad I can get this one off. Jay has not been able to finish his yet. If he doesn't, tell Ronnie not to worry he has written a whole shoebox full. When he gets a chance to mail them she will need a garage to hold all of them.'—That's all I can read to you Ronnie, the rest is personal. Now we know what happened as to why no letters. I'm sure they will write when they get settled. And don't forget Mike said that Jay has written you a lot of letters. He evidently hasn't had a chance to mail them."

# The Fifty-Second Raid

That was the last we heard from the guys for a month. In the meantime we busied ourselves spending as much time as we could with each other and with Rance, Loren, and Lori when she was in town.

The fifth week after my letter from Mike, I got a call from Loren. She had received a letter from Jay. He sent his love and said that everything was well. When I hung up, Ronnie called. She was really excited.

She said, "You won't believe how many letters I received. Mike was right. I've got a shoebox full. I've got forty-one letters. I don't know where to begin. I'm too excited to start. Oh! Jamie, I love my man. Has the mailman come by you yet?"

"Not yet." Just then the doorbell rang. "Hang on," I said. I went back excited. "I haven't got forty-one but there are at least fifteen here. The mailman said the two of us are causing him to earn his pay. He said he was happy for us. Well I guess it's time for us to begin to read."

For eighteen months we received letters from the boys. The papers were full of their exploits. Mike and Jay's company were cited many times. The guys wrote how close-knit they were. How they looked out for each other. Mike wrote as to how Jay was the cause of it.

One day, I told Ronnie, "Mike wrote that Jay refused a field commission because it would have meant his leaving the group so they promoted Jay to Staff Sergeant and promoted Mike to Sergeant. They have begun to do a lot of night raiding. They have been wreaking havoc among the enemy."

Then Mike wrote again that their Lieutenant had been killed and they had promoted Jay to his position and him to staff sergeant. "The guys say that now we are really a tight unit. They really like Jay as a leader. Not that he was not doing the leading anyway."

Mike did not write as often after becoming Staff Sergeant. His letters were fewer but sweeter. He said he did not know what Jay was doing with his letters, but he was writing a ton of them. He mentioned too that, "For the last fourteen months we have been giving the enemy hell. I think that Jay has become a marked man. In fact, I think our whole unit has been marked. Jay says, that tells us we have been really effective. Last night was our fifty-first raid so far. I hear we have to go out again tomorrow. I love you very much. See you kid!" That's how he always ended his letters.

Then the letters stopped coming. Fear rose greatly in Ronnie, Loren, Lori and me. Then the dreaded day came when we got a visit from the military. The news had come that Mike and Jay had been killed in action. Life just seemed to stop. How could it be? Mike and Jay— gone? Lori went to pieces and Ronnie was totally beside herself. How could she go on? She had gone from not being able to stand this man to not being able to live without him. She became totally bedridden.

One day a package came for each of us. The guys had portraits made from one of the pictures they had of the whole unit and sent one to each of us. It said, "Love of God, Country and You." Signed, "The Guys." The name of each was handwritten over each of their pictures. Ronnie's package contained all the letters that Jay had written but had not been able to mail. Loren had to find out how Jay and Mike died so she contacted her friend in Washington.

The guys were to be picked up by a helicopter at a rendezvous point. Jay was covering the hot area and Mike was covering the side where snipers were thought to be. Mike had an uncanny knack of spotting snipers. The unit was almost through the danger zone, when a shot rang out from the rear. They were only thirty yards from the 'copter. One of the guys was hit and Mike being closer ran to help him as Jay continued to yell at him to get down. A mortar hit both of them. When Jay arrived, he was told a mortar had hit Mike. Jay asked, "Is he dead?" and they said, "We're sure he is." Jay ordered the men to board the 'copter and went to get Mike; he said he couldn't leave him there. The guys started to return with him, but he turned to Staff Sergeant Arnett and ordered him, "Get these guys on the chopper and if necessary get them out of here! Their lives are important! See to it that they get that stripe!"

All the men were ordered onto the chopper. They watched as Jay checked both men. He turned, held up two thumbs and then turned both thumbs down indicating both men were dead. He beckoned for one man to help in bringing the men back. S/Sgt Arnett ordered the other men to stay on the 'copter and went to assist Lt. Jay. Lt. Jay was not happy that S/Sgt Arnett had come, but the S/Sgt said he couldn't send anyone else. Lt Jay helped him to get Cpl Gates on his shoulder, and told him to be ready to get those men out of there. He kept watch as S/Sgt Arnett made it back to the 'copter. He then proceeded to pick up M/Sgt Mike. Just as he had shouldered M/Sgt Mike and turned, a shot rang out and they saw what seemed to be Jay's whole side, explode. They surmised it must have been a mortar.

The men started to get off the chopper, but S/Sgt Arnett stopped them and ordered the chopper to lift off. Just after the chopper lifted off a mortar exploded right where the chopper had been. Two other mortars barely missed the chopper in flight. S/Sgt Arnett did just as Lieutenant Jay had ordered, saved the rest of the men. Lieutenant Jay died because he would not leave his buddy there. Lieutenant Jay McFadden six times decorated, M/Sgt Mike West four times decorated, Cpl Charlie Gates two times decorated. Fifty-one raiding missions—no loss of life.

Two months passed and Ronnie had been put in the hospital twice. They had to feed her intravenously as she refused to eat. She looked really bad. Her mother was worried sick. Lori and I had not been much better. It took us almost two months to get to where we could function after Jay and Mike's death. Loren was much better because she had gone through this before with the loss of her husband, her sister and Jay's father. She had finally gotten Lori straightened out and back to work. I continued to spend time with Ronnie. I was the only one she would talk to. I also cried often.

One day, the doorbell rang while I was sitting with Ronnie. Suddenly, standing in the doorway of Ronnie's room were Loren and Lori. Lori was a take-charge type of person. And I soon found out that so was her mother. They both came over to Ronnie, and lifted her up off the bed.

Lori said, "Enough is enough. It is time you let go of this self-pity. You are going to get your self together starting now. And you're coming with us."

Ronnie started to say, "But..." and Loren stopped her.

"No buts about this young lady. It stops here and now. Lori and I got over Jay and so must you. Besides the last thing he said to us was to take care of Ronnie. He would not want you like this and if we have anything to do with it you won't be," Loren said. "You are also my daughter now, and you are going to act like it."

"Lori said, "Yes, and you are my little sister, so let's get cracking."

They bathed and dressed Ronnie, and fixed her hair. When they took her downstairs, her mother and Janis, my mother, who had been sitting with her, jumped up, and Ronnie's mother screamed, "Praise God," and ran and hugged and kissed her baby. With tears running down her face, she hugged and thanked Loren and Lori. She just said, "How?" looking at Ronnie and could say no more.

Loren repeated, "She's also my daughter now" and hugged Ronnie's Mom.

"We are all going for a short walk so get ready." Loren said to Ronnie's mother,

That was the first time Ronnie had been out of the house since Jay and Mike's funeral. It was less than a half of a block to a little park from Ronnie's house. The person who had owned the house and property willed the property to be used for a park for kids. Ronnie could not walk far. She was weak. We all sat on the little benches. Lori retrieved a picnic basket from her car, spread a blanket and we had a picnic. We laughed and talked. Lori was so patient with Ronnie, getting her to eat little bits of food and to drink some broth and juice. Ronnie's mom could not hide her tears of joy and thankfulness as she watched Lori and Loren transform Ronnie. Ronnie began to stand and take short walks. Then taking Loren and Lori with her she walked a little farther to a tree. I knew what she was doing. We watched as they approached the tree. Ronnie began to point to the tree as they walked around it. Then they all three hugged each other and stood there looking at the tree. I'm sure they were all crying. What Ronnie was showing them was the tree that she and Jay had carved their names in a heart and other little love words. It was their tree. Finally they returned.

We enjoyed our picnic and took Ronnie and her mom home. Before they left, Loren asked Ronnie if it would be all right if she visited their tree from time to time. Ronnie said, "Of course!"

Ronnie asked Lori, "Would you go with me to see Rance tomorrow?"

Lori said, "Oh my God, how could we have forgotten about Rance? And none of us have told the Rosses. Of course I will go with you. We had all better go in case they haven't heard! Do you feel strong enough? I can go alone if you don't."

Ronnie said, "I'll be strong enough."

The next day we all went out to the stables. When we drove up, Mr. Ross came out to meet us. He watched as we got out of the car.

He hugged Loren and said, "It's been a long time since we have seen you, Lori! Rance will certainly be glad to see you. He is not doing well."

Lori introduced Mrs. Singleton, Ronnie's mother and Janis, my mother.

He said, "What wonderful young ladies the three of you have, and Jay." He shook his head, "Marvelous just marvelous." "Hi Jamie," he said and kissed me on the forehead. When he saw Ronnie he said, "Oh My Lord, child what has happened to you?" Lori broke the news about Jay and Mike and they had to hold him up or he would have fallen. They leaned his back against the car. Tears streamed down his face. Jay and Mike had been like sons to him.

At that moment, Mrs. Ross pulled up. She had been to the store. She was so glad to see everyone and to meet the mothers. When she got the news about Jay and Mike, she ran into the house crying.

Mr. Ross apologized. "You see we never had any children and Jay and Mike were like our own sons and these are like our girls." He asked everyone to come into the house. It was a beautiful house.

When he and Mrs. Ross, Kathryn or Kate as she introduced herself to the mothers, had got themselves together, Lori explained about Ronnie.

Mr. Ross said, "That's why you have not been to see Rance!" Rance is not doing well at all. I believe he knows."

Mrs. Singleton, who had introduced herself as Beth, said, "A horse?"

"Beth," said Mr. Ross. "There is a bond between Rance, Jay, and your daughter that no man can explain. Ronnie, if you can, the three of you need to go and see Rance. I'll go down and let him out."

Ronnie, Lori and I went down to the corral and the ladies walked from the house out to the grandstand. The grandstand was an extension of the porch on the side of the house, all on the same level as the living room and kitchen.

When Rance came out, he was still as beautiful as ever but that fire and flare he had always showed was not there. I opened the gate to help Ronnie go in. I heard her mother scream "No!" Mrs. Ross calmed her by saying, "It's all right! Rance loves her almost as much as you do."

Rance was sure glad to see the three of us. He kept going from one to the other. He would nuzzle one and then lay his head over her shoulder and then go to the next and do the same.

My mother said, "My Lord, Jamie has told me so often how beautiful he is and how much he loves them but I never imagined!"

Yep, he was really glad to see us. Finally after he had visited with us he went to the fence and began looking toward the car. That brought tears to all our eyes. He was looking for Jay. Mrs. Ross explained that to our mothers. Loren said he is still the most beautiful horse I have ever seen.

Finally, Ronnie called to him and he reluctantly left the fence. We all gave him as much attention as we could.

Beth was saying to Mrs. Ross, "My baby has always been deathly afraid of horses! I didn't believe her when she told me she had a horse as a friend."

Mrs. Ross commented, "See for yourself!"

Suddenly Rance lowered his front legs beckoning Ronnie to climb aboard. The mothers asked, "What is he doing?"

Mrs. Ross explained, "He's asking Ronnie to climb aboard."

Beth gasped and said, "Oh No! She can't. She's too weak!"

Mrs. Ross commented, "Don't worry. The best medicine in the world for those two is each other."

Ronnie tried to climb aboard but couldn't. Rance lowered himself even further. Still Ronnie couldn't make it. She said, "Help me get aboard girls!" Lori boosted her right on up before I could move. Rance walked away with her just as gently as he could. He seemed to sense her frailty at that moment. That was the first smile I had seen on Ronnie's face in a long time.

I said to Lori, "I think she is going to be all right."

Lori said, "Yep, I know!"

As Rance went into a slow canter, Ronnie smiled and waved to her mother, who had her hand over her mouth in disbelief.

"I can't believe what I'm seeing," she said as she clung to Loren. "What wonders your family has done for my baby. I love you all!"

Loren said, "Thank you and we love you!"

The ladies promised to spend time with Mrs. Ross and to visit her often. Ronnie was on her way to complete recovery. We spent as much time as we could with Rance, but he was heartbroken and we could see the changes in him every time we visited.

Ronnie completely recovered and embarked on a career in singing. She had a beautiful voice. I became a real estate broker and was kept quite busy, but we never missed our standing date with Rance.

# Ranceville

It had been two years since Jay and Mike's passing, and Ronnie still said that she felt Jay was alive somewhere.

She looked at the stack of letters he had written, but said, "I can't bear to open them. So I put them away." With tears in her eyes, she would just look off into space.

We encouraged her to get on with her life. We told her that is what Jay would have wanted. Since Lori's talks with her, she had accepted dates but she didn't let them get serious. As soon as they did, she broke them off. There was one person who I thought she really liked and it seemed that it might be getting serious. He was a wealthy Broadway producer. Lori had done a lot of choreography for him, and she introduced Ronnie to him to sing in one of his musicals. He fell madly in love with Ronnie. She was not going to accept the job, but then Lori talked with her and told her she had to get past Jay. She told Lori that she had a feeling Jay was alive somewhere. She told Lori that she was awakened at night to the sound of his voice, as though he were right there in the room. She told Lori that this had started recently. She asked Lori why would it just suddenly start to happen if it had no meaning. Lori reasoned, if it wasn't just her desire, why had it not have happened before. I think she won Ronnie over.

Well, it happened. Ronnie became engaged, and would be married in three months to Len Armontt. We were all elated and got busy making plans. Ronnie and I went shopping one day.

She said, "Jamie I have to talk to you."

I said, "Speak up girl!"

"I had a long talk with Len. I had to be honest with him. I told him about Jay and me. I told him about my feeling that Jay was alive somewhere and about the voice that I hear on occasion. I told him there would always be a part of me that he could not share. I told him that he had to know that about me. If he still wanted me to marry him, I told him I would." Ronnie said.

I said, "Wow! Girl you sure laid it on the line but I am glad you did. This way you have no secrets to hide. Make him the best wife you can."

Ronnie said, "I believe I can love him but I can't give him what I would have given Jay and I wanted him to know that up front. I will be a good wife to him!"

I hugged her and said, "I know you will."

Three years after Jay's death, Ronnie became Mrs. Leonard Armontt. They had a beautiful wedding. Len did not spare any expense. His mother and father were very nice people, a bit stuffy, but nice. I could see why Ronnie could love Len. There seemed to be a wee touch of Jay in him, just a touch. They would be moving to upstate New York. I was going to miss my little friend but I am sure that we would stay in touch. She told me that she still heard Jay's voice from time to time.

One day, the sad news came via the phone that Rance had slipped away. Although we had continued to see him, Ronnie was no longer here to go with us. He had now lost two loves. We think that he just gave up. The pain of a lost loved one had come again. This time it was a horse that we all loved. I decided not to call and tell Ronnie. I would wait until she inquired about Rance. Even the mothers had become attached to Rance and he to them. So we all cried and sorrowed together. Mr. Ross had his hide stretched and mounted. There is a big statue of Rance at the stables, which are now called Ranceville. He is beautifully mounted in his glass case, which is lighted. The stable hands are very proud of the statue. You should see it. It is beautiful. They had a big plaque made and wanted to place it on the case. It says:

*Rance*
*Owner*
*Jay McFadden*
*Of*
*Ranceville Stables*
*Owner*
*Theodore "Ted" Ross*

When they showed it to Mr. Ross, they said he was overwhelmed and said he would be proud to have it displayed on the case. Many people stopped by to look and ask about Rance. They were fascinated about the story of Rance and Jay. When they got a chance to meet us, it was as if we were celebrities. They'd ask for autographs, take pictures with us and ask about Jay and Mike. Rance made Mr. Ross famous. He continually stated that he wished Jay could see this. We all, except Ronnie, continued to visit with Mr. and Mrs. Ross They looked forward to our visits. They missed Ronnie so much. Lori and I had become even closer then we ever were before. She had adopted Ronnie as a little sister, but now she had gone. We both threw ourselves into our work. I made a lot of money and Lori became even more famous than ever.

Five years had passed since Ronnie's marriage. I had been present at the birth of both of her girls. Both were as beautiful as their mother. Ronnie asked that I come spend a couple of days with her. She said she needed to talk to me. So I packed a few things and hopped a plane to LaGuardia where Ronnie's limo met me and drove me to their estate.

When I arrived, Ronnie and the girls were waiting. Beth couldn't wait for the limo to stop. As soon as I stepped out of the limo Beth was all over me followed by Tia toddling along.

They were yelling, "Aunt Jamie we could hardly wait for you to get here." I got more hugs and kisses than I have ever had. Beth was two-and-a-half and Tia about fourteen months. Beth was very outgoing but Tia had a problem. She did not cotton to men. She would not go to any man but her father and grandfather. She had no problem coming to me and I loved it. I enjoyed them so much.

After we had settled in and the girls were taking a nap, Ronnie told me that Len was on a trip for a couple of days. She thought this would be a good time for us to have a chat. We went outside in the garden. It was beautiful out there with all kinds of flowers, green plants and trees. It was very spacious. We sat in the gazebo. I could tell something was lying heavy on Ronnie's heart.

I thought to myself, "Lord, I hope there is nothing wrong with their marriage."

Ronnie was staring out in space. I did not say anything. I waited until she was ready to talk. I was hoping the girls would not wake up too soon.

Finally Ronnie said, "I spend a lot of time here Jamie. Something used to draw me here. I don't know what, but I would have to come here. It's like I was compelled to come here. Sometimes in the middle of the night I had to get up and come out here. Once I got here it seemed like a peace would come over me. I would feel safe. I would feel warm and I would feel loved. It's as though someone or something had its arms around me. At first I was afraid and would run into the house. Finally, I have come to realize that whatever it was, it meant me no harm. I would sit here or sometimes lie here and enjoy being loved. Now here's what really bothers me . . ." She paused. "I'm afraid to say this to you."

I said, "Let it out. That's what I'm up here for."

She said, "I felt that it was Jay holding me."

It startled me but I held my composure. You see I had been hearing Jay call me just like Ronnie had. In fact, I'd been hearing his voice off and on for almost the last two years.

I asked Ronnie, "How long has this been going on?"

Ronnie said, "Shortly after we moved to this estate, that's when it became strong. I had been having lighter tugs before I got married. I paid them no mind."

"Have you always responded to that stronger pull, or whatever it was you felt," I asked?

Ronnie said, "Yes, except for one time."

"When was that?" I asked.

Ronnie responded, "The night Tia was conceived. You see, there were nights when Len wanted to make love and I would be pulled away from him . . ."

I interrupted, "Was it only at night that you got this pull?"

"No said Ronnie. It happened in the morning, afternoon, evening, midnight, early in the morning—just anytime."

"OK," I said. "You were speaking about Len."

"Well the night Tia was conceived I refused to leave Len. I had hurt him enough," said Ronnie. "Jamie am I going crazy?" Ronnie asked, "I feel as though I'm losing my mind sometimes."

I said, "No baby, its just that part that Len cannot touch that's needing love."

"Oh Jamie! Do you think that's all it is?" asked Ronnie.

I said, "I think that is all," and I gave her a big hug. "Are you still having those pulling sensations?" I asked.

Ronnie said, "I haven't had one . . ."

"Since Tia was conceived," I interrupted.

"How did you know that?" questioned Ronnie. "Tell me Jamie. What is it that you know?"

"Nothing," I answered. "I just surmised that once you refused to yield, you broke its hold on you. It's as simple as that."

"Oh you must be right Jamie because it hasn't happened again since. Thank you! You have always been a good friend and helped when I needed it. Thank you for coming. I feel better," said Ronnie.

My mind began to race over everything that Ronnie had told me. I needed to get back home to check some things out.

The next day, Ronnie, the girls and I went into the city to do some shopping. The girls loved to go shopping and were having a ball. We spent some time in the park and at the zoo. Ronnie took me to her favorite store where I met Mrs. Templeton the store manager. It was huge with a lot of different rooms on the first floor of a very high building full of offices, apartments and penthouses. Tia loved Mrs. Templeton, a very professional lady.

Tia stayed with Mrs. Templeton as we continued on our shopping spree. Ronnie had said the shopping was on her and for me not to be bashful. I picked up a nice bag and a jacket I liked, and that was it. Ronnie insisted but I said that was enough. It was time to head back upstate. We picked up Tia, got in the limo and headed back to the estate.

I said goodbye to Ronnie and the girls and headed home. Many things were running through my mind. Mainly, why had I begun to hear Jay's voice about the same time that Ronnie refused to respond to the 'pull' as she called it. The thought really frightened me. There was some reading I wanted to do and I needed to talk to Loren.

It seemed to me that I had read or heard somewhere that men who were prisoners were brainwashed by having their life's routine broken: their sleep would be interrupted many times during the day and night; they would be constantly tortured; they would be allowed to taste food and then it would be taken away; and they lived under bright lights all the time. I wondered if maybe Jay . . .

"Oh," I told myself. "Stop letting your imagination run away with you Jamie Summers." Yet why would the two incidents happen the way they did? I went right to Loren. This strange feeling continued to invade me all the way from the airport to Loren's. As I rang her bell, for some reason, I began to shudder.

Loren answered the door excitedly and grabbed my hand pulling me into the house saying, "You got my message?"

"What message? I asked. "I came straight from the airport." Loren had left me a phone message.

She sat down and pulling me said, "Sit down Jamie!" Loren's heart was beating so strongly, I could feel it in her fingers. My heart began to quicken.

She said, "Jamie, Jay is alive."

I jumped straight up and said, "I knew it, I knew it, I knew it!"

Loren said with a puzzled look, "You knew it? What do you mean?" So I began to tell her the strange story.

"You know how Ronnie used to say she felt Jay was alive and that she could hear his voice in her room? Well once she moved upstate New York some strange force would compel her to the garden gazebo. When she stepped in the gazebo it felt like something would put its arms around her. Frightened, she would run back to the house. However, she was continually summoned back to the gazebo. She stopped being frightened when she realized it meant her no harm. She said she would just sit there and feel loved. It was as if Jay was holding her. She said that she was drawn there at all different times of day and night. This continued until the night Tia was conceived. She said that night she refused to be pulled away from Len anymore. It was about that same time that I began to hear Jay's voice."

Loren stood up in amazement. "You mean you've been hearing Jays voice also?" I said, "And it happened about two years ago, about the time of Tia's conception. I didn't want to upset anyone. I thought it was because I missed Mike and Jay so!"

Loren said, "That is absolute amazing! Now let me tell you about Jay. I got a call from my friend in Washington. He told me that some prisoners have been exchanged and one was a Lieutenant Jay McFadden. He said he was heading to the area personally and would get any details himself. I have been on pins and needles ever since. He called an hour ago and confirmed that it really was Jay. He said that he is seriously ill and that Jay would be in the hospital there until he is stable then he would personally have him shipped to the closest military hospital here. Oh Jamie isn't that the most wonderful news ever? My baby is still alive! I will, with the help of God, do everything in my power to make sure he stays that way. I wanted to fly immediately to where he is but my friend advised me to wait. There is a lot of red tape around his being alive and being kept in the condition he is in. He will let me know when the time is right."

"You must have a lot of confidence in this person. Does he know Jay personally?" I asked.

Loren said, "Yes, I do. He and I were high school sweethearts. He is my late husband's brother. He and Jay's father were army buddies. In fact he was with Jay's father when he was killed. Jay's father once saved his life."

I said, "Wow! Then he is Lori and Jay's uncle? Loren may I ask you something personal?"

"You want to know about Jim? Child, you are like my daughter," said Loren. "As I said, Jim and I were sweethearts. I was a year older but he was one of the sweetest talkers. I met his older brother in college; we fell in love and married—end of story," said Loren.

Then it hit me. Then this will be in the papers!" Loren said, "No, my friend said he would keep Jay's story covered for now. It will have to come out eventually, but for now he will cover it."

"He must be a pretty high person to be able to do that!" I remarked.

"He's a three-star General," said Loren.

I said, "Thank heavens! This is not something Ronnie needs to hear now."

"Right," said Loren. "My baby has gone through enough for now. I hate to think of the time when she has to know. How are she and the girls doing anyway?"

I said, "The girls are doing wonderfully well. The reason Ronnie asked me to go to New York was to talk about what she thought was Jay, and now we can be assured it was. If she realizes that he has been reaching for her all these years, ugh, I shudder to think. She asked me if I though she was going crazy. The other problem," I said, "is Jay! If she is what kept him alive all these years, and only God knows what he has gone through, what will happen to him when he finds out she is married?"

"Don't worry about Jay," said Loren. "We need to get him well and on his feet. Besides he still has you doesn't he," said Loren with a smile? What a wise woman. I guess she knew Jay would always be in my heart especially now that Mike had gone. I asked Loren if Lori knew about Jay.

She said, "Yes, Lori is on her way home from Paris."

The next day Lori arrived from Paris. She was so excited. "Where is Jay? When can we see him? This is for real; it's not a dream is it? I want to see him! When can we go?" She asked question after question.

"Slow down baby," said Loren. "Jim is handling everything."

That was the second time I heard her mention her friend's name.

"Oh Mother! I'm so happy I could burst!" said Lori. "I have so many questions."

"Lori, Lori, said Loren putting her finger up to Lori's lips. There is something I need to tell you baby, sit down." Lori sat down looking puzzled.

"What is it mother?" she asked? "Jay is seriously ill," said Loren.

"Then we need to go now." interjected Lori!

"No," said Loren. "We need to wait until Jim tells us. There is a lot of military red tape around Jay right now. Jim will have him flown to a hospital close to us as soon as he is stable and all right to be moved. Jim said he would be with Jay every minute necessary until he gets him close to home. So don't worry. You know he means every word he says."

Lori said, "It's just that I want so badly to see him."

"We all do," said Loren.

"Oh God—Ronnie!" said Lori.

"Yes," answered Loren, "We have discussed that. Ronnie is not to be told. Jim is going to keep it out of the papers as long as possible."

"Thank God!" said Lori.

True to his word Jim kept Loren abreast of everything that was going on with Jay. We were all upset because we were not able to go see him. But I guess you have to understand military red tape. Each day Jim gave Loren a doctor's report. In fact Jim went against the rules and had the doctor talk to Loren. That helped her feel a lot better. Jay had been badly mistreated by his captors and there was a lot of debriefing that needed to be done and they could only talk to Jay for brief periods at a time. The doctor assured Loren that he was in charge of Jay's recovery and that he would give him the greatest care. He said he was amazed, from some of the things he had heard, that the young man was still alive. He said Jay had done his best to make it back home and he would do his best to see that he did not do what he did in vain. He said Jay was a remarkable young man, not only for what he went through but for what he did for his men. The military had brought his entire old unit in for the debriefing. Jay was an absolute hero.

# Jay's Return

Three months later, Jay was shipped to a Military hospital about twenty miles from us. He could have been shipped to a closer hospital but it was not equipped to handle his special needs. The doctor had kept his word. He had not only given Jay the best care, he had also kept Loren updated and had picked the hospital to which Jay was sent.

We were elated at the opportunity to get to see him. The doctor warned Loren that Jay was a long way from complete recovery and not to be alarmed at his condition. He told her Jay had come a long way from when he first arrived and would continue to improve. He assured Loren that he had picked the doctors for Jay's complete recovery and that he would track his progress. He said, "God bless and good Luck."

As Loren had been told, a doctor called two days after Jay arrived at the new hospital and told her Jay was ready to receive visitors. We hurried and drove the twenty miles and rushed to the floor to which Jay was assigned. We were directed to a large single room where the doctor and General Jim met us. Jim told the doctor that he would talk to Loren and Lori and me before they went into see Jay.

He directed us to a room that adjourned Jay's room. It had lounge chairs and a bed, tables, lamps, all kind of reading material, a refrigerator, and a huge bowl of fruit on one of the tables. Loren introduced me to General Jim. She told him that I was like a daughter and Jay's closest friend. He welcomed me and told us not to be alarmed at Jay's condition. He said he looked great compared to his condition on his arrival. He said his progress had been astounding and with the proper care and he would continue to improve.

He said, "Let's go in now."

When we first saw Jay, Loren gasped, "My God!" The doctor had remained in the room and grabbed Lori as she collapsed. He sat her in one of the lounge chairs that was in Jay's room. He immediately turned to me and asked if I was all right. I just stood there with my hands over my mouth staring at Jay. I nodded my head, yes. He then turned his attention back to Lori. General Jim had his arm around Loren. Her head was lying on his chest. Jay was attached to oxygen; he had had a tracheotomy and a feeding tube inserted. He was just skin and bone. How could he have been any worse than this? General Jim asked Loren if she understood why he did not want her to see Jay before now. Loren said, "Yes, thank you."

Lori had now rejoined us. We were just looking at Jay. Suddenly he opened his eyes. General Jim walked over to the bed and said, "Hi guy! We've got some visitors."

Loren approached the bed and immediately there was a change in Jay. At that moment the doctor approached and removed the oxygen and the feeding tube. Jay was able to talk in a whisper for a short time. Loren lifted his hand and bent over and kissed him her tears falling on his face. As she wiped away her tears from his face, he said in a soft voice,

"No tears I'm all right now!" When Lori approached the bed, it was as though new life was pumped into Jay. They had great love for each other.

He said to Lori, "No tears for you either. I'll be up and around before you know it."

At that moment, the doctor wanted to reconnect Jay's feeding tube but Jay raised his hand to stop him. He could see me in the mirror over his bed. He beckoned for me. I approached his bed. He just looked at me and attempted to smile. Then with his hand he beckoned me down close. He whispered, "I love you my Lady." Something he had always called me, and he kissed me. With tears flowing, I put my cheek against his.

I whispered, "Oh my love, I thought I had lost you!"

"No chance love! Where is Ronnie?" He replied in a weakened voice.

My heart almost stopped! "She's in Europe for the summer." I said quickly. He smiled and the doctor reconnected him. He shortly went off to sleep.

We went into the adjoining room with General Jim. Loren hugged Jim and said,

"Thank you for all you have done."

Jim said, "Remember, he's my nephew." He turned and hugged me and said, "Young lady he must think an awful lot of you, thanks! You are in love with him aren't you?"

I said, "Always have been and always will be."

He asked, "Who is this rival?"

I answered, "She's not my rival. She's my best friend."

He said, "Ouch, that's tough!"

I said, "Not really. You see Jay introduced me to his best friend Mike, who was the man of my life, and who I married."

He questioned, "The young man he was trying to bring back?"

I said, "Yes."

He put his arm around me and hugged me and said, "You have a friend if you are ever in need, remember that. Loren knows how to reach me."

At that moment, the doctor entered the room and said, "The three of you don't know what your presence has done for that young man! We don't have that kind of medicine here."

Loren asked, "Is it possible for us to keep it here?"

He replied, "That why the General had this room provided."

Loren said, "Then I'll go home pick up what I need, return and I'll be here."

Then the three of us decided that we would share the duty, and the doctor said, "Welcome!"

When we were alone, Loren said, "Jamie, thank you for that quick thinking little lie you told in there. In fact it is probably the best one. Hopefully by the end of the summer Jay will be strong enough for us to tell him the truth."

I responded, "That's what I was hoping!"

Lori came over and hugged me and said, "Thanks and we will support what you said when we have to tell him the truth."

Although we had agreed to take turns, we could not get Loren to leave. So we stayed with her when our turn came. Jay was making remarkable progress.

The doctor remarked, "Now I understand what Dr. Rogers—that was Jay's previous doctor, who has been keeping close tabs on Jay's progress—meant by the fortitude of this young man." He told Loren that our presence had made all the difference. We showered Jay with prayers, love and attention and watched him, with the help of God, pull himself up from near death to walking without any help or support after just three months. He looked forward to physical therapy. His face and body slowly filled out and he got stronger by the day. It felt good to have him put his arms around me again. I remember thinking how I wished it could last forever.

We were all taking turns by now and Loren was going home. I was afraid to be left there alone because I knew Jay would be asking about Ronnie before long.

The next time I went, Jay said, "Jamie it's time we had a talk. My heart began to pound. I knew Jay was strong enough to be told about Ronnie, but I didn't want to do it alone. He said, "Come sit here beside me. I need to tell you about Mike." I was relieved but I felt he would ask about her afterwards.

He said, "Mike and I were separated. Whenever we were on patrol I kept him close to me. Whenever we returned, we set up a fence as we neared the rendezvous point. The fence was two lines of men, like the fence post in the corral but staggered. Each man would be watching in a different direction. This would allow us to cover all directions. Mike controlled one line and I controlled the other. He always had the line closest to the chopper. I was always on the opposite side of the field. We would signal to peel and the last two men would peel off and move to the head of the fence. In other words, towards the chopper. The man behind would then turn his eyes in the direction the guy who left had been watching and so on down the line. When the men on my side of the field, who peeled, were parallel to the chopper they would low z, that is, zigzag across the field while the men who reached the chopper from Mike's line covered them. They would then board the chopper as more men moved into position. We did this quickly, but very carefully.

Mike had seven men in his line and four had peeled. Just as the fifth man started to peal a shot rang out and he dropped. Mike started for him. I was yelling from across the field for Mike to get down. He had never made a mistake like that before. Suddenly, a shell burst and Mike went down. I yelled for the rest of my men to peal low z and they headed for the chopper as I headed in a low z for Mike. S/Sgt Arnett was crawling low toward Mike. I ordered him to get the rest of the men on the chopper and get them out of there, if needs be. At any cost to get them out!

The other guys wanted to help, but I ordered them to the chopper. I got to Mike and Gates and l checked both, and both were dead. I signaled to the chopper with two fingers up and thumbs both down, meaning both dead. I could not leave Mike and Charlie, so I beckoned for one man from the chopper. I helped to get Gates loaded on Arnett's shoulder and kept watch while he headed for the chopper. When he was near the chopper, I hoisted Mike on my shoulder to get him to the chopper. I turned to leave. I don't remember anything else. I am so sorry my love I promised to take care of him. I failed Mike and you. I was the cause of Mike's death. I devised that fence. This possibly would have been our last patrol. I let him down! I let him down!"

"No! No! My love," I said. "General Jim said your men defended the fence to the last. At the debriefing they testified that they were under Lt. Quincy for only a short time and using the regular system, they lost four out of the 20-man squad as well as Lt Quincy. They said using the fence that you set up, the sixteen men left, went through fifty-one patrols and didn't lose another man until that last patrol. They said you were always the last man to leave the field. Once the fence had cleared, Mike would stay low and cover you as you crossed the field to him.

One of the guys said Mike was quick to move to the aid of a comrade maybe sometimes too quick, and you would get on him about it, but it was his nature. They counted it as just bad luck. They all agreed to a man that there was not a better platoon leader in the world than you, Jay.

You were right; that was their last patrol. After a record fifty-one patrols without a loss, the entire platoon was pulled out of action. There was not a man in the group under rank of corporal and every man had been decorated at least once. They say that you put every man in for another stripe before that last mission and said they deserved it. Every man who was corporal was given the rank of sergeant.

Jay you are a national hero, not a failure. They are looking at using your fence as part of military operations. Three of the men who have made a career of the military have been asked to give the details and to possibly teach the fence so that they can try it out. General Jim is very proud of you."

I had never seen tears in Jay's eyes before and there had never been such a pain in my heart. After all he'd been through, he was hurting because he had failed to get Mike back safely. I put my arms around him and tried to absorb all the pain he had harbored all those years. At the end of the day, Jay seemed exhausted. His body was still very weak. I waited until he had gone to sleep and went to see Loren. I told her about the conversation. She said that it was lying heavy on his heart. So she had told Jay to just have a talk with me. She said, that she thought it was time for her to tell him about Rance and Ronnie in that order.

I asked, "You told him?"

Loren said, "Yes, I thought that it was my responsibility to tell him."

I said, "He never even mentioned it! How did he take it?"

"When I told him about Rance I thought he was going to fall, but he held on to the bedpost. He said 'I had a feeling because no one ever mentioned him.' I could feel the hurt in him and his tears showed it. Then he said, 'Now tell me about Ronnie. It's long past time for her to have returned from vacation.' I hesitated, and he asked, 'She is all right isn't she?'

I said, 'Yes, but she got married.' I explained what she had gone through and how, thinking him dead, we had encouraged her to date and to marry.

He just sat down, lowered his head in his hands and said, 'thoughts of her is what kept me alive.' I'm happy for her. Let her continue to think that I am dead. When I'm well I won't come back to the city. That way she will never know.' I told him that was not necessary because she had moved out of the state. I also reminded him that she would eventually find out because of the papers. Jim would not be able to keep the lid on him forever. He'd only been able to do it this long because of how ill he'd been.

He asked, 'you mean there has been nothing printed? How did he do that?' I reminded him that his uncle was quite a powerful man!

'Well I'll make my self scarce anyway,' he said. I said, 'Oh Jay!' But he put his finger to my lips and stopped me. I told you that you wouldn't have to worry about Jay. He will be all right. Then I told him that Mr. and Mrs. Ross were anxious to come and see him. I told him that I did not want them to see him until he was up on his feet and that they had agreed to wait, but now they were even more anxious to see him. Jay said he was also eager to see them. So they are coming tomorrow."

When the Rosses saw Jay, they could not stop hugging him or stop shedding tears. They talked for hours. When they were ready to leave, Mr. Ross handed Jay an envelope. In it was the deed to the house, stables and all the property. Jay tried to refuse but they said you are the closest thing we have to a son. The joy that you brought us watching you and Rance we could never repay. And through you we've acquired a family, Loren, Janis, Beth, Lori, Jamie, and Ronnie. Besides we know that when we are gone you will know what to do with the property. We are anxious for you to be able to come out and see it. I told the others not to tell you anything about it before you see it. I'm hoping it will be soon.

Jay spent the next 18 months recovering. While doing so he occupied his mind by studying the stock market. He was like a sponge. He absorbed every thing about the stock market he could. Everything he could read, see on TV, or listen to he absorbed. He said that is where he would make his money.

One day we received a surprise. Jay called me and asked me to tell the others to be at the hospital at noon.

I said, "It's some sort of a surprise." When we arrived, General Jim was there. Jay was dressed. He had been given permission to leave the hospital for a short period. General Jim had arranged for a military staff limo and one of the doctors had to go along. Jay wanted to go to the stables. He couldn't get them off his mind.

When we arrived at the stables there were a few visitors there as usual. The military limo raised quite a stir. This was the first time General Jim had been to the stables. When he got out of the car everyone wondered what was going on. Mr. and Mrs. Ross came out to meet us. When they saw Jay they jumped for joy. Jay stood beside the limo in utter amazement. There was Rance mounted in a glass case looking as though he was alive. He couldn't see the plaque the stable hands had made:

*Rance*
*Owner*
*Jay McFadden*
*Of*
*Ranceville Stables*
*Owner*
*Theodore "Ted" Ross*

Tears filled his eyes. There stood his devoted friend preserved forever. Jay looked at Mr. and Mrs. Ross and all he could do was to give a thumbs-up. Everything was caught up in his throat. He hugged Mr. and Mrs. Ross.

Mr. Ross said, "When I'm gone you can change the owner's name."

Jay responded, "That will never change, never!" Then he asked, "Where are the guys?" At that very moment Sam came around the corner of the house. When he saw Jay he screamed "Jay!" and ran to hug Jay, but the doctor got between them. Sam was full of hay and the doctor was taking no chances with Jay. Sam understood. Then Ben and four other hands came from the back. Ben was running. Excitedly he said,

"I heard you call Jay! Oh my God it's him! Well what do you think of Ranceville?" he asked.

"Ranceville?" Jay asked.

Mr. Ross stated, "Oh you can't see the sign from here. The boys named the place Ranceville. Rance is quite a celebrity. All those people over there stop by to see Rance and ask about you and him.

About that time the visitors realized that Jay was the owner of Rance and rushed him for autographs. The doctor hustled Jay into the limo and explained to the people why. Mr. Ross told the people that when Jay was well enough he would have him here to sign autographs.

We prepared to leave, but Mr. Ross asked for a few moments with Jay. We all got out of the limo and Mr. Ross sat next to Jay. He said, "Son, I know you are going through a tough time right now, but I have something to say to you. When we thought we had lost you, we almost lost Ronnie too. Loren and the girls had to go to her house and literally bathe, dress and almost carry her out of the house. When they brought her out here she was so thin and weak she could hardly stand. Rance wasn't much better off. They both missed you so much. Ronnie and the girls were the best thing for Rance and Rance was the best thing for Ronnie. They supported each other. Rance even began to show signs of his old self. We all encouraged Ronnie to begin her life again feeling that is what you would have wanted her to do.

Jay responded, "Yes you were right."

Mr. Ross said, "Once Ronnie began to sing and travel, it kept her from Rance. She would come as often as she could but Rance missed her. We all encouraged her to get married and she did. She didn't want to leave here. She wanted to stay close to Rance. I told her she had to be obedient to her husband. She said goodbye and moved away. From that point on, Rance went downhill; he was heartbroken. He had now lost both of you. As you see I had him mounted. I could not just bury him. Jay hugged Mr. Ross and said, "Thanks I needed that."

Mr. Ross said Goodbye, to us and Jay said, "I'll make your promise to those people come true."

Mr. Ross said, "I know!"

On the drive back to the hospital, General Jim expressed his amazement at what he had just witnessed and heard. He told Jay that he had no idea of what a beautiful life he had been living. He commented on how much everyone loved and respected him, even a horse that couldn't live without him. He mentioned what a beautiful memorial they had made to his horse. He commented that the plaque too was beautiful and that it was marble inlaid. He said those guys must have loved him and his horse very much because it had to have cost a pretty penny. He told Jay how proud he was of him and said that Jay's father and mother would have been very proud of him too. He told Jay that he was a lot like his father. Jay was occasionally allowed to visit the Rosses at Ranceville.

# Mr.J., JM, Jim Meridith

After twenty-nine months of hospitalization Jay was discharged. The first thing he did was call Mr. Ross and tell him he was ready for the autographing in any way he wanted to handle it. He had Mr. Ross spread the word in the neighborhood to let people know which days Jay would be at Ranceville for autographing. The response was enormous. Jay set up specific times that he would be at Ranceville for autographing. He apologized that he would have to stick precisely to those days and time. Mr. and Mrs. Ross were extremely pleased. Mainly, I think, because they knew they would have Jay for those days and time.

Jay took the back pay that he received, and his nest egg—since Ronnie was married—and invested it in stocks. It paid off better than we believed possible, but not Jay. He said this was only the beginning. Jay was moving his money from one stock to another and in a short time he had become filthy rich. It was unbelievable. One day he ran into one of the guys who had been in his platoon, who pointed Jay to a building in New York, which Jay was able to purchase. Between the stock market and buying property in Manhattan, Jay quickly became an extremely rich man.

Jay and I spent a lot of time together. We began to go to a lot of parties and dances. We were really enjoying each other's company. I noticed that he would get moody occasionally. I knew it was because he missed Ronnie. That was the one thing he would not talk to me about. It hurt me to see the happiest personality I had ever met become moody and forlorn. It was worse to feel helpless and not be able to do anything about it.

One night at a dance, we were having a great time. Suddenly everything changed. The song "Out of Reach" started to play and Jay started to walk off the floor. I grabbed his hand and pulled him back to me.

I said, "Dance with me love." We began to dance. Jay was looking away. He always looked at me when we danced. When the words of the song 'Out of reach of my two empty arms' rang out, I could see his eyes were glassy. I knew the pain he felt and I could not help myself; I took his face in my hands and softly kissed him.

Unexpectedly, he responded with the softest and most blissful kiss I had ever felt. Holding me snugly, but gently I was suddenly in the arms where I had always wanted to be. Just as suddenly he pushed me at arms length. He was shaking his head.

He said, "I will always love you Jamie but you will always belong to Mike." The tears swelled in my eyes; a moment of bliss and then it was gone. I knew then that I could never have him. He wiped away my tears and began to swirl me around the floor until I was totally lost in dance.

He whispered softly, "This couldn't affect us—our relationship, could it?"

I put my arms around his neck and whispered, "Never!" He kissed me gently.

Jay disappeared for quite a while. I didn't know where he was. I worried because this was not like him. Then he called and said he was OK and not to worry. I heard very little from him during the next three weeks. I thought maybe he wanted to put some time between us.

Then one weekend he called and said, "I have a plane ticket at the airport for you. I expect to see you in Manhattan as soon as you can, pack nothing." He had given me a number to call for a limo.

I called immediately and the man said, "Yes, Mrs. West, we were just waiting for your call. And Mrs. West you have a limo standing at your disposal. All you have to do is call. A driver is already on his way."

When I hung up the phone my thoughts immediately went to Mike, then I was overjoyed to hear from Jay, but pondered as to why he wanted me in Manhattan as soon as possible.

When the plane landed I was asked to go to a door where a little shuttle vehicle took me to a waiting limo, which swooped me off to Manhattan. It stopped downtown at a familiar building. The driver said to the doorman, "Mrs. West". The doorman walked me to the elevator. He put in a key, turned it and left. The elevator went zooming up. I was thinking, "What in the world?" Then it stopped. The door opened and there stood Jay.

He said, "Welcome to the penthouse, Mrs. West."

I said, "Jay McFadden what are you up to?" He just smiled, hugged me and began to show me around the apartment. It was breathtaking.

He said, "I have to spend a lot of time in New York. So I needed a base to operate from. I bought this building so I'm making use of the penthouse." Then he said, "Come let me show you why I had you come here." He took me to a door and opened it, and we entered the most beautiful apartment I have ever seen in my life.

He said, "Welcome to your home away from home."

Shocked, I said, "What?"

He said with a disappointed look, "You don't like it?"

"Like it? It's gorgeous!" I responded. "But why?" I asked.

He said, "Since you are going to be handling all my real estate from now on and in time, my stocks, you need a base here and you need to be close by, OK?" I stood with my mouth open. "Better close your mouth before you swallow something." Jay said,

I just threw my arms around his neck and said, "Thank you," and kissed him.

He smiled and said, "Remember you're a married woman."

Then I asked him, "Jay why didn't you let me take time to bring a few things with me?"

He said, "Why don't you look over your apartment." As I went through the apartment, the closets and drawers were full of beautiful things, dresses, suits, lingerie, perfumes, combs and brushes everything a woman could need. With my hands over my mouth I asked, "How did you ever—and my size?"

He replied, "I had it professionally done. As for your size, they just paraded models before me and I picked one."

I said, "Jay you are amazing."

He said, "We have our own private entrance but the elevator services both adjoining penthouses so if you find you don't like something that has been picked out for you or if you want to exchange something or want to add something just take the elevator to the first floor and go to the building next door and see my friend Mrs. Templeton. She is the manager of the store where all these clothes were purchased. Make sure you see Mrs. Templeton don't bother with anyone else."

When Jay said Mrs. Templeton I almost fell over. Luckily his back was turned. Now I knew why this building looked familiar it was next to the one where Ronnie and I had shopped, Mrs. Templeton was her friend. There was no way I was going to return anything or go in that store. She would remember me and definitely tell Ronnie about Jay and me.

Jay said, "Oh by the way, I am known here in New York as JM, for Jim Meridith. Mrs. T, as I call her, calls me Mr. J., or JM. So when the papers get hold of the return of Jay McFadden, they won't associate that with me."

I said, "Jay you have put some thought into this!"

Jay said, "All those years as a prisoner and months in the hospital I had nothing else to do but plan my future. That is part of what kept me alive."

I asked, "Will you tell me about those years sometime?"

He put his arms around me and said, "Sure love."

I said, "By the way, the story was released yesterday."

He said with surprise, "What? I thought they would notify me!"

I said, "I thought you knew! I thought that is why you sent for me. Loren said, she called you and left you a message as soon as General Jim called her. He is in California."

Jay went quickly to his phone and there were a couple of messages. Both were from Loren.

Jay said, "Well that is being taken care of anyway. I have a friend at a paper that will receive a note and will put out a message that will say, 'Jay McFadden flees to South America.' It will also say, 'He said he will return when he is able to rehash the horror of those years.'

Jay asked me to call and have a paper sent up. When the paper came, there in big bold headlines was SOLDIER PRESUMED DEAD FOR 8 YEARS RETURNED. In the text they gave Jay's name and wrote, 'Lt Jay McFadden long presumed dead has been returned to the military. The military said that because of the condition of Lt McFadden, the family had requested the military to not release any information until he was well enough physically and mentally to handle any questions and his doctors agreed. Now that Lt McFadden has been released from the hospital, the complete story will be released tomorrow at a press conference.' There were other stories but no pictures.

"It seems the military has thought this out very well. I think Uncle Jim and the doctors had a hand in this. Now everyone is off the hook. You guys are going to be hammered though," said Jay. "They will be relentless trying to find out where I am. Just tell them I will return when I can face the past and stick to just that. I will call mom and tell her the same and to remove all pictures of me, and not to let them into the house."

I asked, "What about Lori?" Jay just smiled.

"Wait till they ask her!" I got the message. In a short time Jay's home was flooded with mail mostly from his platoon members and their families.

I returned home the next day to set things in order so that I could have things operate smoothly there whenever I was in New York. I couldn't wait to call Ronnie to see if she had read the paper or heard or seen the press conference. As Jay had said, his friend put the story in the paper "JAY McFADDEN FLEES THE COUNTRY." Boy! They bared everything. However, they did not show any pictures of Jay. Jay's thing was that he wanted to make it on his own, and not because he was a war hero or a long lost POW. There was a lot of pride in that guy.

When I called Ronnie, the maid said they were in Paris. They had left two days ago. The maid said that Ronnie had called and left a message when she couldn't reach me. I checked and there was a message, and also one from Loren saying that Ronnie was leaving for Paris and would probably be there most of the summer. Len was doing a musical there. How about that? This time she really was in Europe. Her timing couldn't have been better. Maybe she wouldn't hear or see anything about Jay.

I was now moving between home and New York. Jay was buying more and more real estate. He was also teaching me more and more about the stock market. He had become extremely wealthy and handling his business and real estate had even made me a rich woman. But most importantly, I was with Jay very often.

Whenever I was in New York we had a great time together. We did the clubs, shows, and restaurants. We danced till late in the evening. However, I always made sure Jay got in early enough to get plenty of sleep. He said I was treating him like a little kid. I said, "No like someone who wants to keep you around for a long time." He kissed my forehead and said thanks.

Lori called and said she was on her way to Paris. I told her Ronnie was in Paris. She said she would look them up. She asked how Jay was handling the press release and press conferences, Loren had told her.

I said, "Do you know that guy had planned all this out during his absence?"

She said, "I told you. You didn't ever have to worry about him."

I said, "He is using the name Jim Meridith."

Lori said, "Our mothers' maiden name. Let me speak to JM."

I said, "He's out at the moment but how did you know?" She said, "He's my brother!"

I said, "The two of you are joined at the brain!" She laughed and said, "See you Sis. Tell JM I called."

I said, "Wait!" and I told her about the store and the manager named Mrs. Templeton and that she was Ronnie's friend. I told her that she knew me because Ronnie, the girls and I went shopping there when I had visited Ronnie. Lori said, 'Ouch!' I asked her, if she thought I should tell Jay.

She said, "No! If fate intends for them to meet, it will happen. We can't protect against it. What will be will be. Gotta go kid!"

I thought, "What a wise woman!"

The summer came to an end too soon for me. I was enjoying my time with Jay; especially the times when we would walk though the park in the evening. I told Jay that I would have to be home for the next three weeks. My real estate business there required it. I said, "If there is a need I can hop a plane and get here in a hurry but I can handle most of the things from home." He said, "No problem, kid, do what you have to do. I'll miss you. Get back when you can." One thing about Jay, he meant what he said. When he said he would miss me I knew he meant it. I huddled close to him as we continued our walk. He held me close. I felt so secure.

While I was at home, Ronnie returned from Europe. We talked but I told her nothing about Jay and me. She mentioned that she had seen Lori there and they had spent time together. It was obvious that Lori had not told her anything either. Two weeks passed. Jay and I were just finishing a phone conversation.

He said "I'm to meet a client for lunch but first I have to stop by and see Mrs. T., which is what he called Mrs. Templeton. See you later kid, love you!"

# Tia

I was walking through the store toward Mrs. T.'s office, and I was nearing a large display table when I heard soft whimpering. I stopped and listened. The sound seemed to be coming from under the table. I bent down and there was a beautiful little girl. When she saw me, she drew back further under the table against the wall.

I asked, "What's the matter? Why is such a beautiful little girl like you crying under this table? I won't hurt you. You can talk to me. I would like to help you. Has someone hurt you?" I asked and sat on the floor just as she was. She shook her head, no.

"Are you lost?" I asked. She nodded her head, yes. I said, "I was lost once and someone helped me. Is your mommy in the store?"

She said, "Yes." That was her first word, but she seemed to be loosening up.

I said, "Would you let me help you find your mommy? I have a friend in the store and she can call your mommy and tell her where you are. Your mommy is probably worried about you." I was still sitting on the floor as she was sitting. I said, "Won't you let me help you find your mommy?" She said yes, and I held out my hand and she took it. I got up and sat her on the display table.

On another table nearby was a display of towels. She was still holding my hand. I started to reach for a towels but she pulled on my hand.

I said. "I'm not going to leave you. I just want to get a towel." She loosened her grip.

I looked at her face; she had beautiful eyes. They seemed familiar. I said, "These little eyes are too beautiful for tears." Then I kissed her little forehead, touching my finger to my lips each time. I touched her right eye, her left eye, her nose, and then I touched my finger to my lips and touched it to the right side of her little mouth, I did the same to the left side of her mouth then the same for the top of her upper lip and then under her bottom lip finally, I touched my finger to my lips and touched it to her little mouth.

I said, "Now all the pain and fear are gone. Now we will wipe your beautiful eyes and face so that when your mommy sees you, you will be nice and pretty." I stood her up on the table. I asked, "What's your name?"

She said, "Tia."

"That's a beautiful name; a beautiful name for a beautiful girl." I said. "Now let's go to my friend's office so she can call your mommy. My friend's name is Mrs. Templeton."

Her eyes lit up and a beautiful little smile came on her face. She said, "She is my friend too and my mommy's."

I hugged her and said, "Great. Let's go to her office."

I lifted her down from the table. As we headed for Mrs. T.'s office she tugged my hand and asked, "What's your name?"

I said, "Mrs. Templeton calls me Mr. J. or JM."

"Can I call you Mr. J.?" She asked.

"I would like that!" I said.

She tugged my hand again and said, "Mr. J. I'm tired will you carry me?" I stooped and picked her up and she hugged me tightly around the neck.

We reached Mrs. T's office just as she was rushing out. She stopped in her tracks with her mouth agape.

"Where's the fire kiddo?" I asked. She stood with her mouth open, and pointed at Tia still hanging on tightly to my neck.

Finally she said, "Tia I've been worried sick about you! I just called your mother and she is on her way over here! Where have you been? JM, where did you find her? And how did you get her to hug you?

I said, "She was just walking around and we started talking and I found out that she knew you so I brought her here."

She said, "But she never goes to men! How . . . ?"

I said, "We're friends!"

Mrs. T said, "I thought she was lost, so I called her mother."

I said, "As you should."

She said, "Can you wait? Her mother would like to thank you."

I said, "I would love to, but I'm having lunch with someone and I'm late as it is and I know she is going to be livid."

With her hands on her hips she asked, "All right who is she?"

I said, "No one you have to be concerned about love. You know you will always be numero uno!"

Tia tugged at my hand and said, "You are not going to leave me are you Mr. J? I don't want you to go!"

I bent down, kissed her forehead and said, "Someone is waiting for me little one, and I must go. I'll tell you what; one day I'll take you to see my horses. Would you like that?"

She said, "Yes, when?"

I said, "Soon but we have to ask your daddy and mommy first. OK?"

She asked, "You promise?"

I said, "I promise!"

Mrs. T. pulled me aside and said, "I didn't know you had any horses. You mustn't kid her. You are the first man she has ever trusted other than her father and her grandfather."

I said, "I don't make promises I don't intend to keep. And yes I have six beautiful horses. I'll take you to see them sometime if you like. I've got to run."

I kissed Tia on the forehead and hurried out to my limo.

* * * *

Tia's mother and sister arrived just as Jay's limo pulled off. They hurried to Mrs. T.'s office. When Ronnie entered the office, there sat Tia eating some popcorn.

With a sigh of relief she asked Mrs. T. "What happened?" Mrs. T. explained that she had stepped out of the office for a short time as usual and Tia walked off.

She said, "I was frightened out of my wits, when a friend of mine walked up with Tia in his arms and she, with her arms around his neck."

Ronnie was dumbfounded. She asked Tia, "Who was he?"

Tia responded, "He is Mr. J. and he is going to take me to see his horses. Can I go mommy?"

Ronnie was totally confused. "But you are afraid of horses," she said.

"Not with Mr. J.," said Tia.

Ronnie even more puzzled looked at Mrs. T. Mrs. T. shrugged her shoulders and said, "Mr. J. had to leave for an appointment and Tia did not want him to leave. He told her that he had to go, but he would take her to see his horses if her mommy and daddy said it would be all right. Tia said yes immediately."

Ronnie was trying to understand how her baby, who would not go near any man other than her father and grandfather, could suddenly take to a stranger—a man!

Ronnie said, "Come here Tia." She lifted her to her lap and said, "Tell Mommy how you met Mr. J.

She said, "Well, I went to look for Mrs. Templeton and I got lost. I hid under a table. I was scared so I was crying. Mr. J asked me why I was crying . . ."

Ronnie interrupted and asked, "Did you know Mr. J. before?"

Tia said, "No."

Ronnie said, "He asked you why you were crying? Were you afraid of him?"

"Yes."

Ronnie asked "What did you say when he asked you why were you crying?"

"Nothing," Tia said.

"What did he say then? Tell me what else he said," demanded Ronnie.

Tia repeated the conversation as best as she could, and said, "He told me he was lost once and someone helped him. He said, 'Won't you let me help you find your mommy?' and I said, yes."

Ronnie asked. "Were you still afraid of him?"

Tia said "Yes, at first."

"Then what happened?"

"He held out his hand and I took it. He sat me on the table. He got a towel. He looked at my face and said I had beautiful eyes. He said, 'These little eyes are too beautiful for tears.' Ronnie was startled but kept quiet. "Then he kissed me here," pointing to her forehead, then kneeling in her mothers lap, she kissed her finger and touched her mother's face, right eye, left eye, nose, the sides of her mouth, her upper and lower lips, and her mother's mouth exactly as Mr. J. had done to her.

"He said, 'Now all the pain and fear is gone.' Then he wiped my eyes and my face so that when you saw me I would be nice and pretty. He stood me up on the table. He asked me my name? I said, 'Tia.' He said, 'that's a beautiful name for a beautiful girl. Now let's go to my friend's office so she can call your mommy.' He said, 'my friend's name is Mrs. Templeton. I said, 'She is my friend too and my mommy's.' He hugged me and said, 'Great. Let's go to her office.' He took me down from the table and we were coming to Mrs. Templeton's office. I asked him what his name was. He said, 'Mrs. Templeton calls me Mr. J.' I asked, 'Can I call you Mr. J?' He said he would like that. I told him that I was tired so he carried me. So I hugged him around his neck.

Ronnie was thinking about the way he kissed Tia and remembered how she had been kissed the same way. Was this a coincidence? It had to be. It must be. It couldn't be anything else.

"Who is this man, Mrs. Templeton?" asked Ronnie

Mrs. Templeton replied, "He's a wealthy businessman. In fact, he owns the building next door and lives in the penthouse of that building. He might just own this one also. He is not like the other tycoons around. He keeps a low profile. I've never seen him with women other than clients. He always kids with me that I am numero uno. He's the nicest man I ever met. I wish I were his age and free!"

He's a young man?" asked Ronnie.

"Yes and obviously as smart as a whip," said Mrs. T.

"What is his name?" asked Ronnie.

"Everyone knows him as 'JM' for Jim Meridith."

"I'd like to meet him to thank him for befriending my baby and try to find out how he was able to reach out to her when no other man can, even relatives. It's baffling," said Ronnie.

"You just missed him. His limo just pulled out as you pulled up. A minute earlier and you would have met him. Tia is absolutely mad about him. If he is around the next time you come in town I'll introduce him to you. Remember he made a date with Tia and he won't break it," said Mrs. T.

"See if you can make an appointment with him any day next week at his convenience," said Ronnie.

Mrs. T. called Ronnie later and said, "JM said he would be on the move for the next ten days. He's trying to close a deal on a piece of property and he has some standing commitments at his ranch. He said he had not forgotten his promise to Tia. So if possible, she could see the horses on one of those days or that I could try and catch him as he is coming and going from his office if you are around. He said he would be mostly free that following week."

Ronnie said softly, "Three weeks from now? Len will be gone for the next two weeks that will be the best time for me to get into town. I hate taking the girls away from him after he's been gone for a while. So I'll have to take a chance on one day within the next ten days."

Ronnie called Mrs. T. three days later, and said that the girls and she were about twenty minutes away. She asked if Mrs. T. would keep an eye out for Mr. J. because Tia had been worrying her crazy to see him.

Mrs. T. said, "I wouldn't just happen to see him since he uses the entrance to his building. I would have to call him to see where he is which is not a problem.

Ronnie asked, "Will you do that, please? If his time is tight, we will meet him anywhere."

Mrs. T called Ronnie back and said, "JM said he will be coming into his office in forty minutes, so he will plan lunch for you and the girls in fifty minutes. He said he is anxious to see Tia again."

Ronnie told Tia and then responded, "Tia has a great big smile on her face! Thanks!"

Mrs. T. answered, "I told you she was absolutely nuts about him. Isn't that strange?"

Ronnie said, "It's totally baffling. Maybe we will know more after I meet him." "From the sound of your voice something is puzzling you about him, isn't it dear? I noticed you as Tia was telling you about him. What is it? asked Mrs. T.

Ronnie said, "We are at the building. I'll be right in."

Once in Mrs. Templeton's office Tia was beside herself. "Where is Mr. J?" she asked anxiously.

"Patience," said Mrs. T. "He will be here. Ronnie you didn't answer my question on the phone."

"What was your question?" asked Ronnie.

Mrs. T. asked again, "What is it about him that has you so upset?"

At that moment, Tia leaped from her chair screaming, "Mr. J!" She bolted out of the office running toward a lean figure, neatly dressed in a lightweight black sport coat, a light-blue dress shirt, with the collar open, lightweight charcoal gray pants, and a pair of soft Stacy Adams shoes. He smiled as he stooped to receive her leaping little body. With her little arms in a bear hug around his neck, he approached the office.

Startled by Tia's reaction, Ronnie moved towards the door, looking intently and trying to see the face of this man holding her baby. Tia's head and hair were blocking the view of his face.

He entered the room saying, "I've missed you also little one!" He stooped and placed Tia on the floor. Being aware of the two ladies, standing, he extended his hand as he rose up saying,

"My name is ..." he stopped, startled, as he stared into the face of Ronnie who now seeing his complete face, said, "Jay?" and fainted dead away. Jay caught her and held her and as he looked at her, his eyes watered slightly. He looked at Mrs. T.

Puzzled, she said quickly, "Bring her in here," and opened the door to an office with a couch. He laid her ever so gently on the couch and asked for a damp towel. The girls were quite frightened but in his soft gentle way he calmed their fears saying that she had only fainted, and that she would wake up in a moment. Mrs. T. was going to ask the girls to wait outside, but Jay said no it would ease their fears if they stayed until she woke up.

Tia came close and holding his hand asked, "Why did mommy fall out?"

Jay said, "She did not fall out, she just fainted."

Tia asked, "Why?"

"I don't know. We'll ask her when she wakes up." Jay said.

Jay gently patted her face with a damp towel, and she began to regain consciousness. She slowly opened her eyes. There they were those same beautiful eyes that Tia's eyes had brought back to mind. Looking at Jay, she closed them again for a moment; she opened them and closed them again.

Then she opened them and said, "It is not a dream; you are real!"

Jay said, "Yes love I am. The girls were worried about you. They wanted to know why you fainted." Ronnie couldn't stop staring at Jay.

* * * *

Mrs. T. escorted the girls out of the room. Ronnie raised her hand and lovingly touched the side of my face then she ran her finger over the scar under the eyebrow that caused it to be partially closed.

She said, "It never healed like the doctor said, did it?"

I answered, "No!"

She said, "Jamie was right. It really makes you sexy." Suddenly she was in tears, and her arms were around my neck. She was kissing me with fervor. It was as if she was trying to make up for all those years she had missed.

She said. "Oh my love, my love. I thought you were lost to me forever! Oh I love you, I love you! I felt for years you were alive. I couldn't make myself believe otherwise. Oh my love why did you ever leave me? How, how are you still here? They said you were . . ."

I put my finger against her lips. "You, my love! You were my lifeline! I'd like to tell you about that some time. Right now you have to get back to the girls."

She said, "Now that I've found you again I can't give you up!"

I said, "We have to part now. You have to think about the girls." She stood and straightened her clothes and hair.

She turned to me and said, "Oh Jay, hold me, just hold me!"

I put my arm around her, and it took me back so many years. I thought, "This is what helped me to survive all those dreadful years. I lived just for a moment like this." I could feel her sighing. She raised her face and I let my lips fall softly on her mouth that was still as sweet as the evening honeysuckle I felt her go limp.

As I kissed her, an old song was playing on the radio, to which we had been totally oblivious; I began to move her gracefully around the room. Her body moved and felt the same as though it was yesterday. Suddenly the music stopped. We just stood there in each other's arms. The scent of her and the feel of her soft body were overwhelming. We were lost in each other.

I said, "Love we must go." She clung tightly to me but I knew I had to push her away. I raised her chin kissed her mouth softly and said softly, "We must go." She wiped her eyes straightened her face, and we went into the outer office.

Shortly after, Mrs. T. and the girls returned. They had gone to the ice cream parlor. The girls ran to Ronnie hugging her tightly saying, "Mommy, you are all right!"

She said, "Of course. I guess I got too hungry."

Beth said, "I told you that you hadn't eaten all day."

"Why would she do that?" I asked. "I hope she doesn't do that very often!"

Beth said, "She always does it when she is worried."

I walked over to Beth and said, "I apologize I have not introduced myself and to such a gorgeous young lady. I'm Mr. J. and you?"

She said, "Beth".

I said, "I bet you stole those gorgeous dimples. I'll give you a hundred dollars a piece for them right now!"

Beth smiled for the first time. She said, "You know I can't sell them."

I said, "Why not?"

She said, "Because I can't get them off stupid!"

Ronnie said angrily, "Beth! Apologize!"

She came to me and said, "I'm sorry! I apologize!"

I said, "Thank you Beth." I don't usually go against parents' correction of their children, but I said to Beth, "You were right. I was stupid not to realize that you couldn't take them off. Beside they are much prettier on you. So I apologize for causing you to have to apologize. Am I forgiven?"

She nodded her head, "Yes."

I said, "I know something I can buy. Can I buy a hug?" I winked at Ronnie. Beth shook her head no.

I said, "No?" Then she extended her arms up and I knelt down to receive her hug. She hugged me tightly. I whispered softly, "Thank you!" She kissed me on the cheek. So still kneeling, I took her face in my hands, and I kissed her forehead, I kissed her right eye, then her left eye, then her nose, then I touched my finger to my mouth and touched the right side of her mouth then the left side of her mouth, then her lip under her nose, then her lip above her chin then touched my mouth with my finger and touched her mouth and hugged her. I whispered, "I hope this means we are friends!"

She said, "Yes!"

I asked, "Will you go with us when I take Tia to see my horses?"

She said, "But I'm afraid of horses!"

I said, "That's only because you want to be. You don't have to be. Is your mother afraid of horses?"

She said, "She used to be. But she made friends with a horse named Rance." My head dropped. She raised my head with her little hands and said, "Mr. J. you're crying. Did I say something to hurt you?"

I heard Ronnie say, "Oh my Love!" Then turned her back to hide her tears.

I hugged Beth and said, "No love, something flew in my eyes." I took out my handkerchief and acted as though I had something in my eyes.

Ronnie said, "We must go." I heard her say, "Five minutes." I got up from my knees. Mrs. T. and the girls hugged me and said their good-byes. Beth kissed me on the cheek.

I picked Tia up and said, "Goodbye little trooper until the next time. Don't give all your love away."

She said, "I'll save it all for you."

I said, "You can give some to other people. Just don't give it all to them."

Ronnie and Mrs. T. were talking and I heard Mrs. T. say, "He's a charmer. He could charm the legs off an iron pot. Did you see how he handled Beth? She told me she did not like him when we went out for ice cream. Where do you know him from?" Then I heard Mrs. T. say, "Oh my God!" I turned and she had her hand over her mouth looking at me. Then she whispered for a while to Ronnie and pointed to the TV monitor—she had obviously seen the news release. Ronnie turned and looked at me.

Mrs. T. took the girls out to the limo. Ronnie turned to me. She looked at me for a long time. Then with tears in her eyes, she came to me. She put her arms around me.

She said, "Don't say anything. Just dance with me like we were doing in the other room, I have not danced since I last danced with you." She said, "I've got to see you again. You cannot walk out of my life again. Promise me that."

I said, "There has never been anyone else in my life. You are my life. Where else could I go? I even changed my name—Meridith is my mother's maiden name—and kept my picture out of the paper so that you would not know that I existed. I was happy when I heard that you were in Europe when they released the press conference and news reports. I arranged my disappearance so that they thought that I had left the country, so that you would never know. I just wanted you to be happy. I did not plan or want this to happen. But fate has taken a hand. How could I know that hearing a little girl whimpering under a table would lead to you?"

Ronnie said, "Oh, my love! How could I ever be sorry that this happened? I have only been half happy. I cannot lie about wanting you every day of my life. How could this have happened to us?"

I told her, "I promised you lunch, but under the circumstances, I think it best to put it off till another time—Good-day my love." I kissed her sweetly and escorted her to the door. She held on to my hand as long as she could.

When Mrs. T. returned she closed the door to her office. She stood leaning against the door looking at me. I sat on her desk looking back at her.

She said, "You knew Ronnie before, right?"

I said, "Yes, High School."

She said, "Then you are Jay McFadden?"

I said, "Yes. Am I safe with you?"

Her hands went up to her mouth. She said, "Oh my God!" She put her arms around me. "I never would have believed it. Ronnie has talked to me about you so much. It's like I have known you all my life. She did not exaggerate about you one bit. I can see why she loves you so much just from the little bit I've known about you. You are supposed to be out of the country, and here you are operating right under the nose of the press—wow!"

I said, "When the time is right I will let them know who I am. I would like to share a confidence with you. Am I safe with you?" I asked.

She said, "I would never break a confidence. And respecting you like I do, I would never break one with you."

I told her, "I was hiding out for two reasons. Number two I wanted to make it on my own not because I was a war hero or a returned POW. Number one I wanted to protect Ronnie. Knowing that she was married I wanted her to go on thinking that I was deceased. I never thought I'd run into her. I made a lot of money on the stock market and one of my buddies from my old platoon put me onto my first building in New York City. From there, I found a couple of smaller buildings here in Manhattan. I was able to acquire the building next door and so on. Between the buildings and the stock market I do all right. There are a couple other things I want to accomplish before I let the cat out of the bag because it is going to be a clawing and screeching cat when it does come out.

What is bothering me right now is Ronnie. She doesn't want me to walk out of her life. How can I not walk away? What we had is lost. I made a bad mistake when I left her but it is one I'll have to live with the rest of my life. She has another life now with two darling little girls. I could not mess that up. I won't mess that up. It was she that pulled me through those years as a POW. I owe her everything for that. But I have no choice. I have to walk away.

Mrs. T. came over and gave me a loving hug. She had tears in her eyes. "Ronnie said you were stubborn. Let me point out something to you. Ronnie has a nice husband and he is very good to her. She has some love for him, but she is in love with you. She has always been in love with you. When she thought she had lost you she was willing to give up her life for you, and you were fighting to hold on to your life for her. And from what I've heard you did one hell of a job of it. Did you do that for nothing?

Another thing, as hard as you fought to keep her from finding out that you were alive, you, not someone else, were led to her lost daughter hiding under that table. Do you think that was just an accident? Plus both girls ended up loving you instantly almost like a father and one of them has never had anything to do with a man other than her father and grandfather. Am I going to have to knock you upside that stubborn head?"

"I hear you Mrs. T., but how can I just hang around her knowing all the while she belongs to someone else. I think I'd rather be back in that dungeon. At least there I had something to look forward to. When hope is gone the man is gone."

She asked, "Was she worth hoping for all those years?"

I said, "Of course. As I said, she is what pulled me through."

"Is she not worth hoping for now," she asked?

I said, "Of course!"

She said, "Then hang around and hope! Besides, wherever you go from here, where is your heart going to be? If your heart is going to be with her, you may as well be here. If you could take what they say you went through, you can take this."

I walked over and hugged her. I whispered, "If I ever need a lawyer to plead my case you are elected." I hugged her for a while and released her.

She gave a sigh and said, "Don't do that again. I might not let my husband hug me again as it is. Ronnie is a lucky woman I hope she knows it."

As I was leaving, I looked back winked and said, "You're still numero uno."

She said, "I know better now. I know who is!"

* * * *

Once home, Ronnie was on the phone to Jamie. When Jamie answered, Ronnie excitedly began to talk and so fast Jamie had to calm her down. "Hold it! Hold it! Slow down. I can't understand a word you're saying. What's the matter?" asked Jamie

"Let me catch my breath," said Ronnie. Finally she said, "Jay it's Jay! He's alive and I've seen him! I had my arms around him! So it's no dream! I said all along that I believed he was alive! I just felt it in my heart! And he's right here in New York!"

Jamie said calmly, "I know girlfriend, I know, but I want you to calm yourself. I have to tell you something OK?"

Ronnie said, "Yes."

Jamie began, "It's been about six years since Jay was released. He was barely alive, and hardly conscious. The military held him for a while, something they call debriefing, but always under a doctor's care. When his doctor felt it was safe to move him they shipped him to a military hospital twenty miles from here. He was taken to that hospital because his doctor specified what doctors he wanted to take over Jay's care. I think Jay's uncle was orchestrating all of this from the time they found out Jay was alive."

Ronnie questioned. "His uncle?"

Jamie said, "Yes, you remember the friend Loren had in Washington? Well he is her husband's brother; he's a three-star General and was a close friend of Jay's father. To continue, Jay was skin and bone when we first saw him. It was horrible. When he opened his eyes and saw me, you were the first one he asked for."

"Why . . . ?" Ronnie started to interrupt.

"Just listen." Jamie said. "I told him you were in Europe for the summer. It was the first thing that came to my mind. He had a long road to recovery. We couldn't take any chances on giving him any negative news. When Loren thought he was strong enough, she told him about your marriage. He was devastated. She explained what you had gone through and how we had told you he would want you to go on with your life. He understood and said it was the right thing to have told you. He said he would do everything in his power to keep you from knowing he was alive.

He and General Jim discussed plans to suppress any information about him as long as possible. He then threw himself into studying the stock market. He devoured everything I could bring him. When he was given his back pay, he took a gamble and put it all in the stock market and in a short time he had made a killing. Then one of his military buddies helped him to purchase a small building in New York.

He picked my brain about real estate. From there he went onto purchase other buildings. That's how he happened to be in New York. By the way he did not know where you lived. He changed his name and put things in place so that when the news broke, the newspaper would get the story that he had fled the country until he was able to deal with rehashing the past. He did all this for two reasons; to keep you from knowing he was alive and to make it on his own, not because he was a war hero or POW. So it is important that you don't leak any of this until he is ready, understand?" Jamie said. "Are you still there Ronnie?"

Ronnie finally answered. "I'm just speechless. That man never ceases to amaze me! Oh Jamie what am I going to do? I can't bear to think of losing him again! And the girls absolutely love him especially Tia"

"The girls? Tia?" Jamie asked.

Ronnie said, "Yes! That's how I met him. You know how we left Tia with Mrs. Templeton when we were there? Last week we left Tia with Mrs. T.—that's what Jay calls her—and for some reason Tia left the office and got lost. Jay found her and brought her back to the office. Mrs. T. had just called me and was leaving the office to look for Tia, when she saw Jay approaching carrying Tia, and she had her arms in a bear hug round his neck. He had to leave, but Tia would not let him go. He told her he had to go but promised that he would come back and take her to see his horses. He left just as I was coming in, so I missed him. Isn't that weird about Tia?"

Jamie said, “Yes, but how did you meet him?”

Ronnie said, “Well I was curious as to why Tia was not afraid of this man; so on questioning her, she told me how he had told her that her eyes were too beautiful to have tears, that’s exactly what Jay used to say to me! Then she told me how he had kissed her forehead, her right eye, her left eye, her nose; and she showed me how he took his finger and each time went from his lips to the right and left sides of her mouth, under her nose, her chin, and touched her lips. I almost fainted. That’s exactly how Jay used to kiss me. I had to meet this man. So I asked Mrs. T. to set up an appointment so that I could meet him. I also couldn’t get over how Tia kept asking when she could go see Mr. J. That’s what she calls him.

On the day we met, Tia suddenly yelled, ‘Mr. J!’, bolted out of the door and literally jumped in his arms. Mrs. T. and I had had our backs turned when she ran out. We turned around in time to see her flying into his waiting arms. She had her arms around his neck so her head and hair hid his face. He walked in set her down and started to introduce himself as he stood up. When I looked in his face I fainted. So that’s how I met him.

Jamie said, “That’s awesome! And Tia actually wants to go see horses?”

Ronnie said, “Get this. So does Beth!”

Jamie said, “What? Both of them are scared to death of horses!”

Ronnie said, “Hear this! After I had fainted, Jay assured the girls I was OK. When I woke up Mrs. T. had taken the girls to the ice cream parlor. Beth told her she did not like Jay. But by the time we left, she was hugging and kissing him and said she also wanted to go see the horses. Now they both talk about nothing but Mr. J. I don’t know what to say to Len when he gets back next week. He has to agree to the girls going to see the horses before Jay will take them. You know Len doesn’t care much for horses.

Jamie said, “It sure is weird about both of those girls and wanting to see horses. That’s one for the books. Speaking of horses you should see what Jay has done with Ranceville.”

Ronnie said, “Ranceville?” Jamie said, “That’s right you have not been there since it’s been named Ranceville. Ben and Sam named it Ranceville and it’s a huge tourist stop. Jay has made that large pasture in the back, a wild horse sanctuary. He has six of the most beautiful wild horses there and more coming. You really need to see it.”

Ronnie said, “You know the day I met Jay he asked Beth if I was afraid of horses. She told him I used to be, but that I had made friends with a horse named Rance. He dropped his head and I saw something I had never seen before, Jay crying. He loved Rance so much. My heart bled tears for him. I almost fell on my knees and held him, but with the girls there I could only turn my back. I know how I cried when you told me about Rance. Jamie I love him so much what am I going to do? How could this happen to us? And now the girls adore him! They asked if he could be their uncle. Can you believe that? How can I just let him walk out of our lives?" Jamie said, "Just give it time. But don't do anything stupid or too quickly, without thought."

Ronnie said, "Jamie I've got to see him alone. Do you know how I can get in touch with him?"

Jamie asked, "Do you think that's wise?"

Ronnie said, "What else can I do? After all these years, I've got to have some time alone with him.

Jamie thought, and said, "I work for Jay and have an adjoining penthouse as my office and home away from home."

Ronnie said, "I don't understand!"

Jamie explained, "I handle Jay's real estate business and sometimes I have to be in New York a couple of weeks at a time; so Jay set up that penthouse for me. Since I will be in New York in the next two weeks, if you come by my apartment one day, I can let you into his apartment."

Ronnie said, "Won't I be invading his privacy if I don't call him first? He could have a friend since he knew I am married!"

Jamie said, "For saying that, I shouldn't even help! You can't really believe that can you?"

"No, I really don't!" said Ronnie!

Jamie asked, "When would you like to come by?"

"Tomorrow if you're going to be there!" said Ronnie

"Will you bring the girls?" asked Jamie.

Ronnie responded, "I am not sure what I will do with them. If they get to see Jay, I will never have any time with him. I tell you they are absolutely mad about him especially Tia! He's all she talks about! I don't know what her father will think when he gets home from Paris."

Jamie said, "Why don't you bring the girls with you? I'll fly in tonight, and tomorrow I'll return home and take the girls with me. Loren would just love to see them and I'll bring them back with me the next morning."

Ronnie screamed excitedly, "Jamie that's a wonderful idea. They have been asking when they could go see Grandma Loren and Aunt Lori? I love you Jamie!"

"Ditto," said Jamie.

The next day Ronnie arrived around two in the afternoon. Jamie had left word with the doorman to send them up to her penthouse when they arrived.

When Ronnie entered Jamie's penthouse she was flabbergasted. "What a gorgeous apartment!" she said. The girls were all over Jamie. They had always loved their Aunt Jamie. Jamie showed Ronnie around. Ronnie was stunned to see the clothes Jay had purchased. Jamie explained to her how Jay had told her to see Mrs. T. if she wanted anything else. She explained how she refused to go near the store because she knew Mrs. T. would recognize her.

Ronnie said, "Jay has always loved you and he shows it. You always said Jay was the best friend anyone could have." She hugged Jamie and said, "You deserve it, but can he afford all this?"

Jamie responded, "Like I told you in a short span of time between the stock market and real estate, Jay has become filthy rich! And by letting me handle his real estate, he has made me a very rich woman!" Jamie said, "You should see Jay's apartment. You want me to show it to you?"

Ronnie said, "No I would rather see it with him. Where is it?"

"Through that door," said Jamie.

Ronnie walked over to the door. She touched the door with her hand and laid the side of her face against the door as if she was laying it against Jay's chest.

Ronnie then approached Jamie and whispered, "Don't take the girls to see the horses. They don't know who Jay really is yet. I'm trying to figure out how to tell them or if I should."

Jamie turned on the stereo.

Ronnie listened for a while and walked to the window and stared at a few passing clouds in the sky. "The sky is so blue," she said to Jamie. She listened as a song played and said, "You know Jamie, I hadn't danced since I danced with Jay, other than at my wedding, until the other evening when I met Jay. We danced to a song in Mrs. T.'s office. Oh. Jamie what am I going to do?"

Jamie answered, "You said a few moments ago that Jay was the best friend a person could have. Keep him as a friend."

Ronnie responded, "A friend? I need his love. I need him to love me!"

Jamie said, "You have his love and he will always love you! You have to remember that you are married and have another life now. You have to take that into consideration."

Ronnie dropped her head and said, "You're right! It will be hard to know he is around and not be able to love him." Her eyes began to tear, but at that moment, the girls who had been playing on the computer, asked Ronnie if they could go to see Mrs. T.

Ronnie asked, “How would you girls like to go with Aunt Jamie to see Grandma Loren?”

“Yea!” said the girls.

“Aunt Jamie is going to take you to see Grandma Loren and I want you girls to behave yourselves.”

Jamie and the girls prepared to leave. Ronnie gave them all hugs. Jamie left word with doorman that Mrs. Ronnie was her sister and was to have access to her penthouse at any time. She also told Ronnie that when Jay came home, he always called to tell her that he was in for the evening or he would leave a message on the answering machine.

Ronnie turned on the stereo and listened to music. Old memories caused her to cry herself to sleep. She slept through Jay’s phone call. When she awoke it was almost dark. She turned on the lamp and looked at the answering machine. She listened and Jay said he was in for the evening. Ronnie approached the door to Jay’s apartment, paused and then slowly opened the door to his apartment. There was a soft light on that revealed a beautiful lounge. It was breathtakingly decorated. She heard soft music playing. She turned and followed the music to a large office with a floor-to-ceiling window and she could see a gorgeous view of the lighted city’s skyline.

Jay was standing to the left looking out the window. She called softly, “Jay.” Startled Jay turned and just looked at her for a while. Jay had just been thinking of her.

Finally he asked, “How…?”

Ronnie walked up to him. She placed her finger over his lips. She raised her lips and softly kissed him. Jay took her face in his hands and kissed her the way he had the first time he ever kissed her. As his lips softly touched hers as lightly as a bee landing on a honeysuckle petal, and as she savored the sweetness his kiss with her mouth, her arms fell from around his neck and she went limp in his arms.

Jay gathered her up in his arms and gently laid her on the couch. He stroked the hair from around her face and kissed her cheeks and lips softly. When Ronnie opened her eyes, she looked lovingly at Jay’s face. They looked deeply into each other’s eyes as their lips slowly moved towards each other. They were lost in the sweetness of that kiss for what seemed an eternity. Ronnie refused to release Jay, as if she felt he would disappear.

Jay lifted Ronnie to her feet. She clung to his neck. The song "The Door Is Still Open" began to play and Jay moved Ronnie gracefully around the room both lost in the love and memories of yesteryear. They danced until late evening. Ronnie had given her chauffeur the evening off and told him that Jamie would see them home.

Jay sat in his large lounge chair. Ronnie sat across his lap. She put her hand on the side of his face. Her soft fingers stroked his brow running over the old scar that caused his eyelid to be partially closed.

"Did I ask you if you were sorry it hasn't healed as the doctor said it would?" asked Ronnie.

Jay smiled and said, "Yes."

Ronnie lowered her lips and kissed his neck, then laid her head on his chest. Jay was gently stroking her soft hair, and the dove-like skin of her face, and inhaling her fragrance, when he noticed that Ronnie was fast asleep. He touched a button on the chair and the chair inclined slightly backward. He held her as though she was a little girl asleep in his lap. He continued to stroke her hair, her face and inhale her fragrance. He thought of how this—the thought and scent of her—had been what had helped him to survive those dreadful years. It wasn't long before he fell asleep.

When Jay opened his eyes, the sun was peeking through a small break in a lone cloud. Its rays lay across Ronnie as though it was bathing her. It made a beautiful sight. He watched her slightly sunlit face. "Gosh," he thought. "How gorgeous she has become in womanhood." He wished he had been around to watch this wonderful transformation. He refused to wake her so he continued to hold and watch her.

He thought, "I had better enjoy these moments because it cannot continue. So he continued to hold her and watch her sleep.

Finally Ronnie opened her eyes. "Good morning love," said Jay.

She stretched and snuggled up to Jay and said, "What a wonderful dream! I dreamed I slept in your arms all night," as she kissed him under his chin. Suddenly she realized that she was still in Jay's arms and they were still in the lounge chair.

She said, "Oh Jay I didn't!"

Jay said, "What?"

She said, "Sleep in your lap all night. Oh my love, you must have been awfully uncomfortable!"

Jay asked, "Were you?"

Ronnie answered, "My love that was the best night's sleep I have had in many months. My dream was that I was in your arms and I felt truly safe. Oh my love, my love, my love, don't ever leave me again."

Jay said, "I'm afraid that won't be possible. It won't be long before Jamie and the girls will be getting back. You should be there when they get back, right?" "Jay, Jay, what are we going to do?" asked Ronnie. "How can I give you up now that I have found you again?" Jay said, "The only thing we can do is be friends. We can't continue to spend time together like this." Jay called to have breakfast sent up.

Ronnie asked, "How can we be only friends?"

Jay responded, "That's the only thing left if I am to remain in your life. That's the only way it can be fair to your family."

"But my love I couldn't bear to live and know that I can't touch you!" said Ronnie.

Jay said, "Then I will have to disappear!"

"Oh my God, No!" cried Ronnie. "I will suffer anything rather than have that happen. I'd rather see you and not be able to touch you than not see you at all. Jay, has your love faded for me a little?"

Jay put his arms around her and said, "You are the air I breathe, the sunlight that warms me, the nourishment that strengthens my body. You are the reason I wish to see each day, and the desire to see you and smell the fragrance of you again was the only thing that kept me alive all those years in captivity. Remember you are my lifeline!"

After catching her breath, she kissed Jay passionately assuming it would be the last time. She said, "Will you tell me about those horrible years sometime?

Jay nodded, "Yes."

With tears filling her eyes, she asked Jay to dance with her before she went next door to shower.

Jay turned on the stereo selected a CD and said, "Since I found out that you were married this has been and will always be my thoughts. The song that he played was "Just Out of Reach." He gathered her in his arms as the record began. She listened intently. As the story unfolded, her tears turned to a flood, and her heart pounded for the heartache that he must have been suffering. How could she think only of her pain when this is what he had been living with all this time and would have to go back to? She listened to the words:

*Love that runs away from me.*
*Dreams that just won't let me be.*
*Blues that keeps on bothering me.*
*Chains that just won't set me free.*
*Too far away from you and all your charm.*
*Just out of reach of my two empty arms.*

*Each night in dreams I see your face.*
*Memories time cannot erase.*
*Then I'll awake and find you gone.*
*Then I'm so blue and all alone.*
*So far away from you so sweet and warm*
*Just out of reach of my two empty arms.*

*That lonesome feeling all the time*
*Knowing you could not be mine*
*Dreams that hurt me in my sleep*
*Vows that we could never, never keep*
*So far away from you and all your charm*
*Just out of reach of my two empty arms.*

She looked up at him and said, "My darling I'll do anything you say. I'll even let you go if that will be better for you."

He kissed her tear-filled eyes and asked, "My life, where can I go and not long for you? Where can I go that the air I breathe is not there? Should I not stay here? I would rather stay here and miss you intensely then to be somewhere else and miss you immensely. Besides, I've fallen in love with your darling little girls!"

She put her arms around his waist and hugged him tightly and he flinched but said nothing. She let go quickly and said, "I hurt you! She moved her hand over his side lightly and questioned, My God! What is wrong?"

He replied, "Just an old war wound love!" She said, "Jay that feels like your whole side, Love! Is it healed? And you let me lie on you all night, why did you do that Jay?"

Jay responded, "You did not hurt me and I enjoyed having you there so much I would have let you lie there forever."

She said, "I love you so much and I want you to tell me all about your ordeal. Will you do that some time?"

Jay kissed her sweetly and said, "Yes, as I said before, but right now you'd better take your shower. Do you see that closet there? Go and open it." She opened it and gasped, with her hands over her mouth.

"I somehow had a picture in my head of your size so I hope they fit," said Jay.

She looked at Jay and said, "Why?"

He said, "It was like having you share this place with me. Not ever thinking that you would actually be here."

She said, "Oh sweetheart how could I not love you?" She ran to him and kissed him and ran back to the closet and picked a beautiful pastel orange suit with a pastel green blouse and tan shoes. Looking on one of the shelves she found stocking and on another, lingerie. Looking at the size she said, "Jay these things are beautiful and the right size even the stockings! How could you have known?"

He said, "I'll tell you sometime. Hurry! Go and take your shower." Ronnie kissed Jay and hurried next door to Jamie's apartment.

Ronnie finished her shower, dressed and put on her stockings and one of her shoes. She admired it waving her foot from right to left, and smiled thinking to herself, "How in the world did Jay know my size? He must have had some help." She heard the elevator door and slipped on her other shoe. Jamie and the girls came in.

The girls ran to Ronnie and told her she looked pretty. "Did you go shopping mommy?" asked Beth.

"Uh huh," said Ronnie. She looked at Jamie signaling 'we've got to talk'. She asked the girls if they enjoy their trip to see Grandma Loren. They began to tell Ronnie all about their visit with Grandma Loren. They were quite excited and told her how much they loved Loren.

Jamie turned on the TV and when the girls had finished talking they began to play games on the TV. Ronnie and Jamie went into Jamie's office.

Jamie said, "That's a gorgeous outfit and I really like those shoes. Where did you pick them up, Mrs. T's?"

Ronnie said, "Jamie you've seen these before right?"

Jamie said, "No! Why do you ask?"

Ronnie explained, "I thought you helped Jay pick them out thinking that's how he knew my size. "

"Jay?" Jamie questioned,

Ronnie said, "Yes! You didn't know he has a whole closet full of clothes and shoes, stockings, lingerie, everything and all my size?"

Jamie said. "No!"

Ronnie said, "I thought you were the reason he knew my size. How in the world did he know?"

Jamie shrugged, "He did my closets the same way, but he had seen me and picked a model my size and had professionals pick the clothes. He hadn't seen you so it's a mystery to me. He's just amazing!" They hugged and Ronnie gathered the girls' things, and Jamie's limo took them home.

# Love Can Be a Hurting Thing

Ronnie spent the next three nights with out much sleep. Her thoughts were mainly on Jay. She wondered how and when she would tell Len about Jay. She knew that she would have to tell him about Tia and Mr. J. Then she thought about how Jay had not revealed his identity as yet. She concluded that she had to talk to Jay first. She would have to do it in the next few days before Len returned from Paris, knowing that the girls would tell him about Mr. J. to get his permission to go see his horses.

Jay had given her a passkey to his elevator and apartment. She would use it to see him. Her mind turned back to thoughts of Jay. The words to the song kept haunting her. All night they played over and over in her head. She cried herself to sleep. Her desire overwhelmed the need to stay away. She had to see him. The next evening Ronnie called and asked Jamie to send her limo to pick her up. She did not want to use her own limo. Jamie understood and complied.

At Jamie's apartment, she asked if Jay was in. Jamie said he had called a short time ago. Ronnie disappeared through the door to Jay's apartment. Jay was in the same place looking out the huge window. "Just Out of Reach" was playing again. Ronnie stood there for a while listening and watching Jay. He had his arms folded and he lowered his head for a while, then raised it again.

The ache in her heart from watching him and knowing what he was feeling because she felt the same way was too much for her. She called his name softly. He did not move. She walked to him and slid her arms around his waist just under his folded arms and laid her head against his back. Her tears began to wet his shirt. His hand slid down upon her hands. He patted her hand letting her know that he felt her pain.

He turned to her and lifted her face and said, "I told you long ago—these eyes are too beautiful for tears." He proceeded to kiss her in the usual way until she went limp. He lifted her in his arms and instead of laying her on the couch, he sat in the lounge chair with her across his lap as before. He laid her head against his chest and inclined the chair and stroked her soft hair and beautiful face.

Her eyes opened slowly. Realizing that she was again lying in his lap, she whispered softly, "My love do not be angry with me but at this moment more than any time in my life I want you to make love to me!"

Jay held her close and kissing the top of her head he said, "My love as much as I want to I can't."

She asked, "Is it because of your side?"

Jay responded, "No."

She questioned, "Then why, love? It is not like I have not been with a man before."

Jay said, "But you gave yourself to the right man, your husband. I didn't degrade you before. I certainly won't do it now."

A bit angry, she snapped, "How do you know that I had not already had a relationship before? I did have boyfriends before you, you know!"

"Your anger is showing little one," said Jay softly. "I know, because you complete my spirit. You are part of me. I know you better than you think. If I did what you wish, our spirit would be broken and you would no longer be a part of me. One day you will know what I mean."

"Forgive me," Ronnie said, "But I don't buy that spirit business. I believe you don't want me now because you were not the first." She began to cry uncontrollably.

Jay hugged her close. Although he was hurt, he said nothing. He let her cry. When she finished crying, she pulled away from Jay's arms, stood up and asked,

"What do you want me to do Jay?"

Jay answered, "What do you want to do?"

She responded, I want to tell my husband about you, but I want to respect your secrecy. What shall I tell him?"

Jay said, "Tell him the truth." He rose from the chair, went to the window and stared into the night."

Ronnie watched Jay standing there staring into the night. She was suddenly perplexed. What was this sudden feeling within her? How could she feel this way about Jay? Was it anger, rejection, or self-pity? She wondered why Jay just stood there and did not turn to her. Maybe she was right about the way he felt.

She pondered awhile then she said, "Jay?"

He answered, "Yes?"

She did not respond. He heard the door close and the sound of the elevator.

A month passed since Ronnie walked out of the penthouse. Jay finally closed a deal that he and Jamie had been working on so hard. He had also completed things that he had planned from the start. He gave Jamie a big hug and congratulated her. He told her how he could not have done it with out her.

He said, "Now we can take it easy. I want to spend some time at Ranceville."

Jamie said, "Jay we have to talk. You have worked so hard to accomplish certain things and you have done it. But it is no good if you can't share it with someone. Why don't you try to contact her if for no other reason than the girls? I have been talking to Mrs. T. and she told me Tia calls her crying saying that you promised her. Jay they love you so much."

Jay thought for a moment then turned to Jamie and said, "Ronnie feels it's best that I stay out of her life and I think she's right. So I have no choice but to stay out of the lives of the girls also!"

Jamie asked, "Did she tell you that?"

Jay answered, "Not in words. But the way she left, and her silence for the past month speaks loud enough. I can't just barge into her life. I love those girls, but I told Ronnie that it had to be her and her husband's decision as to whether I took the girls to see the horses or not. They are her children remember! Now before I leave New York I need to set the record straight as to who I really am. Then I will be ready to leave New York for good. You notice that everything has been signed J.M., my real initials, so whether I am Jim Meridith or Jay McFadden the signature is mine. Everything is in order so you can run the business from here or at home."

Wait a minute," said Jamie, "What are you saying?

"It is not that important, said Jay. I have made my mark. I haven't hurt anyone. Now I'm free!"

Jamie said, "I don't understand and you have frightened me. What are you going to do?"

"Please don't worry about me Jamie. I will be all right. I want you to make sure the instructions in that letter I left on your desk, are carried out to the letter for that certain building. The building opens in ten days so I need to complete my business before then. I have a press conference in two days."

Jamie asked, "Jay will you tell me about your ordeal before you talk to the press?"

Jay said, "Then I need to tell you now." He took a deep breath and began:

"I was unconscious for three weeks. They were not sure if I would live. They wanted to give up on me but a certain interrogator named "Mr. Ni" insisted that they continue to try. They pulled me through even though a large portion of flesh from my side had been blown away. Luckily the heat from the shell had cauterized the wound and limited the bleeding. There were a lot of skin grafts. My healing was a long process. They fed me well trying to get me strong enough for me to be able to withstand interrogation.

It took over a year. Finally, one morning this interrogator had me brought to the lab. He had a reputation of never having failed to get information out of a man. He was ruthless, but he started off nice and kind. I would only give my name, rank and serial number. Then he began to turn up the heat. He was a high-ranking individual so he could do anything he wanted. He believed that I had special information because my unit was so successful in our raids. He tried everything, every kind of terrible torture. Nothing worked.

In the third year, they were ordered to turn over all the prisoners. We figured we had made it because we were going to be released. They released the sickly ones and a few of the healthy ones but most of the rest were shot. He shot some right on the spot and had others taken out and shot. He pointed to the dead men and indicated that was what would happen to the four of us who were left. The next five years he continued his relentless pursuit of information. He would move us around so no one could find us.

For two years, he enjoyed toying with us. Then he began to mess around with my side. He would push in on my side until I would yell. I would try not to yell but the pain was more than I could bear. When I passed out he would send me back and would bring in the others. He knew they didn't have any information, but he just wanted to keep in practice trying to see what made them yell the loudest. As soon as I was conscious he would bring me back again. He had no set time for me. I was his pet project. He had to make me talk. He had gotten all he could out of the others but he needed someone to pick on when I was unable to be questioned. He would bring me in morning, noon and night. I had been practicing a mind over matter technique to ease the pain and effectively used it for over three years.

Anytime he felt the urge he would bring me in. He knew my side was my weak spot so he constantly poked at it. He would hit it with his fist, a stick, once with an iron pipe, or anything. He found that pushing in on it was the best so he constantly pushed. Then I began to think about you, Lori, Loren and Ronnie. I found that I could concentrate on Ronnie so hard that I wouldn't feel anything. Early in those last three years I could only see her face but it was enough. Then I got to the point that I would sort of go into a trance and we would be in this garden. It was a huge garden with a lot of trees all kinds of plants and pretty flowers and a beautiful gazebo with climbing roses."

Jamie's hands went over her mouth. She thought, "My God, that's Ronnie's garden. He was actually in Ronnie's garden!"

"The first time I was in the garden, I stood under her window calling her and she came out. She came towards me, but then she turned and ran away. After that she would come out and we would sit in the gazebo, sometimes she would lay her head against my chest, other times she would lay her head in my lap and sometimes I would just hold her— that's how I knew her size. This way I was able to escape the pain. It infuriated him."

Jamie could not believe her ears. This is exactly what Ronnie had told her.

"Some one must have squealed, because they pulled a surprise visit and found the other three guys. But he kept me separated, hidden, so they didn't find me. They warned him if there were and more he had better give them up. After that he got really mean and would constantly bring me in and out of the torture room, but I was spending more and more time with Ronnie so I didn't care. It had become me against his pride. He had to break me. He kept after my side. In spite of my exercising, my body was getting weaker and weaker. This went on for about three-and-a-half years according to my homemade calendar.

Then one night I called Ronnie and she wouldn't come. I felt in my spirit that she had said 'no more'. So for the next eighteen to twenty months or so, I felt myself slipping away. I kept calling her for help. I began to call for you. I seemed to be able to hold your hand."

Jamie thought, "He was actually holding my hand."

"This helped me to hang on even though my body was giving out. Then I remember them finding me and they shot Mr. Ni. They took me somewhere. That's the last I remember until I woke up with my uncle Jim looking over me. They said that I had been that way for three months."

* * * *

I had been looking out the window while I was telling Jamie the story so I did not see her crying a river of tears.

She ran to me and hugged me and asked, "How can I help remove your pain? I will do anything."

I told her, "You've done enough by being there and here for me. I can never repay you."

"You can by staying alive!" Jamie said.

The next day I got a call from Ronnie. She asked if she and her husband could meet with me.

I said, "Either this evening or tomorrow morning."

"We can't make either of those!" She said;

I told her, "Those are the only two times I have available."

She said, "Jay I've never known you to be just plain mean! It's not like you to get back at someone."

I said, "I'm sorry you feel that way but that is the only time I have!" She started to say something, but hung up. Ronnie then called Jamie and asked her about my schedule.

Jamie told her, "He has a press conference with the media tomorrow afternoon and then he's leaving New York."

"Leaving New York? What do you mean?" Ronnie asked.

"I mean he has put all his business in order. He's turned it over to me and he's leaving New York," said Jamie.

"Why would he give up everything he worked so hard for? Can't you talk to him?" asked Ronnie.

Jamie responded, "Jay has been hurt enough. He finally told me about his horrible ordeal, those eight years, and believe me it was horrible. He's too good for this world. I'm afraid for him but I feel that he has had all he can take. I'll tell you what he told me sometime."

Ronnie hung up and immediately called me. I answered.

Ronnie said, "Jay, we cannot make the time frames you gave because of time constraints. Is it possible you could come here?"

"When?" I asked.

"What is your preference?"

"Early morning." I said.

She understood and asked, "Would nine o'clock be all right?"

I said, "Fine. Will you give me directions?"

She said, "Have Jamie's driver bring you, he knows the way."

I arrived exactly at nine o'clock. I heard Ronnie tell the maid, "I'll answer that." Ronnie answered the door. She was looking beautiful in the outfit I had given her.

She looked at me with welcoming eyes and said, "Welcome! Please come in! Len and the girls had to make a short run. They will be back momentarily. Won't you have a seat?

I said, "Thank you. You look absolutely radiant and such a beautiful home."

Ronnie said, "Thank you. You are always the gentleman aren't you Jay? Why do you always have to be a gentleman? Couldn't you have for once forgotten your code and seen me as a woman who loves you and who has a need for you?"

"What you are asking is that I not be me, right?" I asked.

Ronnie did not answer the question but said, "I understand that you are leaving New York?"

I said, "Yes, my time is finished here." Ronnie said, "I didn't know you had a time schedule."

"Only I knew it." I responded

Ronnie began, "Jay, what we wanted to talk to you about is the girls. They want so much to see your horses, and they love you so much especially Tia. You are all she talks about. She wants to see you so badly. So does Beth. I've never seen them take to anyone as they have to you. Jay is there any way we can still be friends?"

I responded, "I always have been and always will be your friend!"

"What happened to us that night?" asked Ronnie

"I guess I was being me as usual, I responded. "But I'm glad it happened!"

"You are glad?" asked Ronnie?

"Yes," I answered. "It put things in perspective. It made me realize that I was an outsider looking in, an interloper, that's not a pleasant picture. I realized that you belong to another man and I was trying to hang on to something that belongs to another man. As you found him, I'm sure there is someone out there for me."

"Oh Jay, you cannot want someone else—you just cannot. I love you," said Ronnie. "Please don't leave New York and all you've built here!" she pleaded.

"What's it all worth if you have no one to share it with you? I answered. "What I built here, I can build somewhere else."

With tears in her eyes she knelt before me and sobbed, "I want to share everything with you," she cried.

I took her face in my hands and said, "You have someone to share with."

She said, "You didn't say it."

I asked, "What?"

She said, "That my eyes are too beautiful for tears."

"When you pushed away from me that night and walked out, you made me realize these eyes were not mine to talk about any more." I told her.

The sound of the car pulling into the garage caused Ronnie to hurry upstairs to straighten her face. The girls and their dad entered the house, the girls bolted for me as soon as they saw me. I dropped to my knees with waiting arms. Tia was first to reach me, and then Beth. Hugs and kisses were plentiful.

Tia asked, "Where have you been? I've missed you so."

I said, "I've missed you too." And kissing Beth I said, "And I've also missed you princess."

Tia asked, "Are you going to take us to see your horses?" I said, "If at all possible my love."

Watching this scene, their father was amazed. He was watching Tia. He just stood there with his jaw dropped. He couldn't believe what he was seeing.

Ronnie came down and said, "Well girls you finally have your Mr. J." and then asked, "Did you introduce Mr. J. to your father?"

They said, "No we forgot."

I said quickly, "It's my fault. I was being as big a kid as they are."

Ronnie said, "Len this is Jay McFadden. Jay, this is my husband Len."

We shook hands. He said, "I'm pleased to meet you."

I said, "Likewise."

Len asked, "What have you done to my daughters? I've heard little else but Mr. J. since I've been home especially from Tia." Tia climbed in my lap as soon as I sat back down.

"I can't believe this scene," Len said, looking at Tia kneeling in my lap with her arms around my neck and Beth leaning up against me with her head on my shoulder. I responded, "Love and tenderness is all I know. No magic spell, no potions just plain love and tenderness."

Ronnie said, "Jay is on a schedule as well, so we'd better get down to facts."

Len said, "I needed to meet the man my girls were suddenly so taken with. I see now it is genuine and I know who you are, so I have no qualms about the girls going to see your horses if their mother agrees."

Both girls bolted to their mother saying, "Can we mommy, can we?"

"Yes, I guess so," responded Ronnie, looking at her husband.

Len said, "You do know that both girls are afraid of horses in spite of what they say, don't you?"

I said, "Yes, but they need not be."

Ronnie asked, "Since you are leaving New York, when will you have time?"

I replied, "I will make time because I promised them and I will not break that promise. I will make it happen as soon as I get permission."

Len said to Ronnie, "If you will excuse us, I would like to have a talk with Mr. McFadden. We're going to take a walk in the garden." Politely he guided me to the garden.

He said, "I understand that you knew my wife before." I said, "Yes from our high school days up until I went into the military."

He said, "Yes, she told me. She also told me that she was very much in love with you."

I said, "We were both very much in love. In fact she wanted us to be married before I left for induction but I refused."

He asked, "May I ask you why you refused?"

I said, "Of course. I read about guys who went off to war leaving young brides, some with a child or children, but who never returned. I did not want that to happen to her. That way, if something happened to me, she would be free to do as she pleased."

Len said, "Thank you for your frankness. My wife said that since you've met, she has spent time with you at your penthouse."

I said, "Yes she has been there a couple of times."

He said, "What bothers me is that she said that she has been in your arms kissing you."

"She is an honest woman, because that is exactly what has happened," I responded.

"She also claims that nothing else happened," said Len.

I answered, "Like I said she's an honest woman. Nothing else happened."

He asked, "You expect me to believe that two lovers who meet after such a long time, spend two nights together and nothing happened except a few kisses? Do you take me for a fool?"

I said, "I take you for a man that loves his wife and takes offense at an interloper. I can't fault you for that. I will tell you this; I could have violated her in high school, in college, before I left for the military, and when I returned on leave. I did not violate her then. I offered my life for this country and the principles it stand for, of which one is the sanctity of marriage. I would definitely not violate her marriage vows and neither would she! I take offense at the idea of your thinking she would!"

Len responded, "I take that as a threat. Let me make it clear to you. I'm telling you to stay away from my wife. I am a powerful man and my father is even more powerful. I could have you disappear!"

I said, "I did not mean that as a threat. I was merely expressing how I felt. Since we are clearing the air, I have no problem staying away from your wife. Not because you say so, but because I desire to. Just so that you might know, I have made many people disappear, in fact complete groups of people."

We walked along in silence for a while. Finally Len broke the silence. He stopped and said, "Jay! Is it all right if I call you Jay?"

I responded, "Perfectly!"

He said, "I apologize. I should not have said that about the two of you. I find you to be an honorable man and I like you. I hope we can be friends." and he extended his hand.

I took his hand and said, "I like a man that puts his cards right out on the table. Friends!"

Len said, "Let's go back to the house."

On the way back I began to notice the garden for the first time. It looked so familiar—the trees, the shrubs, the flowers—and then we came to the gazebo and it seemed to me that I had been here before but when? I pointed to the gazebo and mentioned how beautiful it was. We walked over to it and I looked up and pointed to the roses running across it. Then it all came together. I turned and looked at the house. I saw the windows upstairs. This is where I would meet with Ronnie!

I asked Len, "How long has it been there?"

He replied, "Over twenty years."

I didn't know it then, but Ronnie had been watching us through the window. We continued to the house and entered.

The girls immediately asked their father, "When can we go see Mr. J.'s horses?"

He responded, "Whenever Mr. J. wishes."

I said, "I'd like to do it as soon as possible. How about within the next two days preferably tomorrow? I'd love the two of you to come along." They agreed. I kissed the girls and said my goodbyes. I left to return to the city and a press conference.

# Ronnie's Return to Ranceville

Angie, my newspaper friend, had approached a TV station with the proposal of exclusive rights to Jay McFadden. She left the newspaper and became a news and TV commentator at the TV station. She announced that she had called this press conference because she had a special guest.

She said, "I would like to introduce my mystery guest. Sir would you come out?" So I walked out on the set. She hugged me for about a minute and she asked me to take seat. There was a lot of whispering, pointing, and expressions on the faces of the press. Some even knew me as JM the young tycoon.

Angie took a seat beside me, smiled and gave me a kiss. Then she turned to the audience and said, "I'd like to introduce to you Lieutenant Jay McFadden."

The place went wild. The press people were scrambling trying to get to the stage. However, they had planned for that and the press could not get to me.

Angie got them settled down and said; "This is a very dramatic story so I want Jay, Lieutenant Jay, to tell it in his own way and time." She kissed me again, and said, "Go get 'em tiger. I told my story to the press, but Angie had exclusive TV rights.

After I finished, the press questions started. Questions like: "Aren't you Mr. J. or JM the young Tycoon around Manhattan?"

I said, "Yes, I'm known as Mr. J. or JM.I don't know about tycoon."

"Weren't you supposed to be out of the country?"

I said, "Yes."

"Then why the masquerade? Why did you pose as Mr. J. or JM?"

I asked, "Did you know who Mr. J. or JM was?"

The answer was, "No."

I said, "That's why."

Why did you not want us to know?"

I said, "So that I would not be hounded by you, and so I could do what I wanted to do without interruption, to protect a friend, and to prove to myself that I could be successful on my own and not because I was a war POW or celebrity."

"Who is the friend you were trying to protect?"

I said, "Classified information!"

"You said when you were being tortured, you would put yourself into a trance. How did you do that?"

I answered, "I would think of being with someone or some place pleasant and fall off to sleep."

"What or who would you have been thinking of?"

"Like I said, something or someone pleasant."

"How were you able to lead fifty-one raiding patrols deep into enemy territory without losing a man?"

I asked, "Are you related to Mr. Ni? That's one of the questions he asked me for eight years." There was lots of laughter.

One person asked, "If you were as badly injured as you claim, how did you survive all those years? I don't believe it would be possible to survive with that kind of injury."

Angie hit the floor and yelled, "How dare you?" Angie said, "Jay love, I'm going to ask you something I know you don't want to do, but they've got to know." She turned to the press and said, "Our men give their lives for this country and someone like you questions their honor." With tears streaming down her face she asked, "Where the hell were you when he was going through hell?" She turned to me and said, "Baby remove your shirt. Please love they've got to know." and she began to unbutton my shirt. I tried to resist her but she persisted, and continued to cry, saying, "They've got to know. This will help other returning veterans." With that I ceased to resist.

She finally raised my undershirt and there, for the world to see, was my missing left side. Remaining was a mass of scar tissue.

"This is what men like him give up, for you to be safe and you dare question their honor. How dare you?"

The audience gasped at what they saw. Some turned their heads. I stood there, head hanging down, my arms at my side, too embarrassed to move. She pulled down my undershirt, buttoned my shirt, put her arms around my neck and kissed me knowing how embarrassed I was.

She turned to the person who had asked the question and said, "If I had a gun I'd shoot you and I hope they fire you." She said later that he was fired. She led me off the set to thunderous applause.

Angie had to go back on the set and the press began to question her about our relationship. They asked how she came to know me and why I gave her the story. They questioned her as to how she knew about my side. They hinted that, by her actions on the set, we must have been lovers. She had intended to tell them that it was none of their business. However, she told them that she had been my nurse when I was first turned over to the US military. Then she was asked, again judged by her actions on set, if she was in love with me.

She hesitated and then said, "Yes, ever since I held his near dead body, and when he opened his eyes and said weakly, 'Hello love!'" Here was a man near death and yet could speak kindly to the first person he saw.

I didn't want to go out the next couple days but I had promised the girls. I had no choice. I asked Ronnie and Len to be at the building around one o'clock. The girls wanted to see Jamie so they went up to her apartment. Jamie called me and told me they were early because they wanted to see her. I invited them to come over. Jamie guided them over. I was standing looking out of the window. I was listening to the song "Just Out of Reach." I heard the door and I hit the remote and turned it off, but Ronnie heard it just before it went off. She knew exactly where my heart and mind were. Holding the girls who had rushed to me, I asked if they would like refreshments. They declined. Len remarked on the apartment. I showed him around. I avoided Ronnie's eyes. I was not sure whether she had seen the press conference or not.

Jamie told me later that Ronnie had pulled her into the bathroom, and told her how she felt that she had turned me off her and cried her heart out. I told Jamie it was just that I felt it was best to move on—that I could only cause problems here. She also said that they had not seen the conference due to the office party they had gone to. Jamie said they would probably see it when it was aired again.

"There's so much talk about it, the network is planning to air it several times according to this morning's paper. I suppose you haven't read it?"

I said, "No I haven't."

Ronnie did not see the broadcast for a long time.

Len was impressed with the apartment. We talked about business and he was quite surprised at my success. He congratulated me, as I did him. My limo was waiting and we drove to the airport. We took a short jet ride and then boarded my helicopter. The girls were completely hysterical when they saw the helicopter. They could not believe they were going to get in a helicopter. Ronnie was not aware of my jet or 'copter. It took us only a few minutes and we landed at Ranceville. The girls could see the horses, as we were 'coptering in. By this time I had added 12 more horses. They watched the horses run and kick because of the 'copter. Their little faces were glued to the window.

Ronnie was astonished at what she had seen so far. I had built a helicopter pad and there was an eight-seat club shuttle to take us up to the house. We exited the 'copter and boarded the shuttle. I drove to the house. Mr. and Mrs. Ross were waiting. They had heard the helicopter and were excited to have all of us.

They welcomed us to Ranceville and offered us refreshments.

They told Ronnie and her family, "We know you will enjoy your visit to Ranceville." Ronnie introduced Len and the girls to Mr. and Mrs. Ross.

Mrs. Ross scolded Ronnie saying, "Shame on you for not bringing these beautiful little girls to see us before now. Ronnie just smiled and put her arms around Mrs. Ross and gave her a big hug. Mrs. Ross asked the girls, "How about some cookies and milk?"

The girls looked to their mother, who nodded her head yes, and they ran off to the kitchen with Mrs. Ross. Mrs. Ross loved the girls. She told Ronnie that they were precious. Tia and Beth instantly bonded with Mrs. Ross.

Ronnie heard the girls ask Mrs. Ross, "Are you Mr. J.'s mother?

Mrs. Ross answered, "In a way yes!" Tia gave her a hug. Ronnie smiled.

The girls were finishing their cookies and milk and Tia asked Mrs. Ross, "When are we going to see Mr. J's horses?

Mrs. Ross said, "Soon, but it is customary to meet Rance first."

Tia said, "I know Rance!"

Mrs. Ross answered, "Why sure he is the horse that loved your mother and Jay."

Ronnie still listening, teared. I walked towards the kitchen and heard Ronnie sniffle. I looked in her eyes. I wanted so much to hold her and her eyes said she wanted me too.

I said, "Come girls, let's go meet Rance! Tia and Beth both ran to me anxiously. I asked Ronnie have you seen the front, meaning the front of Ranceville. She shook her head no trying to dry her eyes. Mrs. Ross, that sharp old lady, picked up on Ronnie and whispered to her, "We have to talk!" Ronnie said, "Yes I'll have to call you." They agreed. Len and Mr. Ross were still conversing. They were getting along fine.

We went out to the front and Ronnie gasped placing her hands over her mouth. She looked at Rance and read the plaque with tears running down her face.

She said, "I have never seen anything so beautiful."

Mrs. Ross put her arm around Ronnie and Ronnie laid her head against her.

Mr. Ross said to Len, "She really loved that horse and he loved her. Did you know that when she first came here she was deathly afraid of horses?"

Len answered, I've heard that."

Mr. Ross said pointing to Jay, "That young man is a wonder with horses as you'll see in a few moments!"

"He's pretty good with people also," responded Len.

The girls were looking at Rance and said, "Mommy your horse was beautiful!" She looked at me, and I smiled and she hugged the girls and said, "Yes girls he's still very beautiful!"

Mrs. Ross told Ronnie that Ben and Sam had donated the plaque she read. At that moment Ben, Sam and the crew came up front. When they saw Ronnie they yelled, "Mrs. Ronnie!" Ronnie ran to Sam and Ben and hugged them. She was really glad to see them. They introduced the other hands to her. She introduced them to her family. In the meantime I had been signing autographs for the people that were there.

I had some of the pictures that I had taken of Ronnie, Rance, Jamie Mike, Mr. and Mrs. Ross, Ben, and Sam and had a little booklet made. The hands asked if I would help them put some notes in the booklet with each picture and if they could reproduce the booklet and let the visitors purchase them for a small fee so that they could have a small memento. They would use the fees collected for upkeep of the statue. I thought it was a great idea and agreed.

The hands had told some of the regular visitors about Ronnie and Rance. They asked me if she ever came out to Ranceville.

I said, "Yes. In fact," I pointed to Ronnie, "She is there with her family and that is Jamie beside her." They looked at the pictures in their booklets I had autographed and rushed Ronnie and Jamie for them to autograph their booklets too. Surprised by the sudden onrush, Ronnie looked at the pictures in the little booklet called "Ranceville At a Glance" looked at me and shook her fist as I stood there laughing. Len was looking over her shoulder, and he was laughing too. The girls were saying, "Mommy you and Aunt Jamie are famous!" Ronnie was embarrassed.

Ronnie finished the autographs and I asked her to take the family to the grandstand.

She said, "Come on girls. We're going to see the horses now. Tia screamed "Yea!"

I walked into the corral and headed for the far end to open the gates to the back pasture. Ben beckoned that he would open them. I stood in the center of the corral near the grandstand and whistled. In about thirty seconds the sound of thundering hooves and six beautiful horses came charging in the corral. The girls, frightened, huddled close to their mother as they watched these mighty, powerful animals charge me. I stood still as they charged past me and raced to the top of the corral, turned around and raced to the other end over and over.

After a few minutes they each came to me. I stroked each one individually as I talked very softly to them. After a while I stood in front of each of them and held my hand up like a traffic cop. I then walked over toward the grandstand and picked up a little whip returned and none of the horses had moved. I started at the left and lightly tapped the left front leg of the first horse that bowed down. I proceeded to tap the left leg of each horse until each had bowed. I tapped under the chin of each horse and each one reared on his or her hind legs. Len asked Mr. Ross if I'd had to use the whip to train them to do that.

Mr. Ross said, "Heavens no. Jay would never ever attempt to strike a horse. He does what he does with love only." I put the whip back and picked up a small basket of apples and gave each horse an apple. I petted and thanked each one of them and individually sent five of the horses back to the pasture.

Mr. Ross had been explaining what I had been doing to Len and the girls. Ronnie and Jamie were pretty much aware of much of what I was doing. He also explained that these are wild horses. I kept Lady in the corral because she was the most gentle, a lady. I hugged her and petted her. I turned my back to her and she pushed me out of the way. The girls really got a kick out of that. She followed me around as I walked. I raised my hand up and she reared up and walked on her hind legs. I told her to stay, and walked over to the grand stand; then I called her, picked up an apple and gave it to her.

I raised her chin and said, "Say hello to the people Lady!"

She raised her head and whinnied. I said, "Now give Tia and Beth a kiss." She moved her mouth as if to kiss them. The girls were very tickled. I walked out to the center of the corral and beckoned for Ronnie to come out. She didn't even hesitate. Len meant to stop her but Mr. Ross sort of nudged him and shook his head no.

Ronnie walked right out to the center of the ring to my side. Lady snorted and backed up.

I put my arm around Ronnie and said, "This is my friend Lady, say hello." She pawed with her right hoof and her head down. I said, "Come on say hello!" Lady walked up to Ronnie and nudged her. Ronnie immediately began to fondle Lady's nose softly, then the side of her face, and then her neck. Keeping a hand on Lady, she continued all around her until she was back to Lady's face. She scratched her forehead to see if she liked it; she did. She had made a friend of Lady that quickly.

I told her how proud I was of her. She had remembered everything that I had taught her.

She said, "I love you. I'm so proud of what you have done here. Forgive me for being selfish. I just love you so much."

I said, "Take Lady for a walk." She walked off and Lady hesitated. I said, "Go with her Lady." And she followed Ronnie as she walked around the ring. Ronnie walked over to the grandstand and raised Lady's chin and said give them a kiss and Lady gave then a kiss and Ronnie gave her an apple.

Len said looking over the railing, "I'm proud of you."

Tia asked, "Can I come down mommy?" Ronnie told me that Tia was asking to come down.

I said, "Come on down love!" Len looked at Mr. Ross who nodded his head yes.

Tia came down the steps to the gate. I picked her up in my arms and said,

"Don't be afraid Lady will like you." I called to Lady. "Come here Lady;" She came close and hesitated, I said, "Come on girl!" She came and sniffed Tia. Tia pulled back. I said, "She won't hurt you love. She wants to be your friend. Did you see how she took to your mother? She wants to be the same with you. All you have to do is pet her like you do a puppy dog OK?" I began to rub Lady's head and so did Tia, and as I walked around Lady, Tia began to pet her all over. When I got back to her face Tia began to rub her face and even said, "You are a nice horse I like you." Then Tia asked to get down so I put her down watching to see the reaction of Ronnie. She seemed a bit apprehensive but did not move. Tia began to walk around Lady reaching up to touch her as she went. I walked along with her keeping my hand on Lady all the while. Tia went all the way around Lady and reached up to pet her nose as Lady lowered her head.

Tia walked off and said, "Come on lady!" I followed her and Lady came along with me.

After a while, Tia walked over to the grandstand to get Lady an apple.

I took the apple and said, "I'll have to show you how to give a horse something out of your hand." I broke the apple in half and showed Tia how she had to keep her palm open with her fingers stretched out. I picked her up and watched as Lady took the apple cleanly from the palm of her hand. Tia said, "It tickled! I asked Beth if she wanted to come down. She said no. We said goodbye to Lady and sent her back to the pasture.

Beth ran to me and gave me a hug and asked if I was angry because she would not come down. I said, "Of course not love. When you are ready I'll be ready," and I kissed her.

Mr. Ross said. "Jay you never cease to amaze me."

I said, "It's not me it's my blessing!"

We said goodbye to the Rosses and went back to New York. Len had nothing but praises on the way back. He could not believe what he had seen with Tia. He also praised Ronnie. He was very impressed with Ranceville and teased Ronnie about her celebrity status at Ranceville.

Ronnie claimed, "I'm going to get that Jay McFadden." Ronnie looked at me every chance she had, as if trying to tell me something.

It was evening when we got back to New York so I had a 'copter to fly Len and his family home. I told the pilot there was plenty of room for the 'copter to land on his front lawn, and no wires to worry about. I insisted, so Len thanked me, and we said goodbye.

When we arrived at the building, Jamie got out. There was a mob of people so I instructed the driver to pull around to the side of the next building. I got out and went into Mrs. T.'s office via the rear door. I took a seat in her office and waited for her to return.

When she returned she quickly closed her door and ran and hugged me.

She said, "You darling I had no idea what you had been through, and what the TV showed about you. Oh Jay, what in the world can a person say! I was just watching a replay of your press conference. I wish the hell you had never told them. The world doesn't deserve you. Look out that window. There are more wolves out there, than there are numbers to count; they all want a part of you. Now I understand why you wanted to make your mark before they found out who you were."

I said, "Thank you love. Now I have to find a way to get up to my apartment."

Mrs. T. smiled and said, "I can help you there, but first I want to thank you."

I asked, "For what?"

She said, "For letting me know you. Now I know why Ronnie and the girls love you so much, and Ronnie really does you know?"

I said, "I know, but I have to bow out there. My being around is so unfair to her husband. He is a very nice guy and I like him. I love Ronnie and the girls as you know, but my plans are to leave soon."

"Are you going to throw away everything you have accomplished here? What about your business?" asked Mrs. T;

"I have a very able partner to take care of that. It is all arranged." I told Mrs. T.

She questioned, "A partner?"

I said, "Yes, you remember Jamie? When I get up stairs I am going to have her sign the papers and then take off."

"You know that this is really going to knock Ronnie for a loop," said Mrs. T.

"I don't think Ronnie will be as devastated as you think," I told Mrs. T. "At any rate what must be done, must be done. What I really hate is hurting the girls! How can I get up stairs?" I asked. She showed me some stairs to a walkway connecting the two buildings.

She asked, "Jay can I know where you will be?" I said, "I have a friend in Argentina who wants me to come visit and says he has a beautiful sister. I think I'll go see!" I laughed.

Mrs. T. said, "That's not funny!"

I said, "You're not jealous? I've told you that you are numero uno."

She said, "I'm talking about Ronnie. You can't really love anyone else can you?"

I said with a smile, "I don't know I've never tried,", and started to walk away.

"Mrs. T. asked, "Jay would you mind kissing an old lady goodbye?"

I said, "Old lady! I bet you're not much older then I am." I held her face and kissed her forehead, each eye, her nose, the sides of her mouth, upper and lower lip, and took her in my arms and softly kissed her mouth.

She began fanning her face and said, "Whew!"

I said, "That's so you won't forget me," and laughed as I started down the stairs.

She said, "Yes you'd better go! You would be dangerous to have around."

I continued to laugh and said, "Jamie will give you contact information just in case. Bye!" and I disappeared into the tunnel walkway.

In the apartment I had Jamie sign the papers making her a quarter partner. She tried to refuse. She said I had already made her an extremely rich woman but I insisted. I told her she deserved it. She also tried to talk me out of leaving but she knew I had to go. She asked if Ronnie was to have access to the penthouse I told her of course! She has her passkeys.

"Will she know where you are, asked Jamie? "Not unless you tell her!" I answered. "Give Mrs. T. the contact information." I packed a few things, kiss a teary-eyed Jamie goodbye, and returned to the limo via the tunnel. When I arrived at the airport, I took a flight to Argentina.

* * * *

Five days later the news broke about the last building Jay had purchased. The package that Jamie and Jay had completed also included a building near Mrs. T.'s store. The TV broadcast by Angie, said, "Mr. J., JM or Jay McFadden disappears but leaves behind a legacy. Manhattan now has a remarkable remodeled building showing in lighted letters that says, "Jay McFadden's Children's Memorial Hospital." JM wanted the name to be "Children's Memorial Hospital," however his partner decided to add Jay McFadden to it and she used her own money to add the change to the sign!" Angie said, "The love in that man! He was not satisfied offering his life for this country, he had to leave something for the children. Now here is the clincher, no child will be turned away. Now what I say to you is how can you sit by and watch a man and I emphasize man, give so much. These are our children he is doing this for, because, he doesn't have any. Will we sit by and let this man, who has already given so much, give all? It seems to me we should start a fund to support every child being taken care of!" Angie's words must have hit the right chords, because the response was overwhelming. The fund was set up and named 'JM's Children's Memorial Fund'.

Jay had been on the phone with Lori who told him about the TV program. She said how proud she was of her little brother. He told her that he had not wanted his name on the hospital. He said he had left specific instruction with Jamie as to the name of the hospital.

Lori told Jay, "I guess Jamie had ideas of her own. Hurray for her! Leave it alone Jay!"

When Jay called Jamie, Jamie asked, "Am I fired?" Jay was tickled and just said, "Great Job, I love you!" They talked for a while and Jay hung up.

Ronnie had not known that Jay had disappeared nor had she seen the replay of the press conference. As she sat with her husband watching Angie's broadcast, her heart was overjoyed with the news of his hospital, but ached from the news that he had disappeared and she fought to hold back the tears. She managed to smile in agreement as her husband said, "That is some fellow you know." She wondered where he had gone. She could hardly wait for the next three days to pass when Len would leave for Paris! Her nights were sleepless and full of tears.

After saying goodbye to Len at the airport she went directly to Manhattan. She stopped to talk to Mrs. T. who was very glad to see her. They talked about the news broadcast.

Ronnie asked, "Why would he just disappear. I thought maybe we could patch up our little indifference. I apologized for being so selfish. What will this do to the girls? They have been talking about nothing but him and the horses!"

"Hold it my love!" said Mrs. T. "He did not leave because of you? He left because of all of you, Len, the girls and you! If you truly look at it you will know he was right. He really likes Len and felt you guys were happy before he came back and if he stayed around he could only bring unhappiness to you, the girls and Len."

Ronnie said, "But he could have at least talked to me before he left. To just leave was cruel!"

Mrs. T asked, "Supposing he had talked to you, would you have let him go, be honest?"

Ronnie sat down, put her face in her hands and cried, shaking her head no. "It just hurts too much to lose him again," she said.

Mrs. T. responded, "What about him? What kind of life could he have here? Being around you everyday and not be able to touch you and feeling cheap when he did."

Ronnie bristled, "Feeling cheap! Why? When I wanted him to touch me!"

Mrs. T. asked, "You don't understand Jay at all do you? It has nothing to do with you wanting him to touch you or not. It has to do with right and wrong, moral or immoral. You have no idea of the kind of man you had do you?"

At that moment Ronnie thought back to Denise. She remembered how Jamie had told her why Jay would never go back to her. She was asking Jay to do the very thing he hated. Ronnie was crying uncontrollably by now.

She just shook her head and answered, "I guess not really." She wiped her eyes and said, "I've got to talk to him. I have to tell him that I truly understand now. I have to talk to Jamie and find out where he is." She started for the other building, but Mrs. T. stopped her.

"You will create an uproar if you go into that building! You will be splattered all over the newspaper." Ronnie looked puzzled.

"Ever since the press conference, there has been nothing but reporters hanging around that building. They dig into anybody who goes in or out trying to find out if they have any connection to Jay. I'm sure you don't want your picture all over the paper especially going in or out of there. Come with me." Mrs. T. said, and showed Ronnie the tunnel walkway between the buildings."

Once in the elevator she called Jamie and told her she was on her way up. Jamie was glad to see her and they talked for a while. Finally Ronnie asked about Jay.

Jamie asked, "Did he tell you where he was going?"

Ronnie said, "No! He didn't even tell me he was leaving!"

"Then maybe he didn't want you to know where he was going!" responded Jamie.

Ronnie cried, "Please Jamie I've got to know! I've got to let him know that I finally understand. I want him to know that I release him. Not that I don't love him but that he is free to find a life for himself as tears flowed down her face."

Jamie hugged her and said, "You are really sincere aren't you?"

Ronnie said, "Yes, but you know how hard it is for me to let him go. But he needs a life too."

Jamie gave her a phone number and asked, "By the way where are the girls?"

Ronnie said, "With the maid. Is it all right if I call from his apartment?"

Jamie responded, "Jay said you have your own key?" Ronnie pondered for a moment and began to search through her purse. Her eyes lit up as she held up her passkey. She said, "I had forgotten!" She did not need it from Jamie's apartment.

She walked into the apartment turned on some lights, and began to look around. She cried as the memories of Jay embraced her. She could feel him in every room. Then she went into his bedroom. It was spacious and beautiful.

She realized that she had never been in his bedroom before. She lay across his bed and imagined lying there with him. She could not stop crying. She saw a little remote picked it up and pressed the power button. The song "Just Out Of Reach" began to play. Those were the words that had been haunting her waking hours ever since she had first heard it. "Why can I not have Jay?" she cried. "What ever did I do to deserve this?" Finally she arose and went in and sat in the lounge chair by the window and looked out into the sunlit evening sky and listened as the song played over and over.

She realized she had to call Jay. A lovely voice answered and in a Spanish accent said, "Señor Jay? I will get him."

Jay answered, "Hello."

Ronnie was almost afraid to speak. She finally said, "Jay!"

He answered, "Ronnie? Is something wrong?"

Ronnie said, "Yes you are not here with me! Jay why did you leave without a word? I had to hear it on a TV newscast. Couldn't you have told me? We used to be able to tell each other everything. What happened to us Jay?"

Jay said, "The war. I have no place in your life any more."

Ronnie heard that voice again ask, "Is something wrong Señor Jay?"

Jay replied, "No señorita, just a friend."

"Who is she Jay," asked Ronnie?

"She is the sister of the friend I came to visit," replied Jay.

"I see!" said Ronnie

"Do you really?" asked Jay;

Ronnie said, "Jay I called to tell you that I have been very selfish but I understand that you had no kind of life here, and I want you to know that if I had any hold on you, I release you. I will love you as long as this body draws breath and beyond. I know that love is sometimes selfish so I ask your forgiveness."

Jay said, "Yes love is sometimes selfish. If I have to forgive you, you will have to forgive me, because until time stands still and eternity has an end, I will love you. But I cannot interfere with the sanctity of marriage."

"I understand that now," said Ronnie, "and I love you even more for it."

"Is that music that I hear? Where are you?" asked Jay

"I'm in your apartment," said Ronnie.

"I thought I recognized that song," said Jay. "How are the girls?"

"Like me, wishing for your arms to hold them. They have not stopped talking about you and the horses. Tia is so proud! She wants you to get her a horse and teach her to ride. She asks all kind of questions about you and me and Rance. She sleeps with that booklet from Ranceville. Oh! Love, we miss you so much!" said Ronnie.

Suddenly Jay said, "The apartment! Ronnie did the press see you come into that building?"

Ronnie answered, "No my love. They were there, but Mrs. T. showed me the walkway. No one saw me.

"Thank God!" said Jay.

"You do care, don't you Jay?" asked Ronnie

"Do you ever have to ask?" answered Jay

"I apologize for calling. I guess I was hurt. I won't call you again. Thank you for everything," said Ronnie.

"I have enjoyed your call. I have missed you and the girls and always will. You can always reach me if you need me," said Jay.

"Goodbye my love," said Ronnie.

"See you, beautiful eyes," said Jay.

Ronnie hung up and flopped in the chair and her tears flowed like a stream. She went into Jay's bedroom sat on his bed and looked at the two pictures he had on his dresser. Facing each other were pictures of her and Jay. They seemed to be looking at each other. She thought to herself that's the way it's supposed to be. She straightened her face and went to Jamie's apartment.

Jamie asked, "How did your conversation go? I can see by your eyes that you did a lot of crying."

"Not on the phone. Before and after," said Ronnie.

"Wherever he is, there is a woman. She answered the phone," said Ronnie.

"I know," said Jamie "I have talked with her. She seems to be really nice. She is the sister of one of Jay's service buddies. He was a member of Jay's troop."

"She seemed to be too nice to me," said Ronnie. "I heard her ask Jay, 'Is something wrong señor Jay?'"

"Have you seen Jay's press conference at all?" Jamie asked Ronnie

"No," said Ronnie. "We have always been away or out to something."

"Then you need to see it!" said Jamie. "There are some things you need to know about Jay. And after you see it we have to talk."

"What is it?" asked Ronnie.

"See the press conference," said Jamie.

Ronnie stopped to see Mrs. T. on her way out. They talked about her conversation with Jay and about the señorita who answered the phone. Mrs. T. said Jay had told her that she was supposed to be very beautiful.

"I bet she's probably trying to get her clutches on him!" said Ronnie

"Well you can't do anything about it from here," said Mrs. T.

When Len returned, he said how much Jay was talked about in Europe. He had seen the press conference over there.

"They read every bit of information they can get about him and the ladies are absolutely mad about him. Now the big question is where is he?" Len asked.

Ronnie said that the press conference was to come on in a few minutes and she had not seen it. Ronnie asked Len if he wanted to watch it with her. He said he had a lot of paperwork to do and he would be working late. He suggested that she not let the girls see it.

The girls were in the playroom so she went into the study and watched the press conference alone. Shaking like a leaf she lay on the couch and cried herself to sleep. She awoke to a mind full of questions. She wondered how he had been able to survive. Why hadn't he just told them what they wanted to know? Why had he fought so hard to stay alive in his condition? What kind of a trance had he put himself into? How had he been able to do that? Why had that Mr. Ni hated him so?

What was Jay's relationship with Angie? She seemed too friendly. Why would she embarrass him like that? No wonder he wanted to leave the country. "How could I have been so insensitive about his side? I must have hurt him that night I squeezed his side. He just said an old war wound. Oh love, my love, how could I have only been thinking of myself,? She thought. "It was so thoughtless to ask him to make love to me. I'm sure he would have been too embarrassed to expose his body to me. He has to know that I would love him no matter what!" It was a horrible night for Ronnie she had to lie as though she was sleep. It seemed as though the night would never pass. The next evening Len asked what she thought of the press conference.

She said, "It was horrible."

Len remarked, "That is only because you know him. Everyone is marveling at his fortitude and stamina. They are overwhelmed at the way he took care of his men. It is absolutely miraculous to go on fifty-one patrols, and destroy as much as they did and not lose a man. Every man in his platoon loved him and would have died for him. The man is a genius. And to think I threatened him!"

"You threatened him," asked Ronnie? "When and why?"

Len said, "I didn't mean to bring that up. Can we skip it?"

"Why in the world would you threaten Jay?" asked Ronnie.

"Remember the morning he was here and we took a walk in the garden, I told him I would lay my cards on the table, and that I and my father were powerful men and could make him disappear."

"Why?" asked Ronnie.

"I told him you had told me that you had been with him and that I believed more than kissing took place." Ronnie gasped. "He told me that he would not stand for any man to degrade you and I got angry and said what I said earlier."

"What did he say?" asked Ronnie.

"He said, 'since we are laying our cards on the table, I have made many men disappear.'"

"You didn't believe me?" asked Ronnie. Did you believe him?"

"Yes, I knew that morning that I was talking to a man of honor and integrity. At that moment, we became friends. I guess we were too busy talking when we went out, because on the way back to the house he was admiring the garden. He has an eye for beauty. When he saw the gazebo, he really admired it and asked a lot of questions about it." Ronnie mentioned that she had seen him looking at the gazebo from the window.

She kissed Len and said, "Thanks for being a bit jealous."

He shook his head and said, "That's some fellow you had there."

Ronnie was proud of her husband but she loved Jay all the more. He would protect her honor even in the face of her husband.

The next day Ronnie had to talk to Jamie, She did not want to talk on the phone so she and the girls went to see Aunt Jamie. Jamie was glad to see them and the girls had a lot of questions for her about Mr. J. Jamie explained he had to go on a long business trip like their daddy. She explained that sometimes business takes a long time to complete that's why their daddy went for so long.

"Well Mr. J.'s business takes even longer so he may be gone for a long time." This made Tia very sad. She wanted to see the horses again. Jamie explained that she could take her to see the horses but she could not go in with the horses unless Mr. J was there. Tia agreed. Jamie set up games on the TV and the girls began to play. She and Ronnie went into the lounge and talked.

Ronnie could not hold back her tears and Jamie told her to let it all out. When she was able to talk, she expressed how ashamed she was for being so selfish. She asked Jamie all the questions that had been running through her mind since she watched the program. She told Jamie how she hurt for the embarrassment that Jay must have felt after that exposure.

Jamie said, "If it wasn't for his promise to the girls, he would have been on a plane to Argentina right after the program."

Ronnie asked, "How was he able to survive though all those years in his condition? What kind of a trance did he put himself into?"

Jamie said, "Obviously Jay has not talked to you about what he went through!" Then Jamie asked, "Had Jay ever been to your home before the other day?"

Ronnie said, "No, never, why?"

Jamie said, "Do you remember I told you that we had to talk after you saw the press conference?"

Ronnie said, "Yes."

Jamie said, "Jay promised to tell me about those horrible years. I want you to sit down and listen. I was here with Jay one evening and reminded him that he had promised to tell me about those years. This was just before he was to make his announcement to the press. He had concluded the purchase of the hospital and all the arrangements relative to it, as well as the building near Mrs. T.'s building. He put all his business in order and said he was leaving the country.

He proceeded to tell me the whole horrible story. Mr. Ni as Jay calls him had never had a man that he could not break until he met Jay. So it became his pride against Jay's will. In order to endure the pain, Jay would put him self into a trance. He did this by thinking of you. He imagined you and he would be in a garden. He described your garden to a "T" and had never been there. The first time, he remembers, standing under a window in a high building and calling you. When you came to him, he was standing near a gazebo. You suddenly turned and ran back into the house."

Ronnie jumped up with her mouth open and a shocked look on her face and Jamie pushed her back down in the seat. Jamie continued, "The next time you were not afraid, and came to him and he would hold you. Being with you allowed him to bear the pain. He said they would take him to the torture chamber at all different times of day or night. Sometimes from the punishment, he would start bleeding inside, so they would put him in the hospital until they stopped the bleeding, give him blood, let him heal, and then return him to Mr. Ni."

"Oh God, Oh God, those were the times that he was holding on to me. He said I was his lifeline!" cried Ronnie holding her stomach and rocking as though she was in pain.

Jamie continued, "Only when they were restoring him did he get any relief from Mr. Ni. Those were the times when you said his calls to you would stop for a while and then start up again, remember? He did not have to call on you then."

Ronnie had her face in her hands listening, her heart cracking with every word.

"Do you remember when you said it finally ended completely?" Jamie asked.

"Yes," said Ronnie tears rolling down her face.

"Do you remember when I told you my dreams started?" asked Jamie.

"About the same time," answered Ronnie.

"This is really going to hurt you, but I feel I must tell you. Maybe it will help you understand Jay and yourself," said Jamie. Jay told me, that eighteen months or more before he was released, you stopped coming to the garden. The connection to you was broken . . ."

Ronnie fell from the couch to the floor in a dead faint. In fear, Jamie rushed to the phone and called Mrs. T. who started up immediately. Jamie then quickly got a wet towel and began to wipe Ronnie's face. Jamie let Mrs. T. in and they lifted Ronnie to the couch. Jamie was explaining to Mrs. T. what had happened when Ronnie began to come around. Ronnie had recovered and was lying in Mrs. T's arms.

Jamie told Ronnie she thought she had heard enough but Ronnie said, "No continue I need to know it all!"

"Well," continued Jamie. "After he had lost his connection to you, he needed help in order to hang on . . ." Ronnie turned her head into Mrs. T's breast and groaned out loud and painfully, so Mrs. T. pulled her close.

"So in desperation he turned to me. It was as if I could hear him calling saying, 'I need you' and I would reach out my hand as though he was in the room with me, because that's the way he sounded, and he would hold on to my hand. I guess I couldn't feel him holding it like you would have because there was no strong spiritual connection, but I sensed he was and would leave it extended as long as I felt he needed it day or night. After eighteen or twenty months, it stopped. That's when I got word that Jay was alive. That was right after I returned from my visit with you when you had asked me to come! So it boils down to this; the night you stopped going to Jay in the garden is the night you said Tia was conceived. I believe that is the connection between Tia and Jay, said Jamie.

"Are you crazy?" asked Ronnie, with tears running down her face.

Jamie said, "I know it sounds crazy, but just think about it. Can it be any crazier than Jay describing your garden and the gazebo and never having seen it before or knowing your exact size? Also, he told me everything exactly as you had told me. Remember I asked you had he ever been to your house before. He came to your house for the first time the morning after he had told me what I have just told you."

"Oh my God said, Ronnie tears still running, "That's why he was examining the gazebo and asking Len all those questions about it."

"When was this?" asked Jamie.

"The day he came to visit!" said Ronnie.

"Now think about him and Tia," said Jamie. "Why Jay? She was scared to death of every other man, but gravitates to Jay like a magnet. I tell you there is a spirit connection between them."

Ronnie said, "Oh Lord. Jay mentioned our spirits were connected. I told him that was a lot of bunk. That was the night when things went sour for us. I wonder if I did the same thing I did the night Tia was conceived. I broke that spiritual connection between us. I had never felt what I felt toward him that night. I almost felt hatred. How could I? Now I believe his spirit felt what I felt. Oh Jamie have I driven him away from me. Everything you said is true. I have seen it in my mind's eye but refused to believe it. I told you that I felt at peace in the garden with him. I felt he was holding me and now I know it was true."

Jamie said, "You asked why he held on? He held on for you. He promised you he would come back. And you know he tries never to break a promise. That's why he hurts so much about Mike. You are and will be his life. And now Tia is as much a part of him as you are. Don't ask me how it happened. You have to accept that it did happen."

Ronnie broke into another emotional outburst. Her heart was reaching out to Jay to tell him what she felt, but he was not there.

Mrs. T. who had been sitting and listening in was thoroughly confused and said, "Hold it, just hold it! What is going on here? What is all this about?"

Jamie and Ronnie excused themselves, huddled together and then told Mrs. T., "We've decided to tell you everything and maybe you can help." They told her the whole story. Now she had the TV story plus all the intimate details.

She listened with her mouth open and in utter amazement, and when they finished, Mrs. T. got up with her hands over her face and walked to the window and stared out into space. Finally she turned towards the girls. She looked at the two of them and asked, "Do either of you have any idea how blessed you are? You have been a part of the life of a man that every woman looks for in her life and would die for and both of you have his love!"

Then she turned to Ronnie, "But you are his life! Do you understand what I am saying to you? Now tell me about the spiritual connection you were talking about. You said you think you broke it a second time. You mentioned the night things went sour between you." Ronnie said, "To be truthful, I offered myself to Jay and he refused me again. I guess my pride was hurt and I became angry with him.

He said to me very softly, 'your anger is showing little one. I know because you complete my spirit; you are part of me. I know you better than you think. If I did what you wish our spirit would be broken and you would no longer be a part of me. One day you will know what I mean.'

"Forgive me," I said, "but I don't buy that spirit business. I believe you don't want me now because you were not the first." I began to cry hysterically. Jay hugged me close and I felt that I didn't want him to hold me. I had never ever felt that I didn't want his arms around me. I could feel that he was hurt, but he said nothing he let me cry. When I finished crying, I pulled away from his arms, stood up and angrily asked, 'What do you want me to do Jay?'

He answered, 'What do you want to do?' I responded, 'I want to tell my husband about you but I want to respect your secrecy.' He was not ready to have his identity known as yet. 'What shall I tell him?'

Jay said, 'Tell him the truth.' He rose from the chair went to the window and stared into the night. I watched him standing there staring into the night. I was really confused. I didn't understand this sudden feeling within me? How could I feel this way about him? Was it anger about being rejected, self-pity or a type of hatred? I wondered why Jay just stood there and did not turn to me. I thought, that maybe I was right about the way I thought he felt, that he didn't want me because he wasn't the first. I thought for a while then I said, 'Jay?' He answered, 'Yes?' I didn't say anything. I just left." Ronnie just stood there crying, and shaking her head saying, "How could I? How could I? I must have cut him very deeply. Now I really understand what he meant about our spirits. I know now that he felt my hatred for him."

"No said Mrs. T., "Not hatred I know that you could never feel hatred towards Jay. I'm sure he knew your true feelings. Yes, I believe you hurt him deeply but not beyond repair. What you must never do from now on, is hide the truth from him. So far from what I have heard, you have not withheld the truth. What you haven't told him is what happened the night that you did not go to him when he needed you. His faith was a little shaken there, but it's because he doesn't understand. He will understand that completely when you tell him.

Now this thing about him and Tia I don't believe there is any other explanation. And believe it or not, I believe a divine hand used Tia to bring Jay back into your life for a reason. I don't know what it is but I believe it is for both you and Tia. She has never been this happy in her life. Remember at one time that Len and you were thinking about having her evaluated. Now look at her, all because of Jay. Can you explain that? Can you even explain the fact that she loves horses now? No little one! Jamie is not wrong about your spirits being one!"

Ronnie said, "Mrs. T. you just used Jay's expression. You called me 'little one.'"

"Umph," said Mrs. T., "Now that rascal is messing with my mind! I wasn't going to tell you this, but before he left I asked him to kiss me goodbye. He kissed me just the way Tia said he kissed her, only I got the full treatment Wow! You best be glad I'm not a few years younger."

Ronnie with hands on her hips said, "Mrs. T!"

# Bandito and Hard-hearted Hannah

I had already been in Argentina for three months. My old friend and military buddy Juan Escanaba had warmly received me. Juan had often told of the many times I had saved his life, and everyone on the rancho was very pleased to meet the man who had saved their Patron's life. After returning to Argentina, Juan had become the Patron when his father passed. Juan had given me the run of the rancho and had given orders that everyone was to respect Señor McFadden.

While in the military, Juan and I had had many talks about horses. After a few days, I decided to take a look at the stock. I noticed a beautiful golden palomino in a corral by himself. I stood at the fence looking at the beautiful horse. We both stood staring at each other. I started to open the gate, but a ranch hand rapidly approached me and indicated that this was the señorita's horse and it was forbidden to touch him, besides which he would not let anyone else go near him. Even though he protested, I assured him it would be all right and proceeded into the corral. The ranch hand went to get the head ranch hand who hurried out to protect Señor McFadden. When they arrived, I was standing in the middle of the corral looking at the horse, which had retreated to the far end of the corral. I waved away the ranch hands who were yelling at me to come out. The foreman started to enter the corral but I told him to obey and to stay out.

I stood with my arms folded looking at the big palomino who was in turn looking at me. The palomino pawed at the ground with his right hoof, and snorted a few times. I remained very still constantly looking at the big palomino. Finally the horse started walking toward me. He stopped about three feet from me. He raised his head high shaking it up and down. After a few minutes the horse walked up to me and put his nose into my chest and nudged me. I began to pet his nose, rub and scratch his forehead, and stroke his neck then I rubbed him all over as I walked all around him, keeping my hand on him all the time until I was back at his head.

The foreman and hands were amazed. They could not believe what they had just seen. The best of their horse trainers had not been able to even approach the horse. Their commotion brought attention to the house. Señorita Isabella and Juan hurried to the corral. Jay was still petting the big palomino.

The señorita asked, "What is he doing in there with my horse?" Before the foreman could explain, she had opened the gate and started into the corral. The foreman was trying to explain to Señor Juan but Juan halted him. He wanted to watch the show. Once she had entered the corral the big palomino turned from Jay and started towards her.

She talked to the big horse asking him, "What has he done to you? Has he hurt you?" The big palomino then turned and walked back to me.

Furious, the señorita turned to me and asked, "What right do you have to be handling my horse? I'm sure the vaqueros told you that you were not supposed to touch him. From now on do not touch this horse. You are welcome on this rancho but you are never to touch this horse. Do I make my self-clear?"

Jay said, "Very clear señorita, let me offer my heartfelt apology? You have my assurance it will never happen again. I would like to say in defense of the men they are not at fault. They told me specifically that no one was allowed to touch the horse in fact they said that he would probably kick my brains out. But the lure of his beauty impelled me to take a chance and stroke such beauty. I can see how the two of you go together—such beauty paired."

"Oh!" said the señorita, "I suppose next you will be having a desire to stroke me, as you call it?" "Oh no señorita," I said. "I have no such desire! I would not be so impertinent as to insult someone of your stature with such a thought. To put you in the same vein as a horse would be ludicrous."

I bowed and took my leave and walked towards the gate and winked at Juan who was covering up a smile. The big horse started to follow me but the señorita stopped him. Juan later talked to his foreman about his sister's horse and me.

At dinner, Juan said, "The men are very impressed with you. They say you are a man with the spirit of a horse."

His sister was not impressed; she said, "I hope you did not give my horse sugar."

I said, "Maybe an apple, a pear or carrot but never sugar, señorita!"

"Well," she said. "You must have given him something or he would not have come to you. He never comes to anyone other than Mi Papa, Juan or me."

I said, "Maybe just a little love señorita."

She snorted, "Are you insinuating that my horse is not loved?"

"No love," I said, "And . . ."

She cut me off. "That was impertinent," she snapped.

"You are right señorita. That is an old habit of mine and I have been trying to correct it since I've been here. That just slipped out. I ask your forgiveness."

We said no more to each other during the rest of dinner.

After dinner Juan asked his sister, "Why are you so negative toward Jay? What has he done to you?" She did not answer.

Juan asked me later, "What is this thing you have with horses? Is it just with horses, or with other animals too?"

"I don't know Juan. I just seem to get along with horses and dogs. I don't know about other animals."

Juan said, "I know we talked a lot about horses, but I had no idea you were such a horseman. The men can't seem to stop talking about you."

I told Juan that I would like to take a ride into the countryside.

Juan said, "My friend, it is dangerous to ride alone and you could very easily get lost."

I asked Juan with a short laugh, "Have you forgotten how many times we have been lost in dangerous country?"

Juan laughed and said, "That is funny, me worried about you getting lost!"

The next morning he had a nice horse saddled and brought up. He told me that he had included a rifle with extra shells and a machete in case I ran into large snakes or big cats. I had a compass and a great sense of direction. Unbeknownst to me Juan had one of his men to circle above me to make sure I was all right. I started out about eight-thirty in the morning and at about two o'clock, I found a stream and made a little trap out of branches and small vines, caught a fish, and cooked and ate it.

I traveled up in the mountains. I kept looking behind me. I kept having the feeling that I was being followed but I shrugged it off. I was really enjoying myself. It was like being in back in the military without worrying about being shot. It also brought back a lot of unpleasant memories. The beauty of the mountains revived those memories. I continued to enjoy the scenery. I turned and headed back. I never worried about being lost when I was on a horse because the horse will always know his way back to the stable. I also had to direct the men back from raids under enemy fire and sometimes in the dark so I could always find my way back. Getting lost was not a concern. What was a concern was that this feeling of being followed, had turned into a feeling of being watched. I pulled the rifle out and threw a shell in the chamber. I thought it might be one of the cats that Juan had mentioned. If it was, why didn't the horse react? Then I realized what I felt was at my back and was upwind!

I had just entered a meadow. I kicked the horse into a canter to get away from the rocks. I dismounted in the grassy meadow. Whatever it was would have to come to me. My old survival sense began to tell me it was circling from right to left upwind. If it was an animal I would soon know because the horse would soon pick up its scent. Sure as shooting, the horse began to act up. I caught up her lead-rope short. She kept trying to rear up but I held her tight. Then I saw it coming out of the trees. Walking slowly towards us was a puma. I was having a hard time holding the horse but I kept looking at the puma. Finally it stopped and we continued to look at each other. Strangely, the horse began to quiet down a little.

The puma snarled and fanned its left paw a few times; stood and looked at me for a few moments, then turned and walked back to the trees. About half way back to the trees it turned and looked at me momentarily, and then bounded into the trees and disappeared. I got the horse completely quieted, mounted and rode off. I was glad I didn't have to shoot the puma. I rode down out of the mountains and noticed that the horse was quite lathered. I dismounted, used some grass and leaves to wipe her down. I put the saddle and blanket over my shoulder and walked for about a mile. Finally, I saddled up and rode back to the rancho. Juan asked about the ride I told him it was interesting and beautiful country. I started to unsaddle the horse but one of the hands took over. Juan and I walked back to the house. He asked if anything had happened and I said not really. I took a ride almost every day after that. I used the time to really take a look at my life, trying to decide what I would do. It was pleasant just being alone. Juan seemed to understand that I needed time alone. He had asked me to go to town with him once and to a party another time. I declined both times. I spent a lot of times on the veranda late in the evening looking out into the night thinking about Ronnie and the girls. I hoped that they were doing well.

It was now a year since I had left home. I missed Jamie although I often talked to her on the phone. I missed seeing my family. But here I wasn't being hounded by the press, nor did I have to face the embarrassment of the TV program. My thinking was that if I stayed away long enough they would forget about it. I didn't leave the rancho in case someone recognized me.

Juan came out on the veranda and said, "My friend it's time you stopped brooding and hiding out. The men here have a fondness for you. They talk about you all the time. They talk about your love for animals and how you treat them. They had hoped that you would come to some of the parties. Since you won't go to a party we will bring one to you. We are going to have a fiesta here! You can't refuse to come because you will already be here!

Three days later, I was watching from the veranda as the señorita saddled her palomino for her morning ride. After mounting him, she rode him around the corral for a while. He was a lot of horse for her, but she seemed very capable of handling him. On her way out, she stopped and stared at me as if to say, "What are you looking at?" I continued to look right at her until she decided to ride off.

Later that afternoon, the hands brought in some horses from the range. They put them all in a corral except one, which they chased into a corral by himself. He reminded me of Rance—very stately. Rance had been considered a black. This one was a black. The sunlight sparkled off him. As the men began to work the horses in their corral, I walked over to look at the big black.

As I approached the fence, he charged it; then hung his head over the fence showing his teeth indicating 'don't come near'. I continued my approach and he continued his rage, rearing and stomping the ground. I reached the fence and he went to the far end of the corral towards the end where the other horses and men were. He stood looking at me and I at him. Suddenly, he charged to the other end of the corral and stood looking at me. I continued to stare at him. We stared at each other like this for a number of days. They were going to move the big black but I asked them to leave him there. One day I stood looking at him.

The very next day as I stood looking at him, one of the hands came and stood beside me and said, "Señor I hope you do not plan to go near that man killer. The Patron has offered him to anyone who can tame him. A lot have tried and he has sent many to the hospital. Please do not go near that beast. Señor Juan will be very hurt if anything happens to you on his rancho." I patted him on the shoulder and continued to watch the big black as he stood there, his nostrils expanding and collapsing, looking at me. I continued to stare at him. I continued this for a few more days for a number of hours every day.

Finally, I opened the gate and walked to the center of the corral. As soon as I entered the corral, everything stopped in the other corral and all the men rushed to the corral with the big black and me. Everyone was quiet as a church mouse. It was the sudden quiet that brought señorita Isabella and Juan to the veranda.

I stood there looking at the big black. He stomped his hooves, danced around a bit and made a full charge right at me. I stood with my arms folded and did not move as he passed by close enough for me to feel the heat from his body. He stopped at the other end of the corral and began to snort and stomp the ground with his right hoof. I turned to face him with my arms still folded. Once again he made a charge. I did not move. He passed close enough to leave his sweat on my left arm. Again he stopped at the end of the corral. I turned again and faced him, arms still folded and looking right at him. He made another charge. This time he crossed in front of me and passed on the other side and brushed me just enough to cause me to tilt a little. He stopped at the other end of the corral again but this time I did not turn to face him. I stood there with my back to him. I could hear and feel him pawing at the ground. I did not move. He must have walked very quietly because I could suddenly feel the breath from his nostrils blowing on the back of my neck. Finally he nudged me in the back. I turned and petted his nose, stroked his jaws, scratched his forehead, rubbed his neck and chest, his back, around his rump and up his other side until I was back at his head.

Everyone watching was totally amazed. No one except the men who watched me with the big palomino had ever seen the likes. While the men who were buzzing away went back to work, I stayed with the big black petting, and rubbing him and scratching his forehead and talking softly to him. I continued to work with him until I was able to get him to bow on his left leg from a gentle tap.

The señorita and Juan had come to the corral. They just stood there watching me work with the big black. I had noticed some apples on my way to the corral. As I turned, I realized that Juan and the señorita were standing there with the foreman. As I approached them I asked the foreman if he could have one of his men bring a couple of nice apples. He was so pleased to do it.

Juan just stood shaking his head. He said, "In all my years I have never seen any thing like that. You are truly gifted with horses. I wish you could stay here forever."

I told Juan that I loved it here and thanked him but told him I had to return to the states.

Juan said, "I promised that any of my men who could tame him would own him so he is yours!" I had just found another friend.

The foreman gave me the apples and I called the big black over and began to feed them to him. Juan asked why I broke the apple in quarters before I fed it to him.

I said, "So he doesn't waste much of it." I asked Juan what his name was.

He said, "The men call him "Bandito" because he had been raiding horses from the ranchos. No one knows where he came from. He is an Andalusian."

I countered, "Part Andalusian."

Juan said, "You have a keen eye my friend! They found them in a hidden valley up in the mountains. That's some of his herd the men are working in the next corral. Some of those come from here and the others are wild. The rest of his herd is being sorted out by brand so that they can be returned to their rightful owners."

The señorita who hadn't said anything at all finally said, "Señor Jay, please accept my apology. You were absolutely magnificent with that animal. Forgive me that I don't like you, but I do admire courage."

I answered, "I accept your apology and there is nothing to forgive. You are what you feel. At least you don't pretend and I admire that!"

Juan offered an apology for her words. He said, "She has always been outspoken but I have never seen her attack anyone the way she attacks you!"

I said, "Juan old friend no apology is necessary. I like her honesty and wish more people were like her. Besides, I feel it is time for me to be heading back to the States. You are right. I can't continue to hide."

Juan said, "No my friend you cannot leave. I was hoping you would stay here. I will speak to my sister. She will just have to be more friendly."

I laughed, "I am not leaving because of her, Juan. There are things I have to face back in the States."

As he had said, Juan had a big fiesta that weekend. The hands had worked all week getting the place ready. The hacienda was beautiful and people came from everywhere. The ladies were beautiful and so was their dress. The caballeros were outstandingly dressed. Juan presented me with an extremely handsome outfit. He also presented me as the guest of honor. Everyone was extremely cordial. I had to escort Señorita Isabella to our table. She did not seem pleased. I had her seated and moved to a seat away from her, but Juan told me that it was customary for the guest of honor to sit next to the hostess. Now I understood why she did not seem happy.

The music was playing during dinner and as soon as dinner was finished everyone began to dance. I watched the dancers and thought to myself that Lori had taught me all of these dances. She had traveled all through South America. A young man asked señorita Isabella to dance and she gladly accepted. She stayed on the dance floor. I felt free to leave the table so I began to mingle with some of the hands. They were having a great time. They introduced me to their family and friends. We started talking about horses but that was shorted-lived because the ladies wanted to dance.

One of the ladies, whose fellow was dancing with someone else, asked if I knew the dance. I nodded and we walked out on the floor. When we finished the dance it seemed that every señorita there wanted to dance with this Yankee. I would be talking to one of the men and suddenly, I would be introduced to someone who wanted me to dance with her.

As I danced with the different ladies, I noticed señorita Isabella watching us dance. I was dancing a Tango with one of the ladies and it seemed that everyone left the floor. I danced most of the night it seemed. We danced the Tango, Bolero, Samba, Bossa Nova, Mambo, Guapacha, Salsa, and the Waltz. Seems like I danced with every señorita there, except Señorita Isabella.

I was tired by the time the fiesta ended or should I say worn out.

Juan later said, "You were a big hit at the fiesta with every lady except my sister that is."

"What have I done now?" I asked. "Apparently you spurned her all night," said Juan.

I responded, "I thought I did what she wanted, and that was stay out of her sight!"

"She said, you did not dance with her even once tonight and everyone knew it!"

"I danced with every lady that asked me tonight," I responded!

"Well you're going to run into a hornet's nest when you see her, so stay away," said Juan laughing as he headed for his bedroom.

I sat on the veranda looking into the night. Suddenly an angry voice barked at me. I turned to see Señorita Isabella with her hair down, which I had never seen before. She was very beautiful standing there with the moonlight shining on her.

"How have I upset you?" I asked.

"You know well what you did!" she said angrily. "You embarrassed me out there all evening," she scolded.

"And how did I do that, señorita?" I asked.

"You did not dance with me—not once—all evening!" she fumed.

"I danced with every señorita who asked me!" I answered.

"You expected me to ask you to dance?" she said angrily.

I answered, "Every lady I danced with at the fiesta asked me to dance. I thought that was the custom here!"

"Well, is that how you treat your hostess?" she yelled.

I retorted, "You left the table and never came back. I took that to mean I was free to leave. Besides, did you not tell me that you did not like me? I took that to mean you did not want to dance with me either. Goodnight, señorita." And I went to bed.

The next morning, I was again watching from the veranda as Señorita Isabella was preparing her horse for her morning ride.

Juan came onto the veranda and said, "I heard your conversation with my sister last night. I told you to stay out of her way. You sure were a match for her. I was in my room laughing." He walked back into the house shaking his head and laughing. I continued to watch the señorita. She mounted, and as before, stared at me for a while, this time her look was different or at least it wasn't a scowl. She turned the horse and rode off, but she stopped twice and looked back at me.

That evening after a shower, I was lounging in the recreation room with my eyes closed listening to some music I had brought with me. The music was very low and softly playing. I suddenly had the feeling that someone was there with me. There was this scent of flowers. For a moment I thought that I was imagining Ronnie. I opened my eyes and standing there was Señorita Isabella. She stood gazing at me and I gazed back. She suddenly extended her right hand to me. I took her hand and stood up she pulled me closer and raised her left arm up. I walked into her arms and we started dancing.

Neither of us spoke a word. The music continued to play and we danced for what seemed like hours. Her head was on my shoulder, which she lifted only as I turned her out away from me and brought her back, then her head would go back to my shoulder but she kept her body away from me. Suddenly she stopped dancing, went to the stereo and put on a Tango. She extended her hand and said, "Please!" I took her hand and began to tango with her over and over again. Into the dance I could feel her enjoyment. She became less rigid and began to let her body make more contact as she lay more softly in my arms when we came together. I could sense a smile that did not show on her face.

She changed to a tape that had many different dances. It seemed as though she was trying to find a dance that I could not do. Her body and moves reminded me of Denise. Finally she just walked away. I watched her disappear and I began to listen to my tapes again. I laid my head back and closed my eyes. A while passed and again I felt her presence. There was that scent of flowers again. I did not move or open my eyes. My head was turned slightly to the left. Finally a soft hand laid aside my cheek and turned my head slightly. I continued to keep my eyes closed. My mouth was smothered with a pair of lips. Her lips were soft, her mouth was fresh as morning air and her scent was like a quick breath of a mixture of early gardenia and roses. I continued to keep my eyes closed and her scent disappeared.

The next morning, as usual, I went to the veranda to watch her saddle her horse. When she mounted her horse she stopped to look at me as usual. One of the hands brought another beautiful, almost matching Palomino up to her. She beckoned her head saying come on. I descended from the veranda mounted the Palomino, and side-by-side, we rode off. She showed me where she usually rode each morning. It was a very scenic trail. She never looked right at me as we rode, but I could see her cut her eyes at me from time to time. I wondered what was going through her mind. I wondered what it was about me that she did not like, why she wanted to dance with me, why she kissed me, and why she invited me out on the trail with her. We came to a meadow that was full of beautiful wild flowers. She dismounted, tied her horse to a tree, and walked into the meadow. I sat on my horse watching her among the flowers. She was gorgeous to behold. I dismounted and started toward her, and by the time I reached her, I had picked different colored flowers until I had a bouquet, which I tied with a long strand of grass.

She turned, and I presented the flowers and said, "Señorita, I present this beautiful bouquet to a beautiful lady hoping it will appease the anger that I have somehow invoked in a heart that should know no anger. I ask your forgiveness."

As she held the flowers, she looked at me and her eyes began to tear. She dropped the bouquet and threw her arms around my neck and kissed me. I could not help but respond. The elixir of her mouth was intoxicating as was the softness and warmth of her body.

This person whom I had begun to think of, as hard-hearted Hannah, was all woman. I pushed her away for a moment looking at her then drew her into my arms and kissed her ever so softly.

She said, "Jay I do not hate you! I did not want to give into my feelings because I knew that you would be leaving some day."

I released her and said, "Yes, señorita you are right. I will be leaving some day. I had no right to kiss you. Please forgive me."

"Oh Jay, I would have died if you had not kissed me. I wanted so much for you to kiss me last night while we were dancing but you would not," she purred.

I said, "Senorita, I must tell you . . ." she put her little soft hand up to my mouth and stopped me.

She said, "I know that there is someone back at your home whom you love. I have watched you pine for her. A woman can tell. Let me steal what love I can while you are here. You don't have to love me in return just let me love you. I want to but I will not try to hold you when you have to go, but please do not refuse to let me love you!" I looked deep into those beautiful black eyes and knew that she meant what she said.

I sat on the ground with my back against a tree. She sat down and laid her head in my lap.

She said, "My brother has spoken of you so many times, and of all the times you saved his life."

I interrupted, "He has also saved my life!"

"But you have saved his life over and over, and all of the men in the outfit loved you and would have gladly given their lives for you. When he heard that you were alive, he went immediately to the U.S. Mi Papa wished so to meet you. He would have loved you like a son.

All the men on the rancho think you are the greatest vaquero. They talk about you, and how you are with the horses and how the horses love you. I watched you every day when you went out to ride. You are so gentle with the horses. I saw you take the saddle off the horse and carry it and the blanket on your back as you walked alongside her. Why?" she asked.

"Well," I answered, "The horse was kind enough to carry me for such a long distance, the least I could do was carry the saddle for a while and let her back cool off." She curled up in my lap, put her arms around my necked and kissed me very softly. I raised her face and kissed her teary eyes. She nestled her head against my chest and lay very quietly.

We prepared to leave, and as I was about to help her mount, she kissed me softly and laying her hand along my cheek said, "My name is Isabella." As we rode, she pulled up close and reached for my hand. I extended it. We rode along holding hands.

From then on she invited me to go along each time she went with her friends. We had great times together. All she wanted was to be close to me and I let her. One evening I did not feel like going with her so I declined. That evening when she returned she was visibly shaken. She asked to speak to Juan alone.

After an extended period, Juan came out and he seemed quite upset. He asked me into his office put his arms around me and said, "Old friend I had no idea of the agony you have been through. Now I wish we had all gotten off that chopper like we wanted to. We may have been able to fight our way out of there. As it was, you saved ours lives again, at the expense of your own. We went home and you gave eight horrible years of your life. That is hard to live with my friend."

"My friend," I said. "My orders were to get all of you guys out of there. I gave Sgt Arnett a direct order to save you guys' lives and get all of you that other stripe. He had to follow those orders. That's how we survived all those raids, following orders OK?"

"Thanks old friend!" said Juan. "I think you'd better have a talk with my sister. She saw the program and brought me a tape of it. She hates herself terribly for having treated you the way she has. She's really a good kid Jay!"

I said, "I know! We have come to an understanding."

# Tia's Call

Meanwhile back in the States, Ronnie had been keeping track of the time Jay had been gone. She, Jamie, and Mrs. T. were worried that Jay might never come back. Ronnie also worried about the condition of Tia and Beth. Tia seemed to be on a downward spiral. One day, while the three ladies were talking, Ronnie said that she was afraid that she had lost Jay because she felt that Senorita had gotten her clutches on him. Jamie disagreed strongly. Mrs. T. responded that Ronnie just might be right.

"When he left he said that his friend's sister was supposed to be very beautiful. I have gotten a look at her since, and he was not kidding. The two of them have made a big hit down there in Argentina. I didn't want to tell you but I have some newspapers from down there and it is full of pictures of them dancing and so on."

Ronnie and Jamie said, "We've got to see them." They used the walkway and went to Mrs. T.'s office. The papers were full of the gorgeous Señorita Isabella Escanaba and Jay McFadden. They said that after watching Señor McFadden dance with others she had not wanted to dance with anyone else. She has made all the other señoritas very jealous.

They said that Señor Jay was also an exceptional horseman and they spent many hours riding in the countryside. Immediately, sensing the hurt in Ronnie, the ladies agreed they had to find a way to get Jay home.

Ronnie was crying uncontrollably and said that she was the reason Jay has not returned.

"Oh, what have I done?" Jamie consoled Ronnie and told her that she had to have faith in Jay.

Mrs. T. reminded Ronnie and Jamie, "Our worry now, is how to get him back home!"

* * * *

As I sat in the lounge that evening drinking some orange juice and practicing guitar—one of the hands had been teaching me—a red-eyed Isabella came in and sat on the lounger. She watched me with intensity. She got up, walked around back of me, put her arms around my neck and began to kiss my ear and neck.

She said, "I can't understand you. Nothing seems to upset you. I tried to make you angry and all you did was make me angry the way you responded. Now with all that has happened to you, you sit here hiding. Jay I know they hurt you and made you ashamed with your exposure, but you are a hero around the world. People love you. Stop hiding my love and face them. I will lose you but I will always love you and wherever you are I will be with you. You will never dance another tango and not be dancing with me." She took my hand, walked me to the veranda, sat down and pulled me on the couch. She laid my head on her lap and began to lovingly stroke my head and face. I must have fallen asleep. When I awoke she had gone and there was a note. It just said, "My love, Follow your destiny. I love you. Isabella!"

Juan showed me a note she had left him. It said, "Brother I tried to hate Jay because I did not want to fall in love with him. I knew that he was in love and committed to someone else. I told him that I just wanted to be with him. He graciously consented. He has always been a gentleman, kind and loving even when I was being so ugly with him. How could I not love a person like him? In spite of all that has happened to him, he took all my ugliness and continued to smile. We have become the best of friends. I will be away until he leaves. Do not hurry him. Let him realize when it is time for him to face his destiny. So long for now to both my loves! Your loving sister Isabella! Contact me at Maria's."

I hung my head and apologized for having driven the señorita away.

Juan said, "Jay my friend, my sister has explained everything in her note. I did not show you the note to embarrass you, I showed it to you so that you would know why she left and that I understand. Now I am no longer confused as to the way she was treating you. She has had her first taste of true love and I am glad it was with someone who left a positive taste in her mouth. Thanks for the respect that you showed her. I wish it could have worked out between the two of you. You would have made a great pair.

I was in my second year at the rancho. Juan and I had been having a great time. Although I hurt from missing Ronnie and the girls, I was totally at peace for the first time. Bandito was like having Rance back. We had been spending a lot of time together.

It had been four months since Isabella left home and I missed her. Juan talked to her almost every day. He said she always asked about me. He said that his cousin Maria said that she couldn't wait to meet me, but jokingly said that Isabella was afraid that she might steal me away from her. Isabella would come to see Juan when I was out riding.

I had been out riding and was on my way in when I seemed to hear Tia call me; about the same time one of the hands rode up and said that I must hurry back to the rancho because of a phone call. That was the first time I ran one of the horses. Arriving at the rancho Juan met me and said there had been an emergency phone call and that I should call Jamie immediately.

The operator made the connection and Jamie answered and said that Ronnie and Mrs. T. were there and I should talk to Ronnie.

My heart began to quicken, as Ronnie picked up the phone. She said, "Jay it's Tia she has been slowly slipping back to the way she used to be; then she stopped eating. Oh Jay . . ."

I cut her off and said, "I'm on the first plane out of here," and hung up. I asked Juan, "Where is the nearest Lear jet airport?" Juan was not sure. I asked for the phone number of the airport and dialed and said, "This is Jim Meridith get me Tom Wallenger in a hurry."

The secretary answered, "Mr. Wallenger's office."

I responded, "Jim Meridith here. Let me speak to Tom."

Tom answered, "JM, long time, where the hell have you been?"

I said. "Emergency Tom, need a Lear from here to the States ASAP!"

"Where are you?" He asked.

I said, "Rancho Escanaba." Tom asked, "Do they know Junin airport?" I repeated Junin airport and Juan nodded his head, I responded, "Yes!"

Tom said, "Have one there in an hour!"

I said, "Thanks!"

"Keep me posted, Godspeed," said Tom as he hung up!

"Jim Meridith?" said Juan, puzzled.

"Yes, old friend! I'll tell you about it sometime. Right now I've got to get to the airport how far is it?" I asked.

"About thirty minutes. You've got a little time. What is wrong?" asked Juan.

"A little girl I love very much is in trouble." I answered.

"Is there anything I can do?" asked Juan.

I shook my head and said, "No, just tell Isabella!"

"I called her as soon as I got that phone call." said Juan.

"Thanks," I answered and began to pack my suitcase.

At the airport Juan hugged me and said, "Remember this is always your home. Come back some day."

I started to board the Lear and turned back to Juan and said, "I wanted to make it on my own and not because I was a war prisoner or considered a war hero. So I used the name of Jim Meridith."

"I understand, good luck," said Juan.

As I turned to board I heard my name called. I turned to see Isabella leaving a car almost before it was fully stopped and running toward me with her arms outstretched. She leaped into my arms and kissed me furiously saying, "I could not let you go without seeing you my love."

I took her face between my hands and said, "My little Chiquita no tears for these beautiful eyes," and kissed her lovingly. Then I boarded the plane.

I was sitting at the window with my head down as they waited for the plane to ready for taxi. Then with Isabella, Maria and Juan looking on I held up a cardboard with big letters that said, "I WILL ALWAYS BE DANCING WITH YOU WHENEVER I DANCE THE TANGO! KISS!" Isabella threw her hands over her mouth and with a big smile threw me a kiss with both hands as the plane taxied and took off.

* * * *

Isabella's tears were flowing but they were tears of joy because she knew that she had a part of Jay McFadden.

Maria asked, "Isabella you have been with him all this time? How could you have let him get away?"

Isabella answered but not sadly, "He belongs to someone else!" But she knew that there would always be a part of Jay that was hers. Then she told Maria, "There is so much love in him!" Looking after the plane Maria responded, "I believe you! I saw how he kissed you!"

# Jay Returns Home

I called to let Jamie know when I would be arriving. When the plane landed I tipped and thanked the pilot and hurried to the waiting arms of Jamie, who had missed me terribly. We entered the limo and I asked, "What has happened to Tia?"

Jamie began to tell me how Tia began her slide down after I left. At first she had been satisfied going to see the horses with her, but when he did not return she stopped going to see the horses and eventually stopped eating. I asked why no one had called me earlier and Jamie told me no one really knew how bad she was until she said, 'I want Mr. J.'

"The doctor wanted to know who you were and said we'd better be quick about getting you here.

When we reached Ronnie's home, Ronnie was waiting with Len and his parents. Ronnie rushed me to where Tia was. The Doctor was with Tia examining her. Len's parents wanted to know what this man had to do with Tia.

Len responded, "It's a long story. I'll tell you later."

When Beth saw me she ran and jumped in my arms, saying, "Mr. J. you're back. Tia needs you!"

I said, "I know, love and I'm back." I entered Tia's room and the doctor was standing over her listening to her heart.

Ronnie said, "Doctor, this is Jay, Tia's friend and a friend of the family."

"The doctor said, "She is very weak."

I asked, "Can I speak to her?"

The doctor said, "Please do. I don't think there is any voice she'd rather hear!"

I sat Beth on the bed; then I sat in the chair and pulled it close to Tia's head.

I said softly, "Hey my little lost lady, are you back under the table again? Can I help you? Has someone hurt you? Won't you let me help you find your way back? I've missed you very much!" Tia began to open her eyes. She looked at me and smiled. She put her little hand up and touched my face. I bent over and kissed her forehead, her left and right eye, her nose, I kissed my finger and touched it to the sides of her mouth and to her mouth. I touched her little face and held her small hand. I attempted to put her hand down but she wouldn't let go.

I said, "All right love I won't leave, but I need to take my coat off. Will you let my hand go long enough for me to take my coat off? She didn't let go." I said, "Open your eyes love and look at me." She opened her eyes and I said, "Let my hand go so I can take my coat off and I will stay with you." She let my hand go and I took off my coat and rolled up my cuffs sat down and put my hand in hers and she held on. She smiled and went to sleep. I had no sooner sat down when Beth climbed into my lap, put her arms around my neck and laid her head against my chest. The Armontts asked again who I was.

The doctor checked Tia's heart and put his thumb up and said with a smile, "Nothing like the right medicine."

Len and Ronnie came over, and with Len's parents looking on, said, "Thank you! The girls will be asleep in a little while and you will be able to go and get some rest."

I pointed at my hand and said, "I don't think so!" Len tried to pull my hand loose and could not. He tried to pick up Beth but she wouldn't let go. He shrugged his shoulders.

I whispered, "It's OK, I'll be all right! They're the ones who are important." I pointed to Tia and Beth."

Len and Ronnie came back pulling a big lounge chair, and Len said, "If you have to be here like this, let's make you as comfortable as possible."

I got up still holding Beth and they exchanged the chairs. The lounge chair made it so much more comfortable. As I settled in the lounge chair with Beth in my lap and her arms around my neck I leaned the chair back so that my arm that Tia was holding would be comfortable, I caught sight of Ronnie looking at Beth, being where she was two years ago, in my lap. Her eyes started to tear and she left the room.

I lovingly watched the two girls as they slept. I had missed them so much. I must have fallen asleep because I felt someone lifting Beth from my lap. I opened my eyes and it was Ronnie. She laid Beth on Tia's Bed and covered her. Thinking I was asleep, she lightly ran her hand down my face then very softly laid her lips against mine as she whispered, "My love, my love, how much I love you and how I have missed you. I hope I have not lost you." Then she quietly left the room.

Beth turned over a couple of times, woke up, realized she was not in my lap and climbed back into my lap and went back to sleep. I lay awake the rest of the night thinking of how much I missed Ronnie and how much I loved her. I remembered Isabella's words 'Face your destiny.' I thought I could not run away from her and the girls again no matter what!

Ronnie came in early that morning and found Beth back in my lap. She looked at me and I just shrugged my shoulders.

She came over and kissed my forehead and said, "I'm afraid she might have hurt you lying on you all night like that!"

I responded, "You didn't!"

She bent over and kissed my mouth and answered, "That was before I knew better. Let me put her on the bed."

I whispered, "Leave her here. What the matter, are you jealous?"

She said, "Yes, of any female that gets that close to you. Did any get that close in Argentina?" I smiled and closed my eyes.

She whispered softly. "Don't tease me Jay!" I put my hand on the back of her head and pulled her face down and kissed her very softly.

Beth woke up and looked at me with surprise threw her arms around my neck and said, "Mr. J. I didn't just dream it. You are here!" She hopped down and went to get her mother. Tia was still sleeping when Ronnie came in. She wanted to wash Tia.

I said, "Let her sleep; it is good for her, but I need to shower and shave." Ronnie told me that Jamie had sent a couple of changes of clothes by my limo driver.

"What would I do without her?" I asked;

Ronnie said, "Let me see if I can get Tia to loosen your finger. She was able to loosen her little fingers and replace my finger with hers, and I went to shower, shave and change clothes. I came back to relieve Ronnie but she insisted that I eat first. I told her that I would eat when Tia ate.

I lifted Ronnie from the chair and as I took my seat asked where Beth was.

She said, "In the tub," and sat on my lap. I told her that it wouldn't look good for her husband or his parents to see this. She promptly got up and I was able to put my finger back in Tia's hand. I spent the rest of the day watching Tia squirm and turn, like she was having a dream, and having Beth on and off my lap. I was really enjoying her attention.

The doctor checked on Tia often. He said her heartbeat was getting stronger. He said to let her sleep and call if we need anything before he returned. Ronnie and Len were constantly in and out of the room checking on me, making sure I was comfortable and inquiring if I needed anything. At one time Len had Ronnie fix me a sandwich and juice, even though she told him I would not eat it. He brought it in and I told him the same—I would eat when Tia ate. That night Beth, even after being scolded by her mother, again slept curled up in my lap.

Early next morning Ronnie was again in the room checking on me. "Jay my love," she whispered. "Are you sure she is not hurting you lying on you so long?" I assured her she was not! She knelt beside the chair and put her arms around my neck on top of Beth's and laid her head on my shoulder and whispered her love for me.

The following morning I awoke to the tugging of my hand. I opened my eyes to a beautiful little girl saying, "Mr. J. I'm hungry!" Before I could stretch, Beth had run to tell her mother that Tia was hungry. Ronnie called the doctor and told him that Tia was hungry and asked what she should feed her. The doctor told her to ask Tia but to only let her eat a little. He said he would be right over. Tia wanted cereal and orange juice. Ronnie gave her a small helping of each, which is all she would eat any way. She also fixed me breakfast of cereal, an egg and orange juice, which is what I asked for. I ate as Ronnie fed Tia.

The doctor arrived and checked Tia over and said, "Looks like she's going to be all right." He told Ronnie how to feed her and that Tia should stay in bed for the next couple of days until she regained her strength, but to let her sit up if she felt like it. He said he would check everyday. He told me he had some other patients and asked if he could use me for them? I laughed and thanked him. Tia said "Mr. J!" and I knelt down beside her bed. She kissed me and said, "When I got sick I knew you would come! Mr. J. when I get well, you won't go away again, will you?"

I said, "No love, I won't go away again! I have to go to work but I won't go away." She said, "I'm glad" and went off to sleep. Beth in the meantime was still hugging my neck.

Ronnie put her arms around my neck in front of her husband and said, "Thank you for coming and thank you for my baby."

Len nodded his head in agreement and patted me on the shoulder. I told them to keep me abreast of her condition and call if Tia, Beth or any of them needed me for any reason. I said goodbye, but Beth did not want me to go.

My limo driver was asleep I woke him up and asked how long he had been out there. He replied two nights. He said he hadn't known when I would need him.

I said, "Take a vacation Tom! When you drop me off, you take two weeks and you and your wife go anywhere you want to go. It's on me. You call Jamie and tell her I said to set up an unlimited credit card for a two-week stay. Enjoy yourselves. I don't want to see you for two weeks. Before you leave, call and have them to send me a replacement driver. Pick me a good one OK?"

"OK Mr. J." said Tom. I went to the apartment and went to sleep.

I asked Len and Ronnie if I could have a direct phone line to my office placed in Tia's room so she could call me at any time. My switchboard would ring me wherever I was. They argued the point but my argument was stronger so they consented. The line was installed the next day. That day, I received phone calls from two happy little girls thanking me for the phone. Ronnie told Tia that she must share the phone with Beth. I think in all, I got about nine calls that day. One was from a happy mother who said that she thought the phone was better medicine for Tia than I was. Ronnie had told Tia that she had to eat and build up her strength if she wanted to be able to use the phone. She said that Tia has been eating everything in sight ever since. I reminded her not too much too soon remember? Ronnie also said that Tia wanted to talk with me.

Tia got back on her feet and we spent a lot of time together. The first thing she wanted was a helicopter ride. She loved that 'copter ride, which took us back to see the horses. We spent a lot of time with the horses. Beth graduated to being in the corral with the horses and even riding them with me leading the horse. Gutsy Tia was even riding at a walk by herself. Beth was pretty close to that point. We went fishing in the big pasture pond and I started teaching them to roller-skate.

Len had gone back to work and was traveling again now that Tia had recovered, so Ronnie was able to go with us. Occasionally we would have the girls sit and watch us skate together. The girls were elated to see their mother look so gorgeous out there skating. They ran and hugged her and told her she was beautiful when we came off the floor. She looked at me and silently said thanks. She told them that one day I would have them skating like her.

Tia asked, "Who taught you to skate mommy?"

Ronnie said, "A good friend." Beth and Tia gave me a big hug. We took the girls by the hand and skated around the ring as a foursome. We did a lot of laughing! Once I picked Tia up and took off around the rink with her. She was laughing so hard I thought she would burst. I was dancing to the music, turning around, skating backwards, crossing over and so forth. Skating backwards, I headed for one of the posts I knew was there. Tia was screaming that we were going to hit the post. I waited until we got right to the post and turned around forward, without slowing down.

As Tia saw the post go sailing by she screamed, "How did you do that Mr. J?" When we got to her mother Tia was so excited she could hardly tell her mother and Beth, who saw the whole thing. Ronnie was laughing of course and balled her little fist at me for scaring her baby.

The next time we went skating, Jamie went with us. The girls went wild as we sat and watched Jamie and their mother skating together. They watched as Jamie and Ronnie did all kinds of turns and spins as they danced together. They ran to Jamie hugging her and told her that they didn't know she could skate like that and that she and their mother looked beautiful skating together. Jamie told them that their mother and she used to skate with a good friend all the time when they were in high school and they looked at each other and laughed.

After skating, I took them to lunch and had my driver take them home. Ronnie stated how happy she was to have me back home. In fact all three of my big girls, Jamie, Ronnie and Mrs. T. were glad to have me back in town. Tia called that evening and thanked me for such a wonderful day. She said her mommy enjoyed it also. Later that night her mother called to say that it was so wonderful to be in the rink and in my arms again. She said that having Jamie there brought back so many fond memories. She said that she wanted so badly to go dancing. I expressed the joy of holding her and feeling her softness. I told her how much I loved her and that she was as much a part of me as I was! She said that she needed to come and spend time with me. I agreed.

I finally had to face the media again. I knew that it was coming. I wondered why they had not been around before now. It turned out that after I had flown to Argentina the media kept asking Angie where I was.

Angie aired a program and told the media, "Jay McFadden is not a man that you can charge like a bull in a china shop. He will not tell you anything unless he wants to. His captors found that out. You, the media caused him to disappear and I was the ringleader. I will tell you this. He is a master at disappearing, as you have found out. He disappeared right here under your noses. So take my advice. If and when he returns, give him breathing room. Leave him alone until he is ready to talk to you and you will all get it first-hand. Rush him and he will disappear again. You have been warned."

I had run into a reporter who knew me and wanted to take a picture of Ronnie the girls and myself. I asked him not to take any pictures of us and that I would talk to the media through Angie on Thursday. He agreed. I told him for that I would answer his questions first. I dreaded Thursday but it went off smoothly. I answered that reporter's questions first as I had promised. I answered all of the other questions except the ones I felt were too personal and I told them so. I just told them that some information was not for public knowledge. I was about to leave when one reporter said,

"Mr. J. we've just received some pictures of you and a beautiful young lady in Argentina. The two of you have been seen all over Buenos Aires together. According to the pictures she seems pretty taken with you. Is there something in the making there?

At first I wasn't going to answer, but I thought if I evaded the subject they would make a big blow out of it so I said, "Yes, grateful friendship. We found great pleasure in dancing together, nothing more!"

He asked, "Have you any objections to our printing the pictures?"

I said, "Not if she doesn't!" I laughed as I exited the set. I think I left the press pretty satisfied.

Angie thought so too. She said, "That was masterful Jay!" I kissed her on the mouth.

She said "That's the first time you have kissed me on the mouth. I have kissed you but that's the first time you've kissed me. What gives?"

I said, "That's because you are 'numero dos!'

She asked, 'Numero dos? Whose numero uno?"

"Aha!" I said, exiting the studio. "See you Love!"

Ronnie, the girls and I had been spending a lot of time together visiting the horses, skating, going to the zoo, shopping, fishing and they were very happy days especially for the two of us. One night Ronnie came to the penthouse. I ordered dinner to be sent up. We ate by candlelight and had a soft wine. We danced till almost midnight. I got her to see that we could not see each other any more like this, but that I would continue to remain close to her and the girls. And that's what we did.

I thought that we should try to quell any possible gossip that our togetherness might drum up, so I started accepting dates and began to be seen all over town with different women including Jamie. Of course, only Jamie knew what I was really doing. Besides, Jamie and I loved to spend time in each other's company anyway, especially if we were dancing and we did dance! The press soon picked up on Jay McFadden the eligible bachelor.

Ladies that had been trying to date me found themselves on my arm — one in particular—the lovely Miss Elaine Devout. I became her pet project. She had picked me out as hers and hers alone. When I dated others she let me know in no uncertain words that she did not like it. So as often as I could I dated other girls. I felt it was mean, but I did not want her to believe she had a hold on me. There was only one that had a hold on me and she was quietly fuming. What she didn't understand was that it was for her benefit.

The papers were having a field day guessing this one or that one. They stopped Jamie one day and questioned her about her and me, and Jamie said the she was hoping that I would pop the question at any time. Of course Ronnie called Jamie.

Jamie asked, "Ronnie how many times do you have to be told to trust Jay. Don't you realize what he is doing? He's pulling attention away from you and the girls."

Len came home and before he prepared to go back to Paris, I met him for lunch. We talked about many things.

I said, "Len do you realize that we have talked for an hour and you have not mentioned Ronnie and the girls!"

He said, "Jay you're right. I get so caught up in business and what's going on in the world that I forget about them."

I said, "Why don't you do something with them? Whatever you feel like doing. What ever you like to do. And if all else fails, ask them what they would like to do? Just do something with them. If you need my help ask, but I would prefer that you come up with something."

Len took Ronnie and the girls to a play and they enjoyed it immensely. They went to dinner and Len even took Ronnie dancing. One evening he took them to an opera. That was Ronnie and the girls' first opera, but with Len explaining everything they all enjoyed it. The girls were elated. Len called and said, "Thanks friend."

For the next year when Len was in town he always spent a couple of days devoted only to entertaining his family. When he was out of town, Ronnie, the girls and I spent time together. Beth was riding a horse like a trooper now. We spent more and more time at Ranceville. Mr. and Mrs. Ross were especially glad to see the grandkids as they called them.

The next time Len was in town, he went with us to pick out horses for Tia and Beth. I watched him and the girls laugh as they tried to decide between the horses. Finally with his help they decided. I looked the horses over and decided the one they had picked for Beth was OK, but the one for Tia had a split hoof. Tia was heartbroken. I decided that we would go up in the 'copter and scout out the growing herds from above.

Up in the 'copter we looked over the herds and Tia spotted a young paint pony that had been sired by Prince. Tia would have jumped out of the 'copter if she had not been fastened in.

"That's him, that's him!" cried Tia.

Beth spotted a palomino that she liked better. I landed the 'copter and the hands and I went out and brought the ponies in.

Len excused himself and said he wanted to talk to Jamie and Mr. Ross, and called them aside, and Jamie told me afterward, what he said.

"I've never met anyone like Jay! Ronnie told me that you, Jamie, told her long ago that Jay would be the best friend that anyone could ever have. Jay told me one day that I needed to spend time with my family. He told me that I needed to make money, but not at the expense of my family. He made me see how much I was missing and how much they needed me. That's why I started spending time with them and why I am here to day. I would have missed all that has happened here with my girls had it not been for him."

Jamie hugged Len and said, "And he is sincere when he says that he loves all of you!"

Mr. Ross said, "I second that."

The herds had really grown since I started them. It was nice that the girls had made their choices. Beth picked a beautiful little palomino colt and now Tia had chosen a beautiful paint colt. When the hands brought the colts in they were even prettier than they were from up above. The paint would have been Tia's colt even if he had had a split hoof. But I looked the colts over and they were in great shape.

Tia was jumping up and down. "When can I touch him? When can I touch him", she asked?

I said, "You can touch him now, but you can't handle him. He is completely wild. He needs some special handling first."

I had the hands bring the colts over to the fence and let Tia and Beth touch them. The girls said their coats were as soft as cotton. Tia and Beth were thrilled. So were Ronnie and Len.

Len said, "Jay let me pay you for these horses. I have to do something to repay your kindness."

I said, "Your friendship and the smiles on those three faces are enough! The love they will give those colts will more than pay for them."

Len said, "Too be honest with you Jay, I hated you at one time and wanted you dead as you know. Now that I know you, I wonder how I could ever have hated you."

"Most hatred is about not knowing or not understanding something," I told Len.

"That's pretty sound Jay!" said Len. We hugged each other. We flew back to New York. Len and Ronnie dropped Jamie and me at the penthouse. I kissed the girls and said goodnight and they continued to their home. I think as soon as Tia reached her bedroom she called me. "Thank you for my colt. I love you Uncle Jay."

"Uncle Jay?" I questioned.

"My Daddy said I could call you Uncle Jay. Is it all right if I call you Uncle Jay?

I said, "Yes love if it pleases you."

"Beth wants to thank you also," said Tia.

Beth said "Thank you Uncle Jay for my beautiful palomino colt. I love you also. Good night. My mommy wants to talk to you."

I said. "Goodnight princess!"

Ronnie said, "Jay I don't know what to say. How can we ever deserve you? You have done so much for us and we can give you nothing."

"Wrong my love. The love I have received from those two girls and the friendship of your husband is worth more than all the gold in the world," I told Ronnie.

She asked, "What about me? You mentioned the three of them. Have you given up on me?"

I said, "Not in a million years love!"

She said, "Len told me on the drive home he thinks you are the greatest person in the world. He said it would be a great world if there were more people like you. I wish I could show you the love that is inside of me for you. I am so proud of you and so lucky to have you as a good friend. The girls and Jamie at Roscoe's long ago were right and now I know it. Goodnight my love!"

I said, "Goodnight."

Len left for Vancouver. He would be gone three weeks. Ronnie, the girls and I continued to spend time together. The girls had become good roller skaters and asked if I would teach them to ice-skate as well. I said it was summer so we would have to wait for winter and see but that they were good roller skaters now. We no longer had to keep up with them anymore. They could handle themselves pretty well on the rink. Every once in a while I had to protect them from one of the little show offs on the floor, and they would always give me a hug.

Ronnie and I could really enjoy our skating now. Every so often one of the girls would ask me to skate with her. Ronnie would skate with the other one. Because of their skating ability they had made quite a few friends at the rink. One day one of Beth's friends wanted her to ask me to skate with her. I told Beth to tell her to come over. She came and asked if I would skate with her to the record I skated with Ronnie where I spun Ronnie like a top. I told her I didn't remember which record she was talking about because we could do that to almost any record. I told her that she would first have to learn how to spin. I told her if she heard it or could remember the name of the song, I would skate with her. Tickled she made it to the booth to see if she could get that song played.

Ronnie said, "Looks like you've made a conquest. I hope her friends don't follow suit. This is like the canteen!"

I said, "Now you wouldn't be jealous would you?"

"Yes, I'm jealous of any woman that takes you away from me. Like those ladies you are running around the city with!" I laughed.

Ronnie said, "Jay it's not funny! I'm serious." The young girl came back and said he's going to play the record now.

When the record started, I excused my self from Ronnie and the girls and began to skate with the young lady. She was a very good skater and I got the impression that her purpose was to show me up. I put her through some changes and routines that left her bewildered. She made quite a few mistakes but I helped her cover them up. She knew she was outmatched and thanked me when the record ended. She admitted she did not know how to spin. Ronnie did not have to worry about her friends. Ronnie and I continued to skate uninterrupted; occasionally we had the floor almost to ourselves. The young girl asked Beth if we were professional skaters.

Beth said, "No, that's just my Mom and my Uncle!"

We left the rink and had dinner. While at dinner one lady from another table came over excused herself and said, "Mr. McFadden may I please have your autograph?" Another lady said, "That was a wonderful thing you did for the children donating that hospital building." After signing about eight autographs, we decided to leave.

The girls wanted to know about the building and asked to see it. It was just dusk so when they saw it they were amazed to see the lights saying "Jay McFadden's Children's Memorial Hospital." We sat in the car looking at the sign. Beth asked, "Is that your name? I told her yes. They both unhooked their seat belts and hugged me from behind. Ronnie was beaming with pride and I was embarrassed. We told the girls to fasten their seat belts. We just drove around for a while, stopped for ice cream, and I drove them home and I went home too.

The next eight months I continued to run around the town with Jamie, and different ladies, as well as spend time with Len, Ronnie and the girls.

Angie asked why I did not date her so I did. We went clubbing and dancing a few times. She was great to be with and we had a lot of fun. She knew that there was someone special in my life but not who. She never pushed and just enjoyed the time that we spent together although she would occasionally try to get me to spend the night.

Elaine was a different matter she was a problem. I saw her as little as possible. When she read what Jamie had told the reporter she came unglued. I had to be firm and tell her that no woman had a hold on me, not even her. I had the choice to see anyone that I desired and when I decided on a special lady it would come from me. She was very angry and left but called the next day. I had hoped that she wouldn't. She was a little too possessive for me. I think she was used to bossing the men in her life.

# Bandito at Ranceville

The colts had grown into beautiful young ponies. I spent a lot of time working them and the girls were now handling them well. Len was very proud of how the girls had progressed. He was always willing to go watch them with their ponies. We enjoyed spending time together.

One day while we were at Ranceville, a call came from Juan. He and one of his hands were at the airport and wanted directions to Ranceville. I told him that I would fly over and pick them up in the 'copter, but he said they were driving. The directions were simple so I told him how to get to Ranceville. I was surprised to hear that Juan was at the airport and very excited that I would soon see him. The girls were working with their ponies when a pickup and a horse trailer pulled up. I was elated to see Juan get out. I hurried to the pickup and trailer. Mr. Ross came from the grandstand. Juan and I embraced. We were very happy to see each other. I introduced him and his vaquero to Mr. Ross.

Mr. Ross said, "Welcome to Ranceville."

Juan and the hand walked over to the glass case and Juan said, "So this is Ranceville and this is the famous Rance! What a magnificent looking animal! I can see why you loved him so much Jay!" He began to look around and said, "What a beautiful looking rancho! Then he asked, "What is going on in the corral?"

I said, "Come I would like to introduce you to some friends."

He said, "Just a minute, I have a friend of yours who would like to say hello!"

For a moment I thought it was Isabella, but we walked towards the trailer. The horse in it had begun to really act up. There was Bandito!

I stood there dumbfounded I could hardly speak. I could not believe my eyes—Bandito here at Ranceville!

Juan said, "He missed you. No one else could handle him. So I brought him here. It was a chore loading and getting him here. He only settled down when we pulled up here. I guess he must have sensed you!"

I said, "I have recently finished a special pasture for him. I would have come and gotten him. I have something special for you that I was going to bring!" I backed Bandito out of the trailer and put him in the short corral.

Mr. Ross said, "My word, except for that mane and tail, how much he reminds me of Rance!" When Ronnie saw him, her hands went up to her face.

I went into the corral and like Rance, Bandito was running from one end of the corral to the other. Ronnie came running to the corral with her hand up to her face. She could not believe how much this horse reminded her of Rance.

She yelled, "Jay, he's beautiful! Is he wild?"

I said, "As the mountain scenery!"

She said, "Jay be careful!"

Everyone had come to the short corral to watch the big black." Juan said, "Do not worry señora; they are old friends."

She said, "But Jay said he is wild!"

Juan said "To everyone but Jay. That is why I brought him here. He has missed his friend and no one else could handle him!"

As they watched, Bandito had gotten his run out and walked up to me and started to nuzzle me. He was so happy to see me that he could hardly stand still long enough for me to hug him. He finally put his head over my shoulder and stood still. I hugged him and told him how much I had also missed him. While Bandito and I were renewing our friendship, Juan related the story of how we had become friends, to the others. They were totally amazed. Mr. Ross told Juan how I had had a similar experience with Rance at the age of twelve. Juan almost fell over.

He said, "There is no doubt that Jay is special." He then told them about the puma incident. The others stared in disbelief, and Mr. Ross just stood looking at Bandito and me playing and shook his head.

Len said, "This is unreal, like a fairy tale!"

Finally, followed by Bandito, I walked over to the fence where everyone was standing and said, "Bandito these are my friends, say hello." And I nodded my head up and down. Bandito followed suit. Then I tapped his right knee and Bandito bowed. Ronnie was beside herself.

She said, "It's as if Rance has come back to Jay." She could not hold back the tears in her eyes. When Len went to her she said, "It's like seeing Rance all over again." He understood and hugged her. Len look over at me and Bandito and I felt he truly understood me now. I sent one of the hands for a few apples, broke them and fed them to Bandito.

I introduced Juan to Len, Ronnie, Beth, Tia, Ben, Sam, and the other hands. Juan made a big hit with the girls. I asked Ronnie what she thought of Bandito. She said it was like having Rance all over again. I had a sense that she wanted to get to know Bandito.

I asked specifically, "Would you like to go in and meet him?" Without hesitation she said, "Yes!" Respecting Len's presence, I looked at him. It was obvious that Len had begun to respect my judgment, because he bowed his head in agreement.

As we entered the corral, Bandito backed away snorted and pawed the ground. Juan was watching intently. I put my arm around Ronnie and called to Bandito. He came close, but stopped a few steps away. With my arm still around Ronnie, I put my hand out and beckoned him to come.

He came up and I said, "This is my very good friend, say hello." Ronnie slowly raised her hand to his nostrils. He sniffed her hand as I rubbed and scratched his forehead. Ronnie followed suit and talking very softly to him, she began to rub him all over.

I beckoned for a couple of apples and carrots. Ben quickly brought them. I asked Ronnie to go and get a carrot and an apple from Ben. I broke the carrot into three and the apple into quarters. I asked Ronnie to give Bandito a piece of carrot and a couple of pieces of apple, which she did. She hugged Bandito for a long time as if she was hugging Rance. She had tears in her eyes as Bandito began to nuzzle her. While Ronnie hugged Bandito, I purposely walked over to the fence. Bandito stayed there with Ronnie. Ronnie turned and saw me standing at the fence so she walked over to me. Bandito followed her, came to me, nuzzled me, nuzzled Ronnie and came back to me and put his head over my shoulder. I petted him, hugged him and thanked him for accepting my friend. I gave him a third of the carrot and a quarter of the apple. I gave the other third of the carrot and quarter of the apple to Ronnie who gave then to Bandito. He nuzzled us both.

Ronnie looked at me and with tears in her eyes, and went to Len who put his arms around her. Mr. Ross asked Juan if he had he ever seen the likes. Juan said never in his life. He could not believe his eyes.

Beth and Tia wanted to go in and pet Bandito. I told them they would get to meet him another time. Right now they needed to show Señor Juan their ponies, which they were happy to do. Juan remarked how beautiful the ponies were and asked the girls a thousand questions about them. The girls demonstrated how they had been training their ponies. Juan was quite impressed to see what they had accomplished at such an early age.

They said Uncle Jay taught us.

"Uncle Jay?" He asked.

They said, "He is our uncle."

I asked, Juan if he would like to go up and look over the ranch. I wanted him to see the pasture I had fenced off for Bandito and show him his surprise. I excused us, and Juan and I headed for the helicopter. The girls started to follow but their dad told them to stay with their horses.

We flew over the ranch. First I showed Juan the pasture I had fenced off for Bandito, a high fence separated each of the four pastures and each pasture had a high fenced-off pathway that led to the corrals. There were already brood mares in the pasture for Bandito.

Juan was very impressed. He said, "Bandito will be very happy here. He has plenty of room to roam." I showed him the additional pasture I planned to purchase to, increase the area for the horses to roam. Then we flew over the three herds. The first herd was that of the great paint stallion, Prince. Juan's eyes almost popped out of his head.

"What a gorgeous stallion!" he bellowed.

The second pasture was that of Royal the big golden palomino stallion. He stood on a hill looking over his herd. He reared up at the 'copter.

Juan said, 'Wow! What a magnificently beautiful animal!"

I said, "I am glad you like him because he is the one I am going to bring down to you."

He said, "Jay you can't!"I said, "You won't have any choice once I get him to Argentina!"

Juan said, "Thanks!"

I said, "The same to you, but why did you make that trip just to bring Bandito?"

He said, “We came for the horse show. There are a couple European breeds that I am interested in. By the way Jay, the young lady, Ronnie is she . . . ?”

I said, “Yes!”

Juan asked, “And the husband does he know?”

I said, “Yes, we have talked and I assured him that I was not a threat. We have become great friends and Tia is the reason I left your rancho so suddenly.”

He said, “Be careful my friend.”

“Don’t worry she knows that there can be nothing between us other than friendship while she is married to him,” I assured Juan.

“I am glad amigo,” he said. “I notice the girls call you uncle. By the way we will have a fiesta Saturday, bring your friends.”

I said, “Great, you’ll get a chance to meet Mike’s wife! I’ve talked a lot about you to her.”

“It would be my honor!” said Juan.

We continued to the furthest pasture, which would be adjacent to Bandito’s roaming area once the negotiation was finished for the new pasture. When Juan saw Stars, standing above his herd. I thought his head would go through the top of the ’copter. He almost jumped completely out of his seat.

“That exquisite animal has just graced beauty!” exclaimed Juan.

Standing high above his herd the big white reared as the ’copter flew over. Heading back, Juan could see how each pasture led back to the corral and thought the separate pathways was a marvelous idea. He said he would like to see each of the stallions up close. After landing, I had the hands open three of the gates to the pastures. I placed Bandito in a box stall. I took the megaphone and whistled. Juan asked why the megaphone. I told him if Stars was still on that hill, he might not hear my natural whistle. Shortly, two of the stallions came bounding through their runway into the corral. Moments later Stars came galloping in.

I had never seen Juan so impressed. Juan stepped out of the corral as the stallions entered. I told him that they were completely wild and that they had never been saddled or bridled. Each one was rearing and showing off his power. I called them to me. I held my hand up in front of them indicating stay. I walked over to Juan and asked if he would like to come and meet them. He hesitated, but then said yes.

I picked up the whip and after approaching the horses, who were still standing in their place, I said, “Prince this is my friend Juan say hello,” and I tapped his right front leg. Prince bowed and dipped his head. I did the same with Royal and Stars. I petted them, scratched their heads and hugged each one.

We walked back toward the grandstand. I called the horses and we fed them apples. Juan watched me break the apples and did the same. Juan was truly impressed. He commented that it was hard to believe that the horses were completely wild. He said they were marvelous

The girls had finished brushing down their horses and Ben and Sam had put them up and taken the vaquero with them to bring in the big palomino. When they saw the Stallions heading for the corral they told the vaquero that the loud whistle they heard was me calling them so they gave him a tour of the pastures and the herds. The vaquero told the hands of my exploits with the señorita's big palomino, the puma and Bandito. He told them that all the men loved and respected Señor Jay and were very sad to see him leave their rancho.

Juan was still admiring the stallions. He said, "The stallions are twice as beautiful up close. I thank you for this beautiful palomino!"

Juan's vaquero expressed his delight over the ranch and said he could understand why the men were so happy there. I told them that I had to keep the herds to a certain size due to the size of the ranch. They understood.

Juan and I showed the stallions to the vaquero. The vaquero asked where I had found such beautiful animals. When they had finished admiring and looking over the palomino, I hugged and petted each of the stallions and told them to go home. Each stallion headed for the gate he had come through and went back to his herd. The hands shut the gates. Juan and the vaquero agreed that they had never seen anything like that and they being wild.

I took Bandito out to the new pasture; I petted, and scratched his head, gave him a hug and turned him loose. He nuzzled me, I told him to go and he headed out towards the mares. He stopped, looked back for a few minutes and then went on.

I told Len and Ronnie that we had been invited to a fiesta. They both thanked Juan and said they had never been to a fiesta before. Juan and his ranch hand left and I put my arms around the girls, kissed them and we went back to New York.

Saturday, Jamie and I picked up Ronnie and Len and drove to the fiesta. It was being held at the home of a friend of Juan's who was a horse breeder and auctioneer. A lot of horses came through his farm. The fiesta was being held in the honor of Juan and the buyers from South America. As we entered the home I noticed that it was decorated much like Juan's hacienda. I found out later that the owner had visited Juan in Argentina and had been so impressed with the hacienda that he had to build one like it.

After introducing ourselves as the guests of Juan, we were directed to the garden area where all the guests were gathered. Juan, who had been watching for our entrance, came over the moment he saw us. I introduced Jamie to Juan who found her most charming. In his suave way he told Jamie, "I am capturing all of your dances immediately."

Jamie responded very graciously, "I accept on the condition that I am allowed to save a couple of dances for my escort." Juan agreed.I said, "You've met Len and Ronnie."

Juan introduced me to the host who asked, "Are you, Jay McFadden, Jim Meridith, Mr. J, and JM?"

I said, "I am known by all four. May I introduce my friends?" I introduced Jamie West, Len and Ronnie Armontt. He welcomed them and told Len that he knew his father and mother well and asked after their health.

He said, "It is an honor to have all of you in my home."

He immediately went to the microphone, got the attention of the guests and said, "Ladies and gentleman In addition to my guest from South America, I'd like to take this opportunity to introduce Mr. Jay McFadden and his guests." There was a great 'oohh!' from the guests, and he continued, "I count it a great honor to personally thank him for the great Children's Hospital that he donated to our city. If you have not taken the opportunity to donate to that Children's Hospital fund, this is your chance. Everyone seems to be enjoying the evening!" He came back and shook hands and we had a nice long chat along with Juan, Len and some of the other guests from South America.

After the chat, Jamie found me and said, "Before all those females I have heard talking, get to you, I would like to have our dance." They were playing a Cha-Cha and Jamie loved the Cha-Cha. We let it all hang out and basically cleared the floor. There was great applause when we finished.

Juan captured Jamie and said, "Now you are mine for the rest of the evening!" I knew I would not have to worry about Jamie throughout the evening.

Taking a cue from what Jamie had said, I made it straight to Ronnie, and since Len was already engaged in conversation, I asked Ronnie for a dance and she graciously accepted. It was a medium waltz and we showed out the floor. Ronnie was tickled pink. She was gorgeous and had the eye of all the ladies of all things. I told her that Jamie had overheard talk that there may be a ladies' rush at me, so I wanted to dance with her first.

She responded, "Yes I was with her and heard!"

I needed someone to protect me from the female rush that ensued. I was bombarded with all kinds of questions; from the military, my imprisonment, the ladies I've been dating, how to endorse a check, to 'can I have the last dance'. There definitely was no shortage of dance partners. I had not danced with Ronnie since the first dance and I was looking for an opportunity to ask her.

I took a break to wash my face. When I returned to the dance floor, I saw Ronnie sitting alone. Len was conversing with a couple of men from South America. I was about to seize the opportunity, when I heard this familiar lovely voice ring out. I turned to see Isabella; she had just arrived, with her strikingly lovely cousin Maria. She moved quickly towards me and throwing herself into my arms, her arms around my neck, she pressed her lips softly on mine. There in the sight of everyone, this Argentinean lovely was expressing her love for me. I responded by swinging her around in the air, setting her down and telling her how glad I was to see her.

She said, "I think I have messed up your face!" She wiped the lipstick from my lips with her handkerchief. "But I have missed you so! Why did you not call?"

I said, "I thought you knew why!"

She said, "Yes I did know, but I still hoped you'd call!"

I could see out of the corner of my eye Ronnie watching us intently.

Isabella asked, "Have you missed me?"

I said, "Yes, truly I have!"

Maria was standing there and I asked Isabella, "And who is this gorgeous creature?"

She said looking at Maria, "Please forgive me! This is my cousin Maria. You may have seen her at the plane when you left."

I took her hand, kissed it and said, "For shame I did not meet you before I met Isabella!" Maria said, "Oh he is a sweet one, isn't he?"

Isabella said, "I could scratch his eyes out. Jay, have you danced the tango with anyone since me?"

I said, "No Chiquita!"

"Will you dance with me tonight? And who is the one who dances with Juan but looks at me with steel eyes? Is she the one who keeps you from loving me?" asked Isabella.

I said, "She is just a very close friend."

"No mi amor, she is more than a friend. "She would scratch my eyes out if she could," said Isabella. I just laughed.

When the music stopped, Juan bought Jamie over and introduced Isabella and Maria. Maria went to dance with Juan. I watched her dance. She was as good a dancer as Isabella and maybe a little better. I excused myself and went and asked Ronnie to dance.

I saw Jamie and Isabella talking. Jamie reported the conversation to me afterwards.

Isabella said, "You look at me with eyes of hate but we should be friends. I love him also and neither of us can have him, if you are not the one who has his heart. Are you?"

"No," Jamie said.

"Is she here?" asked Isabella.

Jamie said, "Yes he is dancing with her."

"Ohh," said Isabella. "She is beautiful! Why does she sit with the man who just sat at her table?" She asked.

"He is her husband," Jamie responded.

Isabella replied, "We love him, he loves her; we cannot have him and he cannot have her."

Jamie stated, "She is his soul mate. They are connected spiritually."

"That, I can understand," said Isabella.

"Who is the woman who kissed you?" asked Ronnie when the dance was over.

I said, "That is Juan's sister Isabella." I talked to Ronnie and Len at their table for a while. As I was making my way back to Juan and Jamie, Isabella asked me to dance. It was a waltz and she looked as though she was a part of me the way she stayed close to me. I took her around the floor as though we were on ice skates. She looked into my eyes the whole time except when I spun her out. She was dancing as though we were in a contest, and she was sending a message to the judges,. Everyone had their eyes on us especially Ronnie. I wondered what was going through her mind.

The dance ended, and we were leaving the floor to applause when a Tango started to play. I was going to ask Ronnie to dance but Isabella pulled my hand, spun into my arms and said, "Dance this Tango with me."

We took the room by storm and everyone stopped to watch. Isabella really acted up. I had never seen her dance the Tango like that before. Every move was accented. I was truly enjoying it. Her dance was not lewd, but it was sensual. She danced the way the dance should be danced she just emphasized it because she was dancing it for me. Her beautiful hair was down and the way she tossed her head really showed it off. She moved as if there was a fire in her. When the song ended, I finished with her in my arms after a spin, looking at her as she looked up at me. To thunderous applause she threw her arms around my neck and kissed me with a fire that if I had been, a block of ice, I would have been a pool of water on the floor.

She whispered, "If I can't win you with that, I know you belong to her." We walked back to Juan and the ladies and they all said that the dance was magnificent.

Maria said, "You must promise me a dance before the night is over Jay!"

I said, "At your command señorita!"

She said, "Señora for I am married." I bowed in apology. I noticed Ronnie sitting alone. I excused myself and walked over and extended my hand. She looked up and her eyes were a bit glassy.

I said, "Those eyes are too beautiful for tears especially since there is no reason for them. I have to play the role. I can't help how other women feel about me but only you have what they all want and that's my heart. In spite of what it looks like, none of them get inside. They only have the outside. I've always asked you to believe in me. It is up to you what you do. If every woman that comes near me is going to upset you, then either trust me or free me. If you don't dry your eyes, you will be telling everyone what we have been trying to keep to ourselves."

She said, "I'm tired of hurting, Jay. If you want to be free, go."

I said, "I don't want to be free of you and I can't free myself. You will have to set me free. I've done what you've wanted. I have stayed close. I hurt as much you do. If you can't stand this any longer I will understand. Be aware, if you set me free I will never come back."

I felt her whole body become rigid. I held her close until she relaxed. She asked that I take her back to her table. The song was ending so it looked as though we had finished our dance. I took her back to her table. Len was talking with a man by the door. I asked her if she was all right and she said, yes. I asked if I could get her anything.

She said, "No my husband will get me what ever I need." Then she said, "You are free Jay. Go where and with whom you will."

It was as if a hot dagger had been thrust through my heart. I sat down and looked at her. Her eyes were not teary.

"This is what you want?" I asked. She looked straight ahead and did not answer.

I said, "Since the band is taking a break and I know the DJ, if he has it, I'm going to ask him to play a song. If it doesn't say anything to you, I will do what you say."

As I walked towards the DJ, Isabella rushed up to me and kissed me. I excused myself and looked at Ronnie; who was not a happy camper, and then walked to the DJ. I asked if he had brought "Save the Last Dance for me?" He said he had. I asked him to play it after the next song. He asked if he should, play another song before he played it. I said yes and winked. He said, "Gotcha!"

I then rejoined Isabella and Maria. When he played "Save the last dance for me" I walked over and asked Ronnie to dance and she refused.

I said, "I hope you'll grasp the meaning of this song." I then rejoined Isabella and Maria.

Jamie was dancing with Juan. Maria asked if she could have this dance. I obliged her. I shared the rest of my dances between her and Isabella. When the last dance was announced, I excused myself and asked Ronnie to dance she refused. When it was time to go, I had a chat with the host and we made plans to talk a little business.

I took the time to say good night to Isabella, Maria and Juan. Juan said he had decided to leave the big palomino at Ranceville, because he belonged there. He said he would like to occasionally pick up one of his colts if it was agreeable to me. We shook on it. Isabella and I made plans to talk often. Juan invited Jamie to go to Argentina with him. She declined. We said our good-byes, drove Len and Ronnie home and we headed for Manhattan.

Jamie asked, "What's wrong between you and Ronnie?" I said, "I think she is just tired."

* * * *

Jamie called Ronnie the next day and asked, "What happened between you and Jay?" Ronnie did not want to talk about it.

Jamie said, "You've got to talk about it. I have a feeling that Jay is going to leave here and he might not come back. Did you say something to hurt him?"

Ronnie answered, "I don't care. I set him free. I told him he was free to do whatever he wanted to do!"

Jamie yelled, "Are you crazy? What's the matter with you? Jay has done everything but give his life for you. And if necessary he would do that too. He has done everything you asked? He has stayed close to you and the girls and tried to be a friend, although he was hurting deep inside, and you just toss him aside? Do you realize that if he leaves hurt in this way, he will never return to you? Tell him to leave if that's really what you want, but tell him with love not anger in your heart."

"How could I when I watched that woman make love to him right out on the dance floor and he accepted her?" said Ronnie.

"Oh my God, Ronnie! Listen to your own words. She made love to him, I agree, not him to her and she kissed him at the end. What was he supposed to do, slap her? asked Jamie. "When are you ever going to learn to trust him?"

"He went through hell just to get back to you. He found you had married and still stuck by you. What does he have to do to prove he loves you? You may have already lost him. And what about the girls? You know how much they love him!"

Ronnie said, "Oh Jamie, why do I always do and say such stupid things? I'm not going to call him though. If he truly loves me, he will come back to me."

"You're being stupid again!" said Jamie. "You tossed him away and remember, he said he wouldn't come back. I thought that might bring something back to mind. He told you once before that he would not bother you any more and he didn't! Remember that? I also noticed that you refused to dance with him—why?" asked Jamie.

"I was just not in the mood." said Ronnie.

"Oh my God, girl! I'll talk to you later," said Jamie.

* * * *

I sat in the penthouse that night just staring out the window. I sat in the chair thinking of what had happened tonight. I tried to find a cause for the night's events. I wondered if I had precipitated the way it ended. Should I have shunned Isabella? Should I have ignored all the other women that vied for my attention? Should I not have told Ronnie to trust me or set me free? I wanted the night to end but it seemed to just stretch out. I pressed the remote button to turn on some music but quickly turned it off. I was feeling bad enough. I suddenly wished Jamie were here to put her arms around me. I needed a friend right now.

The night drew on and still I had no answers. I must have fallen asleep because the ringing of the phone woke me. It was daylight I was hoping it was Ronnie on the phone but it was Isabella. They were about to take off to Argentina. She asked if she could persuade me to come along. I was tempted to go but I declined. She threw me a kiss down the phone and was gone. I sat there for a while thinking and decided I would lose my self in my business. I took a shower and prepared to face some appointments I had.

I threw myself into my work so intently that six months passed and I had made a number of deals on buildings one of which was the building across from Mrs. T.'s store. I realized I had not thought much at all about Ronnie, but I had missed the girls. Each time I went to Ranceville and worked with their ponies, which had grown into young horses, I missed them terribly. I often wondered how Tia was doing. I realized that it hurt more missing the girls than Ronnie. Was I getting her out of my system or was this a false front?

I was having great success working with Bandito. We had become great friends. It was almost like having Rance back. The big palomino had sired a set of beautiful twin colts. Juan would be proud of them. Prince, Star and Bandito had also made some beautiful additions to their herds.

I had just returned from Ranceville, and as I was getting out of the limo, I saw Ronnie coming out of Mrs. T.'s. We looked at each other. I thought she was going to say something, but she got into her limo and drove off. I saw Mrs. T. beckoning me. She asked how I'd been. I said well. She asked me into her office and sat me down.

She said, "Jay I want you to tell me what has happened between you and Ronnie?"

I asked, "What has she told you?"

She said, "She won't tell me anything."

I said, "Then neither can I, because frankly I don't know. I have searched my brains and I can't find an answer."

She asked, "What about the girls? Do you know they called me crying and told me that Ronnie had taken away the phone that you gave them so that they couldn't call you? Those girls absolutely love you and those horses and no telling what will happen to Tia if this continues."

I said, "Mrs. T. as much as I love those girls, they are her children. I can't interfere."

"Can't you talk to her husband?" asked Mrs. T. I reiterated, "Like I said, I will not interfere." I left her office and went up to my apartment.

Jamie must have talked with Mrs. T. because she came into my office and said,

"OK enough of this. What in the heck is going on with the two of you? What ever it is, it happened the night of the fiesta so out with it."

I asked, "Don't you two talk any more? What has she told you?"

"She doesn't talk even to me any more. She won't bring the kids around or anything! I saw her coming out of Mrs. T.'s office and tried to talk to her but she said she was in a hurry!" answered Jamie.

I said, "I don't know what happened, Jamie so only she can tell you. All I know is she doesn't want anything to do with me any more. Why? You have to ask her." Jamie went to her apartment.

I was deeply hurt inside. I could not understand Ronnie any more. She was like someone I had never met. I had been reaching for her in my spirit and I could no longer make a connection. I felt that she was no longer my soul mate. I felt lost. I had given her all I could give of myself and I still couldn't satisfy her. Now it seemed I couldn't make any connection with her. I seemed to have sensed anger and hate in her eyes as she looked at me before getting in the limo.

I stood at the window looking out at the evening. I had the music on but I couldn't seem to hear it. Suddenly everything seemed to be closing in on me. It was like being back in captivity. I needed air so I pressed the button that opened the side window. The air rushing in felt very refreshing, so I took off my shirt and sat in the lounge chair and continued to look out at the evening sky. The cool evening breeze was damp, but felt good. I watched the occasional white clouds sailing by and wondered where they were going. I watched one that reminded me of someone in a car and wondered if it was going to meet someone or if was it lost like me? I must have fallen asleep. I remember opening my eyes and it was night, but I must have fallen asleep again.

I thought I could hear Jamie calling me. She seemed so far away and her call seemed urgent, but I couldn't seem to answer her. Then there were bright lights and someone was calling my name, but the voice wasn't Mr. Ni's. I was reaching for Ronnie, but I could not make a connection. I seemed to feel that there was no need to fight any more, so I gave up. Then I heard mother's—Aunt Loren's—voice calling me.

She was saying, "Jay McFadden, I want you to open your eyes and look and me. Do you hear me? Open your eyes and look at me right now!" She seemed to be angry and crying. I had never disobeyed her so I tried as hard as I could to open my eyes.

The lights were bright as I opened my eyes, so I closed them. I heard someone say, "Turn off the overhead." I opened my eyes. Mother and others were looking down at me. One was a doctor. My face was covered with some sort of mask. Mother bent over and kissed me and said, "Oh baby I thought I had lost you!" I was wondering what had happened. Why was I here? Why was mother so worried? Then I saw Jamie. She had tears running down her face. She looked at me and began to smile. Then Lori rushed in, I could hear her saying, "Where is he?" She hurried over to me and began kissing me asking, "Jay, Jay why is all this happening to you?" She told mother that she had called Uncle Jim and he was coming with Jay's doctor.

The doctor in the room came over and said, "Your mother is a strong woman because she refused to give up on you. I thought we had lost you." He thought the pneumonia had been too much for my body to overcome because my body was weak and I needed a lot of fluids and rest. Jamie asked the doctor if she could ask me a question. He said yes.

Jamie asked, "Jay did you open that window shortly after we talked about Ronnie? "Nod or shake your head yes or no."

I was trying to remember. "What window?" I couldn't remember. I felt sleepy. Jamie told the doctor that I must have fallen asleep and had been under an open window for more than fourteen hours. The doctor said that's why the pneumonia had set in so strongly in my body, which was already in a weakened condition. He asked everyone to leave so that he could examine me.

I began to remember what had happened. I had lost Ronnie. I had no desire to live.

The doctor worked feverishly over me most of the day. I was told later that I started to rant and rave. I acted as though I was talking to Mr. Ni. I yelled as though I was in great pain. I kept calling for Ronnie and asking, "Where are you? I need you but I can't find you." I told Mr. Ni that I would not give him any information. The doctor said that I was hallucinating. He asked if any one knew what I was talking about. Jamie told him, 'It sounds as though he thinks he's back in captivity."

I thought I heard Lori. She was crying and telling me to get up. I tried as hard as I could to do as she asked. I fought as hard as I could . . .

* * * *

Uncle Jim called and said that Jay's own doctor was away and it might be a day or more to get there.

The doctor called Loren, Lori and Jamie and told them, "I can provide all the medication required to combat the pneumonia, but I can not provide the will for him to live. Is there was any reason for him to have a death wish?" At that moment Jamie left the room.

Jamie tried to call Ronnie to tell her that Jay was near death with pneumonia. She could not reach her and kept getting a busy signal. When Jamie came back into the room and said that she could not reach Ronnie. Lori went over to the bed and began to yell at Jay. She told him that he had wasted enough time on a woman who never deserved him in the first place. She said that she was not going to stand by and see him throw his life away for any woman especially one that is married. Loren quieted Lori and told her she did not mean what she said, that it was anger speaking. "You know you love her."

Lori agreed, but turned to Jay and told him, "You are not going to lie there and die, so I want you to reach down deep and muster up the strength that pulled you through your captivity. I want you to think of mother, Jamie, the Rosses, Ranceville and me. We are the people who love you and need you. I want you to do this and get up out of this bed. Do you hear me Jay McFadden do you hear me . . . ?"

Uncle Jim and Jay's doctor arrived late the next night. The doctors conferred and told Loren, Lori and Jamie that Jay seemed to do better during the night. He told Lori that her little talk with Jay might have helped. Jay had been fighting for two days, when Jay's doctor came in and said that Jay needed help and asked if there was anyone who might give him inspiration.

Jamie thought of Tia and Beth. She said, "I know someone. I have been trying to reach Ronnie for two days. I can't believe that she won't return my call. I'll call her again."

When there was still no connection, Jamie knew that there was something wrong. She grabbed Jay's army doctor by the arm and said, "We need to go check on someone. They took the limo to the airport and 'coptered to Ronnie's home. The girls came running out thinking that it was Jay.

Jamie asked, "Where is your mother?" as Ronnie came out of the house.

"What's wrong?" asked Ronnie when she saw Jamie. "Why haven't you answered my calls?" asked Jamie angrily.

"Our phones have been out for three days!" responded Ronnie. "There is a whole power grid that is out. They have been trying to get it up again. What's wrong?"

Jamie said, "Get the girls ready I'll explain on the way!"

The urgency of Jamie's voice caused Ronnie not to hesitate. She hurried and readied the girls and they boarded the 'copter for the hospital. On the 'copter Jamie introduced Jay's doctor to Ronnie and the doctor explained Jay's condition. Ronnie looked at Jamie and said, "You thought I intentionally did not answer your call. Oh, Jamie how could you?" Jamie hugged Ronnie and apologized.

The doctor told Ronnie that Jay was extremely ill in fact he was fighting for his life.

"We are hoping for someone who might give him the inspiration to want to live. He has been calling for you and at times, mentally, he has been back in captivity. He has been talking, as though speaking to Mr. Ni, the man that was torturing him. He was calling your name and saying he couldn't find you. He wondered why you wouldn't answer. Do you know what he meant by all this? I was his doctor when he returned from captivity. The answer to these questions would help me understand how he survived the ordeal he went through." Ronnie explained giving the answers to the doctor's questions.

The doctor explained to Ronnie that they had done all they could for Jay. It was now up to him. "He doesn't seem to want to live. It has been suggested that maybe your and your daughters' voices might be might be the inspiration he needs. I know we are asking a lot of you but this seems to be our last hope. Will you try to help?"

Crying almost uncontrollably, she responded, "Yes, yes I will do anything!"

The doctor thanked Ronnie for the information she had given him. He said that it was amazing. He said that he had heard of such incidences, but never met one in real life. The 'copter landed on the 'copter pad on the hospital roof and Ronnie and the girls were rushed to Jay's room.

The doctor seeing Ronnie's eyes and face, talked to her and asked if she was all right. He said that Jay's situation was drastic and that it might frighten the girls. He did not want to dramatize the situation, but if she thought it might be too much for them, he didn't want them to go in there.

Ronnie grabbed the doctor's arm and screamed, "Oh God no! What have I done? What have I done?" she asked again looking at Jamie.

Jamie put her arms around Ronnie and said, "Just help him, please just help him!"

Ronnie ran into the room but Lori stopped her and told her to stay the hell away from him. Loren grabbed Lori and pulled her away.

Ronnie went to the bed and looked down at Jay lying there helplessly. She had never seen him like this before. Her heart was in pieces. All the love she had in her rose to the surface. Her fingertips were on fire with love as she stroked the side of his face.

Her words were wrapped with love as she whispered softly to him, "Oh my love, from the depths of my heart, a jealous woman asks you to forgive her for her selfish ways. But for a love like yours how can one not be jealous of anyone that might be savoring it? However, I would rather know that you are alive and happy with someone else then to see you here like this. My heart is torn into a thousand pieces as I gaze upon you lying helplessly here. Please my love, fight with all your might to get well. I never want to lose you, but go where you can to find the love you deserve. I will cry myself to sleep every night of my life but I will face the next day knowing that you are alive and happy somewhere. Fight my love, fight or I will die here with you!" She kissed every part of his exposed face.

She called for the girls and told them to talk to their uncle Jay.

Tia cried, "Uncle Jay you must get well you must. I love you and I need you. Who will help me with my pony? You promised me remember. I don't want to live without you." She tried to hug and kiss him.

Beth was crying as she spoke, "Uncle Jay, I love you so much. What will we do without you? Who will take us skating? And you promised to teach me to ice skate. You have never backed out on a promise before. Are you going to start now? I love being with you so much. I miss you every day that you are not with us. Don't leave us Uncle Jay please don't!" She continued to cry and laid her head aside his.

Jay raised his hand and patted her arm. Ronnie and the girls prayed for Jay's recovery.

Ronnie prayed, "Lord you know this man better than any of us. You know the love that is in him because you put it there! Can this world afford to be without the love in this man? You must have had a purpose for all that love. I'm sure he hasn't fulfilled that purpose yet. If he has served your purpose, the girls and I have a need for him. I know that I, being a married woman, have no right to ask for him, but my girls need him. Please do not take him away from them."

Loren and Lori listened as Ronnie prayed. They both went to her and hugged her.

Loren said, "That was a beautiful prayer Ronnie. I'm sure God has heard you. Thank you!"

Lori said, "Ditto." Lori told Jamie about the prayer when she came in. She had been secretly praying. Jamie went to Ronnie and just held both her hands and looking in her eyes, said nothing. Ronnie smiled. She understood.

Ronnie spent the night at Jay's side. She refused to leave him. The next day Jay showed some improvement. For three days Ronnie never left his side. One time Jay opened his eyes, saw Ronnie sitting there asleep, grasped her hand and went back to sleep. When Ronnie awoke and found her hand in Jay's hand, she called softly to Loren and showed her. They both smiled. Ronnie looked up and said "Thank you Lord!"

The next day, the doctor announced that Jay was completely out of danger. He was no longer having night sweats and his temperature was down, not too much above normal. Medication was keeping him asleep to rest his body. Lori had apologized to Ronnie and thanked her and the girls for the inspiration and prayer Jay needed. Loren and Jamie also thanked Ronnie and the girls, hugging them gratefully. Ronnie, feeling that Jay was going to be all right, needed to get home because her husband was due home that day. So Jamie had the 'copter readied to take Ronnie and the girls back home.

Before Ronnie left, Jay's army doctor had a talk with her. He told Ronnie that he was finally glad to meet the person who had pulled Jay through those horrible years of captivity. He told her that as a result of the injury to his body he needed to keep his body strong. Ronnie asked about the injury with a puzzled look on her face. The doctor asked her did she not know about the injury to his body. She told him that she knew. The doctor asked her had she seen the TV documentary. She told him that she had. The doctor asked Ronnie if she really knew the extent of his injury. She said only to the extent of the documentary. She had not seen his injury personally. He said I know that the picture was blurry and you could not see the true extent of the injury. He suggested that maybe she should see it again if it ever came back on and take a good look. He said that Ronnie might appreciate the love he had for her even more.

Ronnie went home thinking about what the doctor had said. She knew now why Jay was always going to the health club. She called Jamie and asked how, if Jay was always going to the club, did his body get in such a weakened condition? Jamie said that for the last six months Jay had been to the club only once.

"All he's been doing is working. He was staying up late and sleeping in his lounge chair a lot."

* * * *

Three weeks later, I was back on my feet. The doctors still wanted me to take it easy for a while. I took the time to call and to thank Ronnie and the girls for what they had done. Ronnie asked what I planned to do. I told her I was not sure. I told her that when the doctor gave me the OK, I would take her advice.

"You told me to go where and with whom I wished and I promised you that I would not come back. Well I cannot keep that promise now. I owe you my life again and will always be there if you ever need me but it's time I made a life somewhere for myself." I told her how much I loved her and the girls. I told her that I realized after the fiesta that I could only do more harm by hanging around. It had never been my intention to hurt her.

She begged me not to give up, because she could not bear to lose me. She told me that after sitting at my bedside she had time to think. After almost losing me again, she had decided to give up her marriage.

I told her that she had a wonderful husband and I counted him a friend and I could not be the cause of him losing his family. I told her what we had must stop here and now. I told her I would not see her again. It would be better that way.

She became very angry and said some mean things and blamed Isabella for my decision. I tried to explain that I couldn't destroy their marriage.

"What kind of life could we have with a marriage built on the destruction of another marriage?" It would haunt us until it destroyed us.

"If that's how you feel go and good riddance and don't come back," she responded! I knew it was the hurt in her that was speaking. She had just offered to give up her marriage for me and I had rejected her again. But it hurt me deeply to hear her say that. I said goodbye and hung up.

I felt totally empty inside. There was a huge void in me as if half of me was missing. I sat quietly and tried to think of something pleasant, but all I could think of was Ronnie and the girls. I don't know what Ronnie told the girls about me, but I did not hear anything from them, nor did I try to reach them. Since Ronnie had not tried to contact me, I took it that she still felt the same way and did not want anything to do with me. I knew that it was for the best, but it was hard to give up what had been my life. I still ached for her and did not want to part with such anger spoken. I tried to lose myself in the task of acquiring more property. The more I acquired, the bigger the emptiness. I was asked to speak at an affair for the Veterans Administration, which I gladly accepted. That started a rash of invitations to speak at different functions even a ladies' tea. Five months later I needed to get away.

I had a desire to see Isabella so I had the twin palomino colts shipped to Argentina and went to visit Juan. I didn't even tell Jamie I was leaving. I left a letter telling Jamie I was not sure if I would ever return. With the letter I left some papers and asked Jamie to have Mrs. T. to sign them giving her sole ownership of the store.

# Jay Flees Again

When Jamie gave her the papers Mrs. T. cried. She told Jamie it was not for the store, but because she had lost a friend. She could not bear to think that she would not see Jay again.

She hugged Jamie and said, "I think he's gone for good."

Mrs. T. said it was time for her to have a serious talk with Ronnie. She called Ronnie and told her that either she came to the store or she was going there. Ronnie said she wanted to come into the city anyway so she would come to the store. When Ronnie arrived Mrs. T. told her that she was like a daughter to her so she was going to talk to her like a mother.

"What in the world have you done to Jay?" asked Mrs. T.

"Why see Jay's side and not see my side. Why is everyone so worried about Jay?" Ronnie asked, just as Jamie walked in.

Mrs. T. angrily responded, "Because Jay is gone and he doesn't plan to come back!"

Ronnie jumped up and asked, "Gone? Where? How do you know?" With tears in her eyes, Jamie walked over to Ronnie, put her arms around her and said, "He left a note and he won't be back. He wouldn't even tell me when he left or where he was going. He has never done that before."

Ronnie dropped to her knees and cried uncontrollably, "What have I done? What have I done?"

After getting her under control, they reasoned that if they understood what happened they might be able to put their minds together to get him back.

Mrs. T. asked Ronnie to tell her what happened the last time Jay and her were together.

Jamie hugged Ronnie and said, "Come on sis, we need to work together on this."

Ronnie said she had been so angry about the actions of Isabella that night, that she had not been able to think straight since, and that she had told Jay to go and good riddance!

"What?" asked Mrs. T "Baby I don't believe you! You could not have told Jay that!"

Ronnie dropped her head and said, "But I did."

Jamie asked, "When did you tell him that? He came to you twice. Was it before or after you refused to dance with him?"

"Wa—ait a minute!" said Mrs. T. "You mean you actually refused to dance with Jay!"

"No, no, no!" said Ronnie. "It wasn't at the fiesta at all that I said that. It was when he called to thank me after he got out of the hospital!"

"Hold it," said Mrs. T. "Am I right that this started at the fiesta?"

"Yes," said Ronnie.

"Then we need to start there," said Mrs. T.

Jamie said. "Jay came to you twice. What happened?"

"Well," said Ronnie, "I was angry because that woman made love to him in front of everyone and he did nothing!"

"What did she do?" asked Mrs. T.

"It was the way she danced with him, and then she kissed him, right in front of everyone!" said Ronnie.

"What did he do?" asked Mrs. T;

"He did nothing. He didn't try to stop her!" said Ronnie.

"What happened when he came to you?" asked Mrs. T.

"He came to me and we were dancing and I didn't feel like dancing, so I asked him to take me back to my table. He asked if he could get me something to drink. I told him that my husband would get it for me. I told him I was tired of hurting and sent him away!" said Ronnie.

"Oh no baby, you didn't!" said Mrs. T.

"He knew I didn't like that woman all over him and kissing him like that!" said Ronnie.

"Oh Lord, baby. I haven't heard anything wrong that the man has done as yet!" said Mrs. T.

"What happened when he came back?" asked Jamie.

"Before he walked away he said, 'I'm going to ask the DJ to play a song. Listen to it and if it doesn't say anything to you I'll do as you say.' When the song played he asked me to dance, but I was in no mood to dance so I refused. He said something and walked away," answered Ronnie.

Jamie said, "When the last dance was announced, Jay excused himself and came over to you, what happened?"

"He asked me to dance and I refused. I didn't talk to him again until he was in the hospital," said Ronnie.

"What did he say before he walked away, after he asked for that song to be played and you refused to dance with him?" asked Jamie?

"I don't know!" said Ronnie.

"Think," said Jamie. "It might be important. He came back to you even after you sent him away."

Ronnie thought and said, "I think he said something about the song having meaning to me. I'm not sure what he said exactly."

"What did the song say?" asked Mrs. T.

"I didn't listen to the words," said Ronnie.

"What was the song?" asked Mrs. T.

Ronnie thought, "Something about a dance. I can't remember!"

"Think Ronnie, Jay doesn't just do something like that without a reason," said Jamie.

"Something about going home," said Ronnie. "I remember," said Jamie. "Save the last dance for me."

"Yes," said Ronnie "That was it!"

Mrs. T. said, "There's a record store about a half a block away. Let's get that record and listen to it."

Jamie and Ronnie hurried and purchased the record. Mrs. T. put the record on in her office.

Jamie said, "I know that Jay does not say anything with out a reason." Mrs. T. agreed. They listened very intently to it. When the song was over Mrs. T. said,

"I know exactly what he wanted you to understand!"

"What was it?" asked Ronnie.

"Your anger had your mind clouded," said Mrs. T. "Listen to what the words are saying. The writer of the song is telling the girl to go on and enjoy the night, the music and have fun. He's trusting her to enjoy herself. He says, she can dance and flirt as much as she wants. All of that means nothing, as long as she doesn't give her heart away, and when the fellow asks if can he take her home, she is to tell him no. Because don't forget who's taking her home and in whose arms she's going to be, so save the last dance for him.

Don't you see? He was telling you that's exactly what was going on that night. Regardless of what you saw happening there, his heart was yours and he was taking you home that night. He was also telling you how much he loved you and he didn't want to let you go. That's why he came back for the last dance! I'm gong to play the record again and you listen well."

Ronnie listened and collapsed crying uncontrollably. "Oh my love, my love, why do I do what I always do? I know it's jealousy, but I can't help myself because I love you so much! Oh God bring him back to me! Too late I have learned! Jamie has always told me to trust Jay. Jay was so right. I didn't even read Rance. Rance was always showing me that I should trust Jay as he did."

When they had quieted Ronnie down, Mrs. T. said, "That's just part of the problem. Before we can plan an attack we need to know the whole story. What happened when you told him good riddance? Umph, little one I can't even believe those word came out of your mouth to Jay. Why would you ever say such a thing to him?"

"Jamie would say, I was being stupid," said Ronnie.

Jamie quickly put her arms around her and said, "Oh sis you know I didn't really mean that. I truly love you."

"I know," said Ronnie, "Ditto!"

"Well?" asked Mrs. T., "What happened?"

Ronnie began, "After we had almost lost him in the hospital, I had made up my mind to give up my marriage and be with Jay."

Jamie and Mrs. T. both jumped to their feet with Mrs. T. saying, "Whoa!" Ronnie said, "I know now that I was wrong but when he refused, all I could feel was rejection. So I said some mean things and told him to go, and good riddance." She started crying and said, "I must have hurt him something awful. I guess he couldn't take any more! Oh, what am I going to do?"

Mrs. T said, "All is not lost yet. Let's first see if we can find him."

Jamie said, "I don't think he will go where we might find him, but we can try to see if he is in Argentina. They tried to reach Jay in Argentina, but were told that he had not gone there. He would usually call ahead to let them know that he was coming and someone would pick him up at the airport. They asked if something was wrong and should they tell Señor Juan? The response was no.

Mrs. T. was crying and said, "They have not heard from him. They said he would usually call and let them know he was coming and someone would pick him up at the airport. I think we have lost him!"

* * * *

I flew to Montana to visit Ted for a few days and then headed for Argentina. Juan was elated to see me. He was quite surprised by the arrival of the twin colts. He absolutely adored them. They became his pride and joy.

I told Juan that I did not want anyone from home to know where I was, so I did not want to receive any call from the States except Jamie. If she called it would be important.

Isabella was extremely happy that I had come. I was honest with Isabella and told her that I was not the man for her because I could not shake myself free from Ronnie. Even so she insisted that she would settle just to be in my company.

During the next year, I spent a lot of time with Isabella. We had a lot of fun together and we made each other laugh. I became quite fond of Isabella. She made me feel like I used to feel with Ronnie. We spent a lot of time in that little meadow with all the flowers near where she rode. I would watch her running through the wild flowers with her hair blowing in the breeze. What a beautiful sight. She would hop on my back and I would carry her around the meadow.

I found she was a happy-go-lucky person and very loving. It was hard not to fall in love with her. My feelings for her had grown very strong. I found that my thoughts of Ronnie and the girls had grown faint. The scent of Isabella, the taste of her mouth, the softness of her body and her laughter were overwhelming and had become a replacement.

As happy as I was with Isabella, about four months after I arrived in Argentina something strange began to happen to me. Isabella and I were walking through the meadow when I felt something like an electric shock. Isabella was quick to ask what was wrong. I had a strange feeling but could not explain it.

The electric shock went away but during the next eight months occasionally it would feel like something would tug at me and then it would go away. Once when I was holding Isabella she could feel my body jump and I could not explain it, which caused her to become quite concerned. I asked her to just forget it and we continued to enjoy our time together though occasionally she would ask if I should see a doctor.

One evening as I walked onto the veranda, Isabella was standing looking out toward the horizon. I walked up behind her and put my arms around her. I kissed the side of her neck and turned her towards me and saw the tears in her beautiful eyes. I was about to say, "These eyes are too beautiful for tears." Suddenly it was as though I could see Ronnie standing there before me. I could feel a pain in my heart—Ronnie at that time was crying her heart out as she played over and over a song called "My Special Prayer" that she had purchased after hearing it on the radio—I held Isabella at arms length and asked her why the tears?

She replied, "I love you so much and I want to marry you and be with you for the rest of my life, but I know you will leave one day."

I stood frozen just looking at her. I wanted to put my arms around her and tell her that I would never leave her but the words would not come out. I drew her close and felt her tears wet my shirt as she laid her face against my chest. My mind was racing a mile a minute. I was totally mixed up now. All this time I thought I had gotten Ronnie out of my system. I had felt the love growing in me for Isabella and now suddenly there was Ronnie.

I knew I could not continue to be someone I wasn't. I had to sort this out and I knew that I couldn't do that here. I told Isabella that I needed to get away to sort out my feelings and that I would leave the next day. I spent the night on the veranda with her in my arms kissing away her tears. The next day I caught a plane bound for Paris.

My plan was to go to Paris and try to sort out my feelings but something was pulling at me to go home. The pull was even stronger as the plane neared Paris. I took a taxi from the airport. On the way to the hotel it was as if I could hear Tia and then Ronnie calling me. I had the taxi turn around and went back to the airport and hopped the next flight for the States.

I had totally disappeared for a year. I didn't even call to have my limo pick me up. I had an airport limo take me to the building. The doorman was shocked to see me get out of an airport limo, and began to tell me that everyone had been looking for me. I thanked him and went up to the penthouse.

I took a shower and lay down. I had fallen asleep for a couple of hours and then the phone rang; it was Jamie. The doorman had told her that I was in.

Excitedly she asked, "Where have you been Jay?"

I said, "Jamie whatever happens with the business you are as capable of handling it as I am."

She said, "It has nothing to do with business Jay. Len was killed in a car accident, on his way home eight months ago."

I sat straight up in the bed. "Oh no!" I yelled.

Jamie continued, "Ronnie had to identify the body and she went to pieces seeing the condition of it. She was put in the hospital for ten days, so I took the girls home to Loren because his parents were back in Australia. The girls were screaming for you but we didn't know where you were.

After Ronnie got back on her feet, she took the girls back to the mansion, but the girls didn't want to stay there. They kept asking for you. I told her you had left without telling me. She wouldn't believe me. I went up to talk to her and she was beside herself. She kept saying you deserted her when she and the girls really needed you. She was ranting and raving so I had to slap her to help her get hold of herself. His parents are seemingly blaming her for the condition of the girls and herself. They want to take the girls away from her. You know how straitlaced they are. If she loses those girls I don't know what will happen to her. Can't you do something Jay?" asked Jamie?

I asked Jamie, "Is she at home?"

Jamie answered, "No they're at the hospital. Tia is in a bad way!"

I said, "Get my limo and call and have the 'copter ready."

"You won't need your 'copter," said Jamie. "I had them brought to the Children's Hospital."

I said, "Great girl Jamie. Did you tell the hospital who they were?"

"Yes I told them they were friends of yours," said Jamie.

"Thanks Jamie," I said.

The limo dropped us off at the hospital. I rushed up to the room that they were in. I walked in the room and the doctor was attending to Tia.

Ronnie rushed at me, hitting me in the chest with both fists and screaming, "Where were you? Where were you when I needed you?"

I put my arms around her and held her. I drew her head to my chest and kissed the top of her head saying, "Shush, I'm here now."

Her arms around me she said, "Oh Jay, I missed you so much and needed you and the girls needed you but you were not here. I remembered how you called to me when you were lost and away from me and I tried to reach you the same way. The first time I tried, I received something like an electric shock and after that I would get a jolt! I continued to try and reach you. Then I thought of Tia and we both put our thoughts together to try and reach you like she had done before!"

When she told me that, my guts twisted into knots. All those years I needed her and she was there for me and when she needed me I had rejected her. Now I understood the electric shock and the jolts I had received. I had allowed the connection to my soul mate to partially shut down.

I responded, "I know. I felt the pull from both of you and it's all right now, I'm here."

I asked the doctor how Tia was.

He said, "I had to give her a sedative to calm her down. She will sleep for a while."

I told him, "I'd prefer you not to give her anymore sedatives. I think she will be OK now."

He said, "Sir I think I might be the best judge of that."

I said, "You're probably right, but I prefer it if she doesn't have another sedative unless Dr Houston says so." He responded that he was the doctor in charge, and he made the decisions.

I softly asked Jamie "Is the Tower suite open yet?"

She said, "Yes it was completed a month ago."

I said, "Tell Ronnie to get their things together and be ready to move to the Tower Suite. I'll be back. I have to make a couple of calls."

I walked down the hall to a call station and plugged into a special access port that I'd had installed in certain areas throughout the hospital so that I could have direct access to any place in the hospital for occasions like this. I entered a special code and had direct access to a special hospital panel board. I punched a single digit and rang the director of the hospital. I said, "This is JM. I have some people in suite 2283 that I would like moved to the Tower Suite ASAP and see if Dr. Houston can report there when he's free."

In the meantime the Doctor asked Jamie, "Who is he supposed to be anyway?"

Jamie replied, "He's not supposed to be, he is JM or Jay McFadden!"

The doctor responded, "Well I guess there goes my job!"

Jamie replied, "I don't think so! He's not like that. He's just quite concerned about this little girl."

When I walked back into the room the doctor apologized because he had not known who I was.

I said, "It is I who should apologize. Of course you did not know who I was and I overstepped my authority. You were right you are the doctor."

I walked over to the bed and kissed Tia and asked Ronnie where Beth was. She pointed to the room where Beth was asleep. I looked in on Beth and kissed her forehead, wrapped a blanket around her, picked her up and told the doctor that I was taking them to the Tower Suite. I asked Ronnie if she would care to go up with me or come up when they brought Tia. She grabbed hold of my arm. I could feel her watching me. She watched my every move. She could not take her eyes off me.

I went to a private elevator waved my key card over a sensor and the door opened. We stepped into the elevator and I put in my code and it zoomed us up to the Tower. The door opened and exposed a gorgeously decorated floor. I heard Ronnie gasp as she stepped out of the elevator, but she said nothing. I walked a few feet to a door and punched in a code. The door led to a suite with five rooms each with beds that could be hospital beds or made to look like regular beds, a large living room and a completely furnished kitchen.

I laid Beth in one of the bedrooms and covered her. I proceeded to kiss her forehead and she opened her eyes. She closed her eyes and reopened them. She smiled and suddenly threw her arms around my neck and held on for dear life. I picked her up and held her in my arms.

She cried and said, "I love you, I love you, I love you!"

I said, "I know baby. I love you too." I sat on the bed and held her and told her, "These eyes are too beautiful for tears!" I began to kiss away her tears. She laid her head against my chest and went back to sleep. I said to Ronnie, "She must be really tired!" "She was up all night," said Ronnie.

As I sat holding Beth, they brought in Tia and all of their things. They asked where they should put Tia and I pointed to the big bedroom. Ronnie went to watch them transfer Tia to the bed. I noticed that Ronnie had only a very few of her things with her. I beckoned to Jamie and asked her to go with Ronnie to the penthouse and help her get a few things from her closet. If she needed anything else for her or the girls she could stop at Mrs. T.'s and get it. I told Jamie I would stay with the girls.

About that time Dr Houston came in. He, like Jamie and I had the code to this room. He said, "Hi JM! What seems to be the problem?" I said "The little girl in the A room Ken. Her mother is in there with her." He went in and talked to Ronnie and began to check out Tia. He told me he needed her awake and asked how long she had been asleep. I told him that he had to check with the other doctor.

Ronnie told me that she wanted me to go to the penthouse with her. I told her that I wanted to stay with Tia. She was pleading with me to go with her. Dr Houston came to the door and said that Tia would probably be asleep for another forty minutes and said he would wait with her.

Ronnie took the opportunity and said, "There is no reason for you to stay Jay. Dr Houston will be here with her. Please come and take me there." I relented and we went to my apartment. I went into my office and made a call while she retrieved a few things from the closets.

I was standing looking out the window. A voice softly said, "Jay?"

I answered, "Yes."

She said, "Jay, Please look at me!" I turned and looked in her eyes for a few minutes and turned back to the window. She put her arms around my waist and laid her head against my back.

I could feel her tears as she said, "Oh my love what have I done to you? There is no smile on your face and the light has gone out of your eyes. You didn't even smile at the girls! I have hurt you so! What can I do? Have I killed all the love that you had for me? Is there no hope?"

I had to tell her what was within me. I said, still looking out the window, "There are no more smiles. I can't seem to find one anymore. This may end us here and now, if so, so be it. You pushed me into the arms of another woman. One that I have found that I could easily love." Still holding me tightly, I could feel her tremble when I said that. "Your jealous selfishness hurt not only me, but also the girls. Knowing how much we loved each other you separated us just to satisfy your ego. I asked for trust and you gave me anger and disbelief. I did everything that you wanted me to do. You wanted me to stay in your life so I stayed. I tried to do things as you wished. I could not help it if other women liked me. I told you that I was only playing the part. They meant nothing. I was trying to keep attention away from you. You were my life. Did you expect me to shun every woman that came towards me? All I wanted was your trust and your love. That was enough for me.

When I was sick you and the girls helped pull me through. I was so grateful for that. I hoped that afterwards you might have changed your mind about me. I hoped that you would call me, and when you didn't I felt that you still wanted nothing more to do with me. When I called to thank you for saving my life, I thought you might feel differently. I said I would take your advice and that I would try to find a life for myself. You said that you didn't want me to go away. I appreciated your desiring to give up your marriage for me. It showed me just how much you loved me. I explained that I didn't want to be the cause of Len losing his family. I couldn't bear that. He had become my friend and my staying around would only have made matters worse. But then your anger took over again and you said things that really hurt me deeply. I loved you with every fiber in my body but I couldn't hurt others to get you. What kind of life would we have had? Destroying your marriage would have destroyed us.

It didn't seem to matter to you and that you hurt me deeply. I tried to lose myself in my work and even did some speaking engagements, but nothing seem to help. I decided to get away from here for a while. However, when I left, I had no intention of ever coming back to you.

I spent the last year with Isabella. She and I are like we used to be. I felt alive when I was with her. I could smile with her. She wants me to marry her even though she knows that I am not in love with her. I know now that I can love her! I could feel Ronnie shudder as though I had stabbed her. One evening while holding Isabella, I suddenly saw your face. I knew then that I had to get away and sort things out. The next day I left and headed for Paris. I needed to get away by myself and to be sure in my heart that she was what I wanted.

At the airport, something was pulling me to come home. I knew that I should have come to check on the business but I shrugged it off. In flight to Paris something was pulling at me even more strongly to come home. In Paris I took a cab to the hotel but the pull was so strong that I had the driver turn back to the airport and I got on the next flight for the States. It was not my intention to come home. As it was, I found that Tia really needed me!"

"Not just Tia, thc three of us needed you and I needed you most of all Jay," cried Ronnie. "I had been kneeling all day and night at Tia's bed praying that you would hear me. When you walked away, my life stopped. I've been an empty shell ever since. I had no feelings at all. I apologized to the girls for taking their phone away and gave it back to them after a while, but you had gone. No one knew where you were." She could hardly get her words out for crying. She didn't realize it but she was squeezing me so tight that her nails were digging into my flesh.

"When Len was killed and I had no one to turn to, I almost lost it. Had it not been for Jamie I probably would have. I truly love her." Her arms suddenly dropped and she sat down in the chair. She must have sat on the remote because the song "Just Out Of Reach" started to play.

She was crying and pleading, "Jay we need you so badly. What will we do with out you? Our lives have always been entwined. There is no you and us. There is just us. I deserve to lose you but not the girls." She rose from the chair, and put her arms around me again. I've been an empty shell without you, and so have they. I would rather you took them with you when you leave, than to see them suffer!"

That really hurt me; I had to look into her eyes to know the truth. Knowing how much she loved them, would she really be willing to give them up. I would never take them away from away her and they would never leave her. Still I had to look into her eyes to see the truth. She just kept her arms around me with her head against my back and continued to cry.

About that time another song, "The Door Is Still Open," started playing. She cried, "Have I truly driven you to the arms of another woman Jay? Have I Jay? Oh God! Don't let that be so!" She held on and continued to cry.

The song said, "The door is still open to my heart."

Crying, she asked, "Is the door still open to your heart for me Jay?"

I didn't answer her. She was trembling and as the song ended she pressed her lips to the back of my neck, and "Just Out of Reach" started to play again. I continued to stare out of the window, but I was listening to the music. It was almost as though she had put the song on herself.

She said, "Jay I know now the hurt that you have felt. I have heard you play these songs whenever I came over here. I have purchased each one of them. They have been all I've listened to and I feel what you must have been feeling all those years wanting me. Too late I understood the message you were tying to give me in the song "Save the Last Dance For Me." I have cried myself to sleep every night to that song since you've been gone. I feel that I am being punished for putting you through the torment that I am going through now! Oh my love, please forgive me for the pain that I have caused you. I deserve what I am going through, but you didn't! Can you ever forgive me?"

The next song that played was "These Arms of Mine." Listening to the words of that song, I remembered what hurt I felt in my heart when I was listening to it and wanting her. Then I remembered how when I needed her, I would call to her and she would meet me in the garden. Her call had reached me in Argentina, and I unknowingly ignored it there, on the flight to Paris and in the Paris airport taxi. I realized that we were still connected spiritually. My heart ached from the pain that she was feeling. I knew it all too well.

She continued to cry as she said, "While you were gone I would come here often and play your music and look out the window just as you are doing. Then one day I heard a song that has tormented me every day since. I brought it here and played it continuously. It was then that I knew that I was truly a part of you because I could feel all your years of pain so I played it over and over as I prayed." At that moment the song "My Special Prayer" began to play.

Listening to the words it was as though my insides were being slowly pulled out of me. The singer of the words was saying:

*While the choir sang, Ave Maria*
*I was singing with all my heart*
*And I sent a special prayer*
*Up to heaven*
*That you'll return to me before I fall apart*

*While the choir sang, hallelujah*
*I was singing with all my heart*
*Darling please come back and never leave me again*
*And this will be the answer to my prayer*

*And I'll wait, here for the answer*
*That you'll come back, come back right away,*
*For if you stayed, away another hour*
*I don't think I could last another day*

*While the choir sang, hallelujah*
*I was singing with all my heart*
*Darling please, come back and never leave me again*
*And it would be the answer to my prayer*

I slowly dropped to my knees as my hands slid down the window. Frightened she moved from behind me and tried to lift me up. I put my arms around her waist and buried the side of my face into her stomach trying to absorb the pain she must have been feeling.

I said, "I can't bear to think of you suffering the pain I suffered."

She held my face close to her repeating, "Oh my love, oh my love." I could feel her body trembling.

I rose slowly and lifted her face, but she tried to keep it down.

She said, "I'm too ashamed to look at you."

I held her tear-wet face in my hands, and looking deeply into her eyes I asked, "Are you serious about the girls?"

She said, "Yes, they love you so and would be so much better off with you, I have hurt all of you enough." I could see that she really meant it. She truly loved those girls even to the point of giving them up.

I said, "These eyes are too beautiful for tears," and began to kiss her in the usual way. I kissed her tears that were flowing like a river. Her tears were tearing the heart out of me. I let my mouth settle softly on her lips. I could taste the salty sweetness of her tear-covered mouth. As she responded to my kiss I began to slip helplessly into a sea of almost forgotten love. I began to remember why I fought so hard to hold onto life when all seemed lost. I hung on just for a moment like this.

Holding her close I could feel her heart pounding as though it would come out of her chest. When her arms fell limply to her side I knew that there was no other love that could match this. We were still united in spirit. I picked her up and laid her on the couch. I sat beside her and kissed her lovingly. Her eyes slowly opened and we looked deeply in each other's eyes. She started to softly say something, but I put my finger over her lips and continued to look into her eyes and then kissed her softly and sweetly.

I finally said, "It's time to get back to the hospital."

At the hospital Tia was awake and sitting up.

Dr Houston said, "JM you are all the medicine this little one needs. Ever since her sister woke up and told her that you were here, I've been having a problem keeping her in bed. She's a little weak but her heart and lungs are great. I've drawn some blood and sent it to the lab. I want to have a look at her electrolytes. I have ordered some food for her.

Looking at Ronnie, who was holding and hugging my arm tightly with her head against my shoulder, he said, "Looks like you are good for all concerned."

I went over and picked Tia up and held her close. She put her arms around my neck and held on as though I might disappear. Meanwhile Dr Houston sat down and wrote a prescription and gave it to Ronnie.

She read it, kissed him on the cheek and said, "Thank you doctor."

He said, "Good night. I have to stop and see a patient before leaving and JM make sure she fills that prescription!"

Ronnie showed me the prescription. It read, "A goodnight's sleep for the red eyes and a cup of love in the morning for what ails you."

I finally smiled, and Ronnie kissed me for the first time in front of the girls and of course they giggled.

I told Jamie, "We all might as well spend the night here, so pick a room. You should find everything you need."

Tia said, "Uncle Jay will you stay with me tonight?"

"Of course!" I answered.

Ronnie told the girls, knowing that Beth would sleep in my lap, "Uncle Jay had a long flight and has been up all day. He needs a good night's sleep. We don't want him to get sick do we?"

The girls agreed and said, "Goodnight Uncle Jay!"

I said, "After we say prayers."

Tia's room was so big, because of the equipment that had to be brought in there for patient treatment. I asked Jamie and Ronnie to help me and we rolled Beth's bed into Tia's room. The girls were very pleased.

I taught them a little prayer and said, "We will say this together every night." I kissed them goodnight, selected a room and took a shower.

Jamie decided to spend the night with the girls and share Beth's bed. This really tickled the girls. Ronnie kissed the girls good night. They asked why Uncle Jay had taught them a different prayer.

Ronnie said, "His prayer included everyone." Ronnie selected the room next to my room.

* * * *

Ronnie was right, Jay was very tired; he went right off to sleep Ronnie went into his room and watched him, as he lay quietly asleep. She thought how much she loved him. She unlocked the door in Jay's room to the shared sun porch, softly kissed him and went to her room. She took a shower and lay across the bed. She needed sleep but she could only think of Jay. She took a blanket from the bed opened her door to the shared sun porch and went next door to Jay's room. She lay quietly beside him and pulled her blanket over her.

* * * *

I woke early and saw Ronnie lying asleep beside me. I turned on my side facing Ronnie and resting my elbow on my pillow I supported my head with my hand and watched Ronnie as she slept. I thought how gorgeous she looked lying there.

After a short while Ronnie awoke, stretched and seeing me watching her said, "Good morning love, have I ever told you how wonderful you are?"

I said, "What are you doing here?"

She reached her hand behind my head; pulled my face down and softly kissed me and said, "Don't scold. This was that cup of love the doctor prescribed remember?" She hopped out of the bed and scurried back to her room. I smiled and thought how nice it was to see her there in the morning.

Ronnie told me that she needed to call Len's parents because they did not know where she was and would be worried. She also told me that they did not particularly care for me.

"They have always suspected something between you and me." Ronnie told me. "Len decided not to tell them about us after he got to know you. He really grew to love you Jay."

"Ditto," I responded.

"They may try to use the girls and me being here as a basis for trying to take them," wept Ronnie.

I told Ronnie not to worry about losing the girls. "No one is going to take them from us."

"Us!" exclaimed Ronnie looking at me. She threw her arms around my neck and kissed me passionately.

"Is that a proposal?" asked Ronnie. I just smiled but did not answer. Unaware of the presence of the girls and Jamie, Ronnie refused to break the embrace.

Giggling the girls asked, "Is Uncle Jay going to be our new daddy?"

Startled, Ronnie released her embrace and turned to the girls, embarrassed. "How long have you been standing there?" She asked,

Beth said, "Mommy you said never answer a question with a question. Is Uncle Jay going to be our new daddy?" Ronnie turned and looked at me.

I said, "Don't look at me they asked you not me," and I laughed.

She said, Ja—ay! Then she turned the tables on me and said to the girls, "I don' t know you have to ask your Uncle Jay!"

The girls hurried to me and asked excitedly, "Are you Uncle Jay? Are you? Are you?"

I sat down and pulled them to me and asked, with Ronnie and Jamie looking on anxiously, "How do you feel about it?"

Tia started jumping up and down and Beth threw her arms around my neck and both said, "Oh yes, Uncle Jay, yes, yes, yes!"

I said, "Then we'll see. But Tia, you need to take it easy. You need to be in bed young lady! I want you to get plenty of rest for me, OK love?"

Jamie said, "Come on girls we have some wedding plans and some calls to make." The girls elatedly chased after Jamie. Ronnie walked up to me and put her arms around my neck and kissed me like I had never been kissed by her before.

She said, "I've been saving that and more just for you. Oh, my love is this at long last going to happen?"

I said, "Yes my love if we both want it." and returned her kiss.

Fanning herself she said, "I'd better call Father and Mother Armontt. You know they don't know anything about you Jay. They have been living in Australia for a number of years. Once they know who you are, they may not be so standoffish."

I said, "No, don't tell them anything about me, nothing at all! I'm just a friend. Let it be as Len wanted it OK?"

"Whatever you say my love, I trust in you," answered Ronnie.

I said, "Is that a fact? Come here you!" I kissed her passionately!"

She said, "Jay if you keep kissing me like that, I will never make this phone call and we won't make it to our wedding night!"

I said, "We'll make it!"

Ronnie called her in-laws. They seemed to be a quite upset and said they were coming to the hospital.

The Armontts arrived and were directed to the Tower Suite. I had previously gone to the director's office after he had called. The Armontts had called him and he wanted to know how I wanted him to handle them. I told him to handle them anyway he thought appropriate. However, to tell them nothing about me.

"If they want to know why their daughter in-law and the girls are here, tell them Jamie West brought them here." He handed me an envelope that had been delivered.

The Armontts came in quite upset because they had not been informed as to the welfare of their granddaughters. They asked Jamie why they were here instead of the hospital close to their home and where were the grandkids. Jamie is time enough for anybody if you get her dander up and they had.

Jamie said, "I had them brought here because they are my friends and I wanted them close by. The girls are in their rooms taking showers, pointing to the two rooms, as is Ronnie."

I had come in right behind the Armontts. They had not seen me as yet.

"What right did you have to bring them here without our permission?" asked Mrs. Armontt.

"The right of a friend close enough to be a sister. And I didn't know that I had to get permission to help someone who was in trouble; I wanted them close enough for me to keep a check on them," countered Jamie. "You arrived at their home and found it in disarray and because it was not up to your standards you took it out on Ronnie. You didn't consider what she has gone through. All you could see was that your standards were lowered. What about her? It was she who had to identify your son's body and fell apart when she saw the condition of it. You didn't have to go through that. She also had to go through the pressure of the funeral arrangements and the funeral. When you arrived everything had been taken care of."

I clapped, "Well said Jamie!"

The Armontts looked around and said, "Oh it's you again."

"I'm getting the picture now," said Mr. Armontt. He looked at Ronnie, as she came into the room, and told her to get the girls ready. She could stay if she wanted but the girls were going with them.

Ronnie cried, "You can't take them!"

Jamie said, "They have not been released by the doctor."

Mr. Armontt countered, "My lawyer is below taking care of that now." Ronnie looked at me, but I shook my head, smiled and winked at her.

The girls came out of their bedrooms, saw their grandparents and ran and gave them a hug.

Mrs. Armontt said, "Get your things together girls we're taking you home with us."

The girls screamed "No!" Beth ran and hugged her mother around her waist and Tia ran right to me saying, "Uncle Jay don't let them take us! We want to stay with you and mommy!"

At that moment, Mr. Armontt's lawyer came in followed by Dr Houston who looked at me and I gave him a finger over my lips sign. The hospital director had called Dr Houston and told him the situation. He arrived at the office right after the lawyer. Dr Houston had told the lawyer that he would not release his patients. They had all been under a great deal of stress. The lawyer told him that he was representing Mr. Stanley Armontt and that Mr. and Mrs. Armontt were waiting in the Tower. Dr Houston said he would tell the Armontts himself.

When the doctor told Mr. Armontt he would not release them, he threatened to use his power to crush anyone that stood in his way. He told his lawyer to get Judge Walker on the phone. At that time I handed the lawyer a paper. It was signed by Judge Walker and stated that the girls would remain in the care of their mother until further notice. The lawyer read the writ to the Armontts.

Fuming, Mr. Armontt said, "We will see about this!" They left the hospital.

Ronnie and the girls ran to me. Ronnie kissed me saying, "You were wonderful!" and the girls hugged me.

Dr Houston asked, "When did you get that paper JM?"

I said, "A short while ago, Ken. I called when we went to the penthouse. Jamie told me that they wanted to take the girls away from Ronnie so I called the Judge and asked if he knew Mr. Armontt. He said that they had crossed paths a number of times. I asked would he have a problem going against him. He said not if it would help me. I told him the situation and he sent me the paper.

Ken asked, "How do you happen to know the most powerful Judge in the state."

"His son was one of the men in my platoon. He introduced me." Ken checked the girls and said, "JM you must be the right kind of medicine." Ronnie was leaning back against me. Ken turned Ronnie's face from side to side looking into her eyes and said, "I see you filled half of that prescription."

Ronnie reached both hands back and holding my face said, "The whole prescription!"

Dr Ken said on his way out, "Yep the right kind of medicine!"

I pulled Ken aside and asked him for a moment of his time. "Ken what is the condition of the three of them? I was wondering if it might not be good for them to get away and spend some time at a quiet resort and beach."

"Excellent Idea, starting tomorrow," said Dr Houston.

I walked backed to Ronnie who turned and looked into my eyes and said, "My love, my love, I have so much love in me for you." She put her arms around my neck and said softly, "I bet we will make wonderful babies." I just gathered her to me and kissed her.

I called Jamie and the girls together. I asked, "What do you think of us all finding a nice quiet resort and beach somewhere? You all deserve it." There was a yell of agreement.

I called for the Lear to be ready in the morning. I had lunch and dinner brought in and we spent the rest of the day together. I should say that the girls spent the rest of the day right up under me.

Tia asked, "Uncle Jay, You won't let them take us away will you?"

I said, "No love. You will stay with your mommy."

"And you too?" asked Beth.

"Yes and me too," I responded! I was bombarded with hugs and kisses by a woman and two lovely young girls.

In the morning the girls were up bright and early. Jamie got them ready. I had ordered breakfast to be sent up at seven thirty. The girls and Jamie ate a hearty breakfast. Ronnie also ate a rather good breakfast. I had OJ, a poached egg on raisin toast and fruit. After breakfast, we carried only ourselves to the limo, drove to the airport and the Lear flew us to a remote Jamaican resort and beach. The sand on the beach was white and the water was warm and blue. I hired someone to teach the girls to snorkel. They were having so much fun, and Jamie and Ronnie joined them. The instructor and Jamie got along so well they began to spend a lot of time together. Ronnie and I smiled as we watched them together. They were like two kids having fun.

Ronnie would occasionally have tears in her eyes. I would kiss them and ask her what could be wrong. She told me that they were tears of joy.

She said, "When I think back to the beginning till now and remember how many times I almost lost you I can't help but cry for my blessings!" I could only put my arms around her and hold her. Ronnie reached up and kissed me. Whenever the girls saw Ronnie kiss me they would hug each other in agreement.

I had left our whereabouts with the hospital, Mrs. T, and Angie, so that if the Armontts carried out their threat, I would be notified. We had planned to stay ten days but everyone was enjoying themselves so much we extended the stay. Eleven days into our stay, a message came that Ronnie and the girls were to appear before the court in three days. Ronnie, Jamie and the girls were so sad to be leaving and Ronnie was worried about losing the girls. I told her I understood her concern but not to worry.

Ronnie, the girls and Jamie appeared in court at the set time. A female lawyer met them and took them to their seats. She introduced herself and the panel of defense lawyers. Ronnie began to look around for me and asked the lawyer if she knew where I was. The lawyer hushed her and told her not to even mention my name.

They introduced the judge and Ronnie remembered his name from the other night. She began to relax. The case was read and the charge was that the Armontts thought Ronnie had become an unfit mother to raise their granddaughters because she had become influenced by a man who was only after her money. The man was not only a charlatan, with an act of healing powers, but had created some kind of mind control over their granddaughters.

They said they knew it was true because their youngest granddaughter Tia, who since birth has been afraid of every man, including relatives, except her father and grandfather, suddenly became attached to a total stranger. They brought doctors and psychiatrists to the stand to testify to the nature of a person with a fear of men and how it would be improbable for such a one to suddenly become attached to a male stranger or to overcome that fear.

The defense said that they respected the learned doctors and psychiatrists and did not care to attack their testimony.

"Our defense," they said, "will take a different avenue. We will listen to the testimony of the accused, and her daughters. Then we will prove that the person who has been painted as a charlatan, a mind controller and money-grubber is really one of the bravest, kindest, most loving, generous and humble person that we believe this country has ever known."

Ronnie was called to the stand. She told about her relationship with Jay, and how they had met again by fate through Tia and how, after he and her husband had a man-to-man talk, they had become the best of friends, and that was well known by most people who knew them.

Next, Tia was put on the stand and Tia told how she met the man she called Mr. J. Then Beth was called to the stand and told how at first she did not like Mr. J., but began to like him, because even after she spoke badly to him, he defended her. "He wasn't supposed to do that," she said.

Then the lawyer said, "Ladies and gentleman of the jury and court I call the man who is accused of being a charlatan, a mind controller, and after Mrs. Len Armontts' money. I call to the stand the man who might be known to you as Mr. J., JM, Jim Meridith or Jay McFadden. Jay entered the courtroom to standing thundering applause. Tia screamed, "Uncle J!" And before Ronnie could stop her she ran and leaped into Jay's arms with a stranglehold around his neck. Everyone loved it.

The Judge quieted the courtroom and admonished the attorney for her setting up of a theatrical introduction and said, "JM will you take the stand please?" I put Tia down and kissed Beth on the forehead, winked at Ronnie and took the stand.

The attorney asked if I knew Ronnie and the girls. I acknowledged I did. She asked if I knew the Armontts and I said, "Yes, I have been in their presence three times."

"'In their presence?' Would you explain that?"

"I mean that I was in their son's home and I was in the same hospital suite with them," I answered.

"I take that to mean that you have never been officially introduced to them?" asked the attorney.

"I'm not sure. When I was first in their presence, there may have been an introduction, I can't be sure." I answered.

"Why is that?" I was asked.

I said, "I don't know."

"Why were you at the home of their son?" she asked.

"Tia was ill and I was told she was calling for me," I answered.

"Did you help Tia?" she asked, pointing to Tia.

I said, "I think so."

"Let me understand this. You were in their son's house and helped their sick granddaughter and they did not acknowledge you?" continued the attorney.

I repeated, "Not to my knowledge, but my mind was on Tia as was everyone else's."

"Mr. J.," continued the attorney. "You have been charged with controlling the minds of Beth and Tia. What is your response?"

"Well if offering them love and affection is considered mind controlling, I guess I'm guilty." I responded.

After a recess the attorney continued and said, "Mr. J. you have also been accused of being a charlatan and after Mrs. Armontt's money. Are you after Mrs. Len Armontt's money?"

I don't think so!" I answered.

"How did you happen to be in the hospital suite with Mrs. Len Armontt?" questioned the attorney.

"Mrs. West told me that Tia was ill and Ronnie Armontt was in a bad way. I asked if they were at home. She responded that they were in the hospital. I told her to get my limo and have my 'copter ready," was my response.

"Then what?" asked the attorney?

"She told me that I would not need the 'copter because she had put them in the Children's Hospital."

"So you have a helicopter?"

I said, "Yes."

"It was noted in the paper that you live in a building in Manhattan. Is that correct Mr. J?"

"Yes," was my answer.

"Where do you live in that building?"

"In the penthouse," I answered.

"You mentioned a limo. Do you own it?"

I said, "Yes."

"Do you by any chance own the building you live in?"

I answered, "Yes."

"Is that the only building you own?"

I answered "No."

How many buildings here in Manhattan would you say you own?"

"For the moment, eight," I answered.

"Does that mean you may sooner or later own other buildings?"

"It's likely," I responded.

"Are these small buildings?"

"I suppose so!" I answered.

"Come now Mr. J., aren't those buildings among the largest buildings in Manhattan?"

I said, "I guess you could say that some are?" "Now, Mr. J., is real estate your only source of income?"

I looked at the judge. He nodded his head to answer. I said, "No;"

"Is another source the stock market?" I answered, "Yes."

The attorney said, "In fact I understand that your earnings from stocks are in the multimillions. Is that correct?"

Once again I looked at the judge, who nodded for me to answer. I responded, "Perhaps."

"I have but a few more questions to ask. Mr. J., have you donated something to the city?"

I looked at the judge and said, "Judge!"

He said, "Answer the question JM."

I said softly, "Yes."

"We can't hear you! Would you speak up." said the attorney.

I answered, "Yes!"

"What was it that you donated to the city?"

Again I looked at the Judge. He urged me to answer loud enough to be heard. I said, "The Children's Hospital," and hung my head.

The attorney continued, "Not only did he donate the hospital, the hospital was completely furnished and also included some of the first year's salaries. I ask you again Mr. J., Are you after Mrs. Len Armontt's money?"

I said. "No!"

The attorney said, "The defense rests."

The prosecuting attorney started to get up, but Mr. Armontt grabbed his arm. They withdrew the complaint. Ronnie hugged and thanked the attorneys and ran to me and threw her arms around my neck and kissed me. Tia and Beth had already been hugging and kissing me with the judge looking on. I asked the judge if I could see him in his chambers after he had changed. The judge watched as Tia looking at her grandparents, went to them, took them by the hand and led them to her mother and me.

"What is this hold that you have on my granddaughters? What have you done to them? They used to love us. Now you have taken them away from us. What kind of magic or brainwashing have you used on them?" asked Mr. Armontt.

Unaware that the judge was listening in, I answered, "You may call it magic, mind controlling or brainwashing, and maybe that's what love is, but I repeat, all I offered them was love, kindness and myself."

"Are you insinuating that we didn't offer them love?" Mr. Armontt shouted?

"No sir, I'm only speaking of myself. I know nothing about you, except what I have seen in the last couple of weeks. And I have not taken them away from you and they still love you as Tia has just demonstrated, even though you are trying to separate them from their mother, whom they love very much, which is the worst thing you could do. I believe that if I had been trying to destroy their love for you, I would have destroyed their love for me."

Mrs. Armontt walked over to me and put her arms around me and said, "Whatever it is between you and the girls I thank you for what you have done for Tia. She is now like I had always hoped she'd be."

Mr. Armontt reached out his hand and I accepted it. "I apologize," said Mr. Armontt. "I have seen and heard something here today that I shall not forget. I thank you for being a friend to my son and to his family."

Mrs. Armontt hugged me again and said, "Show us how to be part of what you have here."

I said, "Australia is a long way off! We're all going back to finish our vacation."

The girls began to jump for joy. "We would love to have you come along."

The girls still jumping for joy, yelled, "Yea, yea, yea!" The Armontts accepted.

The judge invited me back to his chamber. I thanked him for what had done. He told me I owed him no thanks. He told me that he would be indebted to me for the rest of his life. I told him that if he felt he owed me anything, it had been repaid by giving me what would be my family.

He said, "JM you gave my son back to me four times. I could never repay you for that, end of conversation. By the way, that was marvelous the way you handled Stan Armontt. My son is right about you. You know how to handle men. You would make a wonderful judge. Now call in that family of yours I want to meet them especially that darling little one."

When we left the judge's chambers we all seven of us, headed back to Jamaica. On the Lear both girls were sitting with me and looking out the window.

I whispered to Beth, "Go over and sit with your grandparents for a while and when you come back, Tia will go over and sit with them for a while." They both took turns sitting with their grandparents who enjoyed having them.

Ronnie whispered, "I love you," in my ear.

I whispered, "Will you marry me?" in her ear and kissed her to muffle her response. I told her I did not want it known as yet. "I will explain later."

She whispered, "Yes my love! Yes!" She could not get the smile off her face. Later I told her I wanted her in-laws to spend some time around us to see how we were together before we let them in on the news. I asked Ronnie if she could keep that to herself and Jamie. She threw her arm around my neck, said yes and that she thought I was a genius.

We all had a great time at the resort. When we left the resort I told the pilot to head for Ranceville. As we circled Ranceville the girls began to jump for joy! They made a beeline for their grandparents and were pointing out the horses. They were so excited their grandparents momentarily forgot that the girls were afraid of horses. We took the 'copter from the airport to Ranceville and took the Club car to the house to meet the Rosses.

Jamie had informed them about Len's death. They offered their sympathy and welcomed the Armontts and told how Len had become one of their adopted children. They said how they always loved to see the girls. They explained how Ronnie and Jamie were their adopted daughters and Beth and Tia, who were showing them plenty of love, were their granddaughters.

Mr. and Mrs. Ross suggested that they show the Armontts around Ranceville. I thought it was a great idea. Mr. Ross enjoyed driving the Club car so the four of them got into the Club car and starting with Rance, Mr. and Mrs. Ross gave them a guided tour.

Mr. Ross loved telling the story about Rance and me and how we became his family as a result, along with Jamie, Ronnie, Len and the girls. The Armontts were so touched that Mrs. Armontt cried. She told them what they had first thought of me. Mr. Ross told her how much her son had come to love me. Mr. Ross later showed them the rest of the ranch via the 'copter.

Mrs. Armontt later came to me and reached for both of my hands. Holding my hands she said, "Thank you for allowing my son to be a part of your life and all this. Mr. Ross told us how much Len loved this place and you.

He said that Len told him that you did him a big favor by telling him that he needed to stop spending all his time making money and spend some time with his family. Len never told us about any of this and knowing how we felt about you, I understand why." With tears in her eyes she hugged and kissed me on the cheek.

The girls were anxious get to the horses. They wanted so much for their grandparents to see their horses. As their grandparents watched from the grandstand, the girls and I went to the stables. The Armontts were telling the Rosses that their granddaughters were afraid of horses. Mr. Ross said not any more, and told them to watch. Much to the surprise of the Armontts the girls came into the corral each leading their own horse. The girls each removed the lead rope and let their horse run free in the corral.

When the girls walked out into the center of the ring while the horses were running and kicking their legs, both Mr. and Mrs. Armontt quickly arose from their chairs. Mr. Ross calmly assured them that the girls were all right. The Armontts sat back down and watched as the girls waited for their horses to get their exercise. Each girl then called her respective horse. Their horses came and nuzzled the girls as they fondly petted them. Each girl tapped the left leg of her horse, which bowed down. Beth was able to climb aboard without help, but I had to give Tia a boost up. The girls rode around the corral bareback holding only a handful of their horses' manes.

The Armontts were standing and applauding. Mrs. Armontt's hands went from applause to over her mouth in disbelief. The girls dismounted and raced to the gate of the corral as the Armontts hurried down the stairs from the grandstand to greet them.

Hugging the girls fondly Mrs. Armontt said she could not believe her eyes. Holding the girls close to her she looked at me and said, "Thanks, you are absolutely amazing!" Mr. Armontt was just shaking his head. He just reached out and shook my hand.

I thought I might have seen the start of a tear in his eye. He just bent down and hugged the girls for a long time. Ronnie walked over to me put her arms around my neck and kissed me tenderly and said "yes." I smiled. I looked up at the Rosses and they were smiling and nodding in agreement. Ronnie had told them that I had asked her to marry me.

The girls then turned and ran to hug their mother. After their mother, they stood looking at me and then ran and jumped in my arms. I told them how proud I was of them. Then I reminded them of their horses. They deserved some love too, I reminded them.

"You forgot to introduce them!" I told the girls. They went over to the fence where their grandparents were standing and called their horses. They introduced their horses to their grandparents, had them take a bow and throw their grandparents a kiss. You should have seen the look on the faces of the Armontts when the girls had their horses execute those two exercises. One cannot describe the joy on their faces and, I imagine, the pride in their hearts.

The girls then ran back to me and asked if I was going to exercise Bandito.

I said, "Not today little ones. The next time we come out."

They said, "But we wanted them, our grandparents, to see Bandito!"

I said, "We have to save something for them to see the next time they come, don't we?" The girls agreed. That of course, aroused the curiosity of the Armontts. They wanted to know who Bandito was. I told them that would cost them another trip.

I said, "A bribe to get you out here again. Besides the two of you are great company for our parents, the Rosses."

The Armontts laughed and said sometimes bribes were not necessary. They turned to the Rosses and said, "It will be a pleasure to come the next time we come, and an honor if we can come visit by ourselves!" The Rosses responded that their door would always be open to them. I reminded the girls not to forget to reward their horses in the excitement. They hurried and got apples; I broke them and they gave them to their horses, again to the amazement of the Armontts.

On the flight back to New York, the girls sat with their grandmother and Mr. Armontt and I sat together. He was so impressed with Ranceville and the Rosses he just had to talk to me about them. He mentioned how the Rosses thought so highly of me, and how I had become such a part of their life. He mentioned how devastated the Rosses were when they thought they had lost both my friend Mike and I.

He said, "You are the son they never had. And you and your horse Rance, have been a blessing to them and brought so much joy in their lives. People come by just to look, see and hear about you and Rance. They told us, that because of you they are not alone anymore. They have a large family now and wish that we would join that family. Have you any idea how that makes us feel?

Mr. Ross showed me how you have expanded Ranceville and built on to their house so that they can go all the way to the stable and the 'copter port without being exposed to the elements. We loved that moving conveyor you provided for them with the start and stop buttons and he truly loves that roustabout you put there. I see now, that there's a lot of love in you! I hope you will invite us here again soon."

I said, "You are invited to come any time we come. The girls love to come often."

Tia came over, kissed her grandfather, and climbed in my lap and began to fall off to sleep. "She certainly loves you!" said Mr. Armontt. "I can even understand that now! I also know now what you meant by just giving them love. I suppose everything responds to love." I said, "Yes, everything that God made." Beth came and curled between the window and me and put her arms around my neck.

"I see now that I don't have to worry about them any more," said Mr. Armontt. "Thank you Jay!" He moved over and sat with his wife and pointed back at the girls. They both smiled.

When the plane landed, we took limos to our respective residences. Ronnie and the girls were still staying at the hospital because the girls were not ready to go back to the mansion as yet. Ronnie called as soon as she had bathed and put the girls to bed. She wanted to know when I would let the world know that I had asked her to marry me? I said, "Soon my love soon."

# Jay Tells Ronnie What He Didn't Tell Jamie

I got a call from a builder who needed money. We made a deal on a piece of property that I had a desire to acquire. It took about two week to get him to come to terms.

Jamie came into the apartment and said, "That was a great closing you made on that piece of property. You have had your eye on it for a long time. He was tying to work you but you showed him why they say you are hard to beat and yet he didn't leave feeling he was a loser."

I told Jamie, "I like win, win situations."

She hugged me and said, "That's what I love about you. You never take advantage!"

Jamie left and I was preparing to take a shower when the phone rang. I answered and Ronnie said, "Hi man of my life."

"Hello beautiful eyes to what do I owe this pleasure?" I responded.

"The fact that I haven't heard from you in almost two weeks."

"Wait a minute, I have talked to you a number of times in the past two weeks." I said,

"Right! You have heard from me but I have not heard from you." She responded,

I hung up and called her right back.

She answered and asked, "JM did you just hang up on me?"

I said, "How else would I be able to call you? Now you have heard from me. So what's with the JM?"

She said, "From now on when I am angry with you, you are JM."

I said, "So you are angry with me, huh?"

She said, "Yes, because I love making up with you! Are you still busy with that deal you and Jamie are working on?" I told her that we had just completed the deal.

Ronnie replied, "Great because I need to talk to you. You can either come here or I can come there but I would rather come there."

I asked, "Why?"

She said, "Because I love being there with you and it feels so intimate and cozy and here, I guess, well I guess it's the ghost." Ronnie and the girls had moved back to the mansion. I chuckled.

She said, "Jay don't laugh, I mean it. That's what I feel."

I said, "I know love! I know exactly what you mean. I want to talk to you too. When do you want to come over?"

She said, "Tomorrow if you are available."

I said, "I am yours to command! Why don't we plan to have dinner with Jamie and the girls and we can talk later. I'll ask Jamie if she is available tomorrow."

Ronnie said, "No Jay! Let me ask Jamie. I want to talk to her anyway. By the way I think you want Jamie and the girls along because you are afraid to be alone with me."

I said, "Boy! There's a brain above those shoes you wear."

She laughed and said, "Goodnight my heartthrob."

I said, "Goodnight love."

The next day after dinner, Jamie and the girls went shopping and to a movie. Ronnie turned down the music. I had been listening to "This Magic Moment." She started to turn it down lower, but then began to listen to the words and said, "Jay that's a beautiful song I haven't listened to the words before."

I told her, "It has a lot of meaning."

She asked, "Why were you listening to it?"

I told her, "Because it says all the things I want to say to you and what I feel inside for you?"

She started the song over and said, "Dance with me Jay!"

We danced to the song over and over again. Then she played the song "My Special Prayer" buried her head in my chest and we just danced.

Softly she said, "After you had gone away and we thought you had gone for good my heart was shattered. Whenever Len was away I would come here play this song and stand and look out that window as you always did. I knew then what you were really feeling. I prayed for you to come back. I promised that I would never act selfishly again. I felt so guilty being here praying for you to return to me. And then when Len was killed that is what almost destroyed me. I felt that it was my fault."

I tried to stop her tears. I just held her close. I whispered softly "You cannot control fate. What will be, will be!"

She was quiet for a long time. Then she said, "Jay, you don't know how I feel when I kiss you now, or when you hold me in your arms. I used to feel so guilty and now I can truly love you freely."

I kissed her without guilt also. "Can you now understand how I felt when you wanted me to be with you," I asked?

Her eyes continued to tear as she answered, "Oh my love how I have hurt you!" and she drew her body closer to me.

She turned the music down low, kissed me softly and said, "Jay, you promised to tell me about those horrible years. I know you have told it before but I want to hear it from you and I have a lot of questions. I hope you want to tell me about it but if you don't I'll understand."

* * * *

Jay walked over to the window and began to look out into the evening. I began to worry that I had asked the wrong thing. I walked up to him and put my arms around him, and lay my head against his back and apologized to him for asking.

He turned around, lifted my face and said, "These eyes are too beautiful for tears," but he just kissed my lips softly.

He sat down with me and said, "You of all people deserve to hear it from me. You said you have questions. What do you want to know?"

I said, "I want to know why they left you out there? Why didn't you tell that man what he wanted to know rather that go though all that pain? How did you survive all that torture?"

Jay looked at me for a while, smiled, kissed me softly, stood up, stared out the window again, and then he turned to me and began to speak.

"I'll start from when I was wounded, he said.

I had gotten to Mike and verified that he and Charlie Gates were dead. I could not leave them there so I beckoned for one man to come from the chopper so we could bring both men back. S/Sgt Arnett came himself. I told him he should have sent one of the other men because I had ordered him to get the other men out of there. He responded, 'you have trained all of us to be leaders. I left someone else in charge.'

I helped to get Gates loaded onto his shoulders and told him to get him to the chopper and no matter what happened get the men out of there and to be sure each one got that next stripe. I kept watch while he headed for the chopper. When he was near the chopper I hoisted Mike on my shoulder to get him to the chopper. I rose to leave. I don't remember anything else. They said they saw what looked like my whole body exploded. They said that just after the chopper lifted off, a mortar hit right where the chopper had been. That's why it's necessary to obey orders and S/Sgt Arnett was ordered to get those men out of there. I was unconscious for three weeks. They were not sure if I would live. They wanted to give up on me but a certain interrogator insisted that they continue to try. You see they had found out that my group was the one they had been looking for and trying to capture. We were marked men and I was number one. They pulled me through even though a large portion of my side had been blown away. I was told that the heat from the shell that hit Mike and me cauterized my wound and limited the bleeding. You see I was blessed because most of the shell hit Mike's thighs and took my flesh. There were a lot of skin grafts. My healing was a long process. They fed me well trying to get me strong enough to withstand interrogation.

It took over a year. Finally, one morning, this interrogator had me brought to a lab. He had a reputation of never having failed to get information out of a man. He was ruthless. He started off nice and kind. I would only give my name rank and serial number. Then he began to turn up the heat. He was a high-ranking individual so he could do anything he wanted. He believed that I had special information because my unit was so successful in our raids. He was trying to get the names of all the men in my group. He tried everything, every kind of terrible torture including a hot pin under the fingernails"—Jay showed me his nails—"nothing worked and after two years of interrogation they were ordered to turn over all the prisoners.

We figured we had made it because we were going to be released. They released the sickly ones and a few healthy ones, but most of those who remained were shot. He shot some right on the spot and had others taken out and shot.

He pointed to the dead men and indicated that would happen to the four of us who were left. He thought that the other three men were part of my group. I told them to tell him that they were not as I had. But they refused to give him the satisfaction.

The next five years he continued his relentless pursuit of information. I always prayed and tried to keep you in the forefront of my mind. I asked God to help me to always keep the picture of you in my mind. The more he tried the harder I tried to keep you in my mind. Whatever he did I kept you there. I think we were wearing him out because he would have to take a break now and then. So we were left alone for a few days.

For two of those years he had tried brain washing, but when that didn't work, he said we would know the meaning of torture. He used to move us around so that they could not find us. For the next three years, he seemed to enjoy toying with us. He had begun to mess around with my side. He would push in on my side until I would yell. I would try not to, but the pain was more than I could bear. When I passed out he would send me back and bring in the others. He finally realized that they didn't have any information, but I think he just used them to keep in practice trying to see what would make them yell the loudest . . ."

I had my hands over my face but Jay could see the teardrops falling from my hand. He told me that I had heard enough.

But I pleaded for him to continue. "I want to know it all!" I said. Jay continued:

"As soon as I was conscious again he would bring me back in. He had no set time for me. I was his pet project. He wanted the information he knew I had. He had to make me talk. He had gotten all he could out of the others but he needed someone to pick on when I was unable to be tortured. He would bring me in morning, noon and night. Anytime he felt the urge he would bring me in. He knew my side was my weak spot so he constantly poked at it. He would hit it with his fist, a stick, an iron pipe or anything. He cracked one of my ribs, so he found that pushing in on it was the best so he constantly pushed . . ."

"Stop! Stop! Stop!" I cried, tears flowing like a faucet. "Oh my love why didn't you just tell him what he wanted to know? Why did you go through that punishment?"

"I will only answer that question for you love. No one else must know this and you may not love me after this, but you must know."

"We were returning from a patrol when we heard voices. Men were yelling commands at people. We crept up and saw soldiers with a lot of villagers on their knees and were about to shoot them. We quickly and quietly surrounded them and on signal suddenly, quickly and quietly killed all the soldiers. We rescued all the villagers and took them back with us. We found out that the soldiers had already killed half of the villagers and were about to kill the rest them. I killed the officer who had his pistol against the head of one of the villagers whose wife and two sons were in that group.

He was very grateful and told me what was going on. He told me that the soldiers were killing all the people in villages and putting other enemy families and people in the villages as though they were the original inhabitants. So that when our small patrols came along they would welcome them into the village, then catch them off guard and kill them all and bury their bodies. That explained why some of our patrols of four to six men were disappearing without a trace. We needed proof to take to the C.O. I asked this person if he knew where any of our men were buried. He and a person from another village showed us two villages where this had happened and the graves they had found. We dug up some of the graves and removed the dog tags we found on the bodies. When we showed the dog tags to the C.O. and explained where we got them and about the incidents, which had occurred in the surrounding villages, he ordered us to completely destroy any of those villages.

The two villagers volunteered to get us information on the villages where these atrocities had occurred, or where they were taking place, and we would intervene if we could get to them before any of the villagers were killed. The two informants grew to seven and they fed us the information. Sometimes we were able to catch the enemy before they killed the native villagers. Other times we were shown where they had buried the villagers. So our raids were in enemy territory and involved destroying those enemy villages. This is why we were marked men. We were destroying the enemy's well-laid plans to take over villages and kill our patrols. This is the information that Mr. Ni wanted: How did we know what villages to target? How were we going undetected? How were we able to get away with it?"

I said, "This is what you meant when you told Len that you have made many men disappear."

"Yes, I was given the task of destroying all of the known villages once I had proof. You see we had even seen young children in those enemy families kill the occupants of the villages they were taking over, so the whole village had to go.

In order to escape, I had each man in the unit to pick a surrounding plant, shrub, bush or some part of the landscape where he could quickly and easily camouflage himself. When a village was destroyed, we were sometimes a long way away and disguised. Other times they would begin an immediate search and sometimes they would be walking right by us. We would be spread out and if it was a small group, we would sometimes spring from ambush and quickly and quietly kill them and move on. So you see we were driving them nuts. Now you understand why I couldn't tell him anything. Ni wanted this information so badly, it got him killed.

What do you think of your lover now?" Jay asked.

"Oh Jay, that was war! You did what you were ordered and had to do. Look at the lives you saved. Baby I am so proud of you."

"You asked how I survived. Well I wanted to see you again and I had promised to come back to you. I prayed a lot. Then I began to think about you, Lori, Loren and Jamie. Then I found that I could concentrate on you so hard that I wouldn't feel anything. Early in those five years I could only see your face but it was enough. Then I got to the point that I would sort of go into a trance and we would be in this garden. It was a huge garden with a lot of trees, all kinds of plants and pretty flowers and a beautiful gazebo with climbing roses. I later saw that garden at your home. I don't know how I was able to see it before but I saw it and you were there.

The first time in the garden I was standing under your window calling you and you came out. You were coming towards me, and then suddenly you turned and ran away. The other times you came out and we would sit in the gazebo, sometimes you would lay your head against my chest, or you would lay your head in my lap and sometimes times I would just hold you. That's how I was able to escape the pain. It infuriated Mr. Ni.

Then one day they pulled a surprise visit and found the other three guys. I suppose Mr. Ni must have crossed someone and they squealed. But he had always kept me separated, and hidden, so they didn't find me. They warned him if there were any more he had better give them up. After that he got really mean and was constantly bringing me in and out of the torture room but I was spending more and more time with you so I didn't care. It had become me against his pride. He had to break me. He kept after my side. My body was getting weaker and weaker. This went on for about three-and-a-half years according to my homemade calendar."

I put my arms around Jay's neck and said, "That's enough my love. It is too hard for me to take." My face was totally wet.

Jay said, "No love you may as well hear it all. It is almost finished."

"Then one night I was very weak. I didn't think I could hold out any longer I desperately needed you. I was calling your name but you wouldn't come. That's when I felt in my spirit that you had said, 'No more!'"

When Jay said that, I fell to my knees and began to cry uncontrollably.

Jay said, "Now I know I must stop," and he lifted me up and put his arms around me and said, "All right my love you have heard enough." He kissed me and wiped my face and assured me that it was all right.

I cried a bit longer and said, "It's important that you go on my love."

Jay asked, "Are you sure?"

"Yes, it's important." I said,

Jay continued where he had left off. "Since I couldn't reach you, my strength and my desire to live began to wane. For the next fifteen or twenty months I felt myself slipping away, but something was telling me to hold on. I kept calling you for help. Then I thought of Jamie. I began to call for her. I seemed to be able to hold her hand. This helped me to hang on even though my body was giving out. I believe the other guys must have told them about me because I remember hearing them saying 'we know he's here' and then they found me. Then they shot Mr. Ni. They took me somewhere. That's the last I remember until I woke up with my uncle Jim looking over me. They said that I had been that way for two months. I remember dreaming during that time that I was still holding Jamie's hand."

When Jay finished, I was still crying. I put my arms around his neck and held him so tight that he told me I was choking him. I released him and apologized.

"What is wrong my love? You are trembling like a leaf." he asked me.

I was silent for a while. Jay started to say something, but I said, "I have to tell you something, but I'm afraid I may lose you!"

Jay told her, "If you can still have me after the kind of person I told you I have been, you won't lose me!"

I said, "The last night when you called me and could not reach me, you said, that's when you felt in your spirit that I had said, 'No more!' Oh my love I know now, how right you were about our spirits being tied together. I was there in that garden with you every time you called. I looked forward to and waited for your call. I did everything you said I did. I wanted to be there with you, but there is another spirit that is tied to you."

"I don't understand," Jay said, puzzled.

"You will in a few minutes," I told him. "You see my love that night that you tried to reach me, that is exactly what I said. 'No more.' And I said more than that. Jay I had been neglecting my husband whenever you called me. There were times he wanted to make love to me and I would respond to your call because I would rather be out in the garden with you. That night when I said, 'No more' and stayed with him and I told you to leave me alone, that was the night that Tia was conceived. But even though I stayed with him I was wishing I were with you. Tia is tied to your spirit too. That is why she gravitated to you, a stranger, when she was afraid of every other man."

Jay listened dumbfounded. He got up and went to the window and stared into the late evening.

I continued. "You brought back to mind high school and college. I had forgotten how we seemed to know what the other was feeling or sometimes thinking. You are right. Our spirits have always been tied together. I realize now that my fear of losing you had paralyzed my mind and turned me into a horrible, jealous individual." I went and put my arms around him and said, "Can you ever forgive me? I let you down when you really needed me. You had to turn to Jamie. She deserves you not me. She has always been there for you when you needed her. Even now."

Jay turned and put his arms around me and said, "Silly girl! It's you I love! You were there for me for when I needed you for over five years. For all that time I could see you as clear as day. That's how I knew your size. You had given me enough. You neglected your husband all those years. He needed and deserved you that night. I love you woman. Will you stop trying to give me to someone else! As for Tia, you are right. The day that Jamie called to tell me about Tia, I was out riding and just before the ranch hand rode up to tell me about the phone call I felt that Tia was calling me."

At that moment I felt Jay wanted to make love to me but he did not say anything. We just held each other and we seem to meld into one.

Later, I asked, "Jay are you ashamed for me to see your body. I know what I saw on TV but I hope that you don't think that I would be offended. I love you, all of you. Remember that, will you? When you feel like it I want you to show me where you were wounded."

Jay held me at arm's length and looked hard into my eyes. I hoped he would see the love that I had for him in them. After a while he let go of me and began to unbutton his shirt. He raised his undershirt and looking away toward the ceiling he stood there. I was watching him. I had not yet looked at his wound. I slowly lowered my eyes and what I saw was more graphic than on

TV. At that moment the doctor's words came to mind, 'Take a good look at his wound and you will know how much he loves you.'

'How could he have lived like this?' was my thought. I knew then that there was a greater force watching over this man. I raised my hand and touched the area. I ran my hand gently over the complete area, which went from just under his left nipple area down to his waist, from almost to his belly button to just under the backside of his left armpit to his waist. His whole left side!

I moved up close to him and touched his side with both hands and pressed my lips to his wounded side. I then reached and held his face in my hands, pulled his face towards me and kissed his sweet lips so tenderly.

I pulled his undershirt down and said, "Thank you." There were tears in his eyes. I said, "My love I am not ashamed of your body. Don't you ever be! I don't believe anyone has given more for his country than you have. I know your great love for me and I will always love you." I began to button his shirt, but he lowered his head and finished buttoning it himself and said,

"Some guys gave their lives." I kissed the tears in his eyes.

He said, "It looks as bad as it does because they had to cut away a lot of the tissue because it was burned." I hugged him close and said, "I know how painful it must be for you love, but we will bear it together from now on."

* * * *

For a while I did not want to look her in the eye.

She lifted my chin and said, "Jay look into my eyes. Do you believe that I love you?

I answered, "Yes."

She asked, "Do you believe that I am not offended by the look of your body… I ask you Jay, do you believe that? I need to know that you believe that!"

She was looking into my face. I raised my eyes to meet hers. I looked deep into those beautiful eyes and I could see to the depth of her.

I said, "I, I, I am the one that is embarrassed not you."

She put her arms around me and laid her head against my side and said, "Oh my love never ever be embarrassed or ashamed with me. I want you to love me right now, but I know you won't. Now what was it you said you had to tell me?"

* * * *

# Big Outing at Ranceville

I sat down and she sat in my lap and put her arms around my neck just like Beth and Tia.

After a period of time I was able to say, "I plan to close a couple of business deals in the next two weeks. After that, I want to throw a huge Bar-B-Que at Ranceville. I want to invite the entire group; you know, the old gang, all the neighbors and people who come to visit Ranceville. I want you to invite the Armontts, your family, especially Alice.

Ronnie looked questioningly at me, and said, "Alice?"

I said, "Yes, I think about her a lot."

Ronnie said, "That's strange. She always asks about you."

I said, "I want my family there. And anyone else you wish to invite. Invite everyone— and since Jamie and I will be busy, I hope that I can impose upon you to handle the whole thing. Maybe you and the girls can go to Ranceville and supervise the entire operation. You know any decorations you desire. Get the Rosses involved. Hire anyone you need to have it the way you would like to see it. I know the hands would love to get involved. I don't need to tell you what to do. I would like to ask if you would care to do that?" Ronnie sat there looking at me with her mouth open.

She suddenly threw her arms around my neck and said, "Oh Jay I would love to do that. I have always wished I could do something with or for you. I have been so jealous of Jamie always being able to work with you. Not an angry jealousy, just a wishful jealousy. I know that the girls are really going to enjoy this. I already have ideas formulating in my mind. Thank you darling for the opportunity. I can hardly wait to get started. Is there a set day and time you want this to happen?" I said, "Other than taking into consideration that people will be working, use your own judgment. Just let me know the date and time."

We danced and talked until Jamie and the girls came home. Ronnie's favorite song now was "My Special Prayer." She would stay close to me with her head laid against my chest. Ronnie told the girls about our plans and asked if they wanted to help. They screamed with joy.

I suggested that they spend the night. This really got them screaming and I got hugs galore. I told Ronnie that I understood about ghosts and suggested that if it bothered her and the girls to stay at the mansion, they could stay at the penthouse. There was plenty of room. Jamie had mentioned that she did not think they should be staying at the mansion by themselves and we had plenty of room here. You should have heard the joy that came out of the three of them and Jamie.

Ronnie really enjoyed herself the next two week. I had never seen her and the girls so happy. They were going to and from Ranceville in the limo, the Lear and the 'copter. She had the Rosses and the girls involved in creating ads for the newspaper and creating posters and fliers. She made sure the Rosses approved everything she did even though they kept telling her that what ever choices she made was OK with them. They were just so pleased to have her and the girls there; they could have done anything they wanted. The hands were elated to have a big outing at Ranceville. They had their wives and kids out helping to get the place ready. Everyone seemed excited. Even neighbors and visitors stopped by to help. Ronnie and the girls were a big hit at Ranceville anyway.

Ronnie and the Rosses pored over the menu constantly. Ronnie even got input from the hands and their wives and kids as to what should be on the menu, and she asked the neighbors and visitors what would be the best day and time. They had two dates and they discussed and voted on it to iron that out. Everyone was so pleased that they were asked to be involved. When everything was set Ronnie told me the date and time and I made a special phone call.

The day of the Bar-B-Que people came from all over. There was a large vacant lot half a block away, which was great for the extra parking. Most of the gang from the canteen and skating rink showed up. Some had been to Ranceville before, but most had not. They were thrilled to meet the Rosses and the Rosses added them to their ever-growing family.

The Rosses asked, "Jay why haven't you had this whole group out here before?" The gang was such a fun-loving group that the Rosses and everyone couldn't help but love them. They bawled Ronnie out for not getting them involved in the setup.

People who came to Ranceville for the first time were absolutely amazed. Everyone fell in love immediately with Rance. There were so many people around the statue you could hardly see it.

The big surprise was Angie and her crew from the TV station. She said, "How could you think that I would miss an event like this especially if you have something to do with it? I came to enjoy myself; thanks for the invite. I brought along my camera people just in case and from the looks of things I'm glad I did."

I said, "Well don't leave before you check with me. You just might miss something important."

"Jay now you know you couldn't pry me away from here now! Where would be a good spot for me to have my camera people set up," she asked? I showed her a spot that would allow coverage of everything.

I had limos pick up Aunt Loren, Lori, Jamie and her family. The Armontts, and Mrs. T. were leered and 'coptered in. Ronnie wanted to pick up her family herself. I had someone announcing who arrived in each limo that pulled up. There was a thundering roar that went up when they announced my mother, Aunt Loren, my sister Lori, and my best friend and business partner Jamie and her family. The Armontts received a loud ovation when they were announced as Ronnie's in-laws. Mrs. T. was announced as "Mrs. Fashion our big city mom." They loved her. I had the announcer give her store a big plug. I also asked Angie to plug her store.

When Ronnie and her family arrived the roar was deafening. They absolutely loved Ronnie and the girls. The visitors wanted so to meet her family. Alice was with them.

Ronnie had hired some clowns and had all kind of games set up for the kids. There were pony rides, cotton candy, candy apples, drinks, hot dogs, hamburgers, and two types of popcorn (buttered and caramel). The meal consisted of steaks, ribs, brisket, chicken, hot dogs, hamburgers, corn on the cob, baked beans, potato salad, green beans, slaw, green salad, pickles, tomatoes, onions and garlic bread. The catering service was outstanding. They cooked and barbecued the meats on the premises. Wow, the aroma! Everything was done in a very orderly way. Ronnie had done a marvelous job.

There were plenty of Ranceville booklets to go around. I had added some pictures of the girls, their dad and their ponies and wow were the girls tickled.

Ronnie and Jamie were being swamped for autographs and the girls weren't doing badly either.

Mr. and Mrs. Ross welcomed all the people and told them about Ranceville. At the end Mr. Ross introduced me as the owner of Rance. When he said 'Jay McFadden', the place went wild. A lot of people had seen me on TV but never in person. I told them a bit about Rance, how I got him and trained him. I pointed out that Jamie was Mike's wife. They gave Jamie a thunderous applause. Then I asked Ronnie to come up and told them how she had become such a part of Rance and me. I introduced Ronnie's girls Beth and Tia and then introduced the Armontts as their father's parents. There was of course special applause for Ronnie and her family! Ronnie punched me.

The girls were anxious to show their horses so I announced, "I now have a special treat for you and I know there will be some very proud grandparents out here to day. I would like the grandparents of these two especially talented young ladies Beth and Tia Armontt to stand up." Ronnie's mother and the Armontts stood up as the crowd applauded. Then I asked, "Will the adopted grandparents please stand up and join them?" Aunt Loren and the Rosses stood up. They were all seated in the grandstand. The crowd continued to applaud. Ronnie, the girls and I were standing on a platform that I had the hands put in the center of the corral. As the crowd was applauding, the hands let the girls' ponies into the ring. The girls hurried down off the platform as their ponies were running free kicking and jumping. The girls stood in the middle of corral away from the platform as the ponies galloped at high speeds pass them again and again. There was a hush in the audience seemingly with fear for the girls. Finally the ponies came to a walk and each went to its owner. The palomino went to Beth and the paint went to Tia. The ponies nuzzled the girls and the girls began their petting routine.

Then each girl began to work the guests. Each took their ponies around the arena and had their pony throw kisses to the audience. Tia started at one side of the corral and Beth started at the other each in a different direction. The audience and the grandparents were jubilant. They did the same with the ponies taking a bow. Each left their pony at the end of the corral and they walked to the other end. Their ponies stayed put. They each called their pony and their pony went to them. When their ponies reached them, they had their ponies lower their front legs and the girls climbed aboard. There was a little stand made so that Tia could mount without help. Watching the girls riding bareback holding just a handful of mane was a treat for the audience. The grandparents were on their feet beaming with pride. Ronnie put her arms around my waist and laid her head against my back. She asked, "Have I told you today that I love you?" She was so proud of the girls.

We left the stand and the girls got off their horses and ran to us with their arms out stretched. We both receive their hugs. They said, "I love you mommy and Uncle Jay!"

The girls fed each of their ponies an apple and the hands took the ponies back to the stables. The hands were introduced to the audience as much a part of Ranceville as we were. It was told that they were the ones who provided the plaque and who had named Ranceville.

The girls ran to their grandparents. The audience was still applauding as the hands removed the stand from the corral. The hands opened the gate to all the pastures except Bandito's pasture and I whistled through the megaphone and before long all the stallions except Bandito came galloping into the corral, Stars, Prince, and Royal showed their grace, strength and beauty as the audience let out loud gasps and 'oaths' and 'hash.' At that moment Mr. Ross identified each stallion and told the audience about the herd of each and that they were completely wild and would respond only to me. I called the three stallions to me and petted and hugged each. I had the three of them stay put while I retrieved the whip. I started back toward the horses, stopped and tossed the whip back towards the fence. I used my hand to tap the leg of each horse to have him bow. The audience was jubilant. I then raised my hands up and the three horses stood up. I stood in front of each horse in turn and had each one rear and walk on his hind legs to the pleasure of the audience.

Mr. Ross announced, "This young man never ceases to amaze me. He never uses the whip on any horse. He just uses it to do what he did with his hands today. He has never ridden any of these horses. Let's give a round of applause for Stars, Prince and Royal!" I broke and fed an apple to each horse and sent them back to their herds. The audience was elated by the beauty and performance of the stallions.

Mr. Ross then announced over the microphone, "Ladies and gentlemen, it's my pleasure to introduce Jay's new friend from Argentina, Bandito! He is part Andalusian and completely wild. Except for Jay, Bandito will not let anyone come near him. Recently Jay has only allowed his friend Ronnie, who was also, Rance's friend, to become friends with Bandito. Today Jay will exhibit what it is to have an animal completely trust you.

They opened the gate to Bandito's pasture. Bandito came charging in; running, kicking, snorting and showing his teeth, and making people back away from the fence. I stood in the corral as Bandito showed himself off. He was really letting off steam. There were 'oohs' and 'aahs' as he passed very close to me at high speed. I just stood still. Finally after he had run enough he walked over to me and nudged me with his nose. I petted him, rubbing his forehead and rubbed him all over. I walked around the corral as the girls had. I had a small mike attached to my lapel so the people could hear as I talked to Bandito. Bandito followed me around.

I asked Ronnie if she would come into the corral. She came in and walked up to Bandito, he nuzzled her and she began to pet him. She hugged him as he put his head over her shoulder. Mr. Ross was explaining what was going on. I left them and went to get an apple. Bandito stayed with Ronnie. I came back with the apple broke it and we each fed him a half. We walked to the gate and left the corral. Bandito followed us to the gate. Mr. Ross announced that in order to show that this horse was wild, others would attempt to enter the corral.

At the far end of the corral another two hands entered the corral. Bandito charged them with a vengeance. The audience let out 'ohhs' and 'ahhs' of fear each time he his charged. Mr. Ross announced that Jay would now give them a demonstration of trust. He would introduce two people to Bandito who had never been in there with him.

I told the audience that depending on the trust that a horse has in you, he would trust you not to bring anything or anybody that will harm him. I asked Tia if she wanted to make friends with Bandito. She answered, "Yes." I carried Tia into the corral and I called Bandito. He reared up a couple of times, came close but was a bit standoffish for a few minutes. I explained to the audience that Tia was new to him and he had to feel the air around her. I held out my hand and called to him. I told him, "This is my friend Tia. She would love to make friends with you." He came but just reached his head to my hand. When he felt safe he walked up to me. Tia began to pet and scratch his head and the side of his face. I told the audience that he was realizing that Tia meant him no harm.

I put Tia down to the gasping of the audience. She began to pet Bandito all over as I walked along with her. She went all around him. Tia got an apple and gave it to him. She told him she loved him. The same thing happened with Beth. I told the audience that when a horse realizes he can trust you, you have a friend. Trust takes a while. I said "He will trust the girls now because I trust them and he can sense their sincerity." Beth was feeding Bandito an apple and I walked out of the corral. He walked over to the gate. I told the audience he came over to me but he trusted having Tia and Beth in the corral with him.

I re-entered the corral, thanked the girls, and started walking around the corral with Bandito following. I stopped occasionally and asked him to throw kisses to the ladies. I saw a young lady in the audience. I told Bandito to throw her a kiss and he did. Then I told him to tell her to come over here motioning my head to the side as if to beckon, come here. Bandito began to toss his head the same way. The guest applauded and the young lady smiled but she didn't come.

I said, "I think she is afraid of you, Bandito." I asked the young lady, "Are you afraid of him?"

She nodded, "Yes!"

I asked Bandito, "Should she be afraid of you?" He shook his head no, as I had. I asked, "Will you let her rub your head?" Following my cue, he nodded, his head, yes. The audience applauded loudly. I asked her to come and pet him. She was reluctant, but came at the urging of the crowd.

I said, "Bandito lower your head so that the pretty lady can pet your head." He lowered his head. She hesitated and then reached and touched his head and then reached again and stroked his jaw and then she backed up a little.

I said, "Bandito how do you thank the lady?"

Bandito bowed. She smiled and the audience let out a roar.

Bandito lowered his left leg and I climbed on and rode around the corral for a short while. As I rode, Mr. Ross told the audience that Bandito had never had a saddle or bridle on him. After a short ride I hopped off Bandito and had him take a bow. During the applause Tia came into the ring and Bandito and I went over to her and she gave Bandito an apple. She walked away and I told Bandito to go with her. He followed her around the corral.

I said, "Ladies and gentlemen I give you Bandito and Tia!" A huge roar went up.

I sent Bandito back to his herd. As usual he started away then turned back, came over to me nudged me, and put his head over my shoulder, then headed back to his herd.

I said, "The show is over let's eat!"

The grandparents came rushing down from the grandstand highly excited and beaming with pride. Mrs. Armontt said her heart was in her mouth when the girls went in with Bandito.

She asked, "He is truly wild?"

I responded, "Absolutely!" Looking at me with tears in her eyes and shaking her head she just put her arms around me and hugged me.

Mr. Armontt just said, "You are truly amazing, thank you."

Everyone was well pleased with the food and really enjoyed Ranceville. There was still a lot of day left. There was dancing. I had hired a couple of extra 'copters, so the adults and the children could take 'copter rides to see the wild herds with Tia and Beth, of course, pointing and giving out information about the herds. Ronnie and Jamie were signing autographs and people were asking about Rance and me and what I would be doing with Bandito.

Angie came and pulled me away. She had a million and one questions. The number one question was, "What is this big secret I would miss if I left early?"

I looked at my watched and said, "It's about to happen shortly!"

She said, "Jay I have so much information from this outing—you, the girls, the families, talking to the visitors, the horses and Ranceville itself. Whatever could you do to upstage this?

I said, "Just keep looking up!" A plane began to fly overhead and then it began to write over and over again.

Suddenly, there was an outburst of yells and commotion from that happy-go-lucky group of my friends. They were pointing up at the plane writing in the sky. They were going crazy, dancing and hugging each other.

Angie looked up and pointing at the sky, yelled to her cameraman, "Get a shot of that!" Then people began looking up in the sky. Beth and Tia ran to Ronnie who was busy signing autographs. They told their mother that her name was in the sky. Ronnie looked up and saw the words, "Ronnie Will You Marry Me!" Everyone around her was shouting at her to say yes. Ronnie was so flabbergasted she could hardly speak.

Angie looked at me and said, "You sly fox you. I'm about to find out who numero uno is!"

I said, "You mean you don't already know?"

Her eyes lit up as she said, "Mrs. Armontt!"

I walked down to the corral and Bandito who had returned, came over and I began to rub his head and gave him a couple of carrots. The plane was still writing above. The old group began to pile around me hugging me and saying where is Ronnie?

I heard someone yelling, "Yes, Yes! Let me through!"

I turned and saw Ronnie hurrying through the crowd trying to get to me. The girls were right on her heels followed by the guest for whom she had been signing her autograph.

They made a path for Ronnie and she hit me at a full run. I thought we were going to go through the corral fence. Her arms were around my neck, her lips all over my face, and her tears flowing like wine. The families were on their feet and Angie had the camera rolling. She and the cameraman had followed Ronnie all the way.

Angie shook her head and said, "The love in that Man!" The guests were going wild. The girls were hugging us both. Ronnie was saying, "You never cease to amaze me Jay McFadden."

I said, "Well at least it isn't JM!"

She said, "I—love—you!"

Finally we were able to get up to the family in the grandstand. They were elated. Aunt Loren and Lori were beside themselves.

Lori said. "It was a long way around but all's well that ends well," and hugged Ronnie.

Ronnie's mother put her arms around me and said, "We lost you but thank God we have you back my son." She kissed me on the cheek as I hugged her closely.

The Armontts said, "I think you already know what we think about you. Welcome to the family."

The Rosses were bubbling over and said, "We have been praying for this. We love you both so much. Now we are really a family!"

Jamie and her family were also happy for us. Jamie's mother said, "The only way I could be happier is if it was happening to my family. Jay you know what I have always thought of you. You have always been special to my baby and have done so much for her!"

I said, "Really she is the one that been taking care of me. I don't know what I'd do without her."

I had to talk to Jamie alone. When we got a chance, I said, "OK love now that it has finally happened how do you really feel?"

She said, "I've loved you as long as I've known you. I've always hoped that one day it would be us. But I knew that would never be after you told me how you felt about Mike. I will love you in silence as you loved her when she was married. I would like for you to kiss me once more."

I put my arm around her and kissed her and she held her lips to mine for a long time. She said, "Thanks that will have to last me a lifetime." I said, "Love is waiting for you and will come to you again."

After all the congratulations, I walked over to Alice and asked her for a dance. She accepted. There was a waltz playing and they gave us room in the dance pavilion and boy did we waltz.

When the waltz ended Alice said, "You still take my breath away. I thought you had forgotten me."

I asked, "What do you think now?"

She hugged me and said, "Thanks! Would you kiss me?" I asked Ronnie if she would mind. I held Alice's face in my hands and gently kissed her waiting lips. I heard a soft lingering sigh as my arms slowly gathered her close to me. Her arms hung loosely at her side as she returned my kiss.

As I gently released her she whispered, "I didn't put my arms around you because I don't think I could have ever released you. I have never forgotten your loving kindness to me. You changed me from a wallflower to a genuine member of the group at the canteen. My life has never been the same since. May God bless you, Ronnie and the girls! How can they not love you?"

Alice told Ronnie, "I'm glad you finally got what you wanted so badly! He's still the nicest person and best dancer I've ever met and what a kisser! I wonder if you know how lucky you are. Treat him well and God bless the four of you." They hugged lovingly.

Ronnie came to me, put her arms around my neck and said, "At long last I can do this openly. Now you need to dance with me," and as the song "This Magic Moment" began to play, there was no doubt that we loved each other.

Later I announced, "You're all invited to our wedding! If the Rosses allow us, we will have it here."

The Rosses said, "Then it will be here and we are honored that you choose to have it here."

"When we set a date we will let you know the same way we did with this affair." There was a big roar of approval from the guests. Ronnie was bubbling over. I knew that I would make her happy this day. Ronnie and I talked and we asked Aunt Loren and Mother Singleton if they would be in charge of putting the wedding together. They were elated that we asked them. I told Aunt Loren they had Carte blanche.

The girls were hysterical. They kept telling everyone, "Uncle Jay is going to be our new daddy." They ran back to me and hugged me often.

Lori came and said, "Come on little brother I feel like dancing. She told me how happy she was for us. She said, "The two of you deserve each other and those are two of the happiest little girls I have ever seen. You are so loving and easy with them and they never want to be away from you. Whenever they come to the house, you are all they talk about. When they first saw your picture on my dresser they wanted to know why I had Mr. J.'s picture. When I told them that you were my brother, they had a fit, they began to jump all over me. Then they ask mother if she was your mother. When she told them that she was, they told her, 'We love him so much!'. At first I worried about that hold situation,; then I thought, something must have pulled them together and I stopped worrying." She kissed me and said, "Live happily my love."

After our dance, I went to find Jamie and we danced. I thanked her for being my friend for all these years. Then I danced with Mrs. T. While we were dancing, she commented that she had heard of my ability to get around the dance floor, but never knew how gracefully.

I said, "I see! You think the ladies have been chasing me for my money!"

She got so tickled we had to stop in the middle of the dance floor. She said, "JM I sure wish I was a few years younger and unmarried."

I responded, "Nope you missed your opportunity. I'm about to be married."

She said, "It's about time! You don't know what you have put that poor girl through and laughed."

When we finished dancing, she told Ronnie, "Little one you need to keep that man from dancing with other women. He is just too smooth."

Ronnie said, "I know Mrs. T. that's how I fell in love with him back in high school."

Ronnie had hired a crew to clean up the place because she did not want the ranch hands or any of the guests to do it. The families of the ranch hands thanked Ronnie for letting them be a part of one of the happiest days of their lives. Ronnie told them that she and I hoped that they would be a part of our wedding. They said they wouldn't miss it for the world. They expressed their happiness that she was marrying the nicest man in the world. The hands said that from the first time Jay brought her to Ranceville they felt we were meant for each other. Sam mentioned that once he saw how Rance took to her he knew for sure that she belonged with Jay. Ronnie hugged Sam and Ben and thanked them for accepting her into the Ranceville family.

We prepared to leave Ranceville and Mr. and Mrs. Ross thanked everyone for coming and making this a day that they would never forget. They hoped that their newfound families would continue to visit whenever they had a mind to because their door would always be open.

As a number of the guests gathered around Ronnie and me, the Rosses told us how we had blessed them, and that they just loved the girls. They thanked Aunt Loren and Mrs. Singleton for visiting them often. They hugged Lori and Jamie and told them they didn't see enough of them but they understood about their busy schedules. They thanked their newfound friends, the Armontts and Mrs. T. They told the Canteen gang that they were now a part of the family and to visit whenever they had a mind to.

Ronnie, the girls and the Armontts stayed the night with her mother after leaving Ranceville. Jamie, her mother, Lori and Aunt Loren went home in a limo. Mrs. T. and I flew back to the city. I had the limo drop Mrs. T. off and I went to my apartment. Ronnie and the girls returned a few days later and we began to make plans for the wedding. We picked a date, then called and told Aunt Loren and Mother Singleton.

Ronnie planned to help them by putting out the information as she had for the barbecue, the rest she would leave to them. They would have the pleasure of working things out with Mr. and Mrs. Ross about Ranceville. They had grown to love the Rosses as much and we did. Ronnie, the girls and I spent as much time as possible together.

# Return to Argentina

One day when Ronnie, the girls and I were at the apartment, I told Ronnie that there was a piece of business that I needed to bring closure to and that I hoped she would not get angry with me.

I said, "I can't just leave it as it is." She became sullen and went to the window and looked out into the evening. I walked over to her and put my arms around her as she did when I was standing at the window. I kissed the top of her head.

I said, "It's something I must do."

She responded, "It's the señorita isn't it?"

I said, "Yes, how did you know?"

She said, "A while back when we talked and I told you that Tia was connected to your spirit, from that time I realized that it was true for me too. You see until we talked, I had refused to accept that. Once I believed what we had before had come back. I have been able to feel that need in you to bring that business to a close. I have been afraid and expecting this."

I said, "Then you understand why I have to go. When I left her it was to get clear in my mind what I really wanted. I can't do this by note or phone call. Do you understand?"

Ronnie turned and put her arms around my neck and said, "Jay I have been so happy!"

I raised her head and said, "Nothing has changed my love. Your happiness is my happiness. You are what I have waited for most of my life!" I kissed her softly and I could feel that her fears had not left her.

I sat in the lounge chair and she sat in my lap. She asked, "When will you leave?"

I said, "The sooner the better." I could feel her shudder."

She said, "We had better tell the girls that you are leaving. You know how they are about you leaving them."

She called Jamie and told her to send them over.

Jamie came over with them and asked, "What's up? I thought you and the girls were going to spend the night?"

Ronnie got up as if she were angry and said, "Their father to be has to go away for a bit." She then turned around bent over and kissed me sweetly.

The girls asked, "Where are you going?" Tia climbed up in my lap and Beth sat on the arm and put her arms around my neck.

I said, "My loves I have to go to Argentina for a couple of days." Jamie looked at me as if to say, you're kidding?

But the girls began to say, "Can we go with you?" Running to their mother asking, "Can we all go mommy? Can we?"

Then, looking at me, Jamie said, "Yes, why don't you all go?"

I agreed and said, "That's a great idea. You too Jamie! Juan would love to see you again?" Jamie declined claiming that she had something important to do.

Then Ronnie said, "Why don't you take the girls with you. I've got a lot to do to get ready for our wedding."

I said holding her gently; "I think it would be a great idea if you came with me. It will give me a chance to show you off."

"No love," she said. "I want you to go. I haven't shown much faith in you in the past. I want to show you that I have faith in you and that I trust you with everything I hold dear in this world, my girls, you and your love. Go do what you have to do and hurry back to me."

I put my arm around her and held her for a long time. I called and had the Lear readied for the morning. The girls went with Jamie. Ronnie got some things ready for the girls' trip and she slept in my lap in the lounge chair. The next morning we said goodbye and flew to Argentina. The girls were very excited looking out the window and commenting on just about everything. We arrived at the ranch and Juan welcomed us and was glad to see the girls again and was surprised that they remembered him. He gave them a hug when they said, 'you are Uncle Jay's friend who brought Bandito to Ranceville. He likes it there.' They were excited about Juan's ranch. The girls were hungry so Juan had some lunch prepared for them. We talked while the girls ate. He told me that Isabella was out riding with Maria.

In the meantime back in the States, Angie had released a whopper of a TV documentary about the Bar-B-Que and my proposal to Ronnie. It had the city buzzing.

When Isabella and Maria returned, Juan and I were on the veranda. There was a handsome escort with them. He was a friend of Isabella whom I had seen her with before we became friends. The girls had finished eating and were down at the corral with the foreman of the ranch. He had fallen in love with the girls and they took to him. When Maria saw them she leaped off her horse and hurried to the corral to meet them.

"She said, "What beautiful young ladies. Where did you come from?" The foreman said, "They are with Señor Jay."

Maria with her hand up to her mouth asked, "Jay is here?"

Isabella arrived in time to hear the conversation. She turned her attention towards the veranda and saw Juan and me conversing. We were quite involved in our conversation and had barely noticed their arrival.

Isabella and her friend went into the house, but did not come onto the veranda. Maria and the girls were making friends. She was enchanted with them. She was married but she had no children. Maria and the girls came up to the veranda. I greeted her with a loving hug and she returned it with a kiss on the cheek. I told her how beautiful she was. She looked at me and told me to save that for the other lady. Juan and I laughed. She told me that it was so good to see me and these two beautiful young ladies. She asked me how long I would be staying and I responded, a couple of days.

Maria excused herself and called the girls to go with her. They looked at me and I nodded my head, yes. So off they went.

Juan and I talked for a long time and then went down to the corral. When we returned Tia came in and climbed into my lap, laid her head against my chest and went to sleep. Juan watched the little girl and smiled.

I had told Juan about the last time when I left. I told him how the call of this little girl was what directed me back home. Juan said he knew that I had that kind of connection to people from their days in the war that is why all the men loved and respected me. When he found that I had that same kind of connection to horses he knew that I was someone special. He told me that there was no doubt left when his ranch hand recanted the story about the puma and I. I was surprised. I was not aware that a ranch hand had seen the puma incident.

Maria came back on the veranda and seeing Tia asleep picked her up and told me that she was going to give the girls a bath and prepare them for bed.

She said, "Both of the darlings are worn out. I'm not sure they will eat supper."

I said, "You would make a great mother."

Maria said, "And you are going to make a great father." I just smiled.

Juan said, "I second that!" I had told him Len had been killed.

After their bath, prayers and kisses the girls went right off to sleep.

Maria said, "Jay that is a beautiful prayer that you taught the girls. If you are not careful I will steal those two. They are absolutely adorable and they love you madly, especially Tia."

After eating, we were on the veranda. I had not seen Isabella since she had returned from her ride. Maria asked if I wished for a glass of wine. I declined. She was pleasant company and had a great sense of humor. Juan had said good night and left the two of us still talking. Suddenly, there was Isabella; I knew she was there although I had not seen her. That gardenia-rose scent that flowed from her was a tell tale. Maria excused herself and said good night. I said good-night to her with a hug.

I turned to Isabella and said, "Hello love!" She stood there momentarily and then rushed in my arms. She had been crying and I could not help but console her. I just held her for a long time until the tears stopped. She turned her face from my chest and pressed her sweet mouth to mine. For a while I was lost in the memory of her.

She said, "Oh my love why didn't you just stay away."

I said, "I couldn't love. I couldn't let it end like that. I had to tell you face-to-face. I knew it would be hard on both of us but I couldn't do it any other way. Please don't hate me for having to personally tell you."

She said, "Oh my love as painful as it will be, I would rather have these last minutes with you than not to have seen you again. How can I hate you for loving me enough to come to me like this? I know now that you did love me and do still, or you would not have come. I also know that you love her more. Just love me for whatever time you will be here and leave while I am out riding. I will ask that you ride with me tomorrow. Will you do that?"

I said, "Yes love." I held her in my arms on the veranda until early morning.

That morning I told the girls that I was going riding with the señorita. Maria had planned to have them ride in the corral and take them shopping. Isabella and I rode to the little meadow where we had spent many hours. We walked holding hands and not saying anything. I picked some flowers and gave them to her. Her tears began to flow. I held her and kissed her soft lips. We sat under a tree and just looked into each other's eyes and came to an understanding of our hearts. She laid her head against my chest and cried herself to sleep. I continued to stroke her beautiful face and soft hair. I watched her and knew how close I had come to not ever leaving her.

I had left her to try and get my mind right. I knew that I made the correct decision, but a sigh of relief still came over me. When she awoke we talked about the girls. She commented how lovely they were and how much they were like their mother and how much they loved me.

She said, "I have to love them because they love you." We held hands as we rode back to the Hacienda.

The girls had a wonderful day with Maria. After dinner Isabella and I spent time with the girls. Isabella took the girls down to meet her horse. The girls talked to her about their ponies and Bandito. Tia told how Bandito would follow her around the corral.

Maria who had come down said, "Not that crazy man killer?"

Tia said, "He is not crazy and he's not a man killer. He is a nice horse and he loves Uncle J., Beth and me." Maria asked Beth does he really follow her around the corral.

Beth said, "Yes and Bandito is Tia's and my friend." Maria commented that Jay must be a miracle worker. She kissed Tia and told her she must have the same kind of love in her as Jay.

Isabella left the girls with Maria and joined me on the veranda. Later Maria put the girls to bed and packed their things. Isabella left for a while to say goodnight to the girls. She came back with tears in her eyes, laid her head in my lap and cried. I lifted her up in my arms and smothered her with kisses. She lay in my arms all night.

Early in the morning she arose and kissed me lovingly and went to her room. After lunch, Isabella took my hand and led me to the veranda. We stood looking out at the blue sky. We said nothing. She turned put her arms around my neck and kissed me and I knew it was for the last time.

I watched her walk down the stairs to the corral, saddle her horse and ride away. I stood there until I could no longer see her. The girls and I said goodbye to the hands, Maria and Juan. The limo arrived and drove us to the airport; we boarded the Lear and flew back to the States.

When the Lear landed, we could see Ronnie and Jamie standing by the limo. The girls were elated to see Ronnie and Jamie standing there waiting for us. They almost jumped off the plane and ran to their mother and Jamie. They were still hugging them when I walked up. They were saying what a wonderful time they had. I stood there watching the girls and their mother. What a sight? When the girls released her she walked into my arms and said, "Welcome home my love! You've been gone for what seemed like forever." And our lips met and no beehive had anything sweeter.

Ronnie hooked her arm through mine as we walked to the limo. Her head was lying on my shoulder and some strange sighs were coming from her.

I said, "What are those sounds I hear coming out of you?"

She responded, "Love and happiness!" The girls were talking a mile a minute to Jamie telling her everything they had done and who they had met. They could not stop talking about Señora Maria and her many gifts.

As we entered the limo Tia and Beth were planning to climb in my lap but Ronnie said, "No, no, girls you have to sit in the seats with aunt Jamie, mommy is going to sit in your daddy's lap this time. Once I settled in the back seat, Ronnie sat in my lap, put her arms around my neck and proceeded to kiss me all the way to the apartment. The girls were kneeling in their seats watching their mother kissing me and were giggling. Jamie kept making them turn around, but she had to do so all the way to the apartment.

When we were getting out of the limo, Tia said, "Mommy you call Uncle Jay our daddy. Is he our daddy now?"

Ronnie hugged her and said, "Not yet baby but soon."

Beth and Tia hugged me and said, "You are our daddy Uncle Jay aren't you?"

I said, "Yes my loves. It's just not official yet!"

They whispered to each other and then whispered to Jamie, "What is official?"

Jamie whispered, "They haven't been married yet." We were tickled at Tia's whispering. Tia said, "I don't care he's my daddy now! Beth said, "Mine too." Ronnie looked at me and I shrugged my shoulders.

In the apartment I sat in the lounge chair and reclined a little and immediately the two little ladies were in the chair with me.

Ronnie looked at the girls shaking her head said, "I think we're going to have to get a larger chair." The girls soon fell asleep. I was almost asleep when I heard Ronnie call Jamie and said, "Look at them. Isn't that a loving sight? He never seems to tire of them! His love has made such a difference in their lives."

"I told you years ago, there's a lot of love in that man!" Jamie said softly,

"Gosh have I been blessed! Pinch me so I know I am not dreaming—Ouch!" Ronnie yelled!

"Well you told me to!" responded Jamie.

I must have fallen completely asleep because Ronnie was softly waking the girls to eat before they showered and prepared for bed. Ronnie and the girls had been staying at the apartments since before the outing. Jamie loved it. Having Ronnie and the girls there all the time had been great company for her. The girls were also able to spend a lot of time with Mrs. T.

I told Ronnie I was not hungry, so she allowed me to continue to rest in the lounge chair while she prepared the girls for bed. The girls came and lay beside me.

Ronnie said, "Girls kiss your daddy good night so you can go to Aunt Jamie's. There was room here but the girls and Ronnie always stayed at Jamie's apartment. The girls kissed me good night; Tia asked if I'd say their prayers with them as usual and after big hugs went next door.

I took a shower and began to look over some papers, when Ronnie re-entered.

"Oh no you don't, Jay McFadden. No papers tonight," said Ronnie. "If you think you're getting out of talking to me, you've got another thought coming!"

"What's up love," I responded?

"What's up? Your trip, that's what's up!" said Ronnie.

"Oh that!" I said.

"Oh that!" chirped Ronnie. "Jay McFadden if you think that we are not going to discuss your little visit, think again!" I was standing at my desk and she was standing by the lounge chair.

She said, "Now put down those papers and come over here." I walked over to the chair and she said, "Sit." I sat down and she sat in my lap and began kissing me so sweetly. While kissing me she said softly, "Now tell me everything that went on down there in señorita- land."

I said, "I thought you trusted me!"

She said, "I do, but trust has nothing to do with it. I'm a woman and if you think I don't want to know what went on between you two, think again. Tell me Jay" and she continued kissing me softly. "Was she glad to see you?"

"Yes."

"Did you kiss her?"

"Yes."

"Did she run to your arms?"

"No."

"You ran to her arms?"

"Nope."

"Then, what happened?"

"Well, she wasn't home."

"She wasn't home?"

"Nope."

"Where was she?"

"She was out riding with her cousin Maria and a boyfriend."

"A boyfriend?"

"Yep."

"Well, what happened?"

"I was on the veranda talking to Juan and the girls were down at the corral with the ranch foreman, when they returned from riding. Maria saw the girls and rushed over to find out who they were. The foreman said they were with señor Jay. Isabella was there when he said that and she saw us on the veranda. Juan and I were in deep conversation but we hardly noticed them when they arrived. Maria fell in love with the girls immediately. She's married but she has no children. They became instant friends."

"What about Isabella did she and her boyfriend come to where you were?"

"Nope. I don't know where they went."

"Huh?" said Ronnie.

I said, "All I know is that Isabella and her friend went in the house somewhere. Later, Maria and the girls came up to the veranda. I greeted her with a hug and she kissed me on the cheek. I remarked how beautiful she was. She told me to save that for the other lady. Maria is a lot of fun. She told me that Isabella had seen me and that she and Antonio were in the lower study. She left and told the girls to go with her. They looked at me and I nodded my head OK, so they went with her."

"Then what happened? Get to when you first saw Isabella," said Ronnie.

"Well Maria had given the girls a bath and put them to bed. She, Juan and I were on the veranda talking. Juan said good night and Maria and I continued to talk. Suddenly I knew she was there behind me."

"Who? Isabella?"

"Yes."

"Did you see her?"

"No I smelled her perfume."

"Oh you could detect her scent?"

"Yep."

"You mean if she walked in this room right now you could tell she was here?"

I said, "Yep."

"Well what happened then?"

"Maria excused herself and left."

"And then?"

"I turned to Isabella and said, 'Hello love!' She stood there momentarily and then rushed into my arms. She had been crying and I could not help but console her. I just held her for a long time until the tears stopped. She looked up at me and kissed me."

"You called her Love?"

I said, "Yep."

"Don't ever call me that again!"

I said, "OK love."

Ronnie said, "Ja—ay! Did she kiss you like this?"

I said, "Umm, yes!"

"Then what happened?"

"She asked me why I hadn't stayed away. I said, 'I couldn't love. I couldn't let it end like this. I had to tell you face to face. I knew it would be hard on both of us but I couldn't do it any other way.'"

"Was it hard on you?"

"Yes."

"What, no yep?" asked Ronnie?

"Yep."

"Oh Jay, you're impossible! What happened next?"

"I asked her not to hate me for having to personally tell her."

"What did she say?"

"Do you want to know exactly what she said?" I asked.

"Yes. I want to know every word."

"Well, she said, 'Oh my love, as painful as it will be, I would rather have these last minutes with you than not to have seen you again. How can I hate you for loving me enough to come to me like this?'"

"She said that?"

I said, "Yep."

"You loved her didn't you?"

"Yes, I think I told you that."

"I don't think I want to hear anymore!" said Ronnie.

"OK."

"Oh no you don't! We're going to finish this! What happened next?" questioned Ronnie?

"Are you sure you want to know?" I asked.

"I want to know every word, everything."

"OK! She said, 'I know now that you did love me and do now or you would not have come. I also know that you love her more. Just love me for whatever time you will be here and then leave while I am out riding. I will ask that you ride with me tomorrow. Will you do that?' I said, 'Yes love.' That night, I held her in my arms on the veranda until early morning."

"You mean she lay in your arms all night like I have?"

I said, "Yep!"

"Jay that's the way you hold me!"

"I'm not two different Jays. Do you want the truth or shall we stop here?"

"Oh baby I know that you know how to love but one way and that's with your whole being. Then you love her as much as you love me!"

I said, "Nope! You are right. I know but one way to love, but not with the same intensity. I recall leaving her and coming to you, staying with you and asking you to marry me. What say you to that?"

"I love you," purred Ronnie! "Now I can understand why you would never go back to Denise or anyone who betrayed you. It's just that it hurts to know that I pushed you to love someone else, so close that I almost lost you. Please continue. What happened then?"

"I told the girls I was going riding with Señorita Isabella in the morning. Maria had planned to have them ride in the corral and take them shopping. The next morning Isabella and I rode to a little meadow where we used to spend many hours. We walked holding hands and not saying anything. I picked some flowers and gave them to her. She began to cry. I held her and kissed her."

"Did you tell her that her eyes were too beautiful for tears?"

I said, "No. That is only for you and the girls."

"Show me how you kissed her." —"Ooh! She must have loved that! What happened next?"

I said, "We sat under a tree and just looked at each other I felt we had came to an understanding of our hearts. We kissed for a long, long time."

"Show me how you kissed her." Then, "Umm don't stop, I love you!"

"Then she laid her head against my chest and cried herself to sleep."

"Did she lay her head like this?"

I said, "Uh huh but I like this better." "

What did you do then?"

"I continued to stroke her face and her hair."

"Show me love! Then what?"

I said, "I watched her sleep and thought how close I had come to never leaving her. Remember I told you when I left her, that I was trying to get my mind right. Sitting there thinking back I knew that I had made the right decision. I felt a wave of relief come over me."

"So you knew then that it was me who you really wanted?"

"No. I knew that before I went back to tell her. What I realized at that moment was that I had not made a mistake."

"What happened then?"

"Well when she awoke we talked about the girls. She commented how lovely they were and how much they were like you and how much they loved me."

"She remembered me from the fiesta?"

I said, "Yep, just like you remembered her."

"What then?"

"She said, 'I have to love them because they love you.' Before she put her hair up she knelt over me as I sat against the tree and kissed me as if she knew that we would never be there again."

"What do you mean 'before she put her hair up'?" asked Ronnie.

"Well, the first time I went to that meadow with her she let her hair down and I commented how beautiful she was running through the flowers with her hair flying in the breeze. So every time we went there she would let her hair down. And before we left she would always kneel over me and kiss me with her hair hanging down covering my head and face—Ouch! What was that for?"

"Did you have to say that Jay?"

"Well you said you wanted to know everything."

"How did she kneel over you and kiss you? Like this huh? Umm. Do you like this?"

I said, "Yes. Give me more!"

"What happened then?"

I said, "She was crying as she put her hair up. I kissed her and helped her on her horse and we rode back to the hacienda."

"Kiss me like you kissed her, Jay because I know you did it sweetly. I love you so much and now you are all mine!"

I told Ronnie, "The question you have in your mind, you have to answer yourself." Ronnie had a perplexed look on her face.

I said, "The question that you have burning in you right now."

She stared in my eyes with amazement and asked, "How did you know Jay?"

"You are my soul mate remember?" I responded.

She said, "I have answered it and the answer is no. I know you didn't."

I said, "Thank you my love. What I have is for you alone."

She said, "Now tell me how did you leave her?"

"Well, back at the hacienda, the girls had had a wonderful day with Maria. After dinner Isabella and I spent time with the girls. Isabella took the girls down to meet her horse. The girls talked to her about their ponies and Bandito. Tia told how Bandito would follow her around the corral. Maria said, "Not that crazy man killer?" Tia said, "He is not crazy and he's not a man killer. He is a nice horse and he loves Uncle J. and me. He follows me around the corral.' Maria asked Beth, 'Does he really follow her around the corral?' Beth told her yes and that Bandito was Tia's friend. Maria said, 'Jay must have worked wonders with that horse and there must be a bit of Jay in you!' and she kissed Tia.

Isabella left the girls with Maria and rejoined me on the veranda. Later that evening Maria put the girls to bed and packed their things. Isabella left for a while to say goodnight and goodbye to the girls. She came back with tears in her eyes, laid her head in my lap and cried. I lifted her up in my arms and smothered her with kisses . . ."

"Show me how you kissed her? Mmh I like that! Then what?"

"She lay in my arms all night."

"Oh Jay it hurts to think of her lying in your arms all night. It's like my privacy has been invaded," said Ronnie.

"Early in the morning she arose and kissed me lovingly and went to her room. After lunch, Isabella took my hand and led me to the veranda. We stood looking out at the blue sky. We didn't say anything. Crying, she turned, put her arms around my neck and kissed me and I knew it was for the last time." "

How did she kiss you, like this?"

I said, "I didn't quite get that. Try it again—Oh, yes!" I said. "That's how she did it!"

"What did you do then?"

"I stood on the veranda and watched her walk down to the corral, saddle her horse and as she rode off she turned, stared at me, threw me a kiss, wiped her eyes and rode out of sight." I looked at Ronnie who had tears in her eyes. I tenderly kissed her tears.

"The girls and I said goodbye to the hands, Maria and Juan. We took the limo to the airport, boarded the Lear and flew back to you."

Ronnie laid her head against my chest and I heard her sniffle. I raised her face and saw her tears.

She said, "These are her tears. I hurt for her because I know she loves you as I do."

I said, "These eyes are too beautiful for tears and began to kiss her until she became listless." Then I held her in my arms, wiped her tearful face, stoked her soft hair and beautiful face and drew her close to me. I looked up and gave God thanks. I just sat holding her. In a short time I felt her soft lips press against my neck.

She said, "I am so happy, I'm afraid! Is it really true that we will soon have what we both have wanted for so long?"

We sat wrapped in each other's arms looking out into the starry night. Angie had the TV and press humming. She had taken the time to put together a humdinger of a TV special with pictures of the barbecue, Ranceville, the Rosses, the horses, the people, the skywriting proposal, Ronnie's acceptance and everything that happened. She didn't miss a thing. The upcoming wedding was included. She mentioned that the wedding and reception would be at Ranceville and that all of the Ranceville regulars and guests were invited. This was as per Ronnie and the parents. All of those people had become our friends and a part of Ranceville. How could something like our wedding not be at Ranceville and they not invited? It was planned to be a gala event!

Ronnie, the girls and I could not go anywhere without being bombarded with congratulations, questions, pictures and autographs. They even wanted the girls' autographs. You cannot imagine the questions we were asked about Ranceville. Everyone wanted to go see it. The girls were asked questions about their horses and their riding. The girls loved the attention. However, we were sort of protective, but I've never seen Ronnie and the girls so happy!

Ronnie and I made plans. We included the girls in just about everything. There were a few things that they were not privy to, but not many. Ronnie and the girls did not want to live in the mansion. She and the girls loved living at the penthouse but when we asked them where they would like to live other than the penthouse, they said Ranceville. I asked Ronnie her choice for a home. She looked at the girls and the three of them began to smile, and she said Ranceville.

I said, "I think there's some collusion going on around here!"

The girls wanted to go to Ranceville the next day, but it was impossible for me to go. I asked Ronnie if she would mind taking them by herself. She hesitated momentarily but smiled and said she'd take them. The hesitation was because they hated to go without me. I had to fly up to Canada for half a day.

When I returned, Ronnie was quite upset. As I kissed her teary eyes, she explained that someone had purchased the property next to the Rosses and was preparing to build a house on it. She said that since the girls wanted so much to live there she hoped that we would build a home there. I held her and consoled her. I told her that it was not the end of the world. We could find another place close by. In fact there was a beautiful spot out in the west pasture that may be even better. I told her that I would show it to her one day. This calmed her.

The next couple of days I spent some time on the phone with some important people: stockbrokers, real estate investments, hospital directors, and bankers. There was a special project that I had been working on and it was coming along well. I had, of course, enlisted Jamie to assist me. Jamie was like my right arm. I don't know what I would have done without her all these years. Jamie had become a very wealthy woman. We have discussed many things over the years. We complemented each other. One of the things I had impressed upon her was that she keep her financial worth to herself. She has done that very well.

We were at dinner discussing the closing of a land purchase and construction of a park for handicapped children. We were waiting for the president of the company who would build the park. Jamie and I were so engrossed in conversation we were not aware of the man who approached our table.

A familiar voice said, "Lieut?" Which is how all the guys had called me.

I looked up surprised and said, "Walt Ryan!" We hugged each other and overjoyed, started talking.

"So you are JM?" He said, finally.

I responded, "Yes! I had no idea you were Ryan Construction!"

We had momentarily forgotten Jamie when Walt asked, "Who is this gorgeous creature you are with?"

I said, "Forgive me Jamie, I want you to meet a member of my old platoon Walt Ryan. Walt this is my partner and confidant Jamie West."

Walt said, "Jamie West! Not Mike's Jamie by any chance?"

I said, "Yes by every chance. Jamie—Mike and Walt were very close."

Jamie responded, "You are the Walt who sent me that beautiful card and note? Now I can thank you personally!" and she gave Walt a kiss on the cheek. I noticed during dinner and the following business discussion, how Jamie and Walt were continually eyeing each other. After we concluded business, Walt asked Jamie if he could see her again. Jamie agreed.

# Wedding Preparations

The girls were spending time with mother Loren and mother Singleton deciding on what they would wear at the wedding and being fitted for their dresses They always came back excited and joyful. With the conclusion of my business, we were able to spend more time at Ranceville, skating, going to movies, dining, dancing and just enjoying being together. The girls wanted to go to Ranceville every chance they could get. Jamie spent more time riding with us and I invited Walt to Ranceville. He was extremely impressed especially watching Jamie riding, and how she was with the girls. He and Jamie seemed to be hitting it off very well. I told Jamie that he had never been married. She smiled.

With all business out of the way, I told the girls that I would be free for the next three weeks. I told them we could do almost any thing they wanted to do. They jumped for joy. They wanted to take a plane ride, go to the amusement park and asked if I would take them for a ride through the pasture at Ranceville. I had promised them that I would when they became good enough riders. We spent a lot of time at Ranceville and the girls had become great riders.

We had been looking at the place in the pasture for our home and discussed how we wanted it to look. Ronnie gave tons of suggestion about how she wanted the house to face and look. The girls also pitched in. However, Ronnie was saddened each time she went to Ranceville and saw them working to build the house on that other lot.

Ronnie was happy when the girls wanted to do something other than go to Ranceville because of the house being built there. I asked Ronnie if she was growing tired of Ranceville. She responded, "Heavens No!" But she said it was just that she did not think she could ever like the people who would be living in that house. She had so wanted for us to build a house there.

Whenever we went to Ranceville she would see the construction going on there. The foundation for that house had been laid and she became even sadder. But we would still ride the horses through the pasture to look at the property near the lake. And each time she liked the area, and the thought of a house there, a little more. We would discuss which way our house would face, the driveway up to the house and how the inside should look. She became more and more used to the idea of the property by the lake.

The girls and I had a ball during those three weeks. We took plane rides, spent loads of time at the amusement park, and roller rink; we went swimming and I even took them golfing with me a couple of times. They loved the putting greens and riding in the carts. But there was no place like Ranceville for any of us.

We ended our three weeks together by riding our horses through the huge pasture. The girls were thrilled to be out of the corrals. Seeing the wonders of the horses in the wild from horseback thrilled them even more. Watching their amazement was truly a treat. When they saw Bandito on a hilltop watching over his herd they went nuts. When I whistled for him and he came running, they thought it was the greatest. He even went to Beth and Tia and nuzzled them. He would follow along with us for a short while and then I would send him back to his mares. He was a beautiful sight with his mane and tail blowing in the wind as he galloped away. You could not keep the girls quiet when we returned home.

The wedding was approaching rapidly. Ronnie had wanted an August wedding. She said that would be the best time because all our friends would be able to make it. Aunt Loren told us that everything was in order. All the invitations had been sent; a notice had been placed in the paper; Angie had been notified and so had all of our Ranceville friends and neighbors and all of the Canteen and skating gang. Aunt Loren said that she had asked a special favor of Uncle Jim.

The girls and Jamie were highly excited. Ronnie was becoming a wreck. The closer the date approached, the more nervous she became. Two nights before the wedding, we had a family celebration with Mother Loren, Lori, Mrs.

Singleton, Mrs. T, Jamie and Mrs. Summers, the Rosses, the Armontts, and Uncle Jim. It was one joyous evening and filled with so much love.

The next morning I took a long walk. Jamie and the girls asked if they could go with me. I really wanted to be by myself but I said yes. Jamie put my arm over her shoulder and laid her head against me. Jamie was holding Beth's hand and I was holding Tia's hand as we walked along. We walked through the park, found a bench and sat there. There were tears in Jamie's eyes.

I whispered in her ear, "I'm only getting married. I am not going anywhere!"

She nodded her head and said, "Yes, I know!"

# Jay Weds His Soul Mate

On the day of the wedding, the limos picked us all up and had us at Ranceville in plenty of time. The Rosses were like little kids, they were so excited. They could hardly wait for us to arrive. The wedding was at one o'clock. I had not seen Ronnie all day! They said that she was like a cat on a hot tin roof. I just wanted to hold her. The girls and Jamie looked beautiful. Jamie was over early and gave me her gorgeous smile and headed for Ronnie. Ranceville was packed. It seemed the whole world was there and still arriving. I hid out for a while. Everyone was asking for me. They were told, "He's around!"

Angie had the whole placed wired for TV. She already had the cameras rolling and talking about and to the people that were there. They even had some of the children from the hospital there. The children were ecstatic about being on the ranch and seeing the horses. When I heard her talking to some of the children, I began to plan in my mind something for them at Ranceville.

Angie found me and wanted a couple camera shots of me before the wedding. Afterwards she told the cameraman that she wanted a couple of minutes with me alone.

When he left she said, "I want you to hold me and kiss me before you get married. Will you do that for me?" For her, how could I not? I held her gently and kissed her sweetly. Her lips were soft and her eyes were tear-filled.

She said, "I have had so many dreams about you. Now I know what I am losing out on. There is so much love in you Mr. J., JM, Jay Meridith, Jay McFadden. I love every one of you. Thanks for letting me know you." Then she went back to find her cameraman.

The whole group from the canteen and skating rink was there. They had come from all over. Some had not seen me since I left for the military. Some had married and moved out of town and had not been able to make the barbecue, but wouldn't miss our wedding. I knew that they wanted to see me and I really wanted to see them.

I told Angie to ask that the old canteen and skating group to please assemble in the dance pavilion for a picture. After they had gathered I came out and the group went wild. It was great to see the whole group together again. After a period of greeting, Angie was able to get us quieted enough to get a group picture.

Tim the DJ came and gave me a bear hug. He had tears in his eyes. He could only shake his head. I went through the group hugging each one individually. When I got to Marge, she asked the whereabouts of Jamie and Ronnie. She introduced me to her husband, whispered something in his ear, kissed him and turned to me. She put her arms around my neck and kissed me like she had always done. Tears were streaming down her face as she laid her face against my chest and hugged me for a long time. I took my handkerchief and wiped her eyes.

Her husband came over and said, "Thank you! She has talked about you so much it's like I know you. She had always told me what a great friend you have always been. I understand now. She loves you very much and so do I!" I said "ditto." We hugged. Then I turned to Ronnie's cousin Alice, and gave her a hug and a kiss. She just held my face and tearfully said, "Thank you so much for the love that is in you."

We heard a helicopter overhead. At first we thought it was a from the TV station. Someone said, "It looks like a military helicopter." It turned out that it was and it seemed to be approaching the 'copter pad. It landed and a mixture of military and civilian men proceeded to unload. They lined up in formation with their backs towards us. Angie and her cameraman had made a beeline for the 'copter pad as soon as she realized that it was going to land and her cameraman had began filming the whole scene.

As I neared the 'copter pad, someone gave the command, "To the rear arch!" I was shocked to see that it was my entire platoon and I stopped in my tracks. Suddenly I heard the command, "Dismissed!" Still filming, the photographer and cameraman caught the entire mad scene that followed. The whole platoon, except Juan, made a mad dash toward me. Most of the guys had not seen me since my release from captivity. M/SGT Arnett and I hugged for a long, long tearful time. The Guys were all applauding.

Uncle Jim had made arrangements for them to be here and had flown them in from all over the country. This was Mother Loren's special request to Uncle Jim. Juan had guided them in to Ranceville. There were tears in the eyes of almost all of the guys and me. What a joy it was to see them all like this. They said, "No way would we miss your wedding Lieut! Where's the beautiful lady?"

I said, "Can't see her yet guys!"

After the embracing and hugging subsided, I walked over to Juan and we embraced. He said, "Two beautiful ladies send their love and wishes for long life and happiness. They thanked you for the invitation but declined." He handed me a letter from Isabella and said "She wanted you to read it before you got married." I thanked him.

The whole platoon was looking around asking, "Is all this really yours?" One of the guys said, "Wow, there's more people here than in the military." We all laughed. I began to explain about Ranceville. They all wanted to see Rance. When I showed him to them they stood amazed and said he really was beautiful. Juan had told them about Ranceville and they wanted to see everything. Some of the guys, who were from ranches in Oklahoma, Montana, Texas, North Dakota, and Arizona, could not wait to go out in the pasture.

One of them asked about Bandito. Juan had told them about Bandito and me. I picked up a megaphone and gave a loud whistle and opened the gate to the lower corral. It wasn't too long before this big, beautiful, black, magnificently powerful horse came charging from the distant pasture. At a full gallop he came charging right up to the fence, slid to a stop and reared up showing off his mighty, powerful body. Except for the guys from the western ranges, most of the platoon scurried away from the corral fence.

Bandito kicked and jumped for a bit and then walked over to me and began to nuzzle me and then laid his head across my shoulder. They commented how much like Rance he was. The guys were quite impressed. Even the guys from the ranches said, "That is a mighty beautiful animal and what a show of love and respect he has for you! Is he broken?"

I said, "No, I really never break horses just gentle them."

Randy from Oklahoma said, "Then you've never ridden him?"

I said, "Yes I have, but only after he learned to trust me. Is that not right Juan?"

Juan said, "I told the guys you got on his back even before you left my ranch and that the two of you are amazing together. It was seeing you work with Bandito that help me to understand the relationship you had with Rance."

Ted from Montana said, "Would you be able to get on him right now?"

I said, "Of course!"

He said, "You know I believe you, but I would like to be able to tell my dad about gentling a horse rather than breaking one and that I had actually seen it."

I said, "He has never had a blanket, saddle or bridle on him so he may shy to start with."

I asked one of the hands to get me a new blanket. I warned the guys not to get too close to him if I was not around. He would attack them!

I approached Bandito with the blanket and as I said, he began to shy away. I stood still and beckoned for him and he approached me looking at the blanket.

Ted mentioned, "You can see the trust he has in Lieut. Even though he's skittish about the blanket he comes to him!"

I slowly lifted the blanket for Bandito to sniff it and he did. I lifted it to his neck and let it rub against his chest. Then keeping it against him I slid it along his side, over his back, down around his rear legs, around his romp, up his other side and back to the front of him. I then dropped it on the ground in front of him and he sniffed it. When he was satisfied I picked it up and shook the dust off of it and laid it across his back.

I tapped his left knee and he lowered his body. I grabbed a handful of his mane and hopped aboard. I told the guys that I did not need the blanket but I wanted to show them that Bandito had never had a blanket or saddle on him. We made a jaunt out in the pasture and returned to the fence where the guys were. Ted was shaking his head in disbelief.

I hopped off, laid the blanket across the fence and went to get an apple. Bandito went to the fence and began to sniff the blanket. One of the guys asked Ted what he was doing. Ted told him he was just getting to know the blanket. He won't be afraid of it anymore. While I had gone for the apple, Bandito satisfied with the blanket, then charged the fence that the guys were leaning against and scattered the group. They got the message that he was wild.

I broke the apple into quarters and fed it to him. Juan asked if Ted had ever seen anyone break an apple up like that before they gave it to a horse and Ted said no, never.

Juan said, "He doesn't want the horse to waste any of the apple. Isn't that something?"

Ted said, "Yes, there a lot of love in that act! Wow! I've seen it all now and I can attest to my dad that he is still wild! Lieut is really something. Now I want to see the herds you've told us about."

Juan said, "If you really want to appreciate seeing them, ask Jay to take you up in the 'copter."

"He flies?" Asked Ted.

"Yes!" responded Juan.

"I'll be darned!" said Ted.

I opened the gate and told Bandito to go home. He started off and as usual, he turned back to nuzzle me, and put his head over my shoulder. I petted his neck lovingly he turned and headed back to his herd. The guys were flabbergasted. I told the guys if I were not here he would not let any of them get any where near that fence.

Juan said, "He showed it already!"

We had time so we loaded both 'copters and flew over the pastures. The guys saw the four different herds, Royal the Palomino, Prince the paint, Stars the big White and Bandito's herd. All the stallions were standing on a hill over looking their herds. The guys commented on how beautiful the layout and the herds were.

After we landed the 'copters, I introduced the platoon to Mike's and my friends from the canteen and skating rink that they had heard us talk so much about, and there was immediate bonding. They also all fell in love with Angie. That was just Angie! They wanted to meet Mike's wife and Ronnie. Most of them had written to Jamie and Ronnie when they lost Mike and me.

Juan said, "Remember guys I have first dibs on Jamie."

Someone yelled, "Not on your life!" I just laughed. If only Jamie could hear this! I told the platoon to enjoy the festivities and began to mingle with the crowd, talking to the people, receiving their congratulations, answering their questions, about the military entourage, signing autographs, and visiting with the neighbors and regular visitors of Ranceville.

I hung out with the ranch hands for a while. I told them they should not be working today and told them to go change and be with their families. They left and washed up but came back in clean work attire. They said this was their life and their families understood that. I said, "Well just act like one of the family which you are and never forget that. They and their families gave me a hug. I told the guys that if the people asked them for anything concerning

Ranceville to feel free to respond in any way they knew appropriate, without asking me.

I said, "You guys know the dos and don't s around here as well as I do. So act accordingly."

I decided to go in and change. After showering I sat and read the letter I had received from Isabella. The letter read:

*"Mi Amor,*

*I must have a last chance to pour out my heart to you. You have completely captured my soul and you did it with simple kindness. The love I feel for you leaves me only to imagine what it would have been like if you had made love to me. You own every fiber of my body. I go to our hidden meadow and each time I see us as we were there together. I think of how I would jump on your back and you would carry me around like a little girl. Oh mi amor, how we would laugh! When you took me in your arms and kissed me so tenderly, my heart would almost stop. The meadow is ours and no one else can ever go there with me. I am not angered by the loss of your love. You were always so honest with me. What you gave me of yourself was true and pure love, no pretense. It leaves me to be able to love again. I never have and never will love again like I love you. Oh, don't worry, I will marry because it's the desire of my family, but my true love will be forever yours. I thought that I might hate her who you will marry but I find that I must love that which you love. I pray for long life, love and happiness to you both and those adorable girls.*

*Eternally loving you,*
*Isabella"*

At that moment I wished that I could just hold and comfort her. I heard laughter and my thoughts returned to Ronnie. Later, as I stood looking at the statue of Rance, and watching the people staring and pointing at him, I thought, "We have come a long way Old Friend. I love you!" Afterwards, I had just started talking to the architect of the house next door, when Uncle Jim tapped me on the shoulder and said, "It's time son. It's a few minutes to one."

The wedding was being held in the corral. Uncle Jim led me to the podium where the minister was waiting. The corral had really been decked out. Everything was so neat. Everyone was in place and we waited for the bride.

The music began to play and the bridal procession began. The ladies-in-waiting with beautiful flowers led the procession. They came out of the house via the grandstand and down the stairs into the corral to 'oohs' and 'aahs' from the guests. Uncle Jim escorted Mother Loren out, down the stairs, and onto the podium—and was she beautiful! Ronnie's mother, looking gorgeous, was graciously escorted out and down and onto the podium by Tim. The bridesmaid Lori, followed by the maid of honor Jamie (since Jamie had been married), were both stunningly beautiful. You should have heard the guys from the platoon especially when they learned Lori was my sister. The girls, Beth and Tia beautifully dressed followed them tossing rose petals. They were absolutely gorgeous. The guests broke into loud applause.

After a few minutes "Here Comes the Bride" started playing. Ronnie appeared at the doorway and paused on the grandstand. There was a hush from the guests, and then tremendous applause. She was radiantly beautiful, dressed in a pastel yellow gown trimmed with red roses. Angie's cameraman and photographer were really at work. Her long flowing train trailing along a wide carpet covered with rose petals, Ronnie proceeded down the stairs, and then was escorted by Mr. Ross up the steps of the podium. Wow! Was she gorgeous!

One of the guys in the platoon said, "Jeez, she's even more gorgeous than her photos!" Just then, there seemed to be about fifty flower girls coming out of the house with all kinds flowers. They seemed to fill the corral; later they gave out the flowers to all the ladies. The applause was thunderous! When things quieted down the ceremony began.

The ceremony was lengthy for TV purposes. I did not know that Angie had made an arrangement to have the ceremony stretched out. However it was marvelously well executed.

At last I heard the words, "I now pronounce you man and wife. You may kiss the bride." I turned to Ronnie and lifted her veil and saw a pair of beautiful teary eyes.

The mike Angie had put in place allowed everyone to hear me softly say,

"My love for you is deeper than the sea. It is as patient as the morning waiting for the night to end. It is warm as the sun. It is yours until the moonlight turns to dust and these eyes are too beautiful for tears." and I took her face in my hands and very slowly and softly kissed her forehead, then kissed her right eye, then her left eye, then her nose, then the right side of her mouth, then the left side, then above her upper lip, then below her lower lip, and like a butterfly landing on a beautiful rose petal, I softly covered her lips with mine.

Her arms rose around my neck, and anticipating what would happen next, my arms fell around her waist and held her tightly. As I expected, she went limp in my arms. Watching me kiss her, the guests were hushed, but then they suddenly gasped, for Ronnie had fainted away in my arms. Picking her up, I carried her up into the house amidst great applause as the guests threw rice and confetti over us.

The guys from the platoon were applauding the whole time. I laid Ronnie gently on the sofa and stayed with her until she opened her eyes. Her mother hugged her and told her that was the most blissful kiss she had ever seen.

"How lucky to have someone to love you like that."

Ronnie said, "Not lucky, Mother but blessed."

As Ronnie and I prepared to return to the reception, Uncle Jim's voice came over the loud speaker, "Ladies and gentlemen I present Mr. and Mrs. Jay McFadden!"

The guests really let out a roar as we stepped out onto the grandstand. Ronnie with her hand over her mouth, kept repeating, "Mrs. Jay McFadden." There was the biggest smile on her face.

The girls came running saying, "You are our daddy now!" and hugged and kissed me like crazy. Ronnie looked on lovingly with a smile. Lori began to remove Ronnie's long train.

We stood in a rose-covered gazebo and received congratulations from the guests for about an hour as pictures were continuously being taken. Afterwards I made my way toward the music pavilion while still accepting congratulations from guests. I had the huge pavilion put in so that there was a dance floor and shade from the summer sun.

I finally made it to the mike and thanked everyone for coming and said, "Food and beverages are being served under each one of the red canopies you see. There are plenty of canopies so no one has to rush or push. Eat, drink, dance and be merry. Enjoy yourselves."

Ronnie made her way to me. She said, "How dare you kiss me like that knowing what would happen!"

I asked, "Do you want a divorce?"

She threw her arms around my neck kissed me and said, "Jay McFadden, don't even say that in jest! I am so happy I could scream!"

I held her and kissed her sweetly and said, "I love you my wife. You are my life!"

She whispered softly as she smiled, "Jay please say that again!"

I repeated, "I love you my wife. You are my life"! She kissed me softly.

Mrs. T. came over to us and put her arms around us with tears in her eyes and hugged us tightly. She said, "I am so happy to have been part of your lives. I have prayed that this would finally happen. Ronnie will never know how lucky she is to have you. I have never seen the love and patience in a man that I have seen in you. When I saw you kiss her I finally understood why she became so upset when Tia described how you had kissed her when you first met her. I've never seen a man love a woman so dearly. No wonder the girls love you so. As for me this is my first opportunity to thank you for giving me the store."

Ronnie questioned, "The Store?"

Mrs. T. said, "Oh little one, you did not know that before Jay went away he purchased the building and gave me sole ownership of the store. You see what I mean by you being such a lucky woman to have a man with so much love." Mrs. T. put her arms around my neck and kissed me softly on the check.

By then, the guys from the platoon had surrounded us. I introduced Mrs. T. to them as my Manhattan mom. Mrs. T. said, "I couldn't be more proud of him if he was my own flesh and blood."

I had them all line up and introduced Ronnie to each of them. She had met a couple of them and already knew Juan. She hugged each one of them. Ronnie was tickled pink to meet all of them in person. She had never dreamed that she ever would. They absolutely loved her. Afterward the guys mingled with the old gang, except for one person, who had rushed to congratulate Ronnie and me.

Jamie was looking for me and came into the pavilion. When she saw Juan and Walt she walked over to them and gave them a big hug. All the guys began to yell 'foul, foul, foul!' meaning unfair. They all wanted to meet Jamie. So, as I had with Ronnie, I introduced Jamie to all of the guys and like Ronnie, Jamie hugged each one of them and thanked them for being a friend to Mike and taking care of him.

About that time, Aunt Loren and Lori came in and all the guys started whistling and yelling but they cut it short when Uncle Jim walked in. They all snapped to attention.

He said, "At ease guys you're here to enjoy yourselves." The guys wanted to know why all the time I had been with them; I had never told them that my uncle was a general. I changed the subject by introducing the guys to my 'mother', Aunt Loren, and my sister Lori. Mother Loren and Lori thanked them for their letters and show of concern during the time they thought that I had been killed. They told the guys how comforting the pictures of us that they had sent during that time had been to them. During the introductions, mother amazed the guys by calling each one of them by name from the pictures they had sent. She hugged each one of them. Lori did the same. They all wanted to get to know Lori and Jamie. They also wanted to get to know the ladies from the canteen and skating crowd. They asked me how I got so lucky as to know so many gorgeous ladies especially Lori and Jamie. They also swarmed all over Alice!

The girls came running over and said, "He's our daddy." They looked at their mother and said, "Oh Mommy, thank you! And you look so beautiful." They hugged and kissed their mother and me.

Ronnie leaned against me and said, "Thank you! I've waited so long for this. Thank you for your love and your patience." The music began to play and Ronnie said, "Dance with me!" The family gathered in the dance pavilion, and watched Ronnie and me as we danced.

Uncle Jim said, "You know, I have never seen him dance before. He is some smooth mover!"

Aunt Loren said, "Before the Bar-B-Que I had never seen him dance except with Lori. After the dance, Lori came over and relieved Ronnie of the short piece of train she had pinned up behind her.

"You can dance a little freer now Sis," she said, as she hugged Ronnie and kissed her on the forehead."

The guys started yelling, "I'll take one of those."

Lori smiled and asked, "Are they always like this?"

I said, "Always Sis." Lori blew them all a kiss.

Lori and I danced next and not a soul came on the dance floor. They all watched Lori and me dance. Uncle Jim was totally amazed and so were the guys in the platoon. They said your sister is gorgeous, but we're afraid to ask her to dance. The two of you are too good.

I told them, "Don't be. She is the easiest person in the world to dance with. Give it a try. Ted said he would brave it and asked Lori to dance and I danced with Jamie.

After the dance, Ted said, "You were right. She made me feel like Fred Astaire." I told him that she was a world-famous professional dance instructor.

He said, "Wow! I'm glad you didn't tell me that at first." After Ted, the entire group wanted to dance with Lori and Jamie.

As people finished eating, they gravitated to the dance floor, and one of the old gang yelled, "This is like being at the canteen!" A big roar went up. And with Tim playing the records, it was like the canteen. I had hired Tim to play the records when the band took breaks. He agreed to play music to suit all the guests. However, the guests were asking for the old songs, so Tim was right at home. All the old gang gathered around us and was congratulating us. Ronnie and Jamie had been so absorbed in meeting the guys from my platoon, that they totally missed one of the old gang who had been unusually quiet and almost invisible.

Suddenly Jamie yelled, "Marge!" Ronnie turned and screamed and they both ran to Marge. They were hugging and jumping and crying. They had lost contact with Marge once she married and moved to Florida. After a jubilant reunion and meeting her husband, they said, "We have to talk!" They all agreed.

Jamie came over and asked me to dance.

But Ronnie said to Jamie, "May I borrow Jay before you dance?"

Jamie said, "Yes," and went back to Marge.

Ronnie said to me, "I've got a surprise for you."

I said, "I've got one for you too." Ronnie walked over to the mike and I walked over and whispered to Tim.

Ronnie had a stool brought out and had me sit on it and said, "I've loved this man since high school. I thought I had lost him in the war. By fate, through my little girl, he reappeared in my life, but I was married. Through all those years he was always a gentleman; so much so that my first husband learned to love and respect him and they became the best of friends. He tried to walk away from our lives a few times but my daughters would not let him. They loved him so much. When my first husband was killed in a car accident, he never took advantage but helped the girls and me to get through the trying times that followed, and never once took advantage of the situation even though I wanted him to. Even when there were accusations, he stood fast and protected my honor. I wanted to get married and he said when the time is right. Well I have waited so long. Now I want to dedicate this song to him."

She had the band come back on just to play the song "At Last" and Ronnie softly sang it to me. It blew the entire crowd and me away. What a gorgeous voice. I had never heard her sing before. When she finished the song, the band stepped down and Tim played the record "At Last" and we began to dance. The applause was deafening.

While we were dancing she whispered, "I used to get paid a lot of money for singing, but for you it was free." No one came on the floor during the dance and we made that dance worth their watching, and I kissed her with fervor afterward, too much applause. Tim did as I had asked and played, "The first Time Ever I Saw You Face" followed by "These Arms Of Mine" and the old canteen gang went wild knowing the meaning of those songs. They joined us on the floor. Ronnie buried her face in my chest to hide her tears as we danced around the floor.

When the dance was over, I took Ronnie by the hand and led her to the mike and said, "I have something for you."

She said, "You've given me all I will ever need."

I said, "Nevertheless . . ." as I beckoned Jamie to come forward. I whispered in her ear and she went over to Tim and came back and stood by me as I began to speak into the mike, "Ronnie wanted to build a house on the lot next to Ranceville. To her disappointment someone had purchased the property and started building a house there. So we looked at a place out in the west pasture where we would like to build, and I think she likes that place better. Is that right?" I looked at Ronnie.

Ronnie said, "Yes, we both like it!"

I put a set of keys in her hand, and said, "Then you can decide what to do with the house on the lot next door!"

Jamie's favorite song started playing and we danced away leaving Ronnie standing there with the keys in her hand and her mouth open. There was silence for a moment and then a roar went up from the guests when they figured out what had just transpired. The old gang gathered around Ronnie, as did the family. They too were shocked.

Jamie said, "Jay, I can't believe you did that to her. Look at her she's just standing there with her mouth open."

I asked with a smile, "Think she'll get over it?"

Jamie responded, "Jay, you are the most lovable person in the world but I think she is going to kill you."

The guys from the platoon went over to Ronnie. One of the guys spoke for the group. He said to Ronnie, "You mentioned that you thought you had lost Lieut. Well so did we. He was the best friend that we ever had and losing him was the saddest day of our lives. We all felt the pain that you felt. Now we are all feeling the joy that fills your heart. You not only have a wonderful husband but you have the best friend that a person could ever have. We share your happiness because we too have found that friend again."

With tears in her eyes Ronnie put her arms around him and gave him a long hug. Then she went through the platoon and hugged each one and thanked him for loving me. One of them yelled at me, "Hey Lieut, for these hugs we'll get you lost again!" Everyone burst into laughter. The song was ending so I told Jamie, "Well, if she's going to kill me, let's go get it over with." We danced over to Ronnie as the song ended. Ronnie just stood there looking at me.

Finally, she walked up to me and asked, "These are the keys to the house?" She pointed to the house next door. I said, "Yes. Happy . . ." I looked at my watch, "One hour and fifty-eight minutes anniversary!" She literally jumped into my arms, and with her arms around me, kissed me passionately, saying, "I love you, I love you!"

I pushed her away, saying, "Whoa, in front of all these people, you want them to think you're a loose woman?"

She responded, "Jay you are the most impossible, lovable person I have ever met."

I said, "I hate to tell you this, but Jamie told you that in the beginning."

Ronnie put her arms around Jamie and said, "Thank you Sis! I love you."

"Ditto," said Jamie.

Ronnie turned to me and asked, "Jay how . . ?" She pointed at the house.

I said, "I was the one who purchased the property, and when they started preparing the foundations, I sent you out here knowing you would be upset. Then I took you out to look at the place by the lake. I knew you would like that place. When you began to tell me how you wanted the house to look, I relayed the information to the architect, except for the shape. Simple!"

Ronnie yelled, "And you knew all the time!" She balled her little fist at me to the pleasure of the guests! "Can we go see the house?"

I responded, "I don't see why not. It's yours."

Ronnie asked, "Where are the girls?"

"Here with me," said Mrs. T. Ronnie ran over and hugged Mrs. T. and asked,

"Can you believe this impossible man?"

Mrs. T. just shook her head, came over and gave me a big hug and said, "I am so happy for you two! You never cease to amaze me JM!"

Ronnie said, "Come on everybody lets go see our new house." She used the keys to open the door and I picked her up and carried her over the threshold to applause. Most of the house was empty except for the chandeliers and upstairs.

I told Ronnie, "I have left decorating the house to you. You can do as you will. There are still some things to be done. They require your input."

Standing in the living room she looked up and saw a walkway surrounded by beautiful railings from the balcony outside the second floor bedroom area across the living room to the upstairs outdoor patio which was closed in by floor-to-ceiling glass and her hands went quickly to cover he mouth as if to stop a scream. She looked at me and said, "That is absolutely gorgeous!"

I said, "I added that, but I left the patio on this level to be done to your liking."

Some of the ladies with whom Ronnie had made friends, and who lived close by offered any help she might need. Anyone who wished could file through the house. They expressed their appreciation for the beauty of the design. They told Ronnie how lucky she was to have a husband who was so thoughtful of her.

They said, "In everything he did, he left something for you to do. How wonderful! He shows a lot of love towards you."

"That kitchen island is the most gorgeous I've ever seen," said one lady. "Cabinets galore, a breakfast nook, recreation room off the kitchen with a window so that you have access from the bar, to the kitchen and what a gorgeous dining room! There is access to the lower patio through the recreation room and the study den."

Ronnie came to me and nestled her head against my chest and said, "How I love you!" Can we see the upstairs now?"

The stairs were spiral and I showed her a small elevator that went upstairs and down to the wine cellar and basement. Ronnie was dumbfounded. Ronnie, Jamie, the girls and Mrs. T. rode the elevator and the rest of us used the spiral stairs.

There was a circular hallway that went almost completely around the upstairs floor and led over the walkway above the living room to the outside patio. There were five bedrooms.

Since the house was semi- circular, the bedrooms were in a row except for the two guest bedrooms, which formed a T to the other bedrooms and were along the outer wall separated from the last bedroom by the hall. Each had its own bathroom. A large picture window exposed the outside view.

The huge master bedroom was on the right, the guest bedrooms on the left and formed the top part of the T leading to the girls' rooms in the middle.

There were bathrooms behind each bedroom. Each had a sunken tub with shower. There was a platform bed area in each bedroom. There were double doors between each bedroom. With all the doors open you could walk from the master bedroom through the girls' rooms to a hall that separated the guest bedrooms. The same was true for the guest bedrooms; you could walk from one guest bedroom to the other. This was in case the guests were related in some way.

The girls were delighted to find that their bedrooms were next to each other. Ronnie was beside herself when she saw the huge living area that fronted all three bedrooms. It was an upstairs living room. There were lounge chairs, desks with reading lamps, tables, lamps and TV's. The girls could come out of their rooms to their desks to do homework or any other activity. I told Ronnie that I had the furniture put in so that she would have an idea of how the room could be used but she was free to change or decorate it any way she thought appropriate. She was absolutely floored. She loved it. Around my neck went her arms and she kissed me.

I said, "If I'm going to keep getting this, I'm going to add a third floor!"

As we stood in the master bedroom, Ronnie whispered in my ear, "Something is missing—the baby's room."

Then Beth came in and said, "Mommy there is a room off Tia's room." The girls had already picked their bedrooms, Tia had the middle bedroom. Beth headed for Tia's room but I walked to the wall and pressed a button and a panel withdrew into the wall, exposing the hidden room that was accessible from the master bedroom and through the door off Tia's room. With the panel withdrawn into the wall, a door was in place to be opened and closed. I pressed a button and a hidden panel in the wall was let down. It became a table that exposed a tiny tub that could be used for changing and bathing the baby, and it then converted to a desk. The guests were very impressed with the thought that had been put into the design.

I explained to Ronnie that the room could be completely hidden until needed and that the elevator was there so that the baby would not have to be carried up and down the stairs.

Ronnie laid her head against my chest and said, "I should have known you wouldn't have left this room out."

I said, "What, no kiss?" Again there were chuckles from the guests. Ronnie turned and kissed me tenderly.

The girls had gone downstairs and now had run back up the stairs and said, "Oh daddy we are going to love living here." Ronnie's hands immediately went up to her mouth at the girls calling me daddy—it pleased her so.

"We'll call it Ranceville number two."

I put my arms around them, kissed them and said, "No girls, just Ranceville, because this place is now part of Ranceville; it's all one now, is that all right?"

"Oh yes daddy! Now we can say we live at Ranceville," they responded.

Tia put her arms around my neck and said, "I love you so much daddy! Thank you for everything."

Hugging her and Beth I said, "I love you both very, very much!"

We left the house and went back to the Rosses. The family was all there. They had not come over to the new house with the others. The guests went back to the music and dancing. Many desserts had been set out to their delight. People had asked to see some of the horses. They wanted to see Ronnie's and the girls' horses. The hands told them that Mrs. McFadden had not picked a horse for herself as yet, but she mostly rode a palomino named Bright Star. They had herded some horses into the short pasture so that people could admire them. The guys from the platoon came over and asked to meet the girls. I introduced them to the girls.

Ted told them, "In the military we all became brothers to your dad. So now you two have a bunch of Uncles. Tia looked at me and asked, "Really daddy?"

I said. "Yes love."

Tia said, "Wow!" and started counting the guys. They loved it.

Ronnie entered the house very excited. She said to her mother and Mother Loren, "You should see the house that Jay has built for us next door! We are going to live here at Ranceville!" She turned and hugged Mrs. Ross saying, "Isn't that going to be wonderful?"

Mrs. Ross was elated. She said, "Just think, having you and the girls here all the time, marvelous! Ronnie asked her mother and Mother Loren why they hadn't come over to the house. They said that they would see it tomorrow when they were alone. "We're going to be around to help you."

Ronnie turned to Mrs. Ross and asked, "Did you know that Jay was building that house next door?"

She said, "No, but I am not surprised that Jay purchased that land. He had mentioned long ago that it would be nice to have it as part of Ranceville.

No, I am not surprised at anything that Jay does, and I'm never disappointed. I'm anxious to see that house tomorrow."

Ronnie said, "Oh how I love that man!"

Mrs. Ross said, "Yeah me too!" Ronnie said, "Mother Armontt do you want to see the house?"

"I know how eager you are to show it off but we have all decided to see it tomorrow," said Mrs. Armontt. She hugged Ronnie and said, "We are so pleased to see you and the girls so happy. Now go and change from your wedding dress."

Ronnie said, "I'm so excited that I had forgotten I still have it on." She went to change.

The girls and Jay had already changed and gone to the pasture with the horses. They and the cowboys from the platoon had saddled some horses and went to look over the pasture. They had to get back because their 'copter would have to leave soon. When they came back Ted told the girls that maybe one day their dad would bring them to his ranch in Montana. The girls asked if I would and I said yes.

* * * *

While Jay was out riding in the pasture, Jamie, Marge and Ronnie had their talk. They asked Marge why she had no longer contacted them after she moved to Florida. At first Marge and her husband had been too busy settling into their new location and then her husband got very ill and they fell on hard times. They asked Marge why she did not let them know. Marge just hung her head.

Jamie asked, "Marge how could you be embarrassed to come to us? We are like sisters!" With tears in her eyes, Marge put her arms around the two of them and apologized.

Jamie said, "Jay was always asking me about you. I told him I had not heard from you after you moved to West Palm Beach."

Marge grabbed the two of them by the hand and walked to the mike, and speaking into it she said, "Jamie and I had always told Ronnie that Jay would be the best friend that anyone could ever have. I came to know just how good a friend. I need to say this while Jay is not here because it would embarrass him. My husband and I fell on hard times and were in dire straits. He had lost his job and ended up in the hospital extremely ill. It was two years before he was able to work again. Being out of work and with mounting hospital bills, our debt was enormous. I don't know to this day how Jay found out. But I got a call from him and he told me to send him every bill that we had to pay. He said, 'and I mean every bill and I don't want an argument. If necessary I will come there and get them. Will I have to do that?' I knew he meant it so I sent him all our bills.

A week passed and I received a phone call from our bank saying that our house note had been paid off and we had a positive cash flow of thirty thousand dollars." Ronnie and Jamie stood there dumbfounded with their hands over their mouths. "He has never returned my phone calls said Marge. I was too ashamed to even tell my sister friends. We made plans to come to the wedding. My husband said 'I have to meet this extraordinary friend of yours.' But before we could make plans, Jay called and said a limo would pick us up and a plane would bring us here. He made arrangements for a hotel and everything. He has never even met my husband until today! I found out that he has also helped other of our friends." Marge asked that no one mention it to Jay. Marge, Ronnie and Jamie embraced for a long time; everyone had tears streaming from their eyes.

When Jay and the guys returned from their ride in the pasture, there was thunderous applause. Ronnie and Jamie ran to Jay wrapped their arms around him and hugged him lovingly and then stood back and looked at him shaking their heads. Jay stood there with a puzzled look on his face and said, "What?" No one told him why.

* * * *

The time had come for the platoon to board the 'copter and all the family came to say goodbye to them. The guys said goodbye to all the old gang and all the friends they had made and people they had met while at Ranceville. They had become a big hit with everyone. No one wanted to see them leave. It was hard for them to say goodbye. These were truly my brothers. We waved until the 'copter disappeared.

Angie had spent the day filming everything she could of all that had happened at Ranceville. I asked her if she thought this was a waste.

"Jay, I may have a Pulitzer here. You may be sorry because this is going to make this place so popular, people will be flocking here just to see the place. It may become the ninth wonder!" She said with a smile.

I said, "Then we'd best go in and talk to Mr. and Mrs. Ross to get their feeling on this. After all it is their home." Angie agreed.

Angie spoke with Mr. and Mrs. Ross and laid everything out. They were delighted.

They said, “Jay and Rance deserve everything that is happening at Ranceville and even more so now with Ronnie and the girls here. What he has done to this place deserves to be told and be seen by everyone who will appreciate it. We couldn’t be more proud of him.”

Angie said, “When I finish editing the film and the documentary is ready I will let you know.”

I said, “Everything factual love, no fluff.”

Angie said, “You know me better than that Jay!”

I said, “Sorry Love, it’s just that, well you know how I hate distortion.”

Angie being Angie, kissed me on the lips in front of everybody and said, “I know Love.”

Ronnie and I went out to the dance floor. Everyone was having a great time. The girls from the canteen surrounded Ronnie. They were constantly whispering and giggling. I did not interrupt them. The family joined us out there.

Marge spoke to Tim and then walked over to me as her favorite song began to play.

She whispered, “I thought that this would never happen again,” as she laid her head on my shoulder for the whole dance. She kissed me for the last time and walked over to Ronnie. They talked for a bit and then hugged each other. Their eyes were teary.

Everyone was dancing and enjoying themselves even Mr. and Mrs. Ross, the Armontts, Mrs. T., Aunt Loren, Mrs. Summers, Mrs. Singleton, Uncle Jim, Lori, Jamie and the girls. I danced with everyone in the family except the men. Ronnie’s mother said she had wanted to dance with me ever since she had seen me dance with Ronnie and Jamie. When Lori and I danced everyone left the floor again. There was a lot of applause and Aunt Loren said we were marvelous. When I danced with Aunt Loren it was for the first time ever. She was a great dancer. She told me that she had taught Lori to dance and then sent her to dance school. I never knew that. Wow!

The band left at ten o’clock and Tim played records until about one o’clock, when he played “Good Night Irene.” Everyone said what an enjoyable time they had had.

The cleanup crew had cleaned everything up. The girls had gone home with Aunt Loren, Uncle Jim, Lori, Jamie, her mother and Mother Singleton. Mr. and Mrs. Ross had long since gone to bed, so we locked everything up and took the ’copter and Lear back to New York. Ronnie huddled close to me all the way. Tom, the Limo driver and his wife, the Armontts and Mrs. T. came back with us. Tom dropped us off at the Penthouse and he his wife congratulated us and said that they knew we would be happy together. I told Tom to drop off Mrs. T. and the Armontts and to take three weeks off and have another driver assigned to us as usual. His wife gave me a kiss on the cheek and thanked me for my kindness to them.

At the apartment door I picked Ronnie up and carried her across the threshold and said, "Welcome home Mrs. McFadden. As I let her down she clung to my neck and her tears flowed.

She said, "I have prayed and waited so long for this moment. I thank God for you and the love that is in you. You were right, you are my husband and it has been worth the wait." She pressed her body close to mine and kissed me unlike any time before.

She drew away and said, "I'm going to shower and change." and disappeared into the bedroom.

I turned on some music and lowered it. I sat in the lounge chair and looked out into the night. The stars were brighter than ever before or at least they seemed that way. The song "The First Time Ever I Saw Your Face" began to play and my thoughts went back to the first time I saw Ronnie—The day I exited the classroom and looked down the hall.

All the years that followed passed through my mind up to Mr. Ni. I don't know how long I had sat there with my eyes closed, when a soft sweet voice said,

"You haven't gone to sleep on me have you?"

I turned, looked at her and found it hard to realize that she was standing there. My look must have been strange because she asked. "Jay is something wrong?"

It was just that thinking back, Mr. Ni had almost become real again. I took her in my arms and held her as though she might disappear.

She said, "Oh my love you are sweating something awful what is wrong?" I explained everything to her. She held me and said, "Oh love I am here and I am going to stay here beside you. That awful man will never come between us again!"

I went and took a shower and returned to her in the bedroom. She stood there with the moonlight shinning through the blinds and landing on her. I watched her beautiful face glow with delight. What a gorgeous sight. I could see the outline of her beautiful body through her sheer gown. I took her face into my hands and kissed her tears.

I said, "These eyes are too beautiful for tears." I kissed her until she collapsed in my arms. I lifted her and laid her gently on the bed. I kissed the tears from her eyes and stroked her face and hair until she opened her eyes.

She asked, "Have I been a bad girl and fainted when you were trying to make love to me?"

I gently ran my hands softly over her entire body for the first time. I watched her beautiful face glow with delight. For the first time I kissed her softly below her neck. I took the time to savor her sweetness, gently stroking her gorgeous body. My hands were as if they had a mind of their own. Touching her ever so lightly they caressed her body completely. Very slowly and tenderly, I tried to make up for all the times I had not touched her body. I could feel her entire body tremble almost convulsively. For what seemed like an eternity I gently caressed her until she pulled me to her. I gently entered her and I could feel her receive me completely as her nails dug deep into my flesh. I whispered softly to her, as we loved each other through the wee hours. I emptied my love into her.

All those years of stored desire I passed on to her. Her hands softer than satin were on fire with love, caressing my body as she received the love that I had saved just for her. Our bodies became one. We loved until our bodies went limp.

She looked into my eyes, smiled, kissed my neck softly, and letting out a gentle sigh she said, "I never knew making love could be so heavenly! Your tenderness raised me to heights I never thought possible. I am so glad it did not happen until now. Just think! I am Mrs. Jay McFadden!" She laid her head on my chest. We both knew that the long wait was worth it. Sleep overtook our weary bodies.

I was the first to wake the next morning. Ronnie was lying on my arm facing me. My arm was slightly asleep but I did not move it. I did not want to waken her. I just looked at her lovely face as I lay there for a long time trying to tell myself this was really true. My heart was pounding! Oh how I loved this woman! She began to move and stretch. Finally she opened her eyes and looking at me she stretched her arms around my neck.

I said, "Good morning love."

She said, "Oh my love I was not just dreaming. You are really here!"

I responded, "Yes, Mrs. McFadden. Where would you like to spend your honeymoon?"

She replied, "There is enough moon here and you are all the honey I need. Let's stay here a couple of days, then collect the girls and go to Ranceville." She kissed me passionately.

I said, "Before we shower there is something I need to show you because I want no secrets between us." A puzzled look came over her face as I handed her the letter Isabella had written. Still puzzled, she opened it and began to read. She paused briefly and looked at me, after realizing it was from Isabella, then continued to read. When she had finished reading she dropped the letter, looked at me and then threw her arms around my neck and sobbed softly.

She began kissing me feverishly and said, "It seems every day there is a reason to love you more. Now I know why everyone says to me there's a lot of love in you. Oh I love you so much. Please don't be angry at what I am about to say. Like you, I want no secrets between us. Until I read this letter I had in the back of my mind, as small as it was, it was there, that you had made love to Isabella. Please forgive me for ever having doubted you." She continued to cry softly, and said, "Jamie, Lori and even Rance always said, trust Jay"

As I hugged her close, I could feel the love rise in her body. It was almost noon before we left the bedroom and went to the shower.

While in the shower Ronnie confessed that she had held a jealous hatred for Isabella.

She said, "If you had married her, I would have hated her! Isabella asked the question, how could she hate that which you love? That caused me to see her in a different light. She must be a very kind and loving person and she must love you very much. So I've asked myself how can I hate her. I wish I could hug her. I know the pain she must feel having lost you."

I pulled Ronnie close to me and kissed her ever so gently. I whispered softly to her, "I was never hers to lose and she knew that. She has never heard the things that I have told you." She backed away, looked lovingly at me, then grabbed my hand and led me back to the bedroom.

We were at the penthouse for four days. On the fifth day we went to pick up the girls. Everyone was extremely happy to see us especially the girls. Everyone commented that Ronnie was beaming. Jamie said she was glowing. Lori said she was now complete. Her mother said that she had never seen her looking so gorgeous. I agreed. The girls could not stop hugging us. Tia never let go of my hand. We stayed with the family for a few days and then we all went to Ranceville.

The ladies—All the ladies in the family including Mrs. Ross, Mrs. T. and Mother Armontt— had been planning the job of furnishing the house,. I had never seen a group of women so happy. They put their heads together and decided that each would take a room and do their own thing. However, Ronnie was asked to give an honest opinion of each room whether she liked or disliked it, or if she wanted to change anything in any of them. Ronnie was pleased with the whole idea. She and Jamie thought it would be wonderful to have a room decorated by each of the ladies. You should have heard the chatter in that house. Ronnie and Jamie were like two kids in a candy store watching the ladies enjoying themselves. They hugged each other continually and plotted how to get Marge to move back home. The girls and I decided to saddle up and head out into the pasture.

The girls and I took an occasional plane ride and did some shopping of our own. We took a trip to a ranch I knew in Mexico for something special, but they mainly wanted to stay at Ranceville. I never dreamed I would find anyone who loved Ranceville the way that I loved it.

I was not allowed to see the house until it was finished. The girls were allowed but they opted to see it with me. One day after riding, and we had cleaned and given the horses their oats, the girls and I were sitting on the corral fence watching Bandito and one of his colts, when an excited Ronnie and Jamie came and told us to come and see the house. As we climbed down from the fence, Ronnie threw her arms around my neck expressing how happy she was that I had allowed her to do the house her way. She said that they all were pleased with the way each room had been done and hoped that the girls and I would like them. She asked us to promise that we would be honest about whether we liked something or not. We said we would.

We entered the house expecting to see all the ladies there but we were all alone. Not even Ronnie and Jamie came in. I was elated and started with the patio. The girls made a beeline for their bedrooms. They were so quiet I rushed to see what had happened. As I approached Tia's room, they were both standing there flabbergasted. They couldn't speak. The room was absolutely gorgeous.

I bent down and kissed Tia on the side of her face and asked, "Like it?"

She said, "Oh daddy it's beautiful."

Then Beth began to inch slowly towards her room. Tia and I watched as she slowly peeped from Tia's room into her room. There was a sudden gasp as her hands went up and covered her face. She slowly removed her hands for a second look and let out a 'Wow—ow!' Tia and I hurried over for a look. The room was breathtakingly beautiful.

Beth threw her arms around my waist and said, "Oh daddy I love you so much. You are so good to us."

I hugged them both and said, "Let's be fair girls. I had nothing to do with this it was your mother, Jamie and the ladies. You owe your thanks to them. Let's see the rest of the house. We went to each of the rooms including the guests' and the hidden baby's room. Each room left us breathless. What a job the ladies had done.

We went next door to the Rosses where the ladies were waiting. The girls ran immediately to their mother and hugged her. They were crying they were so happy. The ladies were looking at me. I just threw my hands up in the air. I didn't say a word. I had this frown on my face and Ronnie asked me what was wrong. I threw my hands up and said there were some things I liked but some things were all wrong. I looked at the disappointed faces of all the ladies. They wanted to know what was wrong.

I paused for a moment, and then said, "Just kidding! I absolutely love it!"

Ronnie and Jamie grabbed throw pillows and began to pound me and then all the ladies joined in. The girls were laughing so hard I thought they would burst. Afterward I went to each of the ladies, thanked them for such a wonderful job and gave them a hug and kissed their cheeks. The girls followed giving each a hug. When they got to Jamie they mauled her. Lori had tears in her eyes. She said I am so happy for the four of you. She hugged me for a long time and then went to Ronnie and the girls.

Tia said, "Aunt Lori you are crying."

Lori responded, "Oh baby, they are just tears of joy!" I ended at Jamie then Ronnie. I took Ronnie in my arms and gave her a kiss that left her breathless.

She caught her breath and said, "You really loved it?"

I smiled and said, "Without a doubt. I just held Jamie!"

I told the ladies that I was going to take them all out to dinner, but they would have to pick the evenings they wanted. I asked what else I could do for them. They agreed that we had already done it. Bringing them all together and allowing them to be part of our lives here at Ranceville was the greatest gift we could ever give them.

They picked the evenings and the Lear took us all to Mexico City for dinner. It was a surprise because the ladies expected to have dinner somewhere locally. Lori was the only one who had known. She had picked the restaurant after I told her we were going to Mexico. The ladies really enjoyed their visit to Mexico. They talked about it all the way back. The dinner, music and the dancing was wonderful. Mr. Ross and Mr. Armontt showed that they still knew a step or two on the dance floor. It was a great night for all. They all enjoyed watching how the girls hung so close to me and slept in my arms whenever they were tired. They teased Ronnie about her competition.

While we were at dinner in Mexico, Jamie and I arranged to have some of the things from the apartment moved to the house, and the special shopping the girls and I had done was also to be delivered to the house as well as the something special from Mexico.

Three nights later we all flew to San Antonio for the second night out. They really enjoyed San Antonio and seeing the Alamo and its gardens, and enjoying dinner on the River Walk especially the night boat rides along the River Walk. When we returned, all the ladies were presented with a bouquet of roses and taken to their respective homes.

Ronnie, the girls and I went to our house. Jamie was invited to spend the night but she opted out, to the disappointment of the girls. They truly love Jamie. They did not want Lori to say goodbye, but Lori had to leave for Toronto and then Venice. Lori hugged Tia and promised to bring her and Beth something back from Venice.

When she hugged Beth, Beth whispered, "You did my room didn't you?" Lori winked at her and smiled.

The girls excitedly told their mother that there was a surprise in her bedroom. Ronnie went to our bedroom and stood looking around. The girls told her to look in her closets. When she opened them she found the closets loaded with the clothes from the apartment and many more that the girls and I had picked out for her. As she went from closet to closet she was absolutely stunned.

The girls said, "Mommy these are gifts from our daddy and us." The tears in her eyes told the joy she was feeling as she hugged each of us.

As she threw her arms around my neck she said, "I have never seen so many beautiful things in all my life. The clothes, shoes, jewelry, and perfumes are exquisite. These pearls can't be real! They would have cost a fortune! When did you and the girls find time to shop for all this?"

The girls said, "Oh, they are really real mommy! It's a secret where daddy bought them!"

I asked the girls if they had told her the big secret. They responded that they had not.

Ronnie asked, "What secret?"

We replied, "That's for tomorrow!"

"Oh no! You are not going to make me wait until tomorrow. Tell me now!" cried Ronnie.

"Not until tomorrow," we said.

"Please tell me girls," pleaded Ronnie!

"Oh no, we promised," said the girls giggling as they ran off to their rooms.

She turned and walked towards me with her hands on her hips saying, "You are going to tell me Jay McFadden!"

We went in to the girls for their prayers and goodnight kiss. Then I prepared for bed, turned out the lights and said, "Goodnight my love!"

She laid her head on my chest and said, "Please tell me Jay."

I said, "I love you three thousand times more then all the stars in the sky!"

She punched me and said, "You know that's not what I meant!"

I said, "Good night my love, pleasant dreams and sleep tight my love. May tomorrow be sunny and bright!"

She said, "Oh Jay, you are impossible. Good night my love," and she kissed me softly."

Ronnie was up early and kept asking the girls but they wouldn't tell her.

She tried to be tough with them and said, "I am your mother and I command you to tell me."

They just giggled. Beth hugged her and said, "Oh mommy you know we can't tell you."

Ronnie asked, "Can't you just give me a little hint?" Beth who had begun to pick up my sense of humor said, "Yes," and whispered, "Wake up daddy!" Ronnie put her hand over her mouth and headed for our bedroom chuckling to herself.

I played as though I was sleep. Ronnie came to the bed leaned over and began to softly kiss the side of my face and softly whisper, "Oh my wonderful love. How can I love you any more than I do? Every time I think that I can't love you any more than I do, you do something to raise the bar of my love a bit higher. What can I ever do to deserve your love"

I interrupted her. "Let me sleep," I said.

She jumped on me yelling, "Oh you impossible man! You were awake all the time;" and she tenderly began to kiss me and then lay her head on my chest." I want to know what the surprise is but I'd rather just lie here close to you. I love you so much!"

Shortly she said, "I must fix breakfast for the girls and if you like I'll serve you breakfast in bed." Ronnie went to fix breakfast and I headed for the shower. I walked into the breakfast nook as the girls were being served. Ronnie said, "I was hoping you would stay in bed so I could show you what a good wife I will be."

I said, "I already know," as I kissed her neck and nibbled at her ear."

"Ja—ay, you are going to make me spill breakfast if you don't stop," said Ronnie!

After breakfast, Ronnie went to dress and I went to the stables.

When she came back downstairs she asked the girls, "Where is your dad?"

The girls replied, "Oh he's around!"

"And what does that mean," asked Ronnie? "We can't say any more," said the girls.

Then they said, "Gosh mommy we hope you will like your surprise!" I came into the house and Ronnie rushed to me and asked, "What is it, what is it?"

I said, "Come on girls it's time."

They grabbed their mother by the hands saying, "Come on mommy!"

Following the girls, Ronnie looked back at me and asked, "Aren't you coming?"

The girls led Ronnie next door to the grandstand where Mr. and Mrs. Ross were waiting. The girls nodded to Mr. Ross and he picked up the phone to the stables and said, "OK." The stable door opened and Ben, Sam and the guys came out leading one most beautiful golden palomino with four white stockings, and a long, flowing white mane and tail and completely decked out with a silver mounted saddle, a beautiful black, white and red rolled blanket, and silver trimmed bridle. They stopped in front of the grandstand and tied her lead rope to the hitching post.

Ronnie was breathless from the time she saw the horse come out of the stable. Mr. and Mrs. Ross and the girls, and the stable hands who had followed the horse said, "Happy birthday Ronnie. Happy birthday mommy!" Ronnie sat down in a chair with her hands over her mouth. She was both crying and smiling at the same time.

Mr. Ross said, "Isn't that the most beautiful creature you've ever seen?"

Ronnie couldn't speak. All she could do was sit there with her hands covering her mouth.

Mr. Ross took her by the arm and said, "Go down and welcome our newest addition to Ranceville. The girls led their mother by the hand down to the corral. Ronnie began to run her hands lightly all over the horse.

When she returned to the horse's head, she laid her face against horses and said, "You are the most gorgeous animal I have ever seen. I welcome you to Ranceville and I hope you will be as happy here as I am to have you here." She then backed away from the horse and just stared.

I was approaching the corral when Ronnie saw me. She walked slowly to the corral gate and leaning against the fence post extended her arms and waited for me to walk into them. Her tears were flowing down her face as I walked into her arms and said, "Happy birthday, Precious Love."

She just repeated, "Oh my love, my love, my love."

I held her face and said, "These eyes are too beautiful even for happy tears," and started to kiss her.

She put her hand over my mouth and whispered, "Please don't kiss me like that! My legs are like jelly from the joy the three of you have given me. If you kiss me like that I will be finished for the day and I want you and the girls to saddle up and ride the pasture with me."

I kissed her lips lightly and said, "The horses are already saddled." The four of us rode every day for the next two weeks.

I told Ronnie that Lori would be in Paris for the next three weeks and that since Jamie had been working so hard, I was going to send her to Europe. I asked Ronnie if she would like to take the girls and go with her.

She immediately said "No!"

I said, "Look love, summer is coming to a close and I need to get back to work. You and the girls will be able to spend some time in Europe and I will still have a bit of time to spend with the three of you when you get back before school starts."

We called the girls in and presented the idea to them. They of course, immediately said no, because I was not going.

Tia threw her arms around my neck and said, "No Daddy don't send us away."

I kissed her softly and said, "Love I would never send you away! Aunt Jamie has been working so hard and I want her to go to Europe for a vacation. Your Aunt Lori is over there but I don't want to send Jamie by herself, so I thought your mother and the two of you wouldn't mind going with her to keep her company. I know you don't want to leave Ranceville but will you do that for me."

Still hugging me Tia smiled and said, "Yes daddy, we wouldn't want Aunt Jamie to be lonesome over there all alone." Beth nodded her head in agreement.

The next day I talked to Jamie and of course she didn't want to go. I told her that Lori would be over there and that I had asked Ronnie and the girls if they would like to go along too. This brought a smile to Jamie's face. She put her arms around my neck and asked if it was all right to kiss me. I kissed her.

Jamie said, "You know I have always wanted to go to Paris!"

I responded, "Why do you think I'm sending you? You don't have to do anything. Everything has been arranged including luggage. You are all packed."

Jamie said, "Oh Jay there is just too much love in you! Where does it come from?"

I said, "By the way Jamie there is going to be a secretary in the office to take over some of the secretarial-type things you've been doing. You can lay them out after you come back. No discussion! I kissed Jamie on the forehead and walked away. I looked back and smiled, as she looked after me with her mouth open and hands on her hips, and I yelled, "You will have to do the hiring!"

It was wonderful to see Ronnie, Jamie, and the girls on their return. I had missed them tremendously. Although Ronnie called me every day, to make sure I went to the gym—. Was her excuse, she and Jamie never let me forget. After hugs and kisses, I thought I had missed them the most but it seemed as though they missed me more than I had missed them. When we reached Ranceville the girls could not wait to get to the corral. Their horses seemed just as happy to see them. Jamie was to spend the night and we would all ride together.

The next morning we were saddling up, and while Jamie was admiring Ronnie's Palomino, Ben and Sam brought out a beautiful paint and presented it to Jamie. Jamie was puzzled, because this was not her usual horse. She looked at Ben. Two years ago Jamie had pointed out a Paint colt that she had liked.

Ben asked, "Remember that little paint you pointed out a couple years ago? Well this is it!" Jamie was beside herself. She could not believe that this beautiful horse was that little colt. It too was decked out complete with a silver mounted saddle and all the trimmings. Jamie looked at me.

I said, "Don't look at me. This is the guys' gift to you."

Jamie turned, ran to Ben and Sam and gave them four hugs each. She said, "Give one of those to each of the other guys!"

Ben said, "Here they come. Give them one of their own. I'm keeping these four. Sam said ditto. So Jamie gave each of the others a big hug.

She then walked over to me as I sat on my horse and looked up at me. I knew what she was saying.

She then walked over to Ronnie who had not yet mounted, hugged her and said, "Do you know how lucky you are?"

Ronnie took her handkerchief and wiping Jamie's eyes said, "Yes! Both of us."

Jamie ran her hands over her horse, kissed it on the nose, mounted and we all rode out to our favorite spot. It was a hill at the farthest end of the range. We could sit there and see all four of the stallions when they were standing on their hills overlooking their herds. It was a beautiful sight. We all sat there for a long time quietly watching the stallions and their herds.

After our ride, Ronnie and Jamie came to me and said that there was something that they wanted to know. They had tried to put it off but they needed to know. They said that I did not have to answer if I did not want to but they hoped that I would. They wanted to know how I knew about Marge's family's condition. I looked at the two of them and saw the need in their eyes.

When she did not show for the Bar-B-Que, I knew something was wrong," I told them. "So I asked Tim if he knew anything about her. He basically told me the same thing that the two of you had told me, except he told me her husband's name. With that information and knowing that they had moved to West Palm Beach, I hired a detective agency to get all the information they could on them as discreetly as possible. They had recently had their phone turned back on so I called her."

Ronnie and Jamie said, "We want her back home

"We understand that you have helped other of our friends as well and you have never mentioned it to either of us. Why?" Asked Ronnie.

"It was their personal affairs," I answered. They just looked at me with tears in their eyes and both hugged me lovingly.

Ronnie, Jamie, Aunt Loren, and Beth, Ronnie's Mother, Jamie's mother, Mrs. Ross, and the other ladies began planning for the house warming. The girls and I were spending our last days of the summer riding together. I had asked them what they wanted to do before the start of school. Riding was what they wanted to do and for all of us to go skating so that's what we did.

* * * *

One day all the ladies were at Mrs. Rosses and Ronnie was looking out the window at Jay and the girls who had finished riding and were sitting on the corral fence watching Bandito running around, Loren noticed that Ronnie was wiping her eyes. She walked over to the window and asked Ronnie what was wrong. Ronnie turned to Loren and buried her face in her chest and cried bitterly.

"What is the matter baby?" asked Loren

Ronnie finally responded, “Oh Mother Loren, it’s just happiness pouring out of me. I’m thinking of how blessed I am. Do you know that I did not like Jay when I first met him?”

“Why?” asked Loren. “I was being the genuine little “B” at that time. I was all hung up on the pretty boy wagon. I did not think Jay was very good looking. Not that he is not nice looking, I was hung up on the pretty boy thing. I had never even given him a smile. He even almost lost his eye and his life trying to keep me from being seriously injured or even killed. Bleeding badly, he even tried to help me up and all I could do was slap his hand away and call him a clumsy ox. It took me a long time and a lot of pain to Jay before I found out what Jamie had been telling me was true. She said it’s what’s in the package that counts not how it’s wrapped! I hurt every time I think of what I almost lost and it’s only because he never gave up on me that I didn’t lose him. That first time he kissed me was a magic moment. I thought Lori was his girlfriend and knew I had lost him. He said, ‘These eyes are too beautiful for tears.’ Then he kissed me and it was like the Fourth of July, explosions all through my mind and body. That’s why every time he says those words and kisses me like that first time, Fourth of July happens all over again and I lose all control! I hurt him so and drove him into the arms of another woman with my jealousy.

I realized that it was because I was married and I could see no hope of us ever being together. So I could only feel that someday some woman would come along and take him. Therefore I was extremely jealous of any woman that got close to him, I just couldn’t help myself. Jamie kept telling me to have faith in Jay.

One of those times that I went by to see Jay, he was as usual, listening to music and looking out the window. He did not hear me come in and I was about to call to him when another song began. The man had such a beautiful voice and he sang, “Trust in me” and I stopped and listened to the song. He sang,

*Trust in me in all you do,*
*Have the faith I have in you*
*Love will see us through,*
*If only you trust in me.*

I listened to the whole song as Jay just stood looking out the window with his arms folded. When the song ended I felt so ashamed that I quietly left without saying anything. I went back home and cried myself to sleep. I kept asking myself "Why can't you just trust in him?" But the answer would always be the same. "How can I when I know I can't have him?" Now my heart aches with the amount of love I have for him!"

Loren said, "Jamie has always been a wise young lady. Dry your eyes baby. You are not the first to have made that mistake. We all went through that stage in our lives. It's what you feel now that matters."

Ronnie stared out the window for a long time as Loren kept her arms around her. Then as tears filled her eyes again, she said, "I think of how we almost truly lost him twice and now seeing him sitting there with the girls, my heart swells with love."

Ronnie was quiet for a few moments waiting to be able to speak without breaking down and then said, "Jamie always told me that Jay is the most thoughtful, kindest, most loving person she has ever known and the best friend anyone could ever have. I have seen that over and over again. The girls love him as much as they loved their father.

I thought Len would be jealous of their love for Jay. He did not like Jay at first because I told him the truth about Jay and me. But he talked to Jay for about twenty minutes and when he saw what Jay had done for Tia and how both girls loved him, he learned to love Jay himself. He told me one time about Jay, 'That is some fellow you have there!' The girls would huddle around their father just like they do with Jay, but when Jay came around they would run to him. Their father would just smile. Jay has so much love for them and they love him so much."

Ronnie paused and stared out the window and said, "He's infectious! Each time I look at him I'm reminded of a time when I walked into his apartment and he was standing in front of his picture window staring into the early night. A song was playing, but I had never paid much attention to lyrics before I met Jay. I walked up behind him, put my arms around him, laid the side of my face against his back and just listened to the song. It said everything I would ever want or need to say. The song was "This Magic Moment."

It takes me back to when he first danced with me, when at the end of the dance he held me in a dip and he looked deep into my eyes; I knew he could see clear to my soul; his lips were so close to mine and I wanted him so to kiss me, but he just smiled and walked away and my heart ached for him every moment afterward. And then the first time he kissed me my heart soared above the stars. No song has ever touched me as deeply as "This Magic Moment."

Her love swelled in her and choked off her words. Finally, Ronnie pointed out the window and said, "Look at that picture—the three of them sitting there—Jay, Beth, and Tia, along with Bandito. They're inseparable. He loves the three of them so much and they love him. Tia and Beth are always lying against him as they are now and his arms around each of them. And look at Bandito; he's as bad as the girls. Plus he's a big tease. See, he's always nuzzling the girls and making them laugh. Where did all that love come from?"

Loren responded, "From God, through his parents. His mother was the most beautiful and loving person I have ever known and so was his father. They were truly a match made in heaven. So he got it honestly."

"Do you know what's missing in that picture?" Ronnie asked, looking at Loren."

"You?" questioned Loren.

"No." Ronnie responded. She looked back at the fence. "A little boy!"

Elated, Loren whispered, "Are You?"

Ronnie turned with a smile and nodded. "Yes!"

Loren put her arms around her and hugged her and told Ronnie how happy that made her.

"Lori is going to go absolutely nuts." she said. Does Jay know?" "No. Ronnie said, "I went to the doctor yesterday when Jamie and I went shopping."

"Jamie knows?" asked Loren. Ronnie nodded again.

"How do you think the girls are going to take this?" asked Loren.

"They're going to love it. They have often asked why they never had a brother. I'm going to tell all three of them soon. I just hope it is a boy. I would love to look out the window and see a little boy sitting there with them. The love in that man!" she shook her head. "All these years he has been giving to me and now I can give back something to him."

"Then we will pray to God that it is a boy!" said Loren and she hugged Ronnie warmly.

# Characters

| | |
|---|---|
| Jay McFadden | A man with a lot of love to give |
| Jamie West née Summers | Jay's best female friend/ Almost girlfriend |
| Ronnie Armontt née Singleton | Jay's love |
| Mike West | Jay's best friend married to Jamie |
| Lori Morgan | Jay's cousin– as close as a sister |
| Loren Morgan née Meridith | Jay's aunt and adoptive mother |
| Marge Lowery | High school friend |
| Mary Williams | Friend |
| Denise Winters | Jay's former girlfriend |
| Tim | The DJ and very close friend |
| Tommy Jordan | Close friend |
| Ben Logan | Once close friend |
| Mr. Ross | Stable Owner |
| Mrs. Ross | Wife |
| Rance | Jay's beloved horse |
| Ben | Stable hand |

| | |
|---|---|
| Sam | Stable hand |
| Roy Arnett | Close friend and army buddy |
| Mr. Ni | Jay's merciless interrogator |
| Leonard Armontt | Ronnie's husband |
| Beth | Ronnie's daughter |
| Tia | Ronnie's daughter |
| Mrs. Templeton | Store owner and Ronnie's friend |
| Angie | Jay's nurse and TV commentator |
| Tom | Jay's limo driver |
| Gen. Jim Morgan | Loren's friend and brother-in-law, Lori's uncle |
| Beth Singleton | Ronnie's mother |
| Janis Summers | Jamie's mother |
| Juan Escanaba | Argentinian ranch owner, close friend and army buddy |
| Isabella Escanaba | Juan's sister and almost loved by Jay |
| The Armontts | Len's parents |

**Jay's Wild Horses:**

| | |
|---|---|
| Bandito | Andalusian stallion (Black bay) |
| Stars | White stallion |
| Prince | Paint stallion |
| Royal | Palomino stallion |
| Bright Star | Palomino mare |
| Lady | Chestnut mare |

# About the Author

Joe Green was born in Baltimore, Maryland.

After high school, he went into the Air Force. He became a medic, X-ray Tech, and Surgical Tech. He was encouraged by one of the doctors to go to med school. He attended college at night while in the service, and then gained his Associates of Arts at Wilson Jr. College in Chicago.

He switched gears from medicine to engineering and drove a tractor and trailer to support his family and pay for college. He then worked for IBM, where he taught, traveled extensively, and then finally retired.

The author has a love of horses, which carried over to his three sons. He also enjoys traveling, hunting, fishing, swimming, and golf.